Life of an EX College Bandsman 7

Nobody's Perfect

Also by Jaxon Grant

Bad Religion
Bad Religion 2: A Sinner's Denial

Crimes of the Heart
Crimes of the Heart 2: The Aftermath
Crimes of the Heart 3: The Resurrection

Incidental Contact
Incidental Contact 2: EX-Factor
Incidental Contact 3: Deadly Intentions

Life of a College Bandsman
Life of a College Bandsman 2: Is This Love
Life of a College Bandsman 3: Stuck on Stupid
Life of a College Bandsman 4: Hell on Earth
Life of an EX College Bandsman 5: Starting All Over
Life of an EX College Bandsman 6: Lovers and Friends

What Webs We Weave
What Webs We Weave 2: Nobody Knows
What Webs We Weave 3: Finding Your Love
What Webs We Weave 4: Don't Look Back
What Webs We Weave 5: Old Terror
What Webs We Weave 6: Could This Be
What Webs We Weave 7: Thought You Should Know
What Webs We Weave 8: Guilty Conscience
What Webs We Weave 9: Exit Wounds

Life of an EX College Bandsman 7

Nobody's Perfect

Life of a College Bandsman Series #7

A BnTasty Novel

JAXON GRANT

@jaxon_grant

JTG Publishing

This is a work of fiction. Names, characters, places, and incidents either are the product of the author's imagination or are used fictitiously. Any resemblance to actual persons, living or dead, events, or locales is entirely coincidental.

ISBN-13: 978-1537628653
ISBN-10: 1537628658

Life of an EX College Bandsman 7

Nobody's Perfect

Prologue:

January 2016

The older I get the more I realize that I have a major void in my life. Maybe some of the reasons why I acted the way I did when I was in my twenties was because of this void. I guess it's nothing I can do about that void as it has always been out of my control. I remember asking my mother about this void when I was a child, but she would always look and me and shake her head.

Even after all these degrees—Bachelor of Science in English Education; Masters of Education in Guidance Counselor Education with a certificate in Educational Leadership; and finally, a Ph.D. in Counseling Psychology—that void is still there. I guess I tried to fill that void with a lot of education, but even after recently obtaining the highest academic degree possible, courtesy of Columbia University, that void still exists.

Isn't it ironic that I obtained my Ph.D. in Counseling Psychology, but I'm the one with the fucking problems? How can I help my students when my mind is leaking with my own troubles?

Whatever. Why am I even thinking about this right now? I have work to do.

I looked down at the paperwork that sat on my desk. I ran my hands over my head before exhaling. I wasn't feeling this shit today. My mind is exhausted. I would go home but I have an appointment and one final class coming up.

I looked outside my office window and sighed. Light snow was still falling. I need a change of scenery. I don't like this place and I know Dray can sense it. I value the education I received while at Columbia, but I'm ready to bounce. I'm southern born, southern raised and the south is where I need to be.

New York has its high points, but this shit is just too busy for me. This just isn't my cup of tea. Especially the weather. I just can't do these northern winters. It's too fucking cold. Not to mention this shit is dirty! I've never seen such a dirty motherfucking city in my life. People are nasty as hell up here. And the public transportation system—Jesus take the wheel.

Dray says I think I'm too good for this place. He's damn right. I am too good for this type of living. He may like it, but it's just not for me.

Take me back to the south. I'll gladly go back to the south. Can a nigga get a little southern hospitality up in this bitch?

I dealt with it—I deal with it—because I love Dray. He's doing big things with his job. He just got another major promotion so trust and believe my baby is making some major dough. This is where he wants to be, so I'm going to stand by him. Well, I'm going to try and stick it out but I don't know how much longer I can live in New York.

Being in New York has allowed for the both of us to mature. We grew closer together. All we had was each other. We depended on each other. We were two small people in a big ass city. I had a culture shock when I moved up here, but I've adjusted. However, I still want to go back to the south.

Dray definitely knows how to the keep the romance alive and that's partly how I managed to stay up here for so long. But not even the romance can keep me up here now. We're also in the process of buying a summer home down in Atlanta. Little does he know but that *summer home* may become my *permanent home.*

I looked at the picture of my grandmother that resided on my desk. Next week marks the tenth anniversary of her passing. My family is having a service for her and I can't wait to get to Florida. I really miss my mom. We've come such a long way in a short amount of time.

I was taken out of my train of thought when I felt my phone vibrating on my desk. It was Dray. I answered, "Sup, baby?"

"Nothing. I'm just leaving the office about to head out for this interview with *GQ* right quick. I told you *GQ Magazine* has me as the cover story in their upcoming edition."

"Yeah, I remember," I replied.

"What are you doing?" he asked.

"Sitting here, thinking and waiting on this next appointment."

"You got another class today?" he asked.

"Yeah. I'm probably gonna cut it short. I'm just not feeling it today."

"What's on your mind, Zach?" he asked.

"That void I was telling you about," I replied.

"Oh," Dray sighed. "Well, I know something that will cheer you up!"

"What's that?"

"Your favorite basketball team is in town for a game with Knicks."

"Yeah, I know," I replied, turning on my iPad.

Dray said, "I got us courtside tickets. The game starts at 7:30 so we've got plenty of time to do whatever else is on our agendas today."

"Thanks, Dray. The Magic haven't been the same since all that shit went down with Dedrick Grant."

"Yeah, I remember. That mess hit the NBA by storm. Nobody saw that coming. That entire situation was fucked up."

"Yeah, but thanks though. Maybe going to the game will get my mind off everything. I really appreciate that baby."

"No problem. You talked to Dwight recently?" he asked.

"I was actually about to give him a call."

Dray paused.

He always does that pause whenever he mentions Dwight's name. I exhaled.

He continued, "Oh, well, I don't want to hold you. Just give me a call around four so we can meet up for dinner before we the game."

"Ight, Dray."

"I love you."

"I love you, too."

I hung up and took a deep breath.

My stomach churns every time Dray mentions Dwight's name. The night I slept with Dwight nearly seven years ago changed things for me. It really changed my life. Nothing has been the same since.

Our relationship as best friends is as strong as ever. We don't talk every day, but that bond is still there. The night I tried to step to Dray about what Dwight and I did—

I took a deep breath.

I don't feel like thinking about that. The entire topic is a touchy subject. I have enough shit on my plate already. I can't get brought back into that bullshit. Maybe one of these days I'll relive that moment with Dray, but until then I'll stay far away from it.

I picked up my cell and phoned my best friend who now lives back in his hometown of Atlanta, Georgia. Hopefully he wasn't at the pharmacy.

"What they do, shawty…well… umm… excuse me… Dr. Finley," Dwight said.

"Whatever, nigga," I chuckled.

"What's up with you though? I ain't heard from you in a couple of weeks. I called you a couple of days ago but you ain't ever return my call."

I answered, "I've been busy, man. I have a lot on my plate trying to meet this deadline and dealing with these classes and working here in the on-campus counseling center. I've been trying to get back to you. I'm just dealing with a lot."

Dwight asked, "Are you still thinking about that void in your life? The last time I talked to you, it was bothering you."

"Somewhat."

"It's nothing you can do about that Zach. That is out of your control."

"Yeah, I know. How is the family?"

"The kids are good. I just had to get at Brennan yesterday for beating up on his brother and then picking on his sister."

I laughed and said, "He was just trying to be the protective big brother."

"Yeah, if you say so."

"How are Ced, Michelle and their kids doing?"

"They just got stationed in Ft. Worth, Texas last week. I don't see how they do the military life, but if they like it, I love it."

"Yeah, I was surprised that Michelle joined Ced in his quest to be all he could be," I stated.

"You'll never guess who I saw yesterday at the mall."

"Who?" I asked.

"Micah."

"Micah?"

"Yeah, nigga. Don't act like you don't know who I'm talking about."

"I know who you're talking about, it's just I haven't heard that name in years, Dwight."

"Yeah."

"What happened?"

"When I walked inside of the store, I immediately saw Micah and he was with Brandon."

"The drum major, Brandon?" I asked.

"Yep. They both greeted me. I must say Micah looks good. He looks like he's stayed off the shit."

"That's good," I said as I heard a knock at my door. "Dwight, somebody is at my door. I'll get back at you."

"Ight, shawty. I love you."

"I love you, too," I hung up the phone and told my visitor to enter.

The young French-American student walked in the office and said, "Thanks for meeting with me, Dr. Finley."

"No problem," I motioned for him to sit down.

As Jean started to explain his situation, I caught my mind drifting back to my own issues. I was listening to him, and I would let him know I was paying attention by nodding my head or asking a few questions here and there, but my mind was elsewhere.

The day Dray came back to Tallahassee from his grandmother's funeral all those years ago sticks out in my head. Upon my first glance at Dray, I knew something was wrong. Something was wrong in his body language. It was as if he was there, but he really wasn't there. I tried to put it off on the fact that they just buried his grandmother, but it was deeper than that and I knew it.

I guess part of me was guilty because I just had sex with my best friend days before, so I tried to convince myself that it was me who thought that Dray was acting different. But as a few days passed, I learned that it wasn't me.

I remembered Dray saying that he had a gift for me when he returned to Tallahassee, but I never got that gift until I got to New York—and it was a long time after I got to New York.

I looked at Jean before glancing down at my gift from Dray—my ring. That ring means the world to me. I love Dray with everything inside of me.

When Dray first got back, we laid in the bed together but he wouldn't touch me. We didn't have sex for a long time. It was on the third day of Dray not touching me that I knew something was up. *He knew something.*

My grandmother used to say what's done in the dark will

eventually come to the light and I'll be damned if—

"Dr. Finley," Jean said he took me out of my train of thought.

"Yes sir?"

"I really appreciate you taking the time to listen to me blab on and on about my problems. You're the greatest. I feel so relieved every time I leave your office."

"It's no problem," I stood up and walked him to the door. "Same time next week?"

"Yes sir."

"See you then," I smiled as he left.

As soon as the door closed, I rolled my eyes and shook my head as I walked over to my desk to grab my things.

On the way to my class, my mind pondered over to Keli. When we first graduated from FAMU we still kept in contact with each other, but just like anything else in life, time changes things. As time passed, so did our relationship.

We've keep in contact, but we're not as close as we used to be. Sometimes I think this is a good thing. At times, Keli was a bit wild for my liking, but I love him anyway. He was a good friend to me during my FAMU days. I hear he and Symon broke up for a bit when they moved to Atlanta. Keli would never explain why, but since the last time I talked to Keli, they are back together and making their relationship work. I only wish the best for them.

As I looked forward to the game tonight, I ended class and headed over to the condo to change clothes. I made everything quick because I didn't want to be late for dinner with Dray.

We went to one of Dray's favorite restaurants that was close to Madison Square Garden. I listened to Dray talk as he explained the interview he had with GQ. Sometimes I can just sit and smile at Dray. He's doing so well from himself. I know I made the right decision to live a life with Dray. We complement each other so well.

Outside of the obvious, even though that issue is years removed, I wonder what is going to happen next. Seems like some sort of curve ball always enters into my life when I least expect it.

Once we took our courtside seats at Madison Square Garden, I felt somewhat at ease. I looked up at the huge arena and shook my head. When I entered college as a freshman nearly fourteen years ago I would have never imaged I would be at this place in my life. I guess you never really know what plan God has for you, that's why you've just got to live life and let things happen as they may.

Seeing one of the Orlando Magic new stars, Victor Oladipo, made think back to Tony. The last time I talked to Tony, Raidon had just gotten a position as the associate dean of the School of Education at Clark Atlanta University. He said Raidon had just moved down to Atlanta and he and TJ would join Raidon once the school year was over. Tony didn't seem too excited about moving to Atlanta, but he was going to support Raidon in his dream as he climbed up the ladder in the field of education.

I can only smile when I look at Tony and Raidon because throughout all their problems they are still together. Tony and Raidon give me hope that my relationship with Dray can withstand anything that gets in our way. Tony and Raidon gives me hope that gay relationships can last long term.

Tony said that TJ was starting to ask a lot of questions and I could sense some nervousness in Tony's voice. He knew that those questions would eventually come. Hell, it's crazy to think that TJ will be thirteen this July. *Damn, how time flies.*

"Relax, boy," Dray whispered in my ear. "Stop thinking so hard and enjoy yourself."

"I am," I said, as I looked at Carmelo Anthony of the New York Knicks take his place at center court along with the rest of the Magic and Knicks starting lineup. I looked over at Dray and said, "Thank you."

"For what?" he asked.

"For being you. For being there for me. For sticking with me when times got rough. For being there for me when I made stupid decisions. Thank you, Dray. You'll never know how much your presence means to me."

He smiled and put his attention back on the ball game.

I have everything, or so I thought I had everything. Even after everything that is right with my life that one void still exists. I've tried to fill this void with everything, but nothing works.

It has nothing to do with my relationship with Dray. It has nothing to do with my friendships because even though Dwight isn't in the same city as me, he is still there. It has nothing to do with my job, because I love what I do. I have my mom and my relationship with God but that one void has such a grip on my life.

Maybe one of these days, I'll get over it. Hell, I'll have to because when it's all said and done it's nothing I can do about it. *Nothing.*

Until then I'll make the best of my life. I have no other choice.

Part One:

Georgia On My Mind

1

Dr. Zachariah T. Finley

New York, New York
Wednesday, July 13, 2016

I took my seat on the huge Delta Boeing 767, looked out of the window and exhaled. I was ready to get in the air and get to my destination. As everyone continued to board the plane, I thought about my life and how I got to this point. Once the plane took flight, I looked out the small window again and sighed. An image of Dray appeared before me. I hope that Dray and I get over this issue. I can only pray that he'll see where I'm coming from. While this December will mark the eighth year of our relationship, everything hasn't been perfect, but we're making it work.

When I get off this plane in two hours and offered this job a little while later, I'm getting the fuck away from New York—forever!

I've never liked it there and I will not continue to live in a city I don't want to be. I'm not getting any younger; I will be thirty-three in a couple of months. I refuse to waste away my thirties in New York the same way I wasted away the latter years of my twenties. Because of Dray, I've been in New York for damn near seven years—seven years too long. Call me selfish, but we did things his way for a long time. I bit my tongue for the relationship. I wanted to make it work so I packed up and moved to New York. I loved that man. I still love him. However, I do not want to live the rest of my life in New York. I hate being stressed and I've got to do something to help my situation. I have no other choice.

I miss my friends—Dwight, Keston and Kris. I miss seeing my family. I miss the south. I really miss my mom. I grabbed my phone and looked at a picture of her. She just turned forty-nine back in April.

I placed the phone back down and exhaled. I felt empty. I felt like something was missing from my life.

There was that damn void again. I hate feeling like this. I hate it! What really can I do though? That shit is way out of my control.

My mom, Paula Finley-Grayson, was something else. After twenty years of shacking up, as my grandma would call it, she finally decided to marry the man that I've known to act as my father, even though he didn't donate the sperm required to create me.

While my mom has grown in some areas of her life over the years, others have remained the same. I love the woman; she is my mother. But I've come to accept the realization that we'll never have the type of relationship that I had with my grandmother. The bond just isn't there. I've learned that you can't force something into existence just for the sake of saying it exists. That's the way I feel about my mom. I love her. I really do. But to pretend that our relationship is so great is a lie and I will not stoop to those levels.

There was one point in our relationship, while in New York, I forced myself to call her every day. The phone calls seemed empty. There was nothing natural to the conversation. We seemed like two strangers talking on the phone. I hated that feeling.

I understand that my relationship with my mom will never be like Dwight and his mom or Dray and his mom. My situation is a little different and I understand that it is ok. I can't go around comparing my life to theirs. Everyone has different circumstances that made them into the people that they are today.

On another note, my mom has always been smart, but her sudden and surprising pregnancy at fifteen years old changed her life. She says she never knew she was pregnant, even though I often question that. I understand that you are young, but if your menstrual cycle hasn't been on in months, were you not going to ask someone what was wrong with that? But then again, maybe it's just me being a little over analytical.

She said she never showed until she was seven months. Ok, that's possible. But did you not feel the baby kicking?

My mom says that, at the time, her first and only time having sex turned into her getting pregnant. My biological father had convinced my mom to have sex. They did it one evening behind the gymnasium of their junior high school. My mom and my sperm donor had been together for a year or so and she felt that the time was right. She wanted to experience what all her home girls were talking about, but it just so happened that she was the only one to turn up pregnant.

After a while of my mom being sick, my grandmother took her to the doctor. It was revealed there that my mom, who had turned sixteen a few months back, was seven months pregnant. My grandmother lost her mind.

My grandma Carrie stressed to my mom that I was her responsibility and she needed to make the necessary adjustments to take care of me. My mom never got to experience her high school years. She quit school and got her GED. Once I was born, she immediately started working. As the smartest woman in the family, she never got the chance to go to college. She was stuck in poverty. She never really recovered from that one moment, that one lack in judgment to have sex with that boy back when she was fifteen.

One thing she said she learned from that was one moment can change your life. I think about the world nowadays and that statement is so true. One moment can change your life.

One moment to lay down with some man you've met off an app can change your life. One moment to take your eye off the road to read a text message can change your life. One moment to go to bed angry with the one that you love can change your life. I've learned that we have to make the best of every moment, because you never know what will happen in the next.

However, that was back in 1983. It's now 2016. At some point you have man up, or in her case, woman up, to your mistakes and move on. You can't dwell in the past.

Out of my own guilt on my existence, I've given my mother plenty of opportunities to go back to school. When I was in undergrad back at FAMU, I once told her that she should look into going to college. She was smart enough to do so. She looked into it but said that her going to school would mess up my financial aid and she didn't want to mess with that so she didn't look any further. I accepted that excuse. She was trying to be a good parent and look after her son needs rather than her own.

When I started my master's degree program, I advised her to look into going to school so she could make the remaining years of her life worthwhile. She never did so. She couldn't blame her not going to school on the financial aid issue because at that point in my life I was very much independent. Even after I completed my Ph.D. at

Columbia a few years back, I said, "Ma, what's the hold up now? There is no more schooling for me to complete. I have the highest academic achievement possible."

With Dray's advice, I even suggested to pay for her education. But she is still sitting in that house in Central Florida wasting her life away. She hasn't worked a consistent job in fifteen years. My stepdad takes care of her and the house. I guess she is ok with her life as it stands. I just don't understand the woman. Quite honestly, I'm tired of trying to understand her.

I looked at the time on my phone. I had another hour or so on this flight. I thought about Tony and smiled. I saw images of our childhood.

I missed my childhood. Life was so free and easy. There were no worries. You never had to think about how the rent was going to get paid, or if there was going to be any food in the refrigerator, or if I would have new clothes for the new school year. Not that I have to worry about any of that, but I have students and associates who do have to worry about those things. I understand the struggle. I once lived that struggle.

Young children aren't burdened with those aspects of life. Children live freely. They conquer anything. They have imaginations that run wild. One day I was Superman saving the world from evil, the next day I was Batman. In my mind, I was the hero; I saved the world from the Russians.

I chuckled.

I really miss my grandmother. Even though she's been gone ten and a half years, I still wish she was here with me. I wish she could see everything positive that I've done in my life. She would be so proud of me.

Images of going to church with my grandmother flooded my mind. There were images of me standing next to her in the kitchen while she whipped up one of her most famous sweet potato pies and sour crème pound cakes. Those were the days. I remembered standing around the kitchen counter waiting for my grandma to pour the batter into the cake pans so my cousins and me could lick the excess batter out of the huge bowls.

There were images of my cousins and me sitting in the back of my uncle's pickup truck, riding with him down to the lake to do some fishing. And then there were the times in the summer when we would sit on the porch with my grandmother and make some homemade ice cream, taking turns, using all of our young energy to churn that old wooden barrel, all while she smiled and downed a fresh glass of lemonade. Down the street, the older boys in the neighborhood would be yelling while playing tackle football in the old abandoned field. Moments later, one of my uncle's classmates would stop over to check on my grandma just to make sure she was ok. That's just how things were in the south. Life was simple down there.

There were images of the family gathering around the dinner table for Thanksgiving, holding hands and giving thanks to God for the wonderful things he's bestowed in our lives. I thought about riding our new bicycles on Christmas with my cousins, playing hide-n-go seek; playing red light - yellow light - green light; playing dodgeball; playing duck, duck, goose; climbing up the tree only to fall and scrape something. All that flashed in my head.

A tear escaped from my eye. I missed my childhood. Life was so free. I wish I was free now.

*****

Antonio "Tony" Shaw

Charlotte, North Carolina

He was pissing me off. He was really starting to royally piss me the fuck off.

"Straighten your damn face!" I stared at TJ.

He just looked at me as if he wanted to say something, but knew for his sake he'd better keep his thoughts to himself.

One of the movers stepped into the house and said, "Mr. Shaw?"

I focused my attention on the middle aged white man that stood before me and answered, "Yes sir?"

He said, "We have everything loaded and are ready to take off."

"Good, we'll be leaving in a little bit," I said.

The mover handed me a clipboard and said, "I need you to sign this form."

I read over paper that took any liability away from the moving company if something were to happen as they drove from Charlotte to Atlanta. Once I signed the paper, he gave me the final instructions and then made his way out of the house. I looked out the window as the moving truck that housed all of our belongings was headed south to Atlanta.

I looked back at my thirteen-year-old son and shook my head. I did feel sorry for him, but he knew this day was coming. He's known for six months that this day was coming.

TJ sat on the floor with his silver Beats by Dre headphones over his ears. I ran upstairs to make sure that I didn't forget anything.

I've come to love this house. We've been here for seven years. Charlotte was my city. I know I once said I would never move to Atlanta, but Raidon is there. He got a job as the associate dean of the School of Education at Clark Atlanta University. I'm here to support my dude. We've been in this thing for almost thirteen years and I'm not letting it go because he has a job in Atlanta.

Raidon moved to Atlanta back in January. I didn't want to interrupt TJ's school year, so Raidon suggested that we join him over the summer once the school year was over. That also allowed me time to secure a job down in the Peach State. Luckily, there was a position in my companies' regional office in Atlanta as the Regional Human Resources Manager. I applied and interviewed for the position. I was awarded the job just three weeks ago and I'll be starting next week. I'm responsible for all the human resource managers for my company in Alabama, Florida, Georgia, North Carolina and South Carolina. This is a huge responsibility that will require me to do a lot of traveling, but I'm up for it. Making a six-figure salary with options for crazy monetary bonuses is an added plus.

I walked down the stairs and looked at TJ as he listened to his music and pouted.

"Ight, Tony," I said to myself. "Just calm down."

I grabbed the couple of suitcases that sat by the front door and headed outside to put them in my car. Just as I was closing the trunk, my phone started to vibrate. It was Raidon. I leaned against the SUV and answered.

He asked, "When are you all leaving?"

"In a second. The movers just left and I just put the last few things in the trunk."

"How is TJ?" he asked.

"He's still pouting and showing his ass."

"Wow," Raidon said, as I could hear the sudden change in his voice. "He'll like Atlanta and he'll have the opportunity to make some new friends."

"You're preaching to the choir, Raidon," I looked back at the house.

He said, "Well, you've changed your stance on it. Just give him some time and he'll change his, too."

I sighed, "I hope so. I hate to see him hurting like this. I just feel there are other ways to show your displeasure with something than dragging your feet, throwing tantrums and pouting. He's been doing this for months and I'm tired of it, Raidon. I've reached my limit!"

"Tony, our son has your personality. Y'all share that same fiery temper. He has the same mentality that you have of act first then ask questions second."

"But still," I said.

"But still nothing," Raidon laughed. "Like father, like son."

"Whatever Raidon," I shook my head.

He laughed again and said, "Don't let me hold you up, baby. I've got an interview in a couple hours, so I want to grab a bite to eat so I can be on time."

"Ight," I said. "I'll get at you when we're close so you can meet us at the house."

"Ok," Raidon said. "I love you."

"I love you, too."

I hung up the phone and headed back to the house.

"HEY, MR. SHAW!" I heard some kid yell. I turned around and realized it was one of TJ's closest friends.

"Sup, Daequan?" I asked.

"TJ still here?"

"Yeah, he's in the house," I pointed for him to go inside.

Out of respect for my teenaged son, I stayed outside so he could have a few more minutes with his dear friend.

I went back to the car and thought about our seven years here. This is really the only home TJ knows. He was six when we left Tallahassee and I'm sure he doesn't really remember much of his time there. He doesn't even remember his mother, April. TJ knows that my relationship with Raidon is not of the norm, but he has never really said anything about it. We've sat down and told him that we're gay, but he doesn't talk about it. I guess it doesn't bother him. We're his parents and that's all that matters. I am afraid, however, that as TJ gets older and as he goes through school, there will be more questions. His friends will start to question our relationship. I can foresee some negative reactions in the future. I don't know if TJ is ashamed or not, but the only friend that he's ever brought to the house is Daequan. So, I really don't know what TJ tells his friends, if he even tells them anything at all. I want to ask him what he feels about everything, but I really don't know how to go about doing it.

I looked at my phone. We needed to get on the road. I hate to interrupt their impromptu meeting, but we've gotta go. I hate driving anyways and the sooner we leave the quicker these four hours will be over and we'll be in Atlanta.

Until last month, Raidon has been living in a hotel. We finally found a house that we both like. Since all of our possessions were here in Carolina, Raidon says the house is empty. He's picked up a few ins and outs, but once our furniture is in place things will probably feel like home again.

I walked back up to the house and told TJ that we had to go. He hugged his close friend.

"Take care, Mr. Shaw," the kid said as he lifted his head. "Hit me up TJ."

"Ight, Quan," TJ replied as he stared at him walk out the door.

As soon as his friend was gone, TJ yelled, "WHY WE GOTTA GO TO ATLANTA? I DON'T WANNA MOVE TO ATLANTA! MY FRIENDS ARE HERE IN CHARLOTTE!"

"We're going to Atlanta because Raidon and I both have good jobs there. We're going to Atlanta so we can continue to spoil your spoiled ass! I know you don't wanna go, but you can and you *will* make new friends down in Atlanta. The move is for the best."

"Yeah, man, whatever," he stormed out of the house.

I exhaled.

Patience, Tony, patience.

I locked up the house and headed for the SUV; TJ was leaning against the side passenger door.

"Get in so we can go," I said, sitting down.

As soon as he got in the vehicle, he slammed the door as hard as he could, showing his displeasure in our decision to leave Charlotte.

I scolded him, "You slam my damn door again and I'ma slam this belt up against your thirteen-year-old ass! You're trying my patience, TJ. You're trying my motherfucking patience!"

He rolled his eyes, turned his head and looked out the window.

I exhaled and said a quick prayer before we pulled out and headed for Atlanta.

2

Dr. Dwight Taylor

Atlanta, Georgia

That sixteen-hour shift just killed me. I was exhausted. The only thing I want to do was go home, grab a quick bite to eat, shower and get my ass in the bed. I finally get a few days of peace and quiet since Lexi and the kids left a few hours ago to see her mom in Savannah.

I got off 285 and merged north onto 19. This traffic was killing me. I hated taking this drive to and from work every day.

I think it's time I really look into getting that forensic pharmacy degree. I'm tired of doing this shit every day. Yeah, the money is good, but I need a new challenge in my life.

After about twenty more minutes, I turned onto my street. I exhaled as I pulled in my driveway, pressing the garage button. I was finally gonna get some rest without hearing, "DADDY, DADDY, DADDY!" I love my kids, but I need a break.

I parked the car and let the garage back down. I exited the car and played with the family dog, Max, for a few moments who had rushed through the doggy door when he heard me. I opened the side door and made my way inside of the house.

I just stopped. I looked at the condition of the house.

"DAMN LEXI!" I yelled. "WHAT THE FUCK?"

There were clothes all over the living room. The kids' toys were in the middle of the floor. The dishes from where she cooked breakfast still sat on the stove. The sink was full of plates. This shit was filthy!

She knows how much I hate fucked up houses. She knows I'm a

clean freak. I can't stay here in this shit.

What the fuck is wrong with that woman? The only thing I ask is that you cook and keep a clean house. What is so damn hard about that? She is so fucking lazy! That shit is really starting to irk my last nerve. I don't know how much more of this I can take. I can't stay here in this shit.

I ran upstairs and grabbed a few clean clothes and my toiletries. I then quickly returned downstairs and got back in my car. I was going to a hotel.

I don't know how much longer I can put up with this shit. Marrying her was a mistake, a big mistake. These past seven years have been the worst of my life.

I can't take too much more of this shit.

I can't.

*****

Zach

Atlanta, Georgia

As soon as I got off the plane, I grabbed my luggage and called my other best friend, Keston Sharpe, who slowly replaced Keli in my life. While in graduate school at FAMU, Keston was one of the student athletic trainers for our football team and has now taken his talents to the NFL where he is a trainer for the Atlanta Falcons. He initially got his student training collegiate start down at the University of Central Florida.

Once Keston arrived, I put my things in his car, dapped him up and said, "My nigga!"

"What they do?" Kes smiled as he pulled off.

Dray often asks me why I chose to talk in such hood language when I have degrees that say I'm above that lifestyle. I just shake my head at him. I feel that when I'm around my friends, I don't have to put up a front. I don't have to show off my education. That is the one opportunity where I can kick back, relax and be myself. When I'm in a professional setting, I will act and speak like the professional that I am. My level of education does not define who I am and where I come from. Obviously, Dwight, Tony, Keston and Kris all feel the same way because we all talk in slang when we're around each other.

"Just ready to get this shit over with," I sighed.

"I feel you. How is Dray?" he asked, merging onto the interstate.

"He's doing well," I said.

"What's wrong?"

"I didn't tell him about the interview," I confessed.

"Why not?" Keston asked.

"I've mentioned living in Atlanta before and I can tell that he really doesn't want to move here. Dray likes it in New York. We got into an argument about it before I left."

"What happened?"

"He said that I never really gave New York a chance. I doubted it even before I got up there."

"Well, you did," Keston stated. "You made it clear that you never wanted to go up there."

"That's true, but I went. I went because I loved him and I wanted our relationship to work." I sighed, "I've tried to do it but I can't anymore. I don't want to be up there. I hope I'm not coming across as selfish, but I did things his way. I love Dray but I don't want to be miserable. I need to get this job; this is my way out of New York."

"Didn't y'all just buy a house down here in Atlanta?"

"Yeah. Dray said it's our summer house. But with me teaching summer school courses in New York, when exactly will I have the time to occupy the house? I think I've spent one night in the place since we purchased it."

"Well, you'll get to spend tonight there."

"Yeah, but then I'm back out in the morning because I have a class to teach."

"Wow," Keston stated as we got off the interstate. "You stay busy."

"Tell me about it."

"When do y'all have time to fuck?"

I laughed and said, "We make time."

A few minutes later, we were approaching the AU Center and the campus of Clark Atlanta University. I searched through my phone until located an email.

"Some kid is supposed to meet us over there," I pointed to the Bishop Cornelius Henderson Student Center, a large building on the corner.

"What for?"

"He is to escort me to the School of Education."

"Do your administrators at Columbia know that you've applied for another job at another university?"

"Hell, naw. I ain't crazy. If they knew I was down here for an interview they would try to find a reason to get rid of me. When I get this job, and yes I did say when, because I am claiming it right now, I'll inform Columbia of my decision to leave."

"I got'cha," Keston said as I saw some young dude in a black suit waiting.

"I wonder if that is him."

"He's cute," Keston smiled.

"Yeah, he is," I said as I got out of the car. I put on my suit jacket and grabbed my briefcase.

"Dr. Finley?" the dude asked, approaching me.

"Yes, sir," I stated. "I take it you're my escort?"

"That will be me. We're called Student Ambassadors," he said as he extended his hands and smiled at me. "I'm Larenzo Wright, but everyone calls me Renzo."

I stared at the young, sexy dude. He looked somewhat familiar, like he could be related to someone I've seen before. By my estimate, Renzo was a little taller than 6'. He had an athletic, basketball build with an almond butter skin tone. He had deep, 360-degree sick sea waves, with a clean shaven face. I could see the veins in his hands from where he works out. He was definitely a pretty boy. *Damn, who did he remind me of?* That shit is going to bother me!

I cleared my throat, started walking and said, "Well, it's nice to meet you, Renzo. Are you from Atlanta?"

"No, sir," he shook his head. "I'm from Chicago. I'm just here for school, graduating this school year."

"Well, congratulations! What is your major?"

"Business, but I have a minor in education," he replied, as we approached a building.

I smiled.

He returned the smile and said, "Well, this is the Rufus E. Clement Hall, the building for the School of Education. The dean had a family emergency he had to deal with, so the associate dean will be handling your interview. Good luck, Dr. Finley."

"Thanks, Renzo," I smiled. "Hopefully, I'll see you around."

"Hopefully," he grinned as he turned around and went inside another door.

Once I entered, the secretary let me know that the associate dean would be with me shortly. I sat down, nervous. I've always hated interviews. A few moments later, she said, "Dr. Finley."

"Yes?" I stood up.

"Dr. Harris is ready for you," she pointed to the office door.

"Thank you," I headed to the office.

Once I stepped inside, my mouth dropped. He smiled and said, "I just happened to look at the name a few minutes ago and said this couldn't be right." Raidon closed the door and motioned for me to take a seat.

"It's been a long time, Dr. Harris," I said trying to keep my professionalism.

"Please, Zach, call me Raidon," he took a seat at his desk. "How has everything been? Tony was just talking about you the other day."

"Everything is ok. I'm just trying to get out of New York."

"What's wrong in the Big Apple?"

"It's just not for me. That's why I applied for the job."

"Yeah. I see that you got your Ph.D. from Columbia and you were teaching and counseling there as well," he said, looking over my resume.

"Yeah, but those aren't *my* kind of people. I just feel like I can be more useful helping *my people* if you understand what I'm saying."

"I understand completely," he smiled. "Black people."

We talked for a few more minutes. Not once did Raidon mention anything really serious pertaining to the interview.

"Well, I think we've been in here long enough," he smiled. "I think it's safe to call this interview quits."

I smiled.

"I have a couple more interviews tomorrow and then I will get with the dean next week when he returns to give him my decision. You'll know something by Wednesday at the latest."

"Ok," I stood up and shook his hand.

"But trust me, you don't have anything to worry about. I'll make sure of that," he winked.

"Thank you, Raidon."

"No, thank you. Having you in town might be what Tony needs to help him get adjusted to the city. He really didn't want to move here."

"Got'cha," I said as he opened the door.

"But, yeah," he said, as his voice changed from casual to a very professional one. I assumed he was putting on the show for the secretary. "We will be in touch next week to let you know of our decision."

"Thanks for your time, Dr. Harris," I said playing along.

"No, thank you, Dr. Finley."

I smiled at the secretary as I left. As soon as I stepped out of the office, I exhaled. I looked up to the heavens and smiled.

Thank you, God. This was nothing but you!

I took another deep breath and then exhaled. I will not be returning to New York to live and that's that—whether Dray is with me or not.

I've had enough.

Enough!

3

Dorian Kierce

Atlanta, Georgia

This traffic was the absolute worst. I just wanted to get home. I exhaled and listened to the soothing sounds of Yolanda Adams, while I sat in bumper-to-bumper traffic.

I really missed my mom. It's days like these when I wish she were here. She was such a good woman whose life was taken too early. Today marks the third anniversary of her passing.

My mom, Dorinda Franklin, died from AIDS. Her story is so typical. She was sleeping with her boyfriend who eventually passed the HIV virus to her. Nothing could be done when she found out she had it because it was too late. She went on to be with God at forty-six years old.

Watching those final stages of her life was too much to bear. So when she perished, I left home for good. That's how I became a resident of Atlanta, Georgia for the past three years.

I'm Dorian Kierce (pronounced like Pierce but with a K) and I was born in Orlando, Florida on October 3, 1985. My mom, Dorinda, and dad, Duane Kierce, met in high school. After he broke up with his first baby mama, he and my mom got together.

My mom and dad had an on-and-off relationship for a period of years. During one of their breakup's, my mom met another dude and from there, she had my baby brother Marquis. My brother and I are four years apart. Since Marquis' dad was a bum, my father decided to take Marquis in and raise him as his own son.

My dad got a job in Jacksonville, Florida when I was seven and that's basically where I grew up. My mom and dad broke up when I was ten, and while my dad moved back to Orlando, my mom stayed in Jacksonville because of her job.

My mom, brother and I moved back to Orlando when I was fourteen because my maternal grandmother could no longer take care of herself. Even after my grandmother died, my mom stayed put in Orlando. She said she was tired of moving.

I spent my high school years in Orlando and graduated from the oldest black school in the county, Jones High School. Following in the steps of my high school band director, I decided to attend Bethune-Cookman University over in nearby Daytona Beach.

I really wanted to go to FAMU. However, Bethune offered me more scholarship money, so I went to Bethune. It had its perks. I was only forty-five minutes from home, so it was nothing to hop on I-4 and grab a hot plate from mom.

While at Bethune, I spent my first two years in the band playing trombone. I was one of five drum majors my last two years in the band. Those were some of the best times of my life and I miss it dearly. If I could relive those years, I'd be one of the happiest men in the world.

My dad was my number one supporter. I really love that man.

Being at Bethune also brought me my greatest pride and joy, my daughter, Dakota Kierce. She will be eight in December. Dakota was one of the reasons why I decided to move to Atlanta after my mom passed. Dakota and her mom, Cecelia, lived here. While I feel nothing sexually for Cecelia, I love my daughter and want to be close by so I can see her grow up. I want her to know that daddy will always be there for her. Cecelia was also a member of the band at Bethune. She was on the dancing girl line also known at the 14-Karat Gold Dancers.

I've always known that I had a thing for dudes. I messed around with dudes long before I started having sex with Cecelia. To me, Cecelia was an experiment—an experiment that gave me Dakota. I really liked Cecelia, but I later realized that my true love was for men.

Cecelia got pregnant two months before we graduated college. That was great for us because nobody had an idea that she was pregnant. That wouldn't be good considering that we were at a private, Christian based college.

After receiving our degrees in business administration, she immediately moved back home to Atlanta and I moved back to Orlando. In Orlando, I attended the University of Central Florida and earned my master's degree in accounting. Even though we were in different cities for the first few years of Dakota's life, I've always been a damn good dad. I'm grateful that Cecelia and I have a working relationship as it concerns our daughter.

While I graduated from a small black college in Daytona Beach, that education has granted me the opportunity to make a decent salary. I'm currently a Budget Analyst for a Fortune 50 company. Since it's only me, and I make sure I take care of Dakota's needs without having Cecelia put me on child support, my $62,300 a year takes me a long way.

After spending at least an hour in traffic, I finally reached my upscale condo in Buckhead. Once inside, I took off my suit and slid into something more comfortable. I stared at myself in the mirror. I looked a lot like my mom, but got my height from my dad. I stood 6'1". I had a low cut with waves that stayed on point. I sported a chin strap beard with a connecting goatee. I was brown-skinned with an athletic body. Many people say I reminded them of NFL star Cam Newton. I knew I looked good and I knew my body could take me places, so I did some modeling gigs back in college to make some extra money. I lifted my shirt and ran my hands across my abs. I smiled. I needed to get to the gym downstairs before bed, but knew I'd probably do it before work in the morning.

I walked into the kitchen and opened the freezer. I looked through the meat and decided to take the easy way out tonight and bake some fish. While the salmon thawed, I went into my living room and flipped on the television.

I'm a sucker for politics so I can find myself watching MSNBC all day, every day. Just as I was getting into the show, my phone started to vibrate. It was my pops. I answered, "How is everything?"

He struggled to say, "Son, you know every day is a struggle, but I'm still living."

"Are they taking care of you down there?"

"Yes. Everything is well."

"Good," I replied.

"I was thinking about your mom. It's been three years. Time really moves fast."

"Yeah," I sighed as I looked at her picture that was hanging on my living room wall. "It's been three years."

"You know I always loved your mother. I always loved her."

"Yes, sir. I know."

"Even though we didn't work out, I had to make sure that I did right by you."

I exhaled.

"Speaking of that, have you done what I asked of you?"

"No sir, not yet," I sighed. "I'm gonna do it."

"Dorian, I can die any day now. Please see that you make this happen. Make this wish come true for your old man."

"I'll try my best. I just don't feel comfortable…you know."

"Do it for me. Let me right one wrong in my life. Please, son."

"Ok…I'll do it," I said getting frustrated.

"Well, let me go. I'll talk to you another day if it's the good Lord's will. Tell Marquis to come by and check on me. I miss him."

"Yes, sir, I will. Take care. I love you."

"I love you, too," he ended the call.

My dad is terminally ill with stage-four colon cancer. He was diagnosed about five months ago. They tried surgery and other options, but there's not much the doctors can do at this point because the cancer has spread to his liver, lungs, bones and distant lymph nodes. They're giving him anywhere from three-to-six months to live.

A few weeks ago my dad had a revelation and decided he wanted to heal some open wounds before he dies and he needs me to help set this plan into action. It's intriguing but I don't feel comfortable doing this.

I look at the number every day, but can never find the nerve to actually dial it. Why did he have to put me in the middle of this shit?

I stared at the number for a moment. I don't know why this was so hard for me to do. I exhaled. I typed the area code into my phone, but was stopped when my ex-boyfriend's name started to flash across the screen alerting me that he was calling.

I sighed and shook my head. Morgan Harris. I don't have time for his shit today. I ignored the call and then got up and went into the kitchen. I needed to prepare dinner.

4

Zach

New York, New York

The elevator opened. I stepped out and headed down the hall to my class where I'm sure everyone would be doing some last minute studying. As I approached the room, I sighed and said to myself, "Ight, Zach. It's game time, nigga. Put on your game face."

I wasn't feeling this shit today; today was just one of those days. I took a deep breath, exhaled, opened the door and headed inside.

"Good afternoon everyone," I stated in a firm tone as I walked directly over to the professor's desk.

All forty students in the class greeted me back. While they looked over their notes, I took out my laptop and let it boot up. I sat the exam papers on the desk and then looked at my phone. I would give them an extra five minutes to study.

I sat down and rubbed my hands through my hair. This potential move to Atlanta is really stressing me. It's been exactly one week and one day since I interviewed for the position at Clark Atlanta University and I have yet to hear anything. I know Raidon said I had the job, but what is taking so long to make it official?

I grabbed my phone and checked the time. Those five minutes were up.

"Ok, you can go ahead and put away all study materials," I stated as I grabbed the exams and stood in front of the class. "If you've had one of my classes before, you know how my exams are constructed. If this is your first time, all of my exams are essay/short answer questions. I don't do multiple choice exams. Either you know the answer or you don't."

I heard a few students moan in displeasure.

I continued, "This is a five question exam. Please take your time and answer each question thoroughly. You have the next two hours to complete. Trust me when I say that there is no reason to cheat as there are five different tests, all with different questions, being circulated."

After I went over the directions and passed out the exam, I went back to my seat and re-read the latest chapter in the book I'm writing. That didn't last long as my mind pondered to Dray. I really needed to figure out what I am going to do with him. He wants to stay in New York but I'm over it. Things are getting tense in the house. Dray says that I have an attitude all the time. We tend to argue a lot now. Nothing is the same and I think it's because I'm fed up. Any little thing pisses me off. I don't want to be in New York anymore.

I suddenly thought about Chaz. Just three months ago, this past April, marked the tenth anniversary of his passing. I wonder where life would be if he was still alive. I wonder what type of father he would have been. At least God spared the life of Chaz's second born child, Elijah, from that accident. That entire scene was just tragic.

Last I knew, Chaz's wife, Genevieve, had gotten back with her first love, my ex house mate and co-worker, Will. I wonder how life has treated them. Are they still together? The last time I talked to Will was seven years ago at the gas station. I remember I told him not to contact me again because he was telling Lexi about my relationship with Dwight. Yes, I was in the wrong for telling Will about the things Dwight and I shared, but I thought I could trust him. I thought Will was different. Ironically enough, that day I cut Will out of my life was also the last time I saw Micah Harris. We met at Red Lobster for lunch. While I was happy he reclaimed control over his life and beat his drug addiction, I was done with him. I just wanted Micah and Will out of my life.

I thought about Keli. I need to call and check on him. It's a shame that we don't communicate like we used to. I guess we all outgrow relationships.

About an hour into the exam, my phone started to vibrate. It was an Atlanta area code. I looked at my students who were busy writing their answers down and then got up and headed out of the class. I answered, "Hello, Dr. Finley speaking."

"Good afternoon, Zach. This is Raidon."

"Dr. Harris," I smiled, relieved he was calling. "Please tell me you've got some good news."

"I told you, don't call me that. Raidon will suffice," he said. "But, I do have great news. We have interviewed all prospective candidates and the dean informed me to call and let you know that we have offered you the position."

"That is wonderful news," I smiled, as for once in the past month, I felt good.

"We would like for you to come back to Atlanta to negotiate your salary and sign the contract."

"We can make that happen, but I'm in the midst of administering a test. Would it be ok if I can call you back to make arrangements?"

"Oh, yes," he replied. "No rush. I'll send you an email with all of my contact numbers. Just call my cell. I'm about to get out of the office in an hour or so."

"Sounds good," I smiled.

"I'll be looking forward to hearing from you soon. Take care Zach."

"Thanks, Raidon."

"No problem," he hung up the phone.

Before I opened the classroom door, I exhaled. I looked towards the heavens and said, "Thank you."

Things were staring to work out. Now I just gotta find a way to break this news to Dray.

*****

Tony

We had been here for about a week, but I was still getting settled into our home north of Atlanta in Sandy Springs.

I didn't want to move to Atlanta, but I am grateful for the opportunity. We all need change and this move was definitely a plus. If I can only get my child to see that this change will be good for us.

I smiled.

I loved that boy. I love TJ with everything inside of me. I'll give him the world if I could. I'm stern with him because while his parents have money, that is our money, not his. He needs to learn how to be responsible. He needs to learn how to take care of himself. He needs to learn the value of hard work. My parents instilled those things in me and I want to teach my only child those same values. He may not like it now, but he'll appreciate it when he gets older.

TJ was in the living room listening to his music. That boy is always listening to music.

He hasn't really said much to me since we've been here. I've been listening to Raidon and I'm just going to let TJ come around. He'll come around. He has no other choice.

Just as I walked into the kitchen to grab a bottle of water, I heard the house phone. I answered, "Hello?"

"Hey Tony, this is Morgan. How are you?"

"I'm good, what's up," I stated to Raidon's younger brother.

"I was just calling to see if Raidon made it home. I need to talk to him. I tried calling his cell but it kept going to voicemail."

"No, he hasn't made it yet, but when he gets in I'll tell him to give you a call."

"Thanks, Tony."

"No problem," I hung up the phone.

When I grabbed the bottle of water, I heard Raidon walking into the house. "Hey baby," he said as he came over and kissed me.

"How was your day?" I asked.

"It was great!" he smiled.

Raidon had this smirk on his face as if he knew something.

"What?" I asked.

"Nothing," he replied.

"Morgan just called."

"What did he want?" Raidon asked, leaning against the counter.

"He wanted you to call him back."

"Ok," he smiled. "Let's go get dinner. I'm starving."

"Dinner sounds good, but not until you say why you're smirking like that. What did I do?"

"I just have some good news."

"What is it?"

"TJ!" Raidon yelled ignoring me.

"He has that music in his ear."

"Oh," he turned around and headed in the living room. I followed. When TJ saw Raidon, he smiled and took off his headphones.

"Hey, Ray," TJ said.

"You alright?" Raidon asked.

"Yeah, I guess," TJ sighed. He cut his eyes to me and said, "It is what it is, right?"

I always admired their relationship. Raidon had a special bond with TJ. It's kinda like Raidon took on the motherly role in TJ's life.

"Why won't you go change clothes. We're about to head out and grab dinner," Raidon stated.

"Naw, I think I'll stay. I'm not really in the mood to go out," TJ replied as he looked at me for my approval.

I didn't reply.

"You want us to bring you something back?" Raidon asked.

"Yeah, that'll be cool," TJ smiled. "Thanks Ray."

"No problem," Raidon winked his eye then turned around to me and said, "Let's go."

"When are you gonna tell me the good news?" I asked as we headed back to the kitchen.

"Well, I've been holding onto it for the past week until it was official, and now that it is official, I just wanted to let you know that one of your best friends is moving to Atlanta."

"Who?" I asked. "Killa didn't get traded did he?"

"No," Raidon shook his head. "I'm talking about Zach."

"Zach?" I said shocked. "How do you know he's coming here? Zach teaches at Columbia in New York."

"He applied for a position in my department. I interviewed him last week and offered him the position today."

"Z is really coming down to Atlanta?" I asked, shocked.

"Yeah, he is," he said.

I smiled. Wow. I missed Zach.

"I figured that would make you happy," he said. "Having Zach around should make the transition a bit easier."

"Raidon, you're the best," I smiled as I kissed him on the cheek.

"I know," he kissed me. "Who's driving—me or you?"

"You," I grabbed my phone.

He smiled as we exited our new home.

5

Antonio "TJ" Shaw

Atlanta, Georgia

Once the front door closed, I walked over to the window and watched them back out of the driveway. I love my parents, but they got me fucked up if they think I'm about to go to dinner with the both of them. I'll never be seen in public with the both of them together, if I can help it.

One? Fine. Two? Hell fuck naw!

As crazy as this situation is, Daddy and Ray are my parents. They're all I know and I do love them. I don't have a problem with them and what they do, but I don't wanna be labeled as gay because my parents are gay. Nigga got life fucked up!

I walked back into the living room and sat down on the couch. I missed my friends back in Charlotte. This shit ain't fair! I gotta up and change my life because my parents decide to get new jobs. What the fuck was wrong with the jobs they already had? They're only worried about themselves. What about me and my feelings? They didn't care that I had to up and change my life? It ain't my fault that none of daddy friends lived in Charlotte. Why I gotta be punished for that? My friends were there. Daddy is so selfish. That shit pisses me off. Everything is always about him.

I looked around the house and exhaled. This shit is boring. It ain't nothing to do here. It takes damn near thirty minutes to get back into the city. If I had a car and could drive it would be ok. But I can't drive because I'm not old enough. This that bullshit I be talking about. What the hell I'm supposed to do out here? I went walking around the neighborhood this weekend but didn't see no other black kids my age.

I rubbed my stomach. I was a lil hungry. I went into the kitchen and opened the fridge. I stared at it for a few moments like something different was supposed to appear out of thin air. I exhaled and shook my head.

I went to my room and put on my shoes. I stared in the mirror to make sure I was looking fresh. I brushed my hair.

I was growing boy. I was gonna be tall just like daddy. I'm only thirteen and already 5'10." I looked a lot like my dead mom. I had her honey brown skin. While I had my dad's facial structure, I had all of my mom's features. I was definitely a looker and I had all the ladies back in Charlotte. The fact that I sported the latest name brand clothes and hottest shoes, and best gadgets helped, too. I never went without.

After I put on my Jordan's, I grabbed my iPod and headphones and headed out of the house. I locked the door and then prepared to take a walk to the store all the way at the end of the road.

I still had a few dollars that Uncle Killa deposited into my account a couple of weeks ago. Maybe daddy will let me go spend some time with Uncle Killa. That's a cool ass nigga right there. Killa my nigga fa sho. I smiled. I really loved Uncle Killa. He be ballin' in the NFL and shit. I wish daddy could still play football. I know he misses it.

I'll be forever grateful that daddy decided I was more important than a game of football. I don't know where I would be if he died playing football because of his heart condition.

My mom—who I don't remember—died when I was two years old. I can't lose my daddy, too. Daddy pisses me off at times, but I love him. I really do.

As I walked down the street, listening to Wale, I saw a dude dribbling a basketball out of his driveway. He started to shoot the ball at the goal that had been rolled out to the side of the road. From a distance, he looked like he could be black. He was very light skinned; I think I'll call him Light Bright.

I pulled the headphones from around my ears and placed them around my neck. I turned around as I heard a car approaching me from behind. As the fancy car passed, I realized that I was about five houses away from our place.

As I got closer, the dude raised up for another shot. I laughed to myself as he bricked it. He rebounded his own ball, looked down in my direction and then began to dribble again. He shot another shot and missed.

I will kill this nigga in basketball.

As I approached him, he dribbled the ball and said, "Sup, Shawty?"

"Sup," I replied, as I continued to walk.

Yeah he was light skinned, but he was definitely a nigga. He was country though. He sounded like he was from Atlanta.

As I continued on my journey, I thought, *'Maybe I should talk to him."*

It ain't like I got friends out here and I needed to make some. I need to know somebody 'round this bitch and he playing ball? A nigga like me love to ball, whether it's football, basketball or baseball. I love sports. I guess I got that gene from my daddy.

If Light Bright is still out playing ball when I come back, I'll try to talk to him.

When I finally reached the store, I searched around until I got a bag of Baked Cheddar and Sour Crème Lays potato chips. Those were my favorite chips. I went into the cooler and picked up an orange Gatorade. This should hold me over until daddy and Ray came back with my food.

After I paid for my snack, I put the headphones back on and left the store. I flipped to my J. Cole playlist. I paused for a second. It was hotter than a bitch out here. I stood there and ate my chips, hoping some clouds would come and cover the sun.

When I finished, I threw away the bag of chips. Just my luck, some clouds moved in and I began my walk back home.

I sipped on my drink and rapped to myself as I walked down the sidewalk. When I turned the corner, I saw that Light Bright was still outside trying to ball. I chuckled. He was pathetic.

As I got closer to him, I placed the headphones around my neck and took another sip of my Gatorade.

"Can I get a shot up, too?" I asked.

"That's what's up," he replied, as he bounced passed me the ball. I placed my drink down on the sidewalk along with my music. I took a couple of bounces and then put up a shot. Nothing but net.

Light Bright laughed, "Shawty out here think he balling-n-shit."

"I don't think, I know," I said as I put up another shot that was nothing but net.

"Whatever, nigga," he laughed as he took his own jump shot that went in the goal.

"Good shot."

"Wanna get in a game of twenty-one?" Light Bright asked.

"That's what's up," I said. "Since it's your shit, you go first."

While we played the friendly game, I felt like a friendship was being formed. Even though I didn't know Light Bright's name, he seemed like a cool dude. He was very friendly, and most importantly, he was black.

"Don't let the skinniness fool you," I said as I backed him down. "I can ball."

"You talking a lot of shit, Shawty," he said, trying to defend me.

When I had him in the right position, I spun off him and shot my jumper.

"Lucky shot," he said.

"Ain't no luck, nigga. It's all skill," I said, as I looked him dead in the eyes. That competitive side of me was at full force. "Skill, nigga!"

"You still talking a lot of shit," Light Bright said.

"Yeah, because next basket is game," I replied as I started to dribble the ball down the road and away from the goal.

"Where are you going?" he asked confused.

"To show you how this isn't luck," I replied, as I stopped about twenty-five feet away from the basket.

"You ain't about to make that shot," he confidently said.

"Watch me," I rose up and took what I imagined to be a NBA style three pointer. A few moments later, the ball dropped through the hoop. "GAME!" I yelled as I jogged over to him.

"Whatever," he replied, as we dapped each other up. "That was all luck."

"Luck don't run in my genes, talent does. I'm TJ, and you?"

"Elijah," Light Bright replied. "Elijah McDaniel. Everyone calls me Eli."

Light Bright…well...umm…Elijah, was about 5'7", and had hair like NFL star Odell Beckham. He wasn't fat, but he had a lil thickness to him. I wasn't gay, but he was attractive. I knew he had females on his dick.

"Man, it's hot out here," I said. "You can come chill with me at my place if you want to."

"You just moved in right, at the house down the street?" Eli asked.

"Yeah," I replied.

"Hold on. Wait for me. Let me go lock up," he ran up to his

house.

I grabbed my Gatorade and finished it off. I picked up my headphones and when he came back out, we started walking towards my house.

"What does TJ stand for?" Eli asked.

"I'm a junior. I was named after my dad," I said. "His name is Antonio, but he just goes by Tony, so that's where TJ comes from."

"Cool," he replied. "My older brother was named after my dad, but they switched the order of the names."

"What is the name?"

"My daddy name was Chaz Xavier McDaniel. My brother's name was Xavier Chaz McDaniel."

"Why do you keep saying was?" I asked as we walked into my place.

"They died," he stated.

"Oh, my bad," I stated.

"It's cool," he said. "It was a long ass time ago. I don't even remember any of them to tell you the truth."

"You were a kid?" I asked as we walked back to my room.

"Yeah. My mom got pictures of them and shit. I look just like my dad. When I was a baby, I looked like my mom, but as I got older, my dad's side became dominate. When my brother was a baby, he looked like him, too."

"Your dad got some strong genes, huh," I smiled.

"Yeah, he does," Eli smiled. "My brother was a year older than me. I was about to turn three when they died."

"What happened?"

"We were in a car accident," he said. "My mom says we were going to Disney World when my dad's car and a tractor trailer collided. My dad and brother died. My mom said she was pregnant at the time and lost the baby, too."

"Damn, man," I replied. "I lost my mom when I was two years old, too."

"Really?"

"Yep. I don't remember her either. I mean there are pictures of her, but that's about it."

"So where you from?" Elijah asked.

"Charlotte," I replied.

"That's what's up."

"Well, I should say I was raised in Charlotte, but I spent the first six years of my life in Tallahassee."

"Are you serious?" Eli said shocked. "Tallahassee, Florida?"

"Yeah."

"Shawty, this is crazy," he said.

"What?"

"I was born in Tallahassee. We lived there until I was eight. My mom and her boyfriend, Will, broke up then we moved up here. She met this dude, Trae. My mom got pregnant with my sister and then my mom and Trae got married. They're still together and we've been here ever since."

"Damn, we were in the same city and we didn't even know. That's weird," I said in amazement.

"When is your birthday?" he asked.

"July 12," I replied.

"This is weird," he said. "My birthday is July 7."

"This is crazy," I replied as it was stated that we were both born in the same year.

"Can I ask you a question?" Elijah asked. "I hope you don't get offended."

"Sup?"

"Do you live with your dad?"

"Yeah," I said, knowing where this was going.

"Is your dad gay? I mean I only ask because I've only seen two dudes go in and out this house."

"Yes, my parents are gay. Is that going to be a problem?" I said getting defensive as I stood up, "because if it is you can just bounce now, homeboy!"

"Naw, shawty, calm down. It's cool. I was just wondering," he said.

"Why does it matter if they're gay or not?" I asked.

"It really doesn't matter," he said.

I just looked at him then reclaimed my seat.

Eli said, "You wanna know something I've never told anyone."

"So why are you telling me?" I asked. "You just met me."

"I feel like I can trust you."

"Ight."

Eli said, "When I was eight, I heard my mom and her ex-boyfriend, Will, arguing one night. I'll never forget this shit. Will was telling my mom that her dead husband was a faggot. He fucked niggas. He told my mom that my dad used to fuck some dude named

Zach. Supposedly Zach and Will were roommates and that's how Will found out. That's when my mom kicked him out and they broke up. Will always said that she was comparing him to my dad and he was sick of it."

"What's your mom's name?"

"Genevieve."

"My mom's name was April," I said. "But how do you feel about that?"

"About what?"

"Your dad allegedly being gay."

"It doesn't bother me," Eli stared at me. "I didn't know him like that, so it doesn't affect me."

"Yeah. I guess so," I stated.

He just looked at me.

"What did I do?" I asked.

"Nothing," he smiled as he stood up.

"You leaving?" I asked.

"Yeah. I just realized I forgot I had to clean the bathroom before *they* get home. I don't wanna get in trouble with him."

"You don't like your new dad do you?" I asked.

"How can you tell?"

"I just can," I replied.

"Yeah, I don't like Trae, but my mom loves him. I miss Will. He was like my daddy. We hardly ever talk anymore. I think my mom had something to do with that. I just don't understand parents. Just because they have problems with people doesn't mean that we gotta have those problems, too."

"Eli, we're gonna get along just fine," I said, as he repeated some of my inner thoughts from earlier.

"Fine," he smiled again. "Yeah, we are."

"What?"

"Nothing, man," he pulled out his phone. "Let me get your number. I'll hit you up later tonight if that's cool with you."

"Yeah, do that," I stated as we exchanged digits, along with our social media handles.

"I'll get at cha," he said as we dapped each other up.

I watched him as he headed back down the street. I shook my head. It is really a small world.

Now if only daddy and Ray hurry up with that food. A nigga hungry as fuck!

6

Zach

It was a quarter to eleven and the moon was glowing. I was in my office supposed to be grading exams but I still can't focus. I loosened the tie from around my neck and exhaled. I looked to the heavens and said, "Grandma, where are you? I really need you right now."

I took another deep breath and then exhaled. I've been in this office for the past five hours. I haven't left except to use the restroom and grab some Chinese food from the delivery man downstairs.

I can't focus because I'm stressed over whether I really want to move to Atlanta. This decision could possibly end my relationship with Dray if he isn't willing to support my efforts to move.

I thought I was ready to go but reality sat in when Raidon called. Am I ready to deal with the possibility of letting Dray go?

His life is here in New York, mine is not. He likes it here, I do not. Despite that, I don't want to give up on Dray. I want this to work. I love him so much. We've been through a lot these past eight years and how could I just let it go like that?

I'll be thirty-three in a couple of months. I'm not getting any younger, so I have to do this for me. I've done things his way for a long time, but now is the time that I take control of my life.

I stared at the exams before grabbing my cell phone. I walked over to my couch and waited for him to answer my call. A few seconds later, Keston said, "What's up, Zach?"

"You got a minute?" I asked.

"Yeah. What's going on?"

"Just thinking about my life and all decisions I've made, whether they be good or bad, and all the decisions I have yet to make. I was thinking how one decision can impact the rest of your life."

"Zach, what's wrong?"

"I'm really stressing about this potential move to Atlanta."

"I thought you wanted to move? What's the problem?" Keston asked.

"I haven't told Dray."

"But you've got the job! How have you not told him?"

"I just haven't," I sighed. "I don't know if I really want to do this now. I don't want my relationship to end for my own selfish reasons. We've been in this thing to long for it to end now. We've been through too much. I've sacrificed so much to be with Dray, more than anyone will ever know. I've let dreams that I have had since I was a freshman in college die because I love Dray. So I'm just supposed to let all that go because I want to move to Atlanta?"

"Zach, you need to tell him how you feel. Dray will understand. Just tell him."

I had another call coming through. I glanced at the phone and it was Dray. I said, "Kes, hold on for a second. Dray is calling now."

When I clicked over and answered, Dray asked, "Where are you?"

"In my office."

"What are you still doing there?" he asked. "It's almost eleven."

"Grading exams."

"Baby, come home. Those exams will be there tomorrow," he said as I got off the couch and headed back to my desk.

"I told my students that I would have this ready for them by the next class meeting. I want to keep my word."

Dray sighed and cut straight to the point by saying, "Outside of this exam shit, what is really the issue?"

"What are you talking about?"

"Zach, don't do that. Something is wrong and has been wrong. I can hear it in your voice, I've seen it in your face. What's really going on?"

"I don't know what you're talking about. Everything is fine."

"Zach, you're lying. I know you."

"Dray, you're worrying about absolutely nothing."

"When are you coming home?" he asked.

"I don't know. I've got to finish this first."

Upset, Dray replied, "Whatever."

"Dray, everything is fine," I tried to reassure him.

"So, you'll be heading home in an hour, right?" he stated.

I didn't reply. I wasn't going to continue to repeat myself.

"Zach?"

"Dray, I'll be home as soon as I finish. I don't know what time that'll be. I have twenty-three more exams to go. I'll be home whenever I finish."

"Whatever," he replied. I could hear the anger mounting in his voice. "I guess I'll just go to bed."

I didn't reply. I stared at the exams sitting on my desk.

He said, "I have a meeting tomorrow afternoon."

"With who?"

"Phoenix," Dray stated.

"Who is Phoenix?"

"Phoenix Cummings, the NBA baller," he replied. I told you we went to high school together. He graduated after year me."

"Oh, you did say that. What's the meeting about?"

"We're working on a business plan for some stuff for the kids back home in Miami. We've been talking about it for a while now, but we're finally meeting up to lay some of the plans on the table while basketball is on break."

"That's cool. Good luck."

"Baby, come home and let me love you," Dray pleaded.

I exhaled and said, "As good as that sounds, I've got to finish this work. I can't let my students down. I expect certain things from them and they expect certain things from me."

"So those students matter more than your relationship? Those students matter more than making sure your man is ok?"

"Dray, don't be like that."

"Be like what?" he said. "You're being *like that*!"

"You're an executive at Rolling Stone," I said upset. "You more than anyone knows how this shit works!"

He just hung up on me. He didn't even say bye.

I held the phone in my hand until I heard Keston saying, "Hello?"

I forgot I had him on hold. I cleared my throat. "Sorry about the wait."

"Did you tell him?"

"No."

"Why not?" Keston asked.

"I just didn't."

"Zach, you need to talk to Dray. You have a good man at home who loves you unconditionally. Communication is key. You've got to communicate with him. Dray is a reasonable man. He can't, however, read your mind. Talk to him and let him know what's going on."

"I hear you, Kes," I exhaled, as I stared at the exams on my desk. "Let me finish this work. I'll talk to you later."

"Ight."

*****

Keston Sharpe

Atlanta, Georgia

When I got off the phone with Zach, I walked into my kitchen and poured a glass of sweet tea. I sipped on the drink as I headed into my living room and flipped the TV to the NFL network. I was so excited that the season was on the horizon. I needed to get in the bed as I have a long day at work tomorrow. I'm one of the team trainers for the Atlanta Falcons.

As I sat on the couch, my conversation with Zach popped in my mind. If I had followed some of my own advice nine years ago, I wonder how my life would be now. I wonder if *we* would still be together. I think about *him* often. I've had a few boyfriends since *him*, but no one has been able to compare to him.

I shook my head. He's doing very well in the NBA. I'm really happy for him. I took another sip and then exhaled.

Having Zach as a friend really helped me through that rough patch in my life. While I haven't told anyone what exactly happened to me on that April night in 2007, I have moved past it.

I was born November 25, 1983, twenty-four days after my cousin, Qier. Even though Qier was my cousin, he has always been like an older brother to me. We both grew up in Miami.

Qier Sharpe is a six-time wide receiver Pro-bowler from the Seattle Seahawks. Qier and I both received our bachelor's degree from the University of Central Florida in Orlando. I went on to receive additional graduate degrees from FAMU in Tallahassee and the University of Georgia in Athens.

I was an athletic trainer at all three of the institutions I attended, which helped land me a job with Falcons. The advisor over the trainers when I was at Georgia was best friends with the head trainer for the Falcons. I maintained a good relationship with my advisor at Georgia and when the Falcons job became available, he recommended me. The rest is history. I've learned in life that it's not what you know, it's who you know.

Besides Qier, I had two other childhood friends, Raheim and Izzy. While Izzy separated himself from the group nine years ago, Raheim and I are still close. Crazy as it is, Raheim, Izzy, Dwight and Zach all joined the FAMU band the same year in 2002.

Nonetheless, both Izzy and Raheim received their degrees from FAMU. While I have no idea what Izzy is doing with his life, I'm really proud of Raheim.

After he graduated from FAMU, he landed a job as a high school band director in Memphis. While in Memphis, he earned his master's degree in music from the University of Memphis.

A few years later tragedy happened. After the annual Florida Classic football game in Orlando between FAMU and our in-state rival, Bethune-Cookman, one of the FAMU drum majors died in a hazing related incident. Nothing has been the same since that night.

I didn't know the guy personally, but it hit Raheim and Zach pretty hard because they both marched in the band with him. I later came to find out that Zach and the dude were close friends. Dwight never had much to say about incident, at least not while I was around. That was shocking to me because Dwight was a former FAMU drum major.

The longtime director of bands, Dr. Edward J. Hunter, retired because of that 2011 event, which started the restructuring of the marching band and the music department. The band was suspended for nearly eighteen months and gutted from the inside out. They haven't been the same since their return in 2013, but we understand because they basically started over from scratch. Sixty-five years of musical and artistic excellence was tainted in a matter of minutes. The new band is steadily building, trying to get back to those glory days. It's not the new kids fault, and they're trying their best, especially with everything stacked against them, but we all yearn for the band that we once knew.

When the new director took the baton, he called on Raheim to come back and join the new band staff. After Raheim went through an intensive and stressful interviewing process by university administration, he was offered and took a position as the director of clarinets and saxophones.

While in Tallahassee, he attended Florida State University in hopes of achieving his Ph.D. He finished the doctoral coursework two years ago and is in the final stages of writing his dissertation. Soon, he will be Dr. Raheim Tyms. Just last month, he was promoted to one of the assistant band director positions.

I love the fact that all my friends are educated.

Now, I've just gotta get Zach to talk to Dray. As educated as Zach is, he really makes a lot of shit harder on himself than it needs to be. He's blown this recent situation way out of proportion. I understand his plight, but the simple solution is to just tell Dray!

I don't think Dray will end the relationship because Zach wants to move to Atlanta, unless there is something Zach isn't telling me.

Does Dray know something I don't?

Only time will tell.

7

Dwight

My little brother answered my call. As I headed home on the interstate, I said, "I'm surprised you're still up."

Ced said, "I'm enjoying the extra free time."

"Where is Michelle?" I asked.

"She's back visiting her mom in Norfolk for the week. Michelle has been spending a lot of time with her mother after their father died some years ago."

"Yeah, I know. How are my nephews?"

"They're doing alright," Ced said. "They just went to sleep not too long ago."

"I've got to get down to Ft. Worth to visit y'all," I said, as I thought about my seven and four-year-old nephews, Cody and Darrin Taylor.

When Ced and Michelle graduated from FAMU, they got married and then both joined the military. Ced and Michelle have both done a few of tours in Iraq and Afghanistan. One year, while they both were on tour at the same time, Lexi and I took care of their kids. I love those two boys like they were my own.

"What are you doing out so late?" Ced asked.

"I actually just got off work. I left a lil early hoping I could spend some quality time with Lexi."

"You're trynna get some pussy from your wife, huh?" he laughed.

"Something like that," I exhaled.

"You know it's a shame that a married man has to beg his wife for sex."

"Who said anything about begging?" I asked.

"Nigga, you know what I'm trying to say."

I laughed.

"Seriously though Dwight, is everything alright at home?"

"Ced, shit ain't been right for a long ass time. I didn't know marrying her came with all this fucking baggage."

"She hasn't had one of her…you know… *episodes*… lately, has she?" Ced curiously asked.

"Naw, she's been good," I replied as I heard the phone beep. It was Lexi. "Ced, let me hit you back up. This is Lexi calling."

"Ight, big bro, get at me," he hung up the phone.

I took a deep breath, clicked over and said, "Yes, beautiful?"

In her ever demanding voice, Lexi said, "Dwight, I need you to stop by Walmart when you get off work and grab a dozen eggs, some milk and sugar so I can make breakfast for the kids in the morning."

"Ok. I left early so I'll pick it up then I'll be home."

"You left early?" she asked with attitude in her voice.

"That's what I just said," I replied.

"Whatever. Just don't forget, ok!" she said.

"Ok, Lexi."

"I'm serious, Dwight. Don't forget."

"I just said I'm about to pick it up now."

She hung up the phone. I exhaled.

This is getting frustrating. I don't know what she wants from me. She's just been rude and nasty. She doesn't talk to me. She barely cooks for me. It's like her only priority is the kids. She has a husband, too—a husband who needs her.

It was nearly midnight when I arrived at Walmart. I grabbed some items for me then searched for what she wanted. When I turned on the aisle for the sugar, I saw a familiar face. I said, "Yo! What's up, Shawty!"

He turned to me and smiled. As we approached each other, he said, "Dwight? What's up!"

"Same ole shit," I dapped him up. "How have you been, Micah?"

"I'm doing good. No complaints. Everything good with you?"

"Yep. Just living and raising the kids."

He said, "You still look the same after all these years."

I smiled and said, "I don't mean to hold you. I gotta get this stuff and head on home before my wife comes looking for me with a shot gun."

He laughed.

"Man, it's rough out here in these streets," I sighed.

"I feel you. Take care."

"You too, Micah," I said as he walked away.

As he exited the aisle, I reached down and grabbed the five-pound bag of sugar. I shook my head and sighed. He's come a very long way.

I approached our home and hit the remote to open the three-car garage. Lexi's 2014 QX60 silver Infiniti was parked in her spot. Once I parked my 2015 black 5-series BMW, I grabbed the bags and headed into the house.

Our dog, Max, met me at the door. I motioned for him to follow behind me and headed into the kitchen to put up the food. I turned on the light and saw the dinner dishes piled into the sink. I exhaled. I looked to the heavens and shook my head. It has to get better. It has to!

As I played with the dog, I realized just how quiet it was in here. It's never this quiet unless I'm here by myself. The kids are always getting into something. Lexi is always on the phone. The TV is always running. It is always something. I guess that's the territory that comes with the family life.

Just thinking about being inside of Lexi was making my dick hard. I left work early because I was horny as fuck! I was getting some pussy tonight. End of story!

As Max headed back over to his make shift bed on the floor, I turned off the kitchen light and began to make my way through the house.

"GOD DAMN IT!" I yelled as my big toe hit one of the kids' toys. I exhaled and then ascended up the flight of stairs.

We have got to do something about this cleanliness. How hard can it be to wash some damn dishes and make sure the fucking house looks good? What if I decide to bring some people over for company and we walk into this mess? We go through this shit too fucking much for this place to still look the way it does.

Before I went into our bedroom, I stopped in and looked at the kids. They always make me smile. They make my life complete. They're some bad asses, but I would give my life for them.

In the room by herself was my princess, Chloe. At four years old, Chloe was the baby of my family. Yes, she was daddy's little girl. Nobody could say any wrong about Chloe. That's just how spoiled she was.

My two boys were in the next room. Brennan was asleep on the top bunk. His bad ass just turned nine a few months ago.

Underneath Brennan was the end result our first week of marriage, Dominic. Nico, as we call him, just turned six in February. Something is different about Nico. I can see it. Ced can see it. Lexi has mentioned something about it, even my mom and dad. Nico is going to be gay.

Even though Brennan is only three years older than Nico, he can sense it, too. Brennan may not know what gay is, but he knows his brother is soft. In turn, Brennan tries to rough him up. As they get older, I can tell Nico's sexuality is going to bother Brennan. That might explain why Chloe and Nico are so close. It doesn't bother me. I love all my kids, regardless if one may eventually live an alternative lifestyle.

I closed the door, turned around and saw the image of the blue TV light flashing under our room door. I walked in the room and Lexi was laying down on the bed looking at an old re-run of Family Matters. She's always loved that show.

"Hey, baby," I walked over and gave her a kiss on the cheek.

"Did you bring the stuff?" she asked voice full of attitude.

"Damn, I can't even get a 'Hey, Dwight. How was your day, Dwight? I love you, Dwight?'."

She just looked at me and then rolled her eyes back to the television screen. I stood there dumbfounded as she acted as if I wasn't even there.

"I love you, too," I replied as I started to undress.

When I was down to my boxers, I headed off to the shower. I had to get this stress off me. I just don't get her. I swear I don't.

The last time I stepped out on Lexi was the night before our wedding and that was with Zach. I've made a conscience effort to do right by her and my family. It's been hard, but I resisted the temptation.

Well, that's somewhat true.

While I haven't had sex with anyone other than Lexi, I have feelings for another person. It eats me up at times and I've even tried to push it there, but have only been met with rejection. I stopped trying after a while. But when she does shit like this, it makes me ask myself why am I really here anyway?

Why? She only treats me like shit. I only provide a roof over her head. I only put food on the table. I only brought her that nice ass car she wanted. I only give her money to go buy whatever she wants, when she wants. I only make sure that she never has to go without. So why do I get treated like I'm the fucking villain?

Is this God's way of getting back at me for all the wrong I've done in my life? Is this my punishment? I know I've made some mistakes in my life, but I've never claimed to be perfect.

I dried off and stepped into a fresh pair of boxers and headed back into the room. It was pitch black, as she had turned off the TV. The red light from the clock on the nightstand read 1:03am.

I eased over to my side of the bed and wrapped my arms around her body. I smiled. She always smells so refreshing and it always sends signals to my dick.

As I tried to kiss her on her neck, she turned her head. I tried to run my hands up and down her thigh and she brushed them away. I tried to run my hands across her spot on her arm and with attitude she said, "Dwight, I'm tired. Go to sleep."

I ignored her and tried to kiss her. I knew she could feel my dick poking at her ass.

I just wanted to make love to my wife. I just wanted to feel her sweet insides. I just wanted to show her how much I still love her, despite all the bullshit, despite her episodes.

As I continued with my advances, she got upset and said with a bit of anger in her voice, "I'M TIRED, DWIGHT! LEAVE ME ALONE AND GO TO SLEEP!"

"SO I CAN'T FUCK MY WIFE?" I yelled back upset.

"You can go fuck yourself! I'm tired. Go to bed."

She jerked on the cover as if she was protecting her body from me.

"Lexi," I said, trying to regain my composure. "We haven't had sex in over a month. I want to make love to you. I miss you."

"Dwight, when you decide to sit home and raise your three kids by yourself, then you can talk to me. Until then, shut the fuck up and take your ass to sleep! For the last time—I'M TIRED!"

8

Dorian

Doing this shit always bothered me, especially after my mom died. I hear the horror stories. Living in Atlanta isn't helping my case either. The HIV rate here is astronomical! This shit is serious.

But all sense of logic goes out the window when that little head down there is hard. This is why I missed my ex-boyfriend, Morgan Harris. He was an exceptional lover, made my body feel shit I've never felt before.

I sighed. I was horny as fuck.

So, despite everything that telling me to get the hell off Jack'd, I continued to look for something. I haven't been laid in about six weeks. I do it all—suck, eat, fuck, get fucked. But I was looking to lay some dick tonight. I needed to feel a tight ass gripped on my dick. I wanted to make someone scream.

Morgan was the last person to take care of that itch for me. He sucked, I sucked. He fucked, I fucked. I knew it was wrong to do since we were over, but damn he takes me there.

That's why I won't entertain him. That's why it's hard for me to answer his calls. Morgan knows how to get me and I'm trying to be strong. I have to get him out of my system.

As I browsed Jack'd, I thought about my dad. He called me today trying to see if I had done what he asked. He wants me to contact some lady for him, but that lady isn't gonna wanna talk to me when she realizes who I am. Why does he have me involved in this shit? This isn't my fight. It's his!

After another ten minutes of looking, some dude finally hit me up. His profile was like mine. Got all the stats and shit. I got a pic of my chest, but that was about it. My philosophy is that you don't need to know me until you see me. I ain't proclaiming to be some ultra DL homothug nigga, but I do like my privacy.

He said his name was Jason. *Yeah, right.* My name is Dorian, but I told that fool my name was Rod. His stats say he was 26 years old. 5'10". Masculine. Discreet. 185lbs. Muscular. The chest pic he had on the profile matched the description. He opened his private pic and it was pic of his ass. I opened mine and it was a pic of my dick. That ass was looking right. Yeah, this was going to be a good fuck.

We chatted and exchanged numbers. I gave him my Google number. I wasn't bringing no random nigga to my apartment. He said he said he lived alone, but I just wasn't going to show up at his place, either. So we agreed to meet at the twenty-four-hour grocery store about fifteen minutes from his home.

I told him to give me forty-five minutes to get dressed and head to that side of town. He was cool with it. It wasn't going to take forty-five minutes, but I wanted to be in place before he got there. I told him I would text him when I was about fifteen minutes away.

When I got to the store, I parked my car in the first space closest to the front door. Luckily, I had tents so no one could see inside. Being that it was dark helped, too. Once I was situated, I sent him a text saying that I was about fifteen minutes away.

"Ight...I'm heading out now," he replied.

"Cool. Just wait 4 me by the benches at the front door. I'll meet you there. I'll lift my head, walk inside, buy something and then head back out. I'll say something so you'll know it's me. I'll have on a black t-shirt and some jeans. What will you be wearing?" I sent even though that wasn't what I was wearing.

"Black wife beater and some black basketball shorts," he replied.

"Cool. Just hit me up when you're there," I sent.

I listened to the radio and waited patiently. A couple of songs later, I got a text that said, *"I just parked. I'm heading to the benches now."*

"Ight. I'm a couple of minutes away," I lied as I looked around.

I saw someone in a black wife beater and some black basketball shorts strolling over to the benches. My mouth dropped open. That couldn't be him.

He stopped and stood there. He looked around, grabbed his phone, played with it for a moment and then put it back into the pockets of his basketball shorts.

In order to make sure it was him, I sent him a text and said, *"You there?"*

I watched as he grabbed his phone and typed on his keypad. A few seconds later, my phone started to vibrate and the message said, *"Yea...where you?"*

"Getting off the interstate," I replied as I got out of my car.

I wanted to see up close and personal if my eyes were deceiving me. I know I was thirty years old, but damn.

As I entered the store, I looked at this faggot dead in his eyes. He stared at me for a second and then turned his head.

I didn't even care if he knew it was me. I had just been played. This faggot just played me.

He was not 5'10". He looked more around 5'7" or 5'8". He was not masculine. He looked to be very much effeminate. Discreet? HELL FUCK NAW. He was not 180 pounds. He looked around 240 pounds and he damn sure wasn't muscular.

I don't have anything against bigger dudes, but don't lie to me. Some big dudes are sexy to me. But this dude lied about everything. His height, his weight, his masculinity. Did he think I wasn't supposed to see that shit?

I bought a soda and left. When I walked back out, he was staring at me.

"WHAT THE FUCK YOU LOOKING AT FAGGOT?" I yelled before I crossed the street and headed back to my car. He looked stunned.

Disgusted, I blocked him and backed out of my parking space.

I knew I shouldn't have gone on Jack'd. I knew that shit!

As I merged onto the interstate, an image of my ex appeared. Reluctantly, I picked up my phone and called him. When he answered, I said, "Yooo…can I stop by?"

Morgan cleared his throat and said, "Yeah, come on."

I hung up the phone and exhaled. I would probably regret it later, but I needed to bust this nut.

9

Zach

When I got back to my office, I pulled out my laptop and searched for flights to Atlanta tomorrow. I know the ticket was going to be a little expensive since it was short notice and tomorrow was Friday. After my trip to Atlanta, I was going to fly on down to Orlando to visit my mom for a few days. All I planned on telling Dray was about the trip to visit my mom. He didn't need to know about my pit stop in Atlanta.

It all hit me when I got home last night. Everything that was stopping me from going to Atlanta went out the door when I walked in the door. That house is cold and empty and doesn't feel like home.

As I searched for times for the short flight from Atlanta to Orlando, I realized that I probably wouldn't come back to New York until Wednesday. It's not like Dray was going to miss me. He's never home anyway. I didn't have any appointments booked and as far as class is concerned, I'll send a mass email letting them know all classes through Wednesday will be held it remotely on the internet. After I clicked submit for my flights, I exhaled. I know I'm doing the right thing. I know I am.

It was almost three this morning before I got home. When I got in the bed, Dray never touched me. Either he was extremely pissed off at me for coming home so late or he didn't know I was there. When I woke up this morning to come to work, he was already gone.

I got up from my desk and walked over to the window. I pulled up the blinds to get a sight of beautiful Manhattan.

I heard my phone vibrating. I looked down and it was Dwight. I smiled and answered, "What's up?" I hadn't heard from him in nearly a week.

"Shit, what's up with you, Big Z?"

I exhaled, sat down and said, "Just in the office."

"Oh. You need me to call you later?"

"Naw," I shook my head. "I ain't doing nothing."

"Dr. Finley, do you talk like that around your students?" Dwight asked.

"Dr. Taylor, no I do not, thank you very much," I replied. "I know the time and place for everything. I swear some people think because I have a Ph.D. behind my name that everything is supposed to change about me. I know when and when not to be Dr. Finley. When I'm not in this office or around campus, I am Zach. That means fitted caps, white tees, jeans, Jordan's. Dray pisses me off with that shit. Always talking about what I need to wear—WHAT I NEED TO WEAR? Are you fucking serious? Nigga, I'm a grown ass man! He's forever saying I need to always dress the part. Some shit I need to do for me. I need to remind myself that I'm still me. My level of education shouldn't determine how I look, what I wear, how I talk around friends. I've never liked wearing all that professional stuff anyway. He may like that shit, but I don't. I was just telling myself if it wasn't for these tattoos—"

I just stopped. I realized that I was venting to Dwight and he didn't have a dog in this fight.

"Sorry," I stood up and walked back over to the window to look at the city.

"Zach, what's going on?" he asked. "And don't lie to me."

"I was just venting. I know you didn't call me for that. How are the wife and kids?"

"Big Z, I'm so over that shit."

"WHOA?" I replied shocked as I turned around and walked to my big couch. "Where is this coming from?"

"Zach, I love my kids. I would die for my kids. But I'm done with Lexi. I can't take too much more of her and her shit. I know what my problem is."

"What's that?"

"You," he said.

I rolled my eyes and thought, "Here we go again."

"I'm serious, Zach. My offer is still on the table. Come be with me. We're only getting older. I know you still love me. I still love you. Is this the reason why you're really coming to Atlanta? You're tired of Dray. You've realized the truth? I've realized it. It took me a long ass time, but I'm there. Let that nigga go and come be with me."

"Dwight, you are out of line," I said upset. "Like I've told yo' ass the last seven times over the past three motherfucking years, I can't and I won't go there with you. You made the decision to marry Lexi. I love Dray. Don't try to bring me down because you're not happy."

He replied, "Yeah, but the real question is, are *you* happy? Yes, you love him. I love Lexi. But are you happy, or is this something you've convinced yourself to believe? Stop lying to yourself, Zach."

I was startled by the knocking on my office door.

"Umm, Dwight, I gotta go," I hung up the phone.

*****

Drayton Wescott

New York, New York

While I waited for Phoenix at one of my favorite New York restaurants, Eleven Madison Park, I sipped on my wine and thought about Zach. What was happening between us? How did it get to this point?

I know it's that damn Dwight. I know it is.

Why is Zach friends with him? What is it about him? I just don't get it.

I should have put a stop to this shit a long ass time ago. I should have nipped this in the bud three years ago. How have I been able to live like this? I don't know.

I love Zach. He stuck it out when shit got tough for us. Through all my faults, he's still here.

I know nobody is perfect. Everyone makes mistakes, as I have done. But something has to be done about his best friend, Dwight.

"DRAY! I heard my guest say as I looked up and smiled.

I got out of my seat and greeted him with a brotherly hug.

"It's been a long time, Mr. Cummings," I replied as we both sat down.

"Yeah, it has been," Phoenix stated.

Phoenix Cummings just finished his eighth year in the NBA, where he is a five-time NBA All-Star and a NBA Champion. He was drafted twelfth overall in the 2008 NBA draft by the Sacramento Kings. After three years in the league, the Kings traded Phoenix to the San Antonio Spurs. That's where Phoenix won his lone NBA championship, when the Spurs defeated LeBron James, CJ Wright and the Miami Heat in 2014. Phoenix left San Antonio after that championship and signed a four-year, 80-million-dollar contract to play alongside Derrick Rose and the Chicago Bulls.

Phoenix was tall and handsome. He was about 6'8" with brown skin and long, neat dreads. His skin was flawless. His teeth were perfect. He looked like he belongs in a magazine.

I knew Phoenix from high school back in Miami. I graduated in 2003 and he in 2004. He was destined for greatness when we were in high school. In addition to playing basketball, he was in the drama club with me. This is where our friendship blossomed.

We lost contact over the years, but ran into each other on the set of a photoshoot three years ago. We've been in contact ever since.

I always liked being around Phoenix. He was one of the good guys. His only child, his five-year old son, Giovanni, was created with a former Sacramento Kings dancer. I knew Phoenix used to mess with dudes back when we were in high school, but I wonder if he still does now. Even though I want to know, I've never had the balls to ask him.

As the waitress left with our orders, he said, "It's amazing that two black kids from the hood in Miami can have the power that we do. You're one of the big wigs, an executive at Rolling Stone and I'm an NBA superstar. Who could've thought two little black kids from Miami could be in a position to influence the lives of others the way that we can."

"Yeah, I think about that a lot," I said. "I've always had big dreams. Even when people would tell me to get real, niggas can't do shit like that, that we needed to know our place and fall in line, I would always say to myself to just watch me."

Phoenix smiled and said, "And that's exactly why we're here today."

"I have so many thoughts in my head," I replied.

"Like what? I've got some ideas. Throw out your ideas," he said.

"I was thinking about starting a scholarship program for our high school, maybe organizing an outreach program, possibly doing workshops in the school. Being that we were in the drama club, maybe help to renovate the African Heritage Cultural Arts Center? Find other successful alums to come back and talk to the kids. Maybe you can do a free basketball camp. Maybe find some corporate company to sponsor it? I can do workshops on design and editing, just putting some ideas on the table."

Phoenix said, "I like some of those. I've got some, so we've got a lot of ideas to build from. I hope you've got a lot of time because I really want to leave here today with something concrete. Whatever we're going to do for the kids back home, I want to get started on it ASAP."

I smiled and said, "Shit, let's get to work."

My phone started to ring. It was one of my former classmates from FAMU, Erwin, who was now living and teaching in Atlanta.

"Hold on, Phoenix," I said. "Let me take this call."

"Sure," he smiled as the waitress brought over his drink.

I answered and he said, "Dray, I know it has been a long time, but I've got an interesting proposal for you. It's something I think you should really look into."

"Ok, what is it?"

10

Zach

I made a serious effort to make sure I got home at a decent hour tonight. I didn't want to hear Dray and his bullshit. Sometimes I feel like he is my mother and everybody knows how I feel about her at times.

It was almost 7:30 when I entered our building. That was good timing. I needed to eat and get packed. I have to be at the airport tomorrow morning at seven.

As I inserted the key card to enter our condo, my nostrils were immediately taken aback. I smiled. Dray was in the kitchen throwing down.

I walked in our home and heard the soulful sounds of Luther Vandross echoing over the surround sound system. Hoping that he wasn't still upset about last night, I exhaled before making my way into the kitchen. With his back to me and the music up so loud, he didn't realize I was standing there.

I stood there and listened as he chopped some fresh vegetables for what seemed like a salad and sang along with Luther. Damn, I loved Dray's voice. When he turned around, he damn near dropped the plate of vegetables. Shocked, he said, "Damn, Zach! You scared the shit out of me! How long have you been there?"

"About a minute or so," I replied as I walked over into the kitchen and kissed him. "What's for dinner?"

"Jerk chicken, rice and peas, cabbage and a side salad."

"Sounds good," I smiled.

Dray looked at me strangely for a moment before putting his focus back to running some water over the veggies.

"What?" I asked.

"Nothing," he replied. "Dinner is almost done, so go ahead and get cleaned up."

I turned around and headed to our bedroom. I really do love this man. He isn't perfect, but he loves me for me. I got undressed and headed into the shower.

I thought about my earlier conversation with Dwight. He had no fucking idea what he was talking about. How dare he tell me that I'm not happy? How dare he compare my situation to his?

And then I could see that night. No matter how hard I tried, I couldn't get those images out of my head. Having sex with Dwight scarred me.

I cried as I tried everything to erase the memories from that night. I love Dray. I want my relationship with Dray to work!

I slid down in the shower and let the water beat against my body.

"I love Dray," I sobbed. "I love Dray!"

After a few minutes of cleansing my soul, I found the strength and stood up. I took a couple deep breaths and got out of the shower.

Once I dried off, I looked at myself in the mirror and said, "Get it together, Zach. That was seven years ago. Get it together!"

I dressed, collected myself and met Dray in the kitchen. He turned to me and started to sing along with Luther, "Here and now, I promise to love faithfully. You're all I need. Here and now, I vow to be one with thee. Your love is all I need."

I just looked at him.

As Luther's hit song, *Here and Now,* continued to play, Dray stopped singing and said, "I was getting worried about you in there. I was just about to come and check on you."

"I just needed to relax my muscles," I replied.

"You feel better?"

"Yeah," I smiled. "A lot better."

"Well go sit down," he said. "Dinner is done."

As I walked to the dining table, he started to sing again, "When I look in your eyes, there I see, all that a love should really be. I need you more, and more each day. Nothing can take your love away. More than I dare to dream. I need you…here and now."

Once he brought both of our plates and drinks over, he sat down and said grace. When he finished I looked down at the colorful array of food.

"Eat up," he smiled as the song finally ended. He got up and lowered the volume as Luther's duet with Mariah Carey, *Endless Love,* started to play.

"This is really good Dray," I smiled.

"Thanks, bae."

"So, how did the meeting with Phoenix go?" I asked.

"It went really well," he smiled. "We got a lot accomplished today. I can't wait to go back home and help the kids."

"I'm happy for you," I took a sip of my wine.

"Yeah, so what's been happening with you? How is everything on campus going?"

"Everything is ok," I said.

He stared at me as he ate some of his salad.

"I'm going out of town tomorrow," I said.

"Oh, really," he perked up. "Where are you going?"

"Back home to visit with my mom."

"Oh. Everything ok?"

"Yeah. I just had the sudden urge to go down there."

"I'm sure she'll like that," Dray said. "So, what else is on the agenda?"

I shook my head and said, "Nothing that I know of."

He just looked at me. *Why does he keep staring at me like that?*

Even though the time seemed perfect to tell him that I was stopping in Atlanta to sign the contract for my new job, I didn't feel comfortable. So, I just continued to eat my food.

Dray changed the subject and started to talk about things at his job. I was listening, but my mind was pondering over if I should just tell him the truth. He'll understand my reasoning for wanting to move to Atlanta. He knew I never wanted to come up here anyway.

As much as I tried, I just couldn't formulate the words. I didn't want to spoil this evening. Everything was perfect.

"So, you're going to Orlando," he said jumping back to our earlier conversation.

"Yeah."

"I think I wanna go," he replied. "I can go ahead and clear my schedule for tomorrow. What time does your flight leave?"

"Dray, you don't have to do that," I replied, as my heart rate started to increase drastically. "Besides, you know how my mom is."

"I'll get a hotel. I don't wanna intrude on your time with moms. When are you coming back? I need a lil vacation anyway."

"Wednesday."

"Oh, that's perfect."

"Dray, you don't have to do that," I said again.

"I think I want to," he insisted.

"It's really not necessary."

"Is there a reason why you don't want me to go? Is Dwight going to be there or something?"

"What? What does Dwight have to do with going to visit my mom?"

"I was just wondering if you were making any pit stops you didn't want me to know about," he replied as he ate a piece of his meat.

"I told you I was going to visit my mom. Dwight lives in Atlanta. Besides, Dwight is my best friend. If I was going to visit Dwight, I don't have to hide that from you. Why would I need to hide that from you?"

He stared at me then replied, "I don't know, you tell me."

"I don't have anything to hide from you, especially concerning Dwight."

"Ok," he took a sip of his wine.

There was an awkward silence.

I listened as Luther's voice filled the room: *"Let me hold you tight, if only for one night. Let me keep you near, to ease away your fear. It would be so nice, if only for one night."*

I took a sip of my wine before grabbing my fork to eat some of my cabbage.

"I won't tell a soul, no one has to know," Luther sang. *"If you want to be totally discreet. I'll be at your side, if only for one night."*

"Don't you just love this song," Dray said staring at me. "Luther's songs tells stories, it spills secrets."

He laughed to himself. I swallowed my spit.

As the song, *If Only for One Night*, continued to play, Dray looked to me and said, "I got a phone call from a friend today."

"Really? Who?"

"This guy we went to school with back at FAMU," Dray said. "You may remember him. He was in the Journalism School with me. He was in the band with you for a year or two. Remember we went to that Christmas party in Atlanta a few years back and he was there."

"The short light skinned dude?" I asked.

"Yeah," he replied. "Erwin."

"Yeah, Erwin," I said. "That's cool. What did he want?"

"He called to tell me I should apply for a specific job," he replied. "A job he thinks I would be perfect for."

"A job doing what?" I asked. "You already have a very important job."

"This would be something part time and temporary. Just something for a semester or two until they can permanently fill the position."

"What is it?" I asked.

"He teaches at Clark Atlanta."

My stomach dropped.

"And," Dray continued. "He figured I would perfect to teach this magazine production and photography class, given my experience at Rolling Stone."

"That's nice," I forced a smile.

"Yeah and you know how us Rattlers are," he said in reference to FAMU's mascot. "We're always looking to help out our fellow Rattler."

"Yeah," I smiled.

"So imagine my response when Erwin proceeded to say that the job would be perfect for me since Zach was going to be teaching permanently at Clark Atlanta. So I said to Erwin, 'Zach who?' And then he said, 'your Zach. Zach Finley.' He said Raidon had told him. And then he asked if we were still together."

I just stared at him.

Dray said, "I know you could imagine my shock. My significant other was moving to Atlanta and I had NO FUCKING IDEA!"

"Dray, I was going to tell you."

"WHEN? AFTER THE FUCK YOU LEFT?" he yelled.

Calm down.

"ZACH, YOU LIED TO ME! I GAVE YOU THE OPPORTUNITY TO SAY IT TONIGHT BUT YOU NEVER DID. YOU SAT THERE AND LIED, TALKING ABOUT YOU'RE GOING TO VISIT YOUR MOTHER."

"I AM GOING TO VISIT MY MOTHER!"

"Yeah, after you stop in Atlanta, right?" he slammed his fist down on the table, stood up and walked into the kitchen.

When he returned, I said, "Dray, don't act like this shit is new to you. You knew long before I brought my black ass up here that I didn't want to be here! I came here for you, because I loved you! I didn't want to give up on us. I've expressed this to you before!"

"Zach, why the hell do you think we got the summer house in Atlanta? That shit wasn't for me. It was for you!"

"Dray, WHEN THE FUCK WOULD I EVER HAVE TIME TO SPEND IN THAT GOD DAMN HOUSE? You knew that shit before you brought it. The only thing buying that house solved was nothing! It was a fucking Band-Aid to the problems that we have here! C'mon Dray. Don't play me for an idiot. I have a fucking Ph.D. I'm not a dummy."

"What the fuck is your infatuation with Atlanta? Why Atlanta? Ok, you don't want to be here in New York but why Atlanta? What the fuck is so special about Atlanta? Ok, you want to go back to the south. Fine. There is Charlotte, Columbia, Dallas, New Orleans, ORLANDO, TALLAHASSEE. But you're stuck on Atlanta. I don't get it."

I just stared at him.

He calmed down and said, "Zach, I love you. I tried to make sure that you were happy up here. Is there something else that you're looking for that isn't up here? Is there someone else? What is it Zach? What do you need? What do I need to do to make you happy? You are the second most important person in my life. I would give you the world if I could. Why do you think that moving to Atlanta is going to give you so much? What do you feel like you're missing that we have to move to Atlanta? Has life been so miserable with me up here?"

"This has nothing to do with you, Dray," I said as I stood up and slowly articulated every syllable in each word. "This is about me and my happiness. I am not happy here. I haven't been for a long time. So, either you're going to join me down there or I will go alone. This is not up for debate. This is the way it is going to be. Tomorrow, I will be boarding a flight to Atlanta, Georgia to sign my contract for my new employment at Clark Atlanta University. And then on Saturday, I'm getting on a flight and going to visit my mother in Orlando. Hopefully when I get back next week, you would have made a decision."

"Well, just to let you know, since you've compromised for so long, you know living up here and shit, and since you seem to be in so much fucking turmoil, I'm going to accept the job if they offer it to me. I have the interview tomorrow," he said as he started to force a laugh. He finished, "You act like we don't have a joint account and I can't see the purchases you make."

"See that's the shit I'm talking about right here," I said upset. "You act like you're my damn mother, watching the shit I do, monitoring my purchases? What the fuck, Dray?"

"You know, Zach," he said, as his eyes pierced my soul. "I'm not about to get into this with you. I just need you to know that lies and deceit are the downfall of any relationship."

I looked him dead in his eyes and said, "That's funny, Drayton. I could have said the same damn thing when I found out that you have a son. So please SPARE ME THE MOTHERFUCKING LECTURE! I'm going to pack. I have a flight to catch in the morning."

Part Two:

Welcome to Atlanta

11

TJ

It was a quarter to eight. Daddy would be leaving for work in the next fifteen minutes; Raidon was already gone. I wanted to ask Ray yesterday but daddy was always around. I really didn't wanna ask daddy, but I guess I don't have a choice now.

I hated asking daddy for anything. That nigga is just mean for no fucking reason. Ray says I act just like daddy but I don't see it. I ain't mean like that nigga. I'll be straight up with yo' ass, but I ain't mean like him. I just tell it like it is.

Sometimes it feels like Ray has taken over the motherly role in my life. I wonder what it would have been like to have known my mom. What type of person was she? Would I have any other brothers and sisters by now? I know I ain't getting no brothers and sisters with Ray and Daddy. They're too busy poking each other in the ass.

That's disgusting.

Ray loves me unconditionally and he's really big on my education. He stays on my case about getting good grades. But he isn't always jumping down my back and he sits and listens to me. I like that a lot. He really cares about me. He's genuine with me.

Sometimes daddy just needs to take a chill pill. Why is that nigga so uptight? I love him though. I don't know what I'll do without him.

A few moments later, I heard his room door close. I jumped out of the bed and slipped into some baller shorts and my slippers and headed out of the room. I heard the refrigerator door close as I arrived downstairs. I stepped into the kitchen in just enough time to see daddy put a handful of pills into his mouth. He swallowed them with some water.

I guess I startled him because he jumped when he saw me.

I asked, "You sick, Daddy? Why you taking all them pills?"

"Boy, I thought you were asleep."

"Naw, I've been up. Just lying in bed."

"Oh," he grabbed a banana and a personal sized carton of orange juice. "What are you doing up so early?"

"Nothing," I shrugged my shoulders.

"What do you want?" he curiously asked before looking at the time. "I know when you want something, so what is it?"

I felt my heart pounding. The fear of rejection was near. I hated hearing him say no.

He just stared at me.

Going out on a limb, I said, "I need some money."

"So you're talking to me because you need some money? You don't talk to me unless you want something."

"Daddy?"

"What do you need the money for TJ?"

"I'm going school shopping with Eli. I think I'm old enough to buy my own clothes now," I said gaining some confidence with each word spoken. "I don't need you or Ray taking me to the store anymore. I'm almost a man."

Daddy smiled and asked, "Eli is that boy from down the street?"

"Yes."

"So he's your friend?"

"Yeah."

"Are you starting to like it down here?" he asked.

"I still miss Charlotte and my friends, but Eli is making it better."

"That's good," Daddy smiled. "I told you it'll be ok."

Even though I was cool with Elijah, I'd say just about anything right now so he would give me some money.

Daddy checked the time on his phone and said, "When I get to work I'll transfer $500 into your account."

"Really?" I said shocked.

FIVE HUNDRED DOLLARS? BITCH, I'M RICH! No… wait… I'M RICH, BITCH!

"Yeah," he replied. "I want you to be cautious and don't spend it all in one place. You're a teenager now and you should be able to buy your own clothes. When I was your age I hated when your grandma would take me to the store. So if you wanna go shopping with your friend, I'm not gonna stop you."

"Thanks, Daddy," I reached over and gave him a hug. "I love you."

"I love you, too. Do you have some cash on you?"

"Like thirty dollars."

Daddy reached in his wallet, pulled out a bill and handed it to me. He said, "Now you've got fifty dollars cash to eat and stuff, maybe catch a movie while you're out. I'll call you when I transfer the money, ok."

"Ok."

"I want you back home by six, no later than seven. So you got all day to do what you gotta do. Your Uncle Morgan is coming over for dinner and I want you here."

"Ok."

"Text me to let me know you're ok."

"Ok," I said as I started to walk towards the door.

"You're rushing me out of the house?" he asked.

"I don't want you to be late to work."

"Umm, hmm," he leaned over and gave me a kiss on the top of my head. "I love you, son."

"I love you, too," I said as he grabbed his keys and headed out of the house.

I smiled.

Daddy isn't as much of an asshole as I thought.

*****

Zach

We were on Southwest Airlines headed to Atlanta. Dray wasn't lying when he said that he was coming. He was sitting next to me typing on his laptop. I looked out of the small window and thought about Dray's son, our argument last night and Dwight.

I exhaled.

I pondered over a conversation I had with Kris awhile back. He really pissed me off telling me that I never gave New York a chance, talking about I was selfish. How the fuck are you gonna tell me what I did or didn't do? How the fuck you gonna call me selfish? I spent seven years of my life up in New York. How the fuck is that selfish?

Whatever.

I thought back to last night when Dray said, *"I just need you to know that lies and deceit are the downfall of any relationship."*

I looked him dead in his eyes and said, "That's funny, Drayton. I could have said the same damn thing when I found out that you have a son. So please SPARE ME THE MOTHERFUCKING LECTURE! I'm going to pack. I have a flight to catch in the morning."

I stormed off to the bedroom. He had me heated. I entered the walk-in closet, snatched my suitcase and threw it on the bed. I was starting to cry. I felt like my world was coming apart. I wanted and needed my grandmother.

I sat down on the edge of the bed to collect myself before Dray appeared in the room a few moments later. He walked over to me and somberly said, "Zach, I'm sorry. I hate it when you're mad at me. We can't go to bed angry." He wiped the tears from my face and said, "I love you. Do you love me?"

"If I didn't love you, I wouldn't be here," I replied.

He kissed me and said, "Zach, you've got to talk to me. You've got to let me know what is going on."

"Dray, please," I said upset. "You've known for a long time I wanted out of New York."

"But I got the house for you down in Atlanta."

"OH, MY GOD!" I jumped up.

"What?"

"Dray, please do not insult my intelligence. You know the reason you bought that house was to shut me the fuck up. You've never wanted to live in Atlanta and you've expressed that fact time and time again. That house was supposed to be our summer home, but you know I work year-round. I've told you plenty of

times before that I wanted to leave New York, and you told me to just wait it out, it'll get better. It'll get better. Dray, it never got better! You knew I wanted to move to Atlanta years ago. When I told you what I wanted to do, you threw a bitch fit. Did you think I forgot about the way you acted back then? I've tried your way for seven years and I can't do it anymore. Dray, I love you, but I can't do it up here anymore. People die every day. No man knows the place, day or hour, but I know I don't want to be unhappy when my name is called. I have to do this for me. Dray, I love you, but I have to do this for me."

"Zach, I just don't understand what it is about Atlanta? Why Atlanta?"

"Why not Atlanta?" I replied. "All of my friends are there. It's the perfect place to advance career wise. I'm close to my family. Why not Atlanta?"

"Is it something I'm not doing up here for you? Is there something I can do?"

"Dray, this has nothing to do with you. This is about me."

He exhaled.

I stood up and said, "Dray, I love you. I want you in my life. I want you to move to Atlanta with me. But if you don't, I understand. Just because I move to Atlanta doesn't mean I don't want us to work out. We can find ways to make this work."

"I'm not giving up on us because you want to move," he said. "I understand how important this is to you, so if you're going to Atlanta, we're going to Atlanta. I'm not about to be in some long distance relationship with you. I guess we're moving to Atlanta."

"What about your job?"

"I'll make it work. I didn't plan on being with Rolling *Stone much longer. You know I have big dreams. I want to start my own publishing company. I want to own my own TV network. I feel like I'm at a standstill with* Rolling *Stone. That's why this teaching opportunity was perfect for me. It gives me something to do to keep my interest. I'm always trying to better myself."*

"So you're just going to quit Rolling *Stone?"*

"Not right now, but I'll find a way to make that work in the short term. That isn't for you to worry about. I'll worry about that. If you want to move to Atlanta, then Atlanta WE go. I love you, Zach. Part of being in a relationship is compromising, sacrificing for the better good. We've been in this too long. We've been through too much just to give up now. I'm not going out like that. I love you."

"I love you, too." We embraced each other with a hug and a kiss.

"Besides, I hate it when you're mad at me," he replied.

I smiled.

"So I guess I need to get packed, too," he said. "I've got an interview tomorrow at 11:30. I think we are on the same flight."

I was brought back into reality when Dray tapped me on my thigh and said, "What are you thinking about?"

"Us," I smiled.

He smiled back and said, "I hope it's good thoughts."

I smiled and turned my head back to the window.

This two-hour trip was almost up.

12

Dwight

As I drove south on Interstate-75, I looked in my rearview mirror and smiled. My baby girl, Chloe, had fallen asleep. When we first left Atlanta, she was playing with her Barbie. Now an hour into the trip, she was gone. Luckily, the trip was almost over.

As we approached the I-75/I-475 bypass, I stayed off in the left lane to continue to Macon, Georgia. After my mom got divorced from my dad seven years ago, she left the house and moved back to her hometown of Macon.

I spent the first ten years of my life in Macon. We moved to Atlanta when my dad got a better job.

I looked in the rearview mirror again.

Across from Chloe was her partner in crime, her older brother by two years, Dominic. Nico had his head turned towards the window as he looked at all the scenery. Even though Nico was only six years old, I can already tell that he is going to be very creative—a musician, an artist, an actor, a fashion designer, something in the arts. Besides the fact that the boy is going to be gay, he's intrigued by colors. He is a perfectionist. He takes his time and makes sure whatever he's working on is perfect. He won't stop until it is right in his own eyes. Even then sometimes it isn't right. Regardless of how different Nico is, I love that boy.

My oldest, Brennan, is a mama's boy. He didn't want to go on the trip so he stayed back with Lexi. Even though he's only nine, I can already tell I'm going to have problems with him when he becomes a teenager.

Within a few minutes, I was approaching my exit. I smiled. I was excited to see my mom. More importantly, I needed a place to vent and there is no love like a mother's love—even when it's harsh.

That's why I love my mama. She has always kept it real with me, no holds barred. She doesn't sugarcoat anything. And if you don't like, you can get the fuck out of her house.

That woman is raw. I smiled. Meredith Taylor. That's my mama and I love her.

As we approached my mom's house, Chloe woke up and she and Nico immediately started talking. Those two have amazing chemistry. Even though Brennan is going to have a problem with Nico's impending sexuality, I don't think Chloe will. She is going to accept her brother with open arms.

When I parked the car, and blew the horn, both Nico and Chloe started to yell, "WE'RE AT GRANDMA'S HOUSE!"

As we got out of the car, my mom walked out of the house and both Nico and Chloe ran over to her yelling, "GRANDMA, GRANDMA!" My mom reached down and embraced the two kids. My mom was hard on Ced and me, but she is as soft and as sweet as a bag of cotton candy when it comes to her grandkids.

"I GOT COOKIES!" my mom happily yelled.

"YAY!" both Nico and Chloe screamed as they started to jump up and down with pure excitement.

I looked at my mom. She often reminded me of an older Omarosa, in both statue and personality. I smiled as I walked over to the group. My mom smiled and gave me a very fulfilling hug. It felt good to be in her embrace.

"C'mon babies, let's go in the house," she said.

Her house was always inviting and colorful. Today, it smelled of freshly baked chocolate chip cookies. When we walked in the kitchen, I reached over to the stove and grabbed a cookie and began to eat it. She immediately slapped my hand and said, "Those are for my grandbabies!"

"But Ma," I pouted.

"But nothing," she replied with a stern look on her face. "Those are for my grandbabies."

"But I'm your baby, first," I pleaded.

"Dwight," she replied.

Both Nico and Chloe started laughing at me.

"That's messed up. Y'all gonna laugh at me?" I asked my kids.

"Umm, hmm," Nico smiled. "Grandma got you."

"You in trouble, Daddy," Chloe laughed as she pointed. "You gon' get a whooping."

My mom smiled then turned to Nico and Chloe and said, "I got a surprise."

"WHAT IS IT, GRANDMA?" they asked.

"Get your cookies," she smiled and then said, "follow me."

As they walked out of the kitchen, I grabbed another cookie and ate it very quickly before rushing off to catch up with them.

When we got to the room, she had purchased more toys which made Chloe and Nico two very happy people. "Now have fun while Daddy and Grandma go and talk, ok," she said.

"OK, GRANDMA!" they said as they immediately began to dive into the toys.

As we walked down the hallway, she said, "I made some sweet tea just for you."

She poured us both a glass and headed into the living room. She handed me my glass, sat down and asked, "So what's going on?"

"I'm just gonna cut right to it," I replied.

"Cut to what, Dwight?"

"I want out of this marriage with Lexi."

She looked at me and then took a sip of her drink. She never said anything.

"Say something."

"You don't wanna hear what I have to say," she shook her head. "No, you don't want to hear that."

I exhaled.

"So, what's the issue now?" she asked.

"It's everything! It if weren't for my kids, I would have left a long time ago. I love my kids and I want them to grow up in a two-parent home, like how Ced and me did."

"Son, let me stop you right there. Yes, your father lived in that house, but he checked out when you and Cedric were preteens. Your father was gay and he was doing the things he wanted to do. He only stayed around for the sake of his family. Part of it was my fault because I wanted him to be around for the family. You live and you learn. You can't make the same mistake twice. Yes, you love your kids. Yes, your father loved you and Ced, but you can still have successful relationships with your children without having to live in the same house."

"Ma, she won't even have sex with me. She doesn't clean. She cooks for the kids, but she doesn't really care about my needs. She always has an attitude. She's demanding. I didn't sign up for this. This is not the woman I married."

"Oh, yes the fuck it is!" my mom said, cutting me deep with her eyes. "She was the exact same way back when Brennan was a baby. You just couldn't see some of the cleanliness things because it was on a smaller scale, or either you were blinded by the sex. That nasty attitude has always been there. And that mother of hers—God be with that family. I can see right through that woman. That old hag of a mother is nothing but a gold digger, a fifty-year-old gold digger. She needs to grow the fuck up. Yeah, I said it, and I'll say it to her God damn face! Son, it ain't no telling what she is telling Lexi. Who knows what kinds of seeds she has planted into Lexi. Her mother cannot be trusted. She's probably telling her to act this way so you can divorce her. She can get half of everything you've worked so hard to achieve. All that education would be for nothing. You'll never see your full paychecks again. Trust, she's taking you to the bank. It's a good thing that you listened to your mother at least one time. Now all that money that you've been 'depositing' into my 'account' over the years will come in handy. Even though the money was never for me, it was for a time like this. You'll be able to breathe when she wipes the bank accounts clean."

I looked at my mom as she continued to talk. That was probably the best advice she has ever given me.

My mom told me to use whatever money on my paycheck for bills, take a percentage out for some extra spending money, and put money into the kids account, as each of the kids have an account with their names for their future. But the rest of my monthly earnings went into a savings account that was in my mother's name. Yes, it was in her name, but it was my account.

My mom was against the marriage from day one, but she said that if this day ever came when I talked about divorce, Lexi was going to be in for a rude awakening because she had no legal right to any money that was in my mother's name. Women think they're smart, but when you have a mother like mine, she always keeps her children one step ahead of the game. It was easy for me to pull this off because I pay the bills. Lexi doesn't know what kind of money I have. Whenever she wants something, I'll get it for her.

My mom interrupted my thoughts and said, "But you see, son,

you still lose. Yes, you have all that money saved up, but she *will* get the kids. She *will* get the child support. She *will* get the house. She *will* get to keep the cars. Before long, you *will* start to feel it in your pockets. I told you not to marry her, but you don't listen. You don't listen!"

"She's not getting my kids!" I confidently said.

"You must not know how the system works," my mom replied. "She's getting those kids. She hasn't worked since the wedding. The courts will rule for you to continue to keep up her lifestyle. It ain't no way around that, son."

"It's not going to happen," I said.

I knew something my mother didn't. I knew something about Lexi that no one knew, well except her mother, Ced and Zach. This revelation, if presented to the court, would allow me to keep my kids.

"If you would've just listened to me before the wedding we wouldn't be talking about this now. I begged you to think about what you were about to do. I begged you not to marry that girl. You were getting married for all the wrong reasons and love was never in the equation. You never loved her. You loved that boy."

"MA!"

"Oh, shut up, Dwight! Now you're 'bout to piss me off. You're just like your damn father. You married that girl because she was the mother of your child. All those wrong decisions are coming back to bite you in the ass and you're going to eat this shit! I told you not to marry that girl. I told you! You're hardheaded just like your father."

Upset, she got up and walked down the hallway. I heard her talk to the kids.

I rethought my plan of action and my mom might have a point. What if everything backfires and she does get the kids, the house, the cars, child support, spousal support?

Man, fuck that! Daddy always said it's cheaper to keep her.

Hell, he might have a point.

13

Zach

Atlanta, Georgia

It felt damn good to get off that airplane and smell the fresh Georgia summer air. For the first time in a long time, I felt good. I felt free.

I felt like a statue in the middle of a busy city as everybody rushed past us as if we didn't exist. It was no biggie though, as I've become quite accustomed to that hustle and bustle. It is the New York way.

I turned to Dray and said, "Keston should be here any moment. What time is your interview?"

"11:30."

"I don't have to be to campus until this afternoon. Hopefully he doesn't mind dropping you off."

Dray said, "No need to worry, I'm getting a rental. I'm just waiting to make sure that you're off ok."

"Oh."

He said, "I have some errands to run while I'm here."

"Are you going to see Nolan?"

"Yeah," he nodded his head. "I sent him a text while we were waiting to board the plane. We're supposed to meet up when I'm done with my interview."

I saw Keston coming around the curve.

"Looks like your friend is here," Dray replied.

As Kes slowed down, I edged closer to the curb. When he stopped, he popped the trunk open and jumped out of the car.

"Zach," Kes smiled as we exchanged brotherly hugs. It felt good to be around my friend.

When Kes realized that Dray was with me, the look on his face said it all. He smiled then said, "Nice to see you again Dray. How is everything?"

Dray answered, "Everything is good and it's nice to see you again as well."

"I didn't know you were coming," Kes said looking at Dray.

"Neither did I," I mumbled.

Dray cleared his throat before saying, "Well, Keston, make sure you get my Zach home safely."

"You're not riding with us?" Kes asked.

"He's getting a rental," I interjected.

Kes looked at me, then to Dray and said, "Oh, ok. Do you want us to wait around until you get the car?"

"Naw, it's ok. I'm a big boy. I think I can manage," Dray replied.

"Ok," Keston said as he started to move towards the driver's door.

I looked back at Dray and said, "Call me and let me know how the interview went."

"Ok. I love you."

"I love you, too," I replied as I got in the car.

As we pulled off, Keston turned to me and said, "Now you know we've got to talk."

I sighed, "I know."

*****

Dray

Atlanta, Georgia

Once I got the keys for the rental, I looked at the time. I had a little over an hour before I had to be on Clark's campus. When I got inside of the car, I adjusted my mirrors and then sent Zach a text to let him know I got the car and was on my way.

Once I left the airport, I merged north onto I-85 and headed towards the campus. I thought about Zach. I'm happy that we worked it out last night. I hate it when we get into arguments.

Zach must not understand how much I love him. I love him so much in fact that I've done things against my beliefs so this could work.

I want this to work. If I have to move to Atlanta, then I'll move to Atlanta.

I'm not ready to give up on what we've built. He's my other half. I feel like we are supposed to grow old together. I feel like God made him specifically for me. We belong together. I understand that he has made some sacrifices for me, and if I have to make some to make this relationship work, I will.

I will not let a job, or a city, come in-between my happiness. I can always find another job. I can always move to another city. But there will never be another Zach.

I thought about my son, Nolan. He and his mother lives here.

The possibility of living here in Atlanta causes a lot of issues, issues that I've never had to deal with before.

I exhaled.

Among the other shit that's going to come up as it concerns Zach and his friends, my son was the main reason why I didn't want to move here. This is why I've avoided living in Atlanta.

This is my problem and guess I'm going to have to face it sooner rather than later.

14

Zach

I looked out the window as Keston drove on the interstate. I wanted to talk to him about Dray, but he had been on the phone with his cousin, Qier. So I just looked and thought about my own life. I thought about Nolan. I've met the boy a few times. There's so much behind it, I don't even know where to begin. I don't know what to think.

That phone call changed everything. It's something I will never forget:

The day was Sunday, July 1, 2012. I was excited because I was looking forward to seeing the Whitney Houston tribute on the BET Awards. I normally don't watch that ratchetness, but seeing who they had to pay homage to Whitney drew my interest.

The weekends have always been our special time together. No matter what we had going on during the week, the weekends were designated for Dray and myself.

Dray was progressing very nicely at Rolling Stone. I, on the other hand, had just completed the coursework for my doctoral program. I was taking the month of July off to relax before I had to start the research for my dissertation. I was happy that I was one step closer to getting this terminal degree, but I was not looking forward to the work that I had to put into it.

Late Saturday night, Dray went out to the Red Box and rented a few movies. We didn't get to watch them, however, because we ended up having lots of sex. So, instead, on Sunday, Dray decided that we could make this day the movie day. I got up and cooked breakfast for the two of us.

In the midst of flipping the pancakes, Dray came into the kitchen with the three discs and said, "Bae, which one do you want to watch first?"

"What are the selections?" I asked.

"21 Jump Street, Tyler Perry's Good Deeds and Eddie Murphy's A Thousand Words."

"Let's do A Thousand Words, first. I wanna good laugh."

"Ight," he kissed me on the cheek and then headed out of the kitchen.

After we ate breakfast, we laid under each other on the couch and watched A Thousand Words first, followed by Tyler Perry's Good Deeds.

Four hours later, at the intermission of the two movies, Dray was hungry again. I smiled because this man knew he could eat. After we decided on what we wanted for lunch and who was going to pick it up, Dray said, "Baby, I'll be right back." He kissed me on the lips and headed out of our condo.

When he was out of the house, I got up and put the final movie into the DVD player. Everything was going so perfectly. After we finished watching the movie, it would be time for dinner and then the BET Awards.

While in the kitchen grabbing something to drink, I heard Dray's phone ringing. I knew it was his because I kept mine on vibrate.

I ignored the call. I figured whoever it was could and would get in touch with him when he gets back home. The phone stopped ringing but started again a few moments later. It stopped and then his voicemail went off.

I walked over and looked out the window. It was such a beautiful day. If I was back in Florida, it would be perfect to go to the beach. Man, I miss Florida; I miss the south. I exhaled.

Just as I was getting ready to take my seat, his phone started to ring again. Upset that the damn phone was bothering me, I stormed over to it. I couldn't wait to tell whoever it was that obviously he was busy and he would call them back when he was able to reach the phone. I grabbed the phone and looked at the name. It read, Natasha.

"Who the fuck was Natasha?" I thought. Dray had never mentioned a Natasha before. Because she kept calling, I decided to answer the call.

"DRAY?" she yelled. She was hysterical.

"This isn't Dray. This is his roommate."

"I need to talk to Dray!" she cried.

"Dray is out of the house right now. Is everything ok? Can I leave him a message? He should be back within the next fifteen or twenty minutes."

"PLEASE TELL HIM TO CALL ME AS SOON AS HE GETS THIS!" she yelled.

"Ok, what is your name and what is the problem?" I asked.

"Tell him his son was riding with my sister and they got into a bad car accident. The doctors don't think Nolan might make it!"

"Excuse me—did you just say Dray's son?"

"Yes," she pleaded.

"And he was in a car accident?" I asked, taken aback at everything presented to me.

"YES!" she yelled. "I'm Natasha. I'm Nolan's mother. Please tell Dray to call me as soon as he gets this."

"Ok, I will."

She hung up the phone. I placed the phone down and stared at the wall. Dray has a son?

DRAY HAS A SON?

This has to be some kind of sick joke. He has a son? Dray has a kid?

I've known Dray for damn near four years now and we've been officially together for three and he has never mentioned that he has a son. When did this happen? He cheated on me?

I sat back down on the couch and turned off the TV. We were done with the movies.

I didn't know what to think. I didn't know what to believe. What was I supposed to say to Dray? More importantly, if this Nolan kid was his son, he needed to get to wherever they were and be with the family.

Mere moments later, I heard the door open. Dray yelled, "I GOT THE FOOD!"

I never replied.

"BAE!" Dray yelled. "WHERE YOU AT?"

I heard him place the food and keys down on the counter and then he came around the corner. When he saw me he said, "What's wrong?"

"Nolan is in the hospital. He was in a car accident and they think he may not make it."

Dray just looked at me dumbfounded. He looked like a deer caught in headlights.

"Natasha called," I continued.

"Bae, I can explain," he said.

"Dray, you need to go see about your son. We can talk about this later."

I was brought back into reality when I felt Keston tapping on my shoulder. I looked over to him and he said, "Zach, are you ok?"

"Yeah."

"Sorry about the phone call," Kes replied. "You know how Qier is."

"Yeah," I forced a smile, as we arrived at my Atlanta home.

Once we got everything out of the car and into the house, I gave Kes a tour.

"Oh, my God, this is nice, Zach. This is really nice."

"You like it?"

"Like it? I LOVE IT!"

As we continued to walk through the home, he said, "It seems like something Dray would get. You know how high class he is."

I smiled.

"I wonder who your neighbors are?" he asked. "Living out here, they have got to have some elite status."

"Probably," I smiled as we headed into the living room.

"So enough about this," he said. "What's the deal with Dray? Did you tell him?"

"Naw, I didn't tell him. He told me," I said.

"Excuse me? Are you telling me he already knew about the job?"

"Something like that," I replied as I replayed last night events to him.

Keston listened in shock as I spit everything like a firecracker. It felt good to get this off my chest. "It's another thing though," I said.

"What's that?" Kes asked.

"The only person I've told this to was Dwight."

"Ok, what is it?"

"Dray has a son."

Keston just looked at me. I stared at Keston. A few moments later, Kes said, "So you mean to tell me that this dude who I thought was damn near perfect, cheated on you?"

"Everything isn't what it seems."

"What the hell do you mean by that?"

I sighed as I told Kes the story of how I came to know of Nolan's existence.

"So did the boy die? How old was he? You said you and Dray had been together for almost four years when you found this out, correct?"

"Yep, almost four years. Nolan was in critical condition and spent a few days in the hospital, but he didn't die."

"So where is he?" Kes asked. "And how is he now?"

"Nolan is just fine and he's right here in Atlanta," I replied.

"Seriously?"

"Seriously," I stated as I was drawn back to the period when Dray returned from seeing his son:

He had been gone for a few days. Everything was ok with Nolan and that was the most important factor in all of this. While Dray was in Atlanta, he tried to explain to me why he never mentioned Nolan and Natasha before, but

I didn't want no fucking explanation over the telephone. I wanted that shit in person. I wanted to be face-to-face so I'll know if Dray was lying.

I heard the door open and I knew it was him. "Yo Bae!" Dray yelled. "Are you home?"

I didn't reply. I figured he would see me when he came into the living room. When he saw me, he reached over and gave me a kiss. "I missed you so much," he said.

"How is Nolan?"

"He's ok. He'll be going home tomorrow."

"That's good to hear," I said.

Dray said, "I'm sorry, but I promise you it's not what you think."

"Dray, you have son. What the fuck am I supposed to think? WHAT THE FUCK AM I SUPPOSED TO THINK?"

"The first thing you need to do is lower your voice so we can have a conversation like two law abiding adults. Secondly, you need to know that I have not cheated on you."

"You have a son," I said. "Something had to be done."

"Like I just said, I have not cheated on you. I love you too much. I would never do that to you."

I didn't say anything, as I've cheated on Dray. Maybe this was karma coming back to bite me in the ass.

"I never mentioned Nolan because when I first met you, I didn't want to run you away, so I just kept it a secret. I always wanted to tell you, but never knew how. I didn't want you to think I was a liar. Time just passed, and passed, and I just never said anything."

"Get to the point, Dray."

"My son is not a baby; Nolan is nine years old."

I just looked at him. Nine?

I guess the look on my face told my question because Dray said, "Yes, he is nine. Natasha got pregnant our senior year in high school. She had the baby weeks after we graduated. I've never cheated on you. Hid the truth, yes, but cheated, no."

I didn't know what to say.

"Natasha stayed in Miami and had the baby. When Nolan was born my mom demanded a DNA test. That only made Natasha and her family upset. I believed he was my son the moment I saw him. But my mom was not taking no for an answer. So we paid for the test and when the results came back it only proved that Nolan Wescott was my child. After Natasha had the baby, she stayed at home with her mom and went to college down in Miami. When she graduated, she and her mom moved to Atlanta to be with the rest of her family.

Her mom wanted to get out of Miami because she said it was a bad place to raise a child. The violence and crime down there was getting out of hand. They've been in Atlanta ever since."

"Were you and Natasha together?"

"Yes. She was my long time high school girlfriend. We started dating when we were in the seventh grade. We started messing around in the eighth grade and started having sex in the ninth grade. She got pregnant around homecoming of our senior year. I was the homecoming king and she was the homecoming queen. We were THE couple in high school. We broke up months before Nolan was born. It took me a long time to tell my mom that I was about to become a father and with good reason. She didn't take it well. Even though Natasha and I had broken up, I knew that I was going to take care of my responsibility. I was going to be a good father to Nolan. Natasha named him and I was cool with that as long as he took my last name. And so there was Nolan Wescott."

"Is this the reason why you've been going to Atlanta once a month for 'work related' issues?"

"Yes. I mean I did work on some of the trips, but they were mostly to visit my son."

"Why couldn't you just tell me, Dray?"

"I just could never find the words."

"Do you still feel something for her?"

"Hell naw!" he said. "That was then. This is now. Those feelings are long gone. Zach, you are the only one for me. She was fun back in high school when I was trying to learn who I was, but I am past that point in my life."

"Does she know about us?"

"No."

"Does she know about you?"

"As in my sexuality?" he asked.

"Yes."

"Hell fuck no!" he replied.

"So what happens now?"

He exhaled, "We'll figure it out—together."

Keston looked at me and said, "So, if my calculations are correct, you're telling me as of today, Dray has a thirteen-year-old son?"

"Yeah. He turned thirteen a few weeks ago, back in June."

"And you're ok with that?" Kes asked.

"It really doesn't have anything to do with me," I exhaled. "I just hate when he tries to get all high and mighty when his shit isn't clean either. I'm not perfect. I've made some mistakes, but he isn't perfect either and I just wish he'd understand that. I love Dray. We've been through a lot. Nolan was here long before I met Dray, and if for some reason Dray and I doesn't work out, Nolan will still be his son. I'm not someone to come between something like that, especially when I didn't have my father in my life. I would never do that to someone. Dray is a damn good father. I can't take that away from him."

Kes smiled and said, "Well, we need to grab a bite to eat then head on over to campus. I don't want you to be late for your meeting."

"Yeah," I stood up. "Let's get going."

15

TJ

Elijah's mom, Mrs. Genevieve, dropped us off at the mall this morning. After daddy transferred all that money into my account, I knew I was going to have a damn good time.

After spending a lot of time with Eli, I've realized that he really is one cool ass nigga. He's real spontaneous though, always doing some shit to get his ass in trouble. I like that though. I like taking risks as long as daddy don't find out. Now, if this nigga would just show me to the pussy 'round here so I can get into something, he'll really be my new best friend.

All the lil chicks must know I'm new because they keep looking at me. Maybe they think I'm a relative of Elijah or something. Naw... I look better than that nigga. It must be my swag. These kids down here in da ATL don't know shit about that east coast swag. They 'bout to learn today. Hahahaha, class is now in session, bitch.

When these niggas see all them chicks on my dick, everybody gonna be mad. I'm taking all their hoes. And I got them condoms that Uncle Killa gave me. Shitttttttt. What we need to do is ditch this mall and find some pussy.

As we walked out of the shoe store, I turned to Eli and said, "Man, where the pussy at?"

He looked at me and started to smile.

"I know you got some pussy 'round here," I said. "I know you know some bout-it, bout-it chicks. Call dem hoes up, nigga. Let's get our dicks sucked or something."

"Man, you wild'n."

"No, I'm dead ass serious," I replied. "Where the bitches at man?"

"This one chick I be messing is out of town," he said.

This nigga lying. I started laughing and asked, "You a virgin, nigga?"

"WHAT? Hell naw, Shawty? I gets mine! You must don't know who I am."

"Nigga, you a virgin," I said very directly. "You probably ain't even smelled no pussy. Don't even know what that shit look like."

"I got some pussy. I always got some pussy on deck," he said.

"Then call them hoes, fool. Fuck this shopping shit. We can do that later. Let's go back to my shit. This is Ray's long day on campus and daddy gonna be out until at least four. We got like three hours to do what we got to do. I got some extra money. We can get these hoes an Uber or something. Call 'em, Eli."

"Man, what if my mom is home or something?" he said.

"Now you getting scared of your mom?" I asked. "All that shit you been having me doing and now you scared. Nigga, you scared of the pussy? It's alright, pussy ain't for everybody. You can at least get some head. Man, where my nigga Quan at? Damn, I wish he was here with me instead of back in Charlotte. We always were getting head together and shit."

"I'm hungry," Elijah said as he saw the food court. "You hungry?"

"Yeah for some pussy."

"I'M SERIOUS, TJ!" Elijah said.

"Damn, bruh. Calm down, nigga. We can wait on the pussy."

I followed Elijah as he headed over to Subway. After we ordered our subs, we found an empty table. Before I could say anything, my dad sent me a text asking how everything was going. After I finished checking in with my daddy, Eli took a bite of his sub then asked, "So you like it down here so far?"

"It ain't Charlotte, but you've helped me to adjust. If you weren't down the street from me, I don't know what I'd do. I probably would have committed suicide or something."

He started laughing.

"I'm dead ass serious," I replied as I stared at him.

He stopped laughing.

"Naw, nigga I'm just fucking with cha," I laughed. "I wouldn't have killed myself, but it would have been torture."

"You ready for school to start back?" he asked. "You know we're in the same grade and shit, so we might have some of the same classes. Shawty, that'll be tight work if we got the same classes and shit."

"Yeah, it would if you're leading me to some pussy. I mean I can pull my own, but I'm trying to see if you scared of pussy."

"There you go with that pussy talk again."

"If you scared, say you scared," I laughed. "Good pussy don't bite. I once heard a song that said good pussy don't ever get tired, good pussy don't ever get tired, I just let a bitch ride."

"Man, you're a trip," he laughed as he shook his head.

"I'ma put you up on that shit, watch nigga," I said as two females came over to the table.

"HEY ELIJAH!" one said. The other giggled.

This hoe was busted. These the type of chicks he fucks with? I see why he don't want me to see. I would be embarrassed too.

"This is TJ," Elijah said. "He'll be going to school with us next month."

"Hey TJ," the other girl said.

"Sup."

I didn't even want to know their names.

The second girl wasn't as bad as the first, but they both needed some major work. They couldn't walk around with me. Hell fuck naw!

They talked for a few more minutes until the busted hoe said, "Well, I gotta go."

"Why?" Elijah asked.

"I'm tired. I didn't get my beauty sleep last night. So I gotta go get it now before everybody comes home."

Beauty sleep? Bitch, yo' ugly ass need to hibernate.

I laughed.

"What's funny?" the girl asked.

"Inside joke," I replied, shaking my head.

"Anyway, bye y'all," she said as they walked off.

When they were gone, I said, "I hope you ain't fucking them gremlin looking bitches."

"HELL NAW SHAWTY!" he laughed. "They just cool people. TJ, you're something else."

Elijah started talking about the school and how things went down. He was telling me about the teachers, who was cool and who wasn't, basically just giving me the run down.

"I'm 'bout to come in and take over yo' school, nigga. They ain't gonna know what hit 'em."

"Whatever," he laughed.

Some dude started smiling as he walked closer to our table. He put his index finger over his mouth motioning for me to be quiet while he snuck up on Elijah. When he reached Elijah, he playfully punched him in the back. Elijah turned his head and started smiling when he saw the dude.

What the fuck is up with these Atlanta niggas? These nigga down here always smiling and shit. Fuck that smiling shit. Where the pussy at? I'll smile after I bust my nut. How 'bout that!

"My bad, TJ," Elijah said.

"Ain't he rude," the dude replied.

"This is my homeboy, Nolan," Elijah replied.

"What up, Shawty," Nolan said.

"Sup, fool," I nodded my head.

"TJ just moved here from Charlotte," Elijah said. "He lives down the street from me. We're all in the same grade and shit, so he'll probably be one of our classmates."

"That's what's up," Nolan nodded his head.

"What are you doing out here?" Elijah asked, looking at him.

"Picking up some stuff for school," Nolan replied.

I stared at Nolan. He looked familiar, like I knew him from somewhere. He was dark skinned and skinny.

"Shit, we are, too," Elijah said. "You should just chill with us."

Here go this nigga inviting more dicks to the damn party. Fuck niggas, we need some pussy in this bitch, and no busted ass hoes either.

"I can't," Nolan said. "I'm supposed to meet up with my dad while he is in town. So I gotta hurry up and get back home."

"Oh, ight," said Eli.

"I'll get at you later tonight," Nolan said.

"Ok," Elijah said.

"Nice meeting you, Shawty. I'll see you at school."

"Ight," I nodded my head as Nolan walked off.

*****

Zach

When I got to Clark Atlanta's campus, Keston decided he would hang out and check out the hot bodies while I took care of my business. I have a pretty good memory, so it was easy for me to retrace my steps back to the education building. As I approached the building, my phone started to vibrate. I saw it was Dray. I answered, "What's up? How did it go?"

"It went well. I'm pretty confident that they will give me the position. I bring a wealth of knowledge from Rolling Stone, and the person over the hiring is an old school FAMU Rattler."

"Damn, we're everywhere," I smiled as I thought about the FAMU network.

"Yep. Where are you?"

"On campus, about to go in this office."

"Ok. I'm about to pick up Nolan and we're gonna get something to eat. I'll call you later."

I checked my clothing to make sure that everything was still in order. Once I was ok, I took a couple more steps and opened the door to the education building. As soon as I walked in I heard him say, "YO, DR. FINLEY? WHAT UP?"

He jumped up from the desk and made his way over to me. I smiled and when we shook hands, I stated, "I'm doing quite well, Renzo. How have you been?"

"I've been great," he said. "It's good to see you again."

"It's good to see you too, Renzo."

"Since you're back, I guess that means you got the job."

I smiled and nodded my head.

"That's what's up," he replied as he walked back over to the desk. "I'm just filling in for the secretary. She wanted to get some lunch, so I told her I'd cover for her."

"That's nice. Listen, is Dr. Harris in?"

"Yep," he stood up. "Let me go get him."

I smiled. Something about this kid was refreshing. He had a certain glow about him. It's hard to explain, but there is a lot of positive energy flowing from him.

A few moments later, Renzo reappeared and said, "Dr. Harris is ready for you."

"Thanks," I replied as I made my way back to his office.

As soon as I stepped inside and closed the door, Raidon said, "Zach, I'm so glad that you made it."

"Me too," I smiled. "I got a quick question before we get started."

"Run it by me," he replied.

"That Renzo kid. Is he always like that?"

Raidon laughed and said, "Yes. Renzo is one of a kind. You'll love him. He's one of the best."

I smiled and said, "Cool. Let's get started."

16

Dwight

I was excited about tonight. I've been waiting patiently for a few days and now it's finally here. I couldn't wait to get out of this house. While I ironed my clothes in preparation for tonight, Lexi walked in the room.

With her usual attitude, she said, "You going somewhere?"

"Yep," I smiled as I listened to one of my old school Marching 100 CD's. Listening to that reminded me of the good days back in college and here she goes ruining the vibe.

"Who said you could go out? You know tonight is always family night."

"First, I said I could go out," I replied. "I pay all the bills in this house. I decide when and where I want to do something. Secondly, I understand that tonight is family night, but we're going to have to push that back a few days. If you would just listen to me and stop bitching all the damn time, you would know that."

"Who's the bitch, Dwight? Who is she?"

"What?" I looked at her.

"WHO IS SHE?"

"Lexi, you need calm the fuck down. I ain't fucking no damn bitch. Zach is in town for the night. We're going out for dinner and drinks."

"I should have known," she said. "He's the only person you drop everything for. I should have fuckin' known!"

I just looked at her.

"Well, I want to go," she replied.

"And who's supposed to watch the kids? Whenever you want to

go out with your friends I have no issue staying here and watching the kids, now it's your turn."

"I WANT TO GO, DWIGHT!"

"Lexi, you are not invited. Tonight is for the dudes and unless you've magically grown a dick in the past six weeks, you don't qualify. Wait—is that why you've been holding sex from me? You got a dick now?"

"FUCK YOU, DWIGHT!"

"That's the problem—you don't."

She stuck up her middle finger and stormed out of the room. I rolled my eyes and continued ironing my clothes.

*****

Zach

I don't know where Dray was and I didn't care. I hope he stayed out until I was gone. I really wanted to go on this trip alone. Kes said he would be leaving in about twenty minutes to come pick me up. I tried to get in touch with Kris to hang out with us tonight, but he was out of town on business.

I was so excited. Things were finally going my way. I signed the contract and while I took a pay cut to teach at Clark Atlanta, it was worth it. My happiness and my freedom is worth more than any number on a paycheck. I guess it all averages itself out. The cost of living in New York is high as hell. Atlanta is high, but it's manageable. I ain't worried. Money is the least of my worries.

I couldn't wait to kick back and have a good time with the boys. I really didn't want Dray interfering with that. If he comes, we won't be as loose as we normally are.

When I got out of the shower, I wrapped myself in the white towel and walked into the room. I instantly heard my phone vibrating on the nightstand. I still had to get used to living in this house. It feels so different than our condo back in Manhattan.

I grabbed my phone and it was a text from Keston. Just as I was reading it, Dray opened the door.

"Damn, what a sight," Dray licked his lips.

I turned to him and smiled and put my focus back to Kes' text that said he was on the way.

Dray saw the clothes laid out on the bed and asked, "Are we going somewhere for dinner? Ain't shit in here to cook, so going out is perfect. I passed a few restaurants that I wanted to try."

I just looked at Dray.

"What?" he asked as he sat on the bed.

"Dray, I have plans."

"So where are we going?" he asked.

"I'm hanging out with the boys."

"Who? Dwight and who else?" he asked.

"Keston. Kris was supposed to come but he's out of town."

"Why didn't you tell me this?"

"I didn't know you were coming to Atlanta," I rolled my eyes.

"I wanna go. I wanna see Dwight, too," he said. "You can't leave me in this house with nothing to do."

"Dray," I pouted. "It's the boys."

"Is there something you don't want me to know? Why can't I hang out with y'all? It ain't like I'm trying to be part of y'all click. I just wanna get out of the house. My friends aren't here in Atlanta; they're in New York. I mean if we're going to be living in Atlanta, I think it's only right that I—"

"OK, FINE!" I yelled in frustration. "Damn!"

"I don't have to go if you don't want me to go," Dray replied.

"Dray, just hurry and up and put on your damn clothes," I grabbed my phone to send Kes a text letting him know that he didn't have to pick me up anymore.

"I don't want to intrude," Dray said.

"Hurry up and shower before we're late."

While Dray was in the shower, I tried to call Dwight to let him know that Dray was coming but his phone kept going directly to voicemail. I sent him a text to call me ASAP. I never got a reply. I knew he was going to be upset. Dwight was not going to be happy to see Dray…not one bit. This was supposed to be a night for the boys.

I looked over at Dray whose attention was focused on the drive ahead. He knew he was intruding. He knew he was. The car ride was quiet and awkward.

I exhaled then turned my head to face the window. I loved Atlanta's sky line; It is so beautiful at night.

We listened to the radio for a while before Dray started to talk about his interview. I nodded my head a few times letting him know I was paying attention, even though at this moment I didn't give a flying fuck on what he had to say. Yes, I was being selfish right now.

"It was great seeing Nolan today," he said. "That boy is getting taller by the day."

I forced a smile.

"He looks just like me when I was a kid," Dray smiled. "He's the greatest son a man could have."

"That's great, Dray."

I wanted my own child. I exhaled.

"He's so intelligent," Dray raved. "He reminds me of myself. He really is a good kid."

He turned his head and looked at me. I turned my head and looked out the window. He mumbled something under his breath that I couldn't make out and then turned up the radio.

I grabbed my phone to check and see if Dwight replied to my text message but there was nothing.

"Are you ok?" Dray asked.

"I'm fine."

As we pulled into the parking lot, he said, "Do you just want me to drop you off and go back home because I ain't feeling this attitude right now."

"You're here now, so what the fuck does it matter? You might as well just stay. You gotta eat and we're already here."

"I really don't want you being mad at me," he parked the rental car. "I feel like I've been apologizing since before we left New York."

"Dray, it's really not that serious. Just try to enjoy the night."

17

Dwight

As soon as I walked in about ten minutes ago, I started downing the beers. I was enjoying myself, sitting across from Keston laughing and drinking.

I've been looking forward to this night since the moment Zach told me he'd be here. I guess it reminded me of the times Zach and I shared in college. We would often have our drinking nights. We would go out, grab some dinner, maybe even a movie, stop by the liquor store, grab a bottle or two, come back to his place, sometimes mine, and just get white boy wasted. That was back when life was free. That was back when you didn't have to worry about anything but school.

That was a long ass time ago.

I wish Keston were in our life back then. He was really one cool ass dude.

I remember the first time I met Keston. It was in September 2007. We were going to Birmingham for a football game against our arch rival, Southern University, and Zach invited Keston to ride with us. At the time, Kes was still in undergraduate school at the University of Central Florida, but he was a major FAMU fan. He moved to Tallahassee in January 2008 for grad school and it has really been a great friendship from then on out.

As Kes and I talked and laughed, I thought about Kris. Damn, I wish he were here, but he was out of town on a business meeting.

"Damn, where Zach at?" I asked.

"I told you he said that I didn't have to pick him up. They got a rental this morning, so Zach is probably just gonna drive the rental,"

Kes replied.

I nodded my head and downed some more of my Corona.

Then my eyes happened to cut across the room and everything just stopped. I saw them walking, looking around and then Zach pointed in our direction.

HELL NAW. I KNOW HE DID NOT BRING THIS NIGGA TO OUR NIGHT OUT!

What the fuck is he doing here? Why didn't Zach tell me this bitch nigga was coming? If he told me this nigga was coming I would have stayed my black ass at home. I would rather deal with Lexi.

"What's wrong, Dwight?" Keston asked. "Why are you looking like that?"

When I didn't reply Kes turned around and saw for himself.

"Oh, he brought Dray," Kes said.

When Zach saw me, he started smiling. Seeing him smile made me feel good. But still, he was wrong for this shit. He was wrong for bringing him.

*****

Zach

Seeing Dwight made me feel good. I really missed him. I missed being around him. We've been tight for fourteen years—that's almost half our life.

"WHAT UP, DWIGHT?" I said as he got up and gave me a brotherly hug.

"What's up, Big Z?"

When we finished greeting each other, he sat down and said, "What's up, Dray?"

"Sup," Dray replied as he sat down.

"Well, we've already seen each other earlier," Kes stood up and moved on the same side with Dwight.

"Thanks," Dray replied as he sat across from Kes. I sat across from Dwight. My back, along with Dray's back, was to the front door. I hated sitting on this side. I wanted to be where Dwight was so I could see everybody as they walked in the bar.

"I didn't know you were coming," Dwight said looking at Dray.

"It was a last minute thing," Dray stated as the waitress walked over.

"Can I get you two started with something to drink?" she asked.

As she went into the specials, I looked at Dwight and I knew he was pissed.

I kicked him under the table and mouthed, "I'm sorry." He rolled his eyes before starting to look through the menu.

Dray ended up getting a soda and I took a Long Island Iced Tea.

"Are you ready to order, or do you need more time?" the waitress asked.

"I'm ready," Keston replied.

"Me too," Dwight stated.

Dray looked at me and I nodded my head. He said, "Yeah, we can order now."

While Keston and Dwight placed their order, I quickly glanced through the menu. When the waitress got to me, I just decided to settle on some buffalo wings and fries. Dray took a chicken burger and fries.

"It'll be right out gentlemen," she smiled as she walked away.

Keston being Keston, he immediately sparked up a conversation.

Dray being good friends with Keston, immediately began to engage him in the conversation. I looked at Dwight and I could tell that he was still pissed as he downed his Corona.

I looked around the establishment. The Braves were on TV. People were smoking and drinking, while others were playing pool off on the opposite side of the room. Most importantly, everyone seemed like they were having a good time. It was a Friday night, the end of the work week. Why not sit back and relax? Well, I was mistaken. Everyone was having a good time except Dwight.

He's going to have to get over it. I have.

Just enjoy the damn night.

18

TJ

I was in my room listening to my music when the smell of daddy's cooking filled my nostrils. I was hungry and couldn't wait to tear into that food. I looked at some of my new school clothes and smiled. I'm going to be the best dressed nigga at that school.

I took the headphones off and walked out of my room. Before I walked downstairs, I could hear them talking. I stopped and listened. I didn't want to walk in on no nasty shit.

"How is Micah?" I heard Uncle Morgan say. Morgan and Micah were Ray's younger brothers.

"Micah is fine," Ray said. "He's still growing strong with Brandon. Micah actually came by the office today and we chatted for a few minutes."

"That's good," Uncle Morgan said.

"Speaking of that," Daddy said. "What happened to you and Dorian? The last I remember Raidon saying y'all were on good terms, now it's just over?"

I felt my stomach sink.

"It was probably Morgan being Morgan," Ray said.

"Whatever, Raidon," Uncle Morgan replied.

"I'm just saying," Ray said. "We know your track record."

"It wasn't a healthy relationship," Uncle Morgan stated. "We needed to split, but you know after you break up you still have your needs."

"So y'all still fucking," I heard daddy say.

"Something like that," Uncle Morgan replied.

I swear everybody in Ray's family is gay. What the fuck is up with that?

I shook my head then headed downstairs.

I really didn't say much at dinner. Uncle Morgan would ask a question and I would answer it. I wanted to eat and get the fuck away from this table. I didn't want these niggas breathing that gay shit on me. I love all of them, but I ain't gay and I don't want them breathing that shit into my life.

I was looking forward to getting up with Raven, Uncle Morgan's only daughter. I loved hanging out with my cousin. She was fly as shit.

I felt my phone vibrating. While I put some veggies into my mouth, I read the text message from Elijah. He sent, *"SHAWTY!"*

"What's up?"

"I got this chick who said she would suck us both up at the same damn time!"

"FA REAL?"

"Hell yeah!" he sent.

"Shit…set that shit up!" I replied.

"I will. I'm about to eat though. I'll get at you later."

"Fa sho!"

When I looked up, daddy was staring at me.

"Sorry," I mouthed as I placed my phone down and prepared to finish my meal.

*****

Zach

The entire time we had been here, Dwight hadn't said much. He just looked at the Braves baseball game on TV and drunk his drink. It was very tense. I would chime in here and there, but the night was mostly Keston and Dray talking.

"So how did it go today?" Keston asked Dray.

"Kes, it went well. I think I'm going to get the position."

"Get what position?" Dwight finally spoke.

Dray turned his head to face Dwight and then said, "A teaching position at Clark Atlanta."

Dwight looked to me and said, "Are you fucking serious? He's moving here, too?"

Dray said, "I have no reason to lie. I hope I get the position."

"Was I talking to you?" Dwight cut his eyes to Dray.

Kes interjected, "This is going to be great! Both of y'all are moving to Atlanta."

Dwight downed the rest of his beer.

I touched Dray on the thigh and he looked at me. I pleaded with my eyes for him not to say anything.

Dray is a ticking bomb, just waiting to explode. I know how to deal with him and he knows how to deal with me, but he isn't going to take some bullshit from anyone else.

Right on cue, the waitress and another dude walked over with the food. Once all the food was placed down, Dwight said, "Can I get another bottle please? Two bottles."

She smiled and said, "Sure thing. Anybody else need something?" After she took the extra orders, she walked away.

Just like any other time when black people gather, when the food comes, the talking ceases. I ate my fries and exhaled. I just wanted to go home to Orlando. I'd rather be with my mom right now. I couldn't wait to see her tomorrow.

Slowly but surely, Keston started up another conversation with Dray. Dwight ate his food in silence. I forced some laughs even though it was all phony.

In the midst of the conversation, Dray grabbed his phone. When he saw the name, he stood up and said, "I've got to take this call."

He excused himself from the table.

19

Dray

When I stepped out of the bar, I picked up the phone and said, "Man, you called right on time."

"What's wrong?" he asked as I saw a dude standing outside talking on his phone. He looked over at me and lifted his head.

"Just in a situation I shouldn't be in," I replied as I lifted my head back to the stranger. "You're like an angel."

"Well, I'm happy I called," he said. "I just wanted to tell you about some of the things I found out today, but I can call you back later if you're busy."

"NO!" I pleaded. "They don't want me there anyway. They won't miss me. Go ahead and talk."

"Damn, it's like that?" he asked.

"Yeah, it is," I replied. "I don't know what I was thinking coming here, but what's going on?"

*****

Zach

As soon as Dray was gone, Dwight said, "WHAT THE FUCK, ZACH?"

"Dwight, you need to stop acting like a damn bitch! So fucking childish!"

"Whoa," Kes interjected.

"Who invited him?" Dwight asked. "Why didn't you let me know he was coming?"

"Nigga, I called you and I sent you a text. You never replied."

"No, you didn't," he stated. "I didn't get a call from you."

"Check your phone, Dwight."

"Am I missing something?" Keston asked. "What is wrong with Dray being here?"

"This was supposed to be a night for the boys," Dwight said as he grabbed his phone.

"It is the boys," Kes replied.

"Dray is not a boy of mine," Dwight replied as he pressed a button. "Damn, somehow my phone got cut off."

"But Dray is Zach's dude," Kes said.

"Zach is my friend, not Dray," Dwight said.

"Dwight, you need to stop acting like a child," I said. "Act like you got some sense. Dray hasn't done anything to you, but you've done everything to him and you know what I'm talking about."

"Zach, don't go there, ok," Dwight replied.

"Then you need to act like the man and friend I've come to know and love these past fourteen years."

He looked at me. Kes didn't say anything.

Suddenly, Dwight's phone started to vibrate.

*****

Dwight

I looked at the phone. I didn't want to answer the call, but even talking to her was better than being here right now.

"Hello," I answered.

"How is your little dinner going?" she asked.

"Lexi, what do you want?"

"Is your boyfriend there?"

"Lexi, why the fuck are you acting so damn dumb? You're really starting to piss me off."

"Oh, yeah," she said. "He's there. Yep, he's there. You get balls and shit when he's around."

"Lexi, I'm about to go."

"FUCK YOU, DWIGHT!" she yelled. "FUCK YOU!"

She hung up the phone.

20

Dorian

I stood outside the bar and waited. I just got off the phone with this nigga. He said he was around the corner but that was five minutes ago.

I shook my head. It's a good thing I had this chocolate beauty standing outside talking on the phone to look at. I didn't want to be obvious, but he was sexy. He was the kind of nigga I can vibe with.

When I saw my co-worker's car zoom into the parking lot, I smiled. It was time to eat! When he approached me, he said, "Sorry DK, got stuck in traffic."

He was the only person who called me DK.

"Whatever, Brandon," I replied, as we started to make our way towards the front door. As I passed the dude on the phone, I lifted my head again. He smiled and lifted his back.

"Which side?" Brandon asked when we walked inside.

I looked around the bar then saw an empty table over in the corner. "Over there," I pointed.

"Ight," he started to head in that direction.

This was our normal Friday. We meet up at this bar and get wasted.

I had the pregame festivities in my car. When I parked at the bar, I started taking shots of Patron. I wanted to get fucked up tonight and I was already feeling good. My vision was getting a lil blurry. I had to squeeze my eyes a few times to focus.

Brandon Brunswick and I had become very good friends over the years. When we started working together, I instantly knew I knew him from somewhere, but I just couldn't place it. It wasn't until one day after work, he was in the car in front of me and I saw the FAMU license plate and it all hit me. He was a drum major at FAMU during the time I was a drum major at Bethune-Cookman. The next day at work I asked him about it and we've been tight ever since. We even confided in each other about our sexualities. He knew about Morgan, and I knew about his longtime boyfriend, Micah Harris. Go figure, Morgan and Micah are brothers. How small can the world be?

Nonetheless, Brandon and I are best friends and I really value having him in my life.

"OH, SHIT," he said, as he kept walking.

"WHAT?"

"THAT'S MY NIGGA!"

As we approached the table, the dude stood up and smiled.

Brandon said, "WHAT UP, D. TAYLOR?"

"Look at my lil protégée," the dude, D. Taylor, stated as they embraced each other with a brotherly hug.

I looked at the other dude at the table as he lifted his head and smiled. I lifted my head and smiled back.

By looking at the table, it was clear that two other people were eating, too. I wonder if the dude talking on the phone outside the bar was part of this group.

Brandon said, "DK, this was my mentor when I made drum major. He taught me everything there was to know about being a drum major. His expertise eventually helped me land the head drum major position when I was at FAMU."

"That's what's up," I replied.

Brandon's friend was sexy, but that was irrelevant right now. While, on one hand, I was happy that he was having a reunion with his FAMU peeps, on the other hand, I was hungry and ready to eat and drink.

"Yeah, he was a drum major at Cookman," Brandon said to the dude as he pointed to me.

"Cool, cool," D. Taylor said as he sat back down.

"Well, I don't wanna hold y'all up because we're hungry, too," Brandon laughed. "But it was good seeing you again."

"Same here," D. Taylor replied. "Nice meeting you."

"You too," I said as the other dude at the table lifted his hands to say bye.

*****

Zach

When I got back to the table, Dwight said, "You just missed Brandon."

"Who is Brandon?" I asked, looking at him like he was stupid.

"Brandon Brunswick," Dwight said.

"That name sounds very familiar, but I can't put a face to it right now," I said.

"He was a drum major," Dwight said.

"Oh, yeah! He's in here?"

"Yeah. He just stopped over for a second. He was out with some dude who was a drum major in Cookman's band."

"Oh, I guess," I replied.

"I hope Dray didn't leave," Keston cut into the conversation. "He's been gone for a minute."

"I hope he did," Dwight said. "Then maybe we could enjoy our night like we intended."

"I don't know what the hell wrong with y'all, but I'm enjoying my night," Kes said as he took a sip of his drink. "Y'all need to let all the petty shit go and just be free." Moments later, Kes said, "There he goes."

I turned my head and saw Dray smiling as he headed over to the table. As he sat down, he said, "Sorry about that. I had to take that call. It was my homeboy, Phoenix, trying to get some stuff straight for something we're doing back home."

"You know what," Dwight interjected. "I'm tired of biting my tongue. You're the third wheel. Nobody wanted you here. This was supposed to be a night for us, the three of us—Keston, Zach and myself. Not us and you."

"Dwight, you need to chill the fuck out," I said. "You need to watch it. Why are you being so rude?"

"Don't nobody got time for that fuck nigga," Dwight said as he stared at Dray.

Dray cut in by saying, "Keep on bruh. Keep on and I will show you who's a fuck nigga."

"PHOENIX?" Keston yelled in a tone that garnered all of our attention.

We all looked to Keston. He had a look of shock on his face.

"Dray," Kes said. "What is Phoenix's last name?"

"Cummings," Dray replied as he had a blank look on his face.

"The NBA player?" Kes said.

"Yeah, the NBA player. He plays for the Bulls," Dray said.

"How do you know Phoenix?" Keston asked.

Dray said, "I went to high school with him. Do you know him or something?"

"Naw," Kes shook his head. "I mean I used to see him on campus when I was at UCF, that's about it. What are y'all working on, if you don't mind me asking?"

"Some stuff for the kids back home. We have a lot of ideas. He was just telling me that he secured a corporate partner to sponsor a free basketball camp for the kids. We have a lot that we want to do. If everything goes to plan, I will spend one day a week back in Miami doing stuff for the kids. We really just want them to know that you can make it out of the hood. You don't have to sell drugs or your body to make money."

"That's wonderful," Kes said. "If you need anything, just hit me up. I would love to help in any way I can."

"I'm sure we can use you," Dray smiled. "This is great! Just great!"

"HOLD THE FUCK UP!" Dwight interjected. "How do you plan on being there for Zach and you're gone every which way? When will you ever be home to take care of his needs? You're talking about teaching here in Atlanta while you already have a lucrative job at Rolling Stone in New York. Now you talking about going to Miami. Nigga, you're in New York, Atlanta, Miami, probably D.C. and New Orleans, too. While you're traveling the country, he will be lonely."

Dray looked at Dwight and said, "You don't need to worry about that. I takes care of mine. I've been taking care of it for eight years now."

"Well, you ain't been taking care of it to well if he's down here now. He must have been very unhappy with something up there, or maybe it was just you."

Dray said, "If I wasn't secure in my relationship...ugh…you know what… I don't have to explain shit to you. As long as MY dude tells me the truth about what HE feels then I am good. We're good. He's good so let's just worry about something else, like your scandalous ways."

"OH, MY GOD!" I yelled. "I CAN'T TAKE THIS SHIT! Both of you are about to piss me the fuck off. Dwight, why are you acting a fool? Dray, why are you entertaining this? Both of y'all just chill the fuck out, have some drinks and enjoy the rest of the damn night."

"I need a drink," Keston said as he flagged the waitress.

When she walked over, Keston ordered another round. Dray, who doesn't normally drink, said, "Can I have a crown on the rocks?"

When she walked away, I turned to him and said, "Why are you drinking?"

"What, I can't drink now?" he asked. "I thought everybody at this table was a grown man—at least in age anyway."

The rest of the night was cordial, even though the tension at the table was thick.

Once the tab was paid and the waitress was tipped, we headed out. I dapped up Dwight and Keston. Dray dapped up Keston. We said our goodbyes and then Dwight and Keston headed to one side of the parking lot and we headed to the other.

21

Dwight

I was pissed the entire ride home. Pissed at Zach. Pissed at Dray. More importantly, pissed at myself for letting Zach slip away. Pissed at myself for not being a man years ago and grabbing hold to Zach when I had the chance.

I love him so much, it hurts. Sometimes it feels like he doesn't love me back.

This shit hurts. It hurts badly.

I was out of line tonight. It's just when I see Zach with him, it eats me up because I know that's supposed to be me. I am supposed to be the person holding him tight at night, making sweet love. That's supposed to be me.

Now, I'm stuck in this marriage with Thing 1 and Thing 2 all rolled into one body. I love my kids, but I want out of this marriage. I want to be with Zach. I love him.

When I got home, I parked and ran into the house. I was so horny right now. I needed Lexi. I needed her body bad! The fact that I had all these drinks in my system wasn't helping either.

Like expected, the kids were put to sleep. I hurried off to the room and Lexi was in the bed. I didn't say anything. I just got on the bed and started to place kisses on her body. I wanted to fuck my wife.

Well, I wanted to make love to Zach, but fucking Lexi would have to work in the meantime. I didn't get very far though.

"Dwight, please get off me," she pushed me away.

"Lexi, I need you," I pleaded. "I need to feel you. I need to love you."

"Dwight, get off me and take your drunk ass to bed!"

"LEXI!"

"Dwight, I'm not playing with you. I'm not in the mood."

Upset, I got off the bed and grabbed the first thing I could touch, which happened to be the lamp on the nightstand.

From the rage that had overcome my body from tonight at the bar and being rejected by my wife again, I screamed at the top of my lungs, "YOU FUCKING BITCH!" I snatched the lamp out of the socket and with all my force threw it across the room. The glass shattering the wall before it touched the laminate wood floor, sounded like a series of firecrackers being set off at a 4th of July event.

She screamed in fear as I stormed out of the room and out of the house.

I had to get out of there before I do something I'd regret.

*****

Zach

The ride home was just like the ride to the bar—filled with tension and silence. The radio was playing but I knew Dray was dying to say something.

I just wanted to go visit my mom. I wanted to get out of here. I couldn't wait until my flight takes off in the morning.

Tonight was not supposed to be like this.

The closer we got to the house, the more I could feel Dray on the verge of speaking his mind. In an effort to get this over with, I said, "Just say what the fuck you've got to say!"

"YOU JUST LET YOUR HOMEBOY COME AT ME LIKE THAT! YOU JUST LET THAT NIGGA GO IN!" Dray said upset.

"How the fuck you think he's gonna act, Dray? You know he doesn't like you. Don't act like that is some new information. You've known for a long time that Dwight doesn't care for you, but you still just pop out of nowhere and decide to tag along. And while I don't have a problem with you, or with you coming, he obviously does. Dray, you were not an expected companion."

"I asked you if you—ugh," he said before he stopped. He redirected, "I could have stayed home, Zach."

"Dray, we need to figure out how to have lives with each other and outside of each other. You had your friends up there in New York and I didn't barge in when you went out with them."

"But I invited you though," he interjected.

"Yes, but I knew those were times for you to hang with your friends. Key word Dray— YOUR FRIENDS! They were not my friends. Now that we're moving to Atlanta, I'm coming back to my friends. Like I just said, we need, well, you need to figure out how to have lives with each other and outside of each other because when I wanna hang with my friends, I wanna hang with my friends. You have to understand that it's not gonna always be with you."

"Damn, you make it seem like I'm trying to fucking interfere with your life. DAMN! You know what… whenever you wanna do shit with your friends, do shit with your fucking friends and just let me know when you want to key me the fuck in!"

I didn't reply.

And then he said, "I fucking up and changed my life to move to

Atlanta and I don't wanna live here."

"Oh, I'm sorry," I sarcastically replied. "You know I did the shit for SEVEN YEARS when I didn't want to be up there."

"You act like I'm asking to spend every night with your damn friends. I wanted to go because I didn't want to be in the house alone tonight." He parked the car at the house and said, "I feel like I've been becoming a bitch lately. I feel like I've been doing too motherfucking much to please your ass. I've been doing too motherfucking much. FUCK IT! WHATEVER, ZACH! YOU TAKE THE BEDROOM, I'LL TAKE THE GUEST BEDROOM!"

He got out of the car and slammed the door and headed for the front door. Upset, I jumped out and said, "You just don't get to walk away. We're not done!"

"WHATEVER, ZACH!" he yelled as he continued to walk towards the front door.

"AND YOU'RE STILL WALKING!" I replied upset.

Dray turned around and said, "WHAT THE FUCK DO YOU WANT FROM ME? WHAT THE FUCK DO YOU WANT ZACH? I DON'T GET IT! I JUST DON'T GET IT!"

I stared at him.

"You know what," he replied. "Just leave me the fuck alone. Go call Dwight and Keston and whoever the fuck else and go back to the bar and enjoy your God damn night, because at this point I really don't give a fuck about you or anyone else right now."

"Dray, you're acting like a bitch."

"You know what Zach," he said as we stood at the front door. "Why won't you and Dwight just… UGHHHHHH… YOU KNOW WHAT ZACH, FUCK YOU! FUCK YOU! FUCK YOU AND THAT BITCH ASS NIGGA! FUCK YOU!"

Dray inserted the key and forced the door open.

When he was inside, he slammed the door as hard as he could dead in my face. The entire doorframe vibrated.

I took a deep breath and looked around to make sure nobody saw or heard our altercation. When the coast was clear, I turned the doorknob and entered.

I hope this was the best choice.

I hope coming to Atlanta was the best choice…

Part Three:

Family Matters

22

Zach

Orlando, Florida

Once the plane touched down, I turned on my phone and sent Dray a text that I had made it. I spent the entire fifty-minute flight thinking about last night's fight. I hate when we argue, but that has been a trend of late. We've argued more in the past year than we have over the entire duration of our relationship.

My phone vibrated and Dray replied, "Ok."

I stared at the phone for a second, rolled my eyes and thought, "Whatever."

I didn't even wake him this morning when I left. I just caught an Uber to the airport. I figure I'd let him sleep it off. Once I gathered my luggage, I caught another Uber to my mom's house.

I was low-key excited about spending some time with her. Something about seeing her face made me feel good inside, especially because she didn't know I was coming. She hates surprises, but she'll love this one!

I was reminded of my life here as we rode through the city. Ever since my grandma passed away ten and a half years ago, nothing has been the same. When she died, it was like a part of me died too, a part of my life in this city died. Once she was gone, I had no reason to come back. I had no aspirations to ever come back and live. I miss her so much.

I know I have to stop by and visit Chaz's grave while I'm here. I really miss him, too. If he was living he'd be around thirty-eight years old. Wow. Man, where does the time go?

I took in the sights as the Uber driver zipped through the city. It was almost eleven and seems like everyone was out and about taking advantage of the tax-free shopping weekend around the state with school getting ready to start back up.

Sometimes when I look at Dray and Dwight I get jealous because I wonder what it would be like to have my own kid. I've spoken to Dray about having my own child, but the conversation never got very far.

Being that my mom doesn't have any other kids, it's not like I have any nieces or nephews I can raise.

There goes that void again. There goes that empty feeling. I sighed.

Before long, the driver was turning on her street. I smiled as I saw her car parked in the driveway. Once he completed the trip, I grabbed my luggage out of the trunk and headed up to the front door. I guess my Rottweiler could hear and smell me coming because he started barking crazily. I rang the doorbell. The dog barked harder. My mom opened the door and screamed. I heard my stepdad ask, "What's wrong?"

She yelled, "My baby is home! My baby is home!"

We embraced for what seemed like an eternity. Having her arms wrapped around my body made me feel like a kid again. It felt so good to be here. It felt damn good to feel loved.

My stepdad turned the corner and said, "Hey, it's Zach!" We embraced with a hug. My dog wanted to get into the action, so I reached down and hugged him for a few seconds.

"What are you doing here?" my mom asked as my stepdad brought in my luggage.

"I just wanted to surprise you."

"Well, I am surprised."

"It's great to have you home, Zach," my stepdad replied. This was the only man I've ever known to act as my father. Even though I wasn't his biological son, he was my dad. Hell, he's been here since I was about seven years old.

"It's great to be home," I smiled.

My mom asked, "How long are you here?"

"Four days. I gotta head back to New York on Wednesday."

"This is great!" she smiled.

I didn't even get to put my things down before she said, "I was just about to head out to the church."

"What's going on at the church?" I asked.

"We're selling dinners for the building fund."

I shook my head. They've been raising money for the building fund since I was a baby and ain't shit been done on that church.

She added, "Everybody would love to see you. They're always asking about you, so you know you've got to come with me."

"But y'all gonna be there all day!" I pouted.

"Oh, stop, boy," she shook her head. "You can take the car and drive around. Just come on out here with me for a few minutes and say hey to everybody. That way they can ask you all the questions and stop asking me every Sunday."

I sighed and said, "Yes ma'am."

My stepdad smiled and said, "Dear, I've got bowling tonight. I don't know what time you'll be back, but if I'm not here that's where I will be."

She grabbed the keys, looked at me and said, "Ok. C'mon, Zach. Let's go!"

*****

Dwight

It was a little past noon when I woke up. I squeezed my eyes shut and opened them again. I exhaled then moved to the side of the bed.

I don't know how I got here. I was so angry last night I must have drove straight here.

I looked at the phone again and I saw that I had some missed calls from Lexi.

"Fuck her," I said as I put back on my jeans and a wife beater, opened the door and walked across the hall to the bathroom.

I knew she was up because I heard the TV in the living room. I was surprised she hadn't woken me up earlier.

After I took a leak, I brushed my teeth and washed my face. When finished, I stared in the bathroom mirror and sighed as images from last night appeared.

Who was this person? What was happening to me? Who had I become?

I grabbed my phone and took a deep breath before I headed up front. I really didn't want to answer a bunch of questions.

Fuck my life.

When I got to the living room, she turned and looked at me. I said, "Good morning."

She replied, "More like afternoon. You slept all morning."

"Sorry."

"You missed breakfast, so I went ahead a made you a turkey sandwich. I figured you would be hungry whenever you woke up. It's in the fridge along with some fresh fruit and sweet tea."

"Thanks, Mama."

As I opened the refrigerator, she said, "You almost got your brains blown out last night."

"What?"

"Coming in my house like you live here," she said. "I had my shot gun ready and you know I ain't afraid to use it."

I grabbed the food and placed it on the counter. As I grabbed the glass to pour my drink, she said, "When I realized it was you, I put the gun down but you were moments from being in the morgue."

"Whatever, Mama."

"You say whatever now, but I ain't playing, Dwight."

I grabbed the drink and food and sat down at the table.

"Why are you coming down here that time of night? More importantly, why didn't you call me first?"

"Mama, I don't know why I didn't call."

"What made you come down here?"

"I went out with Zach and our other homebody."

"Zach—" she cut me off. "Hmmm."

I rolled my eyes and said, "Anyway, when I got home, Lexi pissed me off and instead of doing something I would regret, I just got in my car. I don't how I got here."

"So you were that mad you didn't know where you were going?"

"Yeah, I guess so."

"You were drinking?" she asked.

"I had a few drinks."

"And you drove an hour down here to Macon under the influence? You're too old to just be thinking about yourself. Dwight, you have THREE children at home. What would they do if they lost their father to some stupid stuff? YOU'VE GOT TO THINK, SON. THINK!"

I didn't reply.

She shook her head and then said, "Gone 'head and eat your food. I'm gonna watch TV. I don't feel like telling your ass something you should already know. I should have put that bullet through your head, 'round here drinking and driving and shit. DA FUCK WRONG WITH YOU?"

I sighed. I wasn't in the mood for any fucking lectures. Luckily, she didn't say anything else and continued to watch TV.

As I sat at the table and ate the sandwich, I realized I'm so over this shit. I'm over Lexi. I'm over Zach. I'm over it all.

I just don't understand why Zach is still with Dray? I've expressed my love to Zach time and time again after we had sex.

That night changed me. Why can't he see that? That night made me realize who I really wanted. I fought with this revelation for a few years but then I got tired of fighting. I wanted to give my heart to Zach.

I've reached out to Zach plenty of times and every time I do, he strikes me down. I don't get it. I thought Zach said he loved me. He's told me he loved me time and time again.

In the midst of our love making, he told me he loved me. Did he not mean it? Was it a ploy? What gives?

What's different now? Why won't he be with me now?

I wanna be with Zach. I'm willing to risk everything for a chance to be happy with him. Why can't he see that? What's his problem?

Over the years, I've thought about trying it again. I wanted to see was it just Zach or was I really attracted to dudes. Sometimes I've been so tempted to just…NAW… let me stop right there.

I can't. I won't even put that shit into my head. I can't go there. I ain't crazy… or am I?

I need to get back to Atlanta. I wanna get some rest in before I have to go to work tonight.

23

Dray

Atlanta, Georgia

I was happy that Zach was gone. We needed this break. The fucking audacity of him. Sometimes I don't know why I'm even here.

I love Zach, but at some point in the very near future he's going to have to make a decision. It will either be me or *him*. There is no way we'll be able to co-exist in the same city.

As I edged closer to my destination, I sighed. I don't think I really mean that.

It's just I'm frustrated. I'm frustrated with Zach and the lies. I feel like I'm stuck on stupid for Zach. What kind of hold does he have on me? Why do I love him the way I do?

This shit hurts. Love isn't supposed to hurt.

I need to re-think my plan of action. Is moving to Atlanta something I really want to do? Do I really want to have to see and deal with Dwight on a continual basis?

I parked the rental car and exhaled. I took a few moments to gather myself and then got out of the car. I rang the doorbell. She opened the door, looked at me and smiled.

"What?" I smiled back, nervous.

"I swear you get sexier every time I see you," she said.

"Whatever Tasha," I shook my head.

"I'm just saying," she replied. "Living in this city, it's hard to find a successful, handsome black man who isn't already married or gay. You're about your business. I appreciate that and you take care of your son."

"Tasha, where is my son?" I asked trying to get out of this conversation.

"You're not gay are you, or in some marriage that I don't know about?" she quizzed.

"TASHA!"

"Sorry," she shrugged her shoulders and moved aside to let me inside of the house.

She knew she was something sexy. Tasha reminded me of Olympic track star Allyson Felix. She had her looks and her amazing body.

Natasha Greene had done well for herself. After receiving her college degree, she and her mom moved to Atlanta to get out of Miami. They already had family here and figured it would be a better place to raise Nolan. Tasha's mom passed away two years ago, so a lot of the help Tasha had with Nolan is now gone.

"NOLAN, YOUR FATHER IS HERE!" Tasha yelled, before offering me something to drink.

"I'm not thirsty," I said sitting on the couch.

"Dray, I don't know if I've ever really told you, but I really appreciate you being a part of our son's life. I have some sisters and friends and I see the struggles they go through with their children's fathers. I'm so grateful that you're nothing like that."

"Speaking of that," I interjected as I saw Nolan coming down the stairs.

"What?" Tasha asked.

"I might be moving to Atlanta."

"FOR GOOD?" Nolan asked, happy.

"Possibly," I replied as I thought about Zach.

"Wow, Dray, this is great news!" Tasha smiled.

"Some other things have to work out first, but this is the temporary plan."

"If you move, when will you be here?" she asked.

"It'll be in the next few weeks. I have to figure out something about my job at Rolling Stone because I'm not quite ready to give it up yet. Nonetheless, when I figure everything out, I'll let both of you know."

"DAD IS MOVING HOME!" Nolan yelled. "YOU GONNA GET YOUR WISH, MAMA!"

I cut my eyes to Tasha. She cut her eyes to Nolan.

Realizing he just fucked up, in a grave voice, he said, "Sorry."

Embarrassed, she turned to me and said, "Well, I guess y'all better get going."

"Yeah, I think so," I stood up.

"Where are y'all going?" she asked.

"To grab something to eat," I replied. "And do a little school shopping."

"Yeah, c'mon, dad," Nolan said as he walked to the front door. He was ready to get out of here.

"Don't keep my baby all day," Tasha said as I followed behind Nolan. She was behind me.

"MAMA!" Nolan pouted. "I'm chilling with dad today. I'll be ok. You'll have me back tomorrow, dang."

She sighed.

I shook my head, smiled and said, "We'll be back Tasha."

"Be safe with my baby," she walked us out the door.

*****

Zach

I had been at the church for about an hour. All the deaconesses and the other church ladies were very happy to see me. I must say, it felt good at first. Everybody was asking me a thousand questions at once. I knew it made my mom feel equally as good, too. I saw her off in the church kitchen smiling. Above anything else, I knew she was very proud of me and all my successes. That had me feeling like I was on a natural high.

I sat in the empty sanctuary and hopped on the grand piano. I hadn't played the piano in years. For some reason, Smokie Norful's *I Need You Now* started to flow through my veins. As I played the song, I thought about my grandmother.

I was raised in this church. We were here every Sunday, Tuesday, Wednesday, Thursday and Saturday, until her health started to fail. It was Sunday school and regular service on Sunday, some Sunday's even had night service. There was bible study on Tuesday, prayer meetings on Wednesday, choir rehearsal on Thursday and just like today, a dinner sale on Saturday.

I loved Saturday's the best because since we lived so close to the church, I could just walk back home. Besides, the food was always great. They would alternate the Saturday's selling different meals like ribs, fried chicken, fried fish, spaghetti and chitterlings. They always had a bunch of sides to choose from and a lot of cakes and pies to top off desert. I smiled. Those were the days.

Now some twenty years later, they're still doing the same things. Some of the same old women are still slaving in the kitchen for that building fund. My mom has taken my grandmothers role and is responsible for doing the desserts. Wow, how times change. When I was a teenager, you couldn't get my mom up here, but now it seems like she is here every Saturday.

I finished the song and headed back out to meet my mother. Some of the ladies' grandkids, who were playing in the lobby, had no idea who I was. I didn't know who they were either. As I headed to the back of the building, I heard the ladies talking and laughing as they prepared the food.

"Awe, look at the doctor!" one of the ladies said.

I smiled.

"So you know how to perform surgeries and stuff?" another one asked.

I smiled and said, "I am not a medical doctor."

"Yeah, girl," another smiled. "He one of them smart people, you know, those college professors and stuff. Zach is one of those types of doctors."

"Oh. Well, I'll be. This whole time I thought you were the doctors in the hospitals. Chile, you learn something new every day."

I smiled.

"I know Carrie is in heaven smiling down," Sister White said. "Your grandmother was always real proud of you as you were the star in her life."

"Lord knows I miss my friend," another lady said. "God bless the dead."

"Everybody knew you were going to do good things," Sister White continued. "We knew you were going to make it out." Sister White turned to my mom and said, "Paula, you should be equally as proud. You and Sister Carrie raised him well."

"Thanks," my mom smiled.

"But Dr. Zach, when are you going to get married and have some babies?" another lady asked. "You're getting up there in age."

I forced a smile and said, "When the time is right."

"Chile, the time will never be right," another said. "But you know what's best for you."

"Umm hmm," Sister White chimed in.

"Excuse me," my mom said as she motioned with her eyes for me to follow her. We both knew where this conversation was headed and neither one of us wanted to go there.

When we walked outside, I said, "I want to take a drive around town, go visit a few places."

"Ok," she reached in her pockets and handed me the keys. "Don't wreck my car and make sure you put the gas back in it."

I smiled and said, "Yes ma'am."

"I'll be here for most of the day. If you get hungry just stop by and get something to eat. I'll call you when I'm getting ready to leave so you can come back and pick me up. I love you and I'll see you soon."

"I love you too," I kissed her on the cheek.

After I left the church, I visited my old neighborhood. I passed my grandma's house. It had a new paint job, but it still looked the same.

I drove by my old high school. I had great memories there. That was back when I was in love with Tony.

I drove around town, taking in the sights. It just felt good to be free for a moment. I ended up stopping by Chaz's gravesite. Seeing his son's, Xavier, tombstone really put everything into perspective.

Grandma used to always say, "Tomorrow isn't promised to anyone; live everyday like it is your last."

My final destination was to the park my uncles used to take my cousins and me to every Friday when I was a kid. It felt really good to just sit there and clear my mind.

While I was there, I sent Dray a text but he never replied. I thought about last night.

I don't know who to be mad at. Dwight was wrong, but Dray was wrong, too. This is why I didn't want Dray to go. I expressed to him that this was a night for the boys. Why couldn't he understand that? Even if Dwight behaved himself, the night still would have been awkward. Dray was the elephant in the room.

Having Dray there was like having your mother or girlfriend intrude on your conversation while you're hanging with friends. With them there, you can't really fully relax. You have to watch what you say and what you do. The point of a *boyz night out* was to let it all go and be free without restrictions. The point was to have fun.

The significant other stopped that from happening. Dray coming to the dinner was like Lexi being there. How strange would that have been?

As I sat on the bench and watched the kids run up and down the court playing basketball, my phone started to vibrate. I thought it was Dray getting back in touch with me but I quickly realized it was Dwight. I answered and he asked, "Did you make it?"

"Yeah, I'm here."

"How is your mom?"

"She's cool. What's up?"

"Sorry about last night," he said. "It's just I wasn't expecting to see him."

I didn't reply.

"You mad at me?" he asked.

"Dwight, why do you have to show your ass every time something doesn't go your way? Dude, you are rude as fuck!"

"Damn, Zach, that's how you feel?"

"Dwight, it's the truth. I love you, but you're rude. Do you remember when we went to President Obama's inauguration parade and we met up with Eric and went to dinner?"

"Yeah," he said.

"Do you remember how you acted? Do you remember how rude you were to Eric until he got rude with your ass right back?"

He didn't reply.

"Dwight, that was eight years ago. You haven't changed. At what point do you grow up? I know I'm not perfect and I've done things that I'm not proud of, and I still have a lot of growing to do. I admit that, but c'mon Dwight. You're my best friend. You're smart as hell. You're one of the smartest people I know, but you can't continue to do shit like that."

"Zach—"

"Let me finish," I cut him off. "You may not like Dray, but I need you to respect him. There is a difference."

"Za—"

"I'M NOT FINISHED!"

He exhaled.

"Dwight, Dray is my dude. He has been for a very long time and he will continue to be. I need you to get that through your head. As my best friend, I need you to respect my relationship with my partner. Dray isn't going anywhere. Do you understand what I'm saying to you? Dwight, I will not let you fuck up my relationship. Do you understand? I will not… I AM NOT… going to allow you to come in-between Dray and I. You had your chance, Dwight. You had chance after chance after chance. The world doesn't revolve around you. I waited for you, Dwight. I waited years. I held out hope. Through all the bullshit you put me through, I held out hope. In my heart, I knew that you would come."

"I'm here now," he said.

"It's too late, Dwight. It is too late," I sighed. "What you want is not going to happen. There is a reason why I've rejected your continual advances over the years. I fucked up and cheated on Dray. I FUCKED UP! I live with that shit every fucking day. EVERYDAY! Dray is important to me and I'm not going to let you fuck us up. Dwight, I love you. You know I do. Hell, Dray knows I love you. But Dwight, I'm telling you right now, your ways have to change. There is no other way around that. Dray and I have been together damn near eight years. You need to respect that. I need you to be the man I met fourteen years ago. I need you to be that Dwight. Can you be that Dwight?"

He didn't say anything.

"Can you?" I asked.

"Zachariah, I gotta go. I just got back home. I'll holla at you." He hung up the phone.

I exhaled.

I know I did the right thing.

I know I did.

I hope I did…

24

Zach

I picked my mom up from the church and headed back home. As we were holding small talk, her phone started to ring. She ignored the call and said, "I see you're still very much the same."

"What do you mean by that?" I asked.

"You're still very much to yourself. Very introvert. Some of the ladies at the church said the same thing. They were talking about how handsome you were and how you had grown up, but how you were still very quiet and shy."

"I don't know if I would call myself shy," I stated.

"You're not very outgoing."

"I guess," I replied as we approached a red light.

She began to gossip about the ladies at the church. I would nod my head and say, "umm hmm" to show that I was listening, but I really could care less about the ladies at the church. I'd prefer to stay away from the gossip shit. She loves it though. Hearing other people's issues keeps her going. I just don't understand that for the life of me. I know I have enough issues of my own to deal with instead of being worried about the next person.

She told me to hold on as her phone started ringing again. She spent the rest of the ride on the phone gossiping.

As we got closer to the house, I was reminded of how she really didn't want to move to this nice house. I wanted my parents to get out of the old neighborhood and move them somewhere a little high class. It's not over the top, but it's in a great neighborhood where crime is a foreign word.

My mom loved the house but she didn't want to move. Her

biggest gripe was that they couldn't afford it.

With them living on just my stepdad's salary, I could understand her concern. When I told her I was willing to pay the mortgage, she told me that she couldn't allow me to do that. They'd stay where they were. After a few months of debate, we finally agreed to go half and half on the mortgage.

I could easily afford it. Working at the university in New York was very prosperous for me. After taxes, I brought home exactly $7000 a month. Dray's monthly salary almost tripled mine. This move to Atlanta will cause my salary to decrease a little. By my estimations, after taxes I'll bring home about $5330 a month. Even if Dray and I were to split, I can still take care of myself and help my parents in the process.

I just lost $20,000 a year by taking this job at Clark Atlanta. If that doesn't explain how important it is for me to be somewhere I want to be, I don't know what else to say. Some people don't make $20,000 a year and I just gave it up to move.

When we arrived home, my mom got off the phone. My stepdad was gone bowling. He's been bowling faithfully every Wednesday and Saturday night since I was a kid.

As she checked the mail on the counter, I said, "Ma, I need you to take a shower and get dressed. I'm taking you out."

"Zachariah, I don't have no money for that."

"Ma, take a shower, put on some clothes and meet me back out in the living room in thirty minutes!" I demanded.

"Who you talking to?" she asked looking at me as if I was a child.

"I'm talking to you," I said in a joking way to lighten the mood. "Gone and clean up and put on some clothes and stop playing. We're gonna miss the movie."

"Chile, these kids these days think they grown, demanding me to do something," she said as her phone started to ring. She reached for her phone and said, "Who is it now?"

She just stared at the number.

"Why are you staring at the phone like that? Who is it?" I asked.

"I don't know," she shrugged her shoulders and charged her phone. "You know I don't answer numbers I don't know."

"I guess," I replied. "I'm 'bout to hop in the shower. Thirty minutes, Ma. Thirty minutes."

*****

Keston

I laid in the bed and sighed. I could hear those words as if he just spoke them yesterday:

"KESTON, PLEASE!" he yelled. It sounded like he was crying, too. "PLEASE, KESTON! I DON'T KNOW WHAT ELSE TO DO. I DON'T KNOW WHAT TO DO, KES. WHAT DO YOU WANT ME TO DO? WHAT DO I HAVE TO DO TO MAKE THIS RIGHT? I LOVE YOU. I WANT TO FIX THIS. JUST TALK TO ME. PLEASE, KESTON. TALK TO ME!"

I remembered everything so vividly. I remembered sitting on the floor crying as he yelled through the front door. I remembered hearing his tears. I remembered his cries for me to talk to him.

I remembered when I made the decision to let it all go:

"Phoenix, I've made up my mind. There is nothing you can say to me right now that is going to change that. Maybe sometime down the road when I am at a better place in my life, who knows what can happen. But right now, given everything that has happened and where I'm trying to go in my life, I can't do this. I need to back away now before I go insane. This is about me and what is best for my life going forward. I'm sorry, Phoenix. But please don't contact me anymore."

"Kes, please don't do this."

"Goodbye, Phoenix and good luck in your future endeavors."

"KESTON!"

Now, here I am, lying in bed, Googling pictures of my old lover. My mind has been going in circles all day.

Ever since Dray mentioned Phoenix's name last night at the bar, my mind has been fucked. It's been nine years since I last saw him in person or even talked to him.

It's been so long that I've put him out of my head. I really don't even think about him anymore. I mean I see him on Sports Center and I was always proud of him for making it to the NBA, but I had put all things about Phoenix out of my mind.

But last night was crazy. Hearing Dray mentioning Phoenix's name moved me. It sent a chill through my body.

Phoenix.

Wow.

That was so long ago though. I wonder if he still talks to Kory.

I exhaled.

Nobody still knows what happened that night. I suppressed it all and moved on, but last night brought all that shit back up—EVERYTHING!

Phoenix Cummings. He was still sexy as hell to me.

Thinking about those dreads and how my body was sensitive to their touch caused an arousal inside of me.

"Ok, Keston," I said to myself. "Get it together. That shit is your past."

I've had a few boyfriends since Phoenix, but no one has compared to him.

I admit I went about that situation the wrong way. At the time, I did what I thought was best for me. Now that I'm older, I wish I would have reacted differently. If I saw him today, I don't know how I would react.

Phoenix.

Wow.

I thought about my cousin, Qier's, significant other, Kookie. I could just contact Kookie to get Phoenix's number.

Naw, let me leave that alone.

"Let that shit go," I told myself. "That was way back when you were in college."

That was the past. The past is to remain in the past. Besides, he might have somebody.

Damn.

Phoenix.

Phoenix Cummings.

25

Dorian

I sat at home, surprised that I actually attempted to make the phone call my dad has been begging me to do. Of course, she didn't answer. I didn't expect her to do so. If she did, I really don't know what I was going to say. I guess I was going to wing it.

That was none of my concern anymore. I tried. She didn't answer. End of story.

I sat in my condo and exhaled. It was a Saturday night and there was nothing to do. I couldn't chill with Brandon tonight because he and his dude, Micah, had plans. I was a home body and haven't really befriended many other people up here. I can't go get Dakota because she is with her mom in Alabama for a family reunion.

I flipped through the TV. Nothing good caught my attention. I wasn't in the mood to go to the gym. I walked over to my bookshelf and grabbed the newest book by my favorite author. I haven't had time to read it because I've been so busy with work.

Prepared to do some reading, I sat on the leather couch and opened to the first page. While I'm sure it was good, I couldn't get into the book because my mind really wasn't there. I forced myself to finish the first chapter and then I put it down. I would have to restart it when I was ready to really read. Tonight was not that night.

I thought about going to the movies, but then realized I didn't want to go alone, so I erased that thought from my mind. I was miserable.

I sat on the couch and pouted. It was a Saturday night and I was stuck in the house with nothing to do.

I exhaled then got up and went to the kitchen and fixed a frozen cocktail. I tasted the drink and smiled. This was just what the doctor ordered. I flipped on my surround sound to my Musiq Soulchild and Frank Ocean mix. While the music played moderately in the background, in nothing but my baller shorts, I grabbed my phone and drink and headed to the balcony. I sat at the patio table and exhaled. There was a small breeze blowing in and that was strange since it was the end of July.

I logged into my Jack'd account and figured I would give it one more try. I would give this shit with niggas one more chance.

I thought about that dude I saw last night at the bar talking on his phone. Damn, he was sexy. Maybe it'll just be my luck that I'll come across him on here.

"Yeah, right," I said as I took a sip of my drink. "Get real, Dorian."

So I browsed Jack'd, clicking on profiles that garnered my attention. Maybe I was being extra picky, but I would always find something that would turn me off. Who do these dudes think they're fooling?

I played on the app for about forty minutes, browsing and chatting with some people. I scrolled and then came across a profile with no picture. I'm a visual creature so I want to at least see a chest or something, and under normal circumstances, I would just bypass profiles with no picture, but something told me to click on it.

Nothing was there other than he was in Atlanta, 33 years old and a Sagittarius. At least he was in my age bracket. His profile stated that he was wasn't really looking for anything, just checking out the app.

Something about this profile aroused my curiosity. What if this was the dude from last night? What if God were answering my prayers? What if this was him? Won't know unless you try.

"Oh, what the hell," I said.

I wasn't looking for sex tonight. I just wanted to vibe with another dude who looked and acted like me. I just wanted some company, some entertainment to pass away the rest of this forgetful Saturday evening.

"How are you this evening?" I sent.

I waited for a response. Then I heard the alert indicator that I got a reply back.

"I'm doing ok. How are you?" he sent.

"Bored out of my mind" I replied.

"Lol. I guess," he sent.

"What brings you on here?"

"This is actually my first time on here and I really don't know why I'm here," he sent.

"Interesting."

"What's so interesting about that?" he asked.

"Just a word I like to use."

"Lol… I know someone who uses that word a lot. I never quite understood his infatuation with the word but whatever lol."

"Lol," I sent back. "But not to sound cynical or anything like that, but are you masculine? Are you out? There is nothing on your profile so I really don't know what to think of you."

"Just because I say I'm masculine doesn't mean that I'm masculine. I could say yes but it doesn't mean I'm telling the truth."

"Interesting," I sent back.

"But if you must know, I am very much a man."

"So why are you really on this app?" I sent, ignoring the other messages I was getting from the other dudes.

"Curiosity. I've never done this before."

"You've never been with a dude before? LOL that's what everyone says."

"That's not what I said."

"Umm hmm," I replied.

"Lol… I like your candor. But check this. I've got to get off here. I want you to call me in exactly thirteen minutes."

"Why thirteen? And what's the digits?" I sent back.

"Because I said thirteen, that's why," he replied and sent the number back.

"Ok."

"The time starts now," he replied.

I grabbed my phone and set the timer. I was not going to fuck this up. I was so engaged in the conversation, I forgot about the drink that awaited me.

So, I sat on the balcony, sipped my drink and waited.

Thirteen. That was such a random number. Normally someone says ten or fifteen, but thirteen?

It intrigued me though. This dude was a mystery to me.

What was once a grave Saturday now seemed like it had life and I was really excited.

I looked at the time. I grabbed my drink and walked over to the side of balcony and looked down at the traffic that passed beneath me. I took a sip. I couldn't taste the alcohol and normally that was a good thing, but with this phone call looming, I'd better slow down.

This was the longest thirteen minutes of my life. And after an eternity, the timer on my phone started to beep. Time was up. I input the numbers into my iPhone and without thinking, pressed talk.

"Why wasn't it this easy to call that lady?" I thought.

Within a few rings, he said, "I see you can follow directions. Good sign."

I was immediately taken aback by his voice. Hearing him talk instantly caused my dick to stir.

"You said call you in thirteen minutes, so I called you in thirteen minutes."

"You sound like a man," he replied.

"Trust, I am all man."

"That's good to hear," he replied as I heard music playing softly in the background.

"For this to be your first time you're pretty open to this stuff."

"I see that you hear what you want to hear," he replied. "What's that called, selective memory?"

"How long have you been in Atlanta?" I asked.

"Long enough," he replied.

I held the phone. He really wasn't giving very much information.

"Why did you ask me to call?" I quizzed.

"I wanted to see what you sounded like. Is there something wrong with that?"

"No, not at all," I replied.

There was silence. I wanted to push it, but I didn't want to run him off. I exhaled and figured I would go for it anyway. "So, I'm not twenty anymore and I've matured a lot since then."

"That's nice to hear," he replied. "So what is your point?"

Damn, he was direct. That shit was turning me on. I collected myself and said, "My point was I don't have time to play phone games. I'm too old for that."

"Ok?"

"I wanna meet up."

"Ok."

"Okay?" I asked, shocked at his response.

"What—you don't want to meet now?" he asked.

"I didn't expect you to be so forthcoming."

He said, "Then stop expecting. And don't expect any sex because I'm not fucking you either."

"That wasn't even in the game plan, homeboy."

"Ok, just putting it out there," he replied.

I rolled my eyes and said, "So let's meet up now. I ain't doing shit."

"Right now is a negative," he replied.

"Why not now?" I asked.

"I'm actually kinda busy and will be for the next few hours. We can get up when I'm done though."

"What time will that be?"

"Around six," he said so nonchalantly.

"SIX IN THE MORNING?"

"Six in the evening has already passed," he replied. "So the next six would be six in the morning."

"You have a slick mouth."

"You like it," he laughed. "However, we can catch breakfast at the Waffle House or something."

"What the hell are you doing where you're out all night? You don't have a dude or something like that do you?"

"I work," he replied.

"At ten at night? You sell drugs or something?"

"You know you ask a lot of questions," he replied.

"What kinda work you do?"

"It's not important."

"You work at McDonald's or Walmart or something? I can't think of anything else open this time of night."

"You ask a lot of questions," he said. "Just know what I do is legal and I make more money in a year than the average American will make three years. I am the boss, and tonight I have work to do. I took some time off work to tend to some stuff and now I have to play catch up. Now, if you want to join me for breakfast, you are welcome to do so. If not, another time."

"Which Waffle House?" I asked.

"You pick and just text me the location."

"Ok. You got a picture so I'll know who I'm looking for?"

He laughed and said, "You get no pics from me. When you see me, you'll know it's me."

"You talk with a lot of arrogance."

"You call it arrogance; I call it confidence. We should all be confident, correct?"

Damn, he was so smooth.

"So, what's your name?" I asked, deciding to go in a different direction.

"You ask a lot of questions," he said again. "Hell, what is YOUR name?"

"Dorian," I replied. "So what's yours?"

"Is that your real name?" he asked.

"Yes," I stated, getting upset. "What's your name?"

"D—… ummm Douglas."

"Douglas?" I said in response to his hesitation.

"Yeah. You can just call me Doug, though."

"Is that YOUR real name?" I returned.

"Yeah," he stated. "Text me though. I gotta get off the phone."

"Sure," I hung up the phone.

Douglas.

Yeah right.

26

Zach

We had been seated and orders had been placed at her favorite restaurant. I smiled as my mom rambled on about the movie we just saw. It made me feel good to know that she was enjoying her night with me. She didn't know it yet, but tomorrow after church, I was going to take her to get a manicure and pedicure. On Monday, I would drop her off so she could get a deep tissue massage. On Tuesday, we would go visit my grandmother's grave. On Wednesday, I would head back home to New York.

Soon, the waitress returned with our drinks. "A Virgin Strawberry Daiquiri for the misses," she replied as she placed the drink down in front of my mom, "and a Strawberry Banana smoothie for the gentleman."

"Thanks," I took a sip.

When the waitress walked away, my mom said, "Ever since you were kid, you have loved a strawberry-banana anything."

"I can't help it," I smiled. "It's my favorite fruit mix."

She smiled and said, "No matter what, I love you."

"I love you, too."

She smiled and continued to stare at me.

"What?" I asked.

"Nothing," she shook her head. "Just admiring how successful you've become."

I smiled and replied, "How are Kyle and Langdon? I haven't seen my stepbrothers in so long."

"They're doing well," she replied as she started to ramble on about their lives.

I met Kyle and Langdon when I was seven. Kyle is three years younger than me. Langdon is a year younger than Kyle. Both Kyle and Langdon have different mothers, but they are as close as brothers can be. My stepdad has two other kids from a relationship when he lived in Mississippi, but I never quite knew them like that.

Kyle, Langdon and I, along with Tony, were pretty close growing up. Kyle and Langdon treated me like I was their older brother, but there was always something missing. I loved them. I still love them, but when I went off to college fourteen years ago our relationships just kinda dwindled. If I'm home visiting and they're at our parent's home, we'll talk for a little, but we really don't keep in communication.

They both had grown up. They both were married with families of their own. Since I couldn't and wouldn't produce any grandchildren for my mother, she took in Kyle and Langdon kids as if they were her blood. In some ways it bothers me, but I just let it go. It is what it is.

I looked at her as she kept talking. Now, the focus of the conversation was on her siblings. I nodded my head and listened as she talked about them.

She said, "So your aunt knows she irks my nerves. She's always got something to say about you. Most of the time, I don't even bring the nonsense your way. I know you have real important things to worry about then that woman."

I stared at my mom.

"I swear she has been jealous of you from the day you were born. She's jealous of the fact that mama raised you. She's jealous that mama wanted you in the will and not her children. She's jealous of the fact that you brought us that house and that you brought us those cars. She's jealous of all your accomplishments. But you know what I tell her ass—it ain't my damn fault and it damn sure ain't my son fault that your children ain't mount to be nothing but some fucking bums!"

"Ma?" I said hushing her down. She was getting louder as she spoke every word.

"Sorry," she took a sip of her drink. "Then she wants to bring up my relationship with you and how rocky it has been and I tell that woman to kiss my ass and go to hell. Then she tries to bring up your sexuality as if that shit is supposed to hurt my feelings. She's supposed to be my sister. We came from the same woman. That's why I don't do her. She can keep her distance over there and I'll keep mine. From the moment mama died, her true colors shined."

I took a sip of my drink.

"Let me tell you something, Zachariah. You press on, you hear me. You do you, son! Don't entertain that negativity. Don't listen to it. Continue to do the things that you have done that has gotten you this far in life. I haven't been the perfect mother, but no one is perfect. Everyone makes mistakes. But you are my child and I'll be damned if I let someone bad talk my child—gay or not. Our relationship isn't for them to understand. This is why we are mother and son."

I exhaled as I saw the food coming in our direction. She said a quick prayer and we began to eat. While we ate, she said, "Your aunt said something to Maurice and Maurice told me."

"What was that?" I asked as I thought about my uncle, my grandmother's youngest child.

"Your aunt said that you act like you're too good for the family. You act like you can't come down to the family functions."

"Ma, do you want to know a story?" I asked as I ate a piece of my fish.

"I'm all ears."

"I've always loved my family," I replied. "I've always loved each and every one of you and no one can tell me any differently. However, I knew I was different and I knew y'all knew I was different."

She stared at me.

"It's hard to put into words, but I knew I loved y'all. I still love y'all. I just felt…feel…strange being around y'all after grandma died."

"I'm not following."

"A few years back in 2011, it all hit me."

"What happened back then?" she asked.

"Uncle James passed away." Uncle James was my grandmother's oldest brother.

"Yes, I remember," she commented.

"Even though I really didn't know him like that, and as much as I hate funerals, I figured I'd fly down from New York to be with the family. While I was down there, I could catch the FAMU football game later that afternoon. So I flew down, excited to see everyone, even though it was under dire circumstances. I got off the flight Saturday morning in Tallahassee and got a rental car and took forty-minute drive to be with y'all. I was excited the entire time, happy to see the family. Then when I got to the church everything changed."

"What changed?"

"So I sat there next to you and it all started to hit me. Those happy feelings had dissipated. When we got back to the Big House for the repast, I got excited again. I was in dire need for some of our cooking. After I got my plate, I sat at the table across from you. I remember like it was yesterday. All of your brothers and sisters and their families were at the same table. You kept looking at me as if you were trying to read me. I couldn't enjoy the food anymore. Other people in the family would look at me. I'm not stupid. I knew what they were thinking. I sat there at that table and really didn't say much. Someone would ask me a question and I'd answer it. I didn't engage in much conversation. My body was tense. I wasn't happy. I was ready to go. When you went back into the house, your sister, my aunt, would maliciously ask questions about me and a girlfriend. She was just trying to start trouble. I smiled and played it off. She would make snide remarks about what I was doing in New York. I even heard she say that she hoped I didn't end up like Uncle Alan."

My mom's face was emotionless.

"You do understand that she was hinting at the fact that Uncle Alan passed away from AIDS?" I stated.

"Umm, hmm," she replied.

"So I stayed a bit longer and hung out with your brothers. The first topic of discussion was, excuse my French, whose pussy was I banging out in New York. Everything they talked about had something to do with the fact of me and my sexuality. It was like my known but unknown homosexuality was the elephant in the room. Ma, I don't have time for that. I'm too old for that. So, a stayed a few more minutes, then I got in the car and drove back to Tallahassee to go to the football game. But, it was in the ride back when I realized—"

"What did you realize?" she asked.

"Family is supposed to be a warm and inviting group of people. When I first see y'all after a long period of time, I feel that way, but within a few minutes, it goes away. I hated the feeling. Every time I would come home to Orlando for a break or something, I would feel strange. I could never put my finger on what the issue was, but after all this time I realized that I don't feel comfortable around my immediate family. I feel uptight and as if the weight of the world is resting upon my shoulders. And I don't like it. Whenever I go home, I feel as if I have to watch everything I say and do. Ma, why do I feel like this?"

She didn't say anything.

"Exactly," I replied. "You don't know and I don't know. I can't explain it either because you and dad know about my sexuality. I don't like the feeling."

She didn't say anything.

"When grandma was here, I didn't feel this way. When she passed, I felt as if I was out here by myself and ten years since her passing, at times, I still feel as if I'm in this big world by myself with no family members to lean on. All I have is three of my closest friends and Dray and I don't like it. I feel as if my three closest friends know me better than my own family and I don't like it, but enough about that."

"How is Dray?" she asked.

"He's ok," I replied.

She stared at me.

"What?" I asked.

"I know my son and I know when something is wrong. I saw it in the car ride to the church. I noticed it when we were at the church. I saw it in the car ride back to the house. I saw it in the car ride to the movies and I see it right here, right now. Now, are you gonna lie to me or are you going to tell me the truth? Something is going on."

"We had an argument last night. Nothing major."

"Umm hmm."

I ate some of my food.

"Dray is a good dude," she said.

"Ma, trust me, I know."

"How is Dwight?" she asked.

"Dwight is Dwight."

"Was he the cause of the argument between you and Dray?"

"Ma, I really don't want to get into that."

"He's still married, correct?" she asked.

"Yes," I cut my eyes to her.

"Ok."

"Oh, yeah, I'm moving to Atlanta in a couple of weeks."

"You're leaving New York?"

"Yep."

"And Dray?"

"You think I'm leaving Dray for Dwight?" I asked.

She never replied, but the expression on her face told her story.

"Ma, I've told you time and time again, Dwight is just my best friend."

"Ok," she said.

"Dray is moving to Atlanta, too. I got a job at Clark Atlanta University so I'll be working there starting next month."

"Congratulations," she smiled as her phone started to vibrate. She looked at the phone.

"What?" I asked.

"It's that same number again."

"Answer it," I replied. "It might be important."

"There is nothing more important than spending time with my son," she smiled as she put the phone down. "If it's really important, they'll leave a message."

I took a sip of my drink.

"However, let's be real, Zachariah. You're not going to have Dray move down to Atlanta and then you leave him for Dwight are you? That boy is married with kids. It's one thing to be gay and it's another to wreck a home."

"Ma, you are out of line! I've told you a thousand times that Dwight is just my best friend."

"While I have you here," she said changing the subject. "I guess I might as well tell you."

"Tell me what?" I cautiously asked.

"Your Uncle Maurice was out and about running the town earlier this week and he ran into Angelica."

"Angelica? Who is that?" I asked.

"Angelica!" she said again with a bit more force in her voice.

Then it all hit me. My eyes got wide and I said, "My Aunt Angelica?"

"Umm hmm," she rolled her eyes. "Her extra phony ass."

Angelica was my birth father's older sister. If Angelica was in this restaurant, I wouldn't be able to point her out. That's how long it has been since I've seen her. The last time I saw her I think I was thirteen or fourteen years old. That was damn near twenty years ago.

"Anyway," she said. "You know Maurice is cordial with everyone. I don't have time to be phony with people, especially those people."

"What did she say?" I asked before she started going off on a tangent again.

"Duane is sick," my mom said in a very nonchalant tone as she ate some of her food.

My stomach churned.

Duane.

Duane Kierce.

I hadn't heard that name in years.

"What's wrong with him?" I asked about as nonchalant as my mom.

"He has some type of cancer," she said. "I really don't know and I really don't care."

"Oh," I replied. "So what is she telling Uncle Maurice for?"

"I guess it was to get the message to you," my mom shrugged her shoulders. "I don't know."

"I guess," I sighed. "I hope he makes it through, but that doesn't have anything to do with me."

She stared at me.

"Ever since that day he stood me up—"

"Stood you up?" she asked, cutting me off.

"He was supposed to take me to meet my brother for the first time, but of course Duane being Duane, he never showed," I said.

"Oh, I remember that," she said. "I told you not to get your hopes up dealing with him. I sat right there in mama's house and told you not to fall for it, but you were so happy that you were getting a brother, a blood brother, that you tuned me out. You HAVE brothers—Kyle and Langdon. But you choose to deal with Duane, so you got what you deserved. He hasn't been there your entire life and then he pops up and you act like shit was just supposed to change overnight. I never thought you could be that damn gullible."

"Kyle and Langdon don't count," I said as I felt tears building up inside of me. "The only thing I've ever wanted in life was to have a brother or sister. You never gave that to me. I begged you for a sibling. I begged you. I knew I had a brother somewhere. I'd never seen him. I never knew his name until Duane told me that day at grandma's house. Dorian."

"What?"

"Dorian," I replied. "I'll never forget it. Dorian. That's his name. That's all I know about him other than he is two years younger than me. I don't know his last name. I don't know what he looks like or nothing. The one thing I wanted exists and I don't know how to reach him. I've tried Facebook and Twitter and MySpace when it was popular, but the problem is I don't know his last name. I don't know how to properly spell his first name, as there are some variations Dorian. So I'm stuck. I stopped looking and stopped worrying about it. There is a void in my life, Ma. I want a sibling and I'll never be able to have my own. So, yes, I got excited when Duane wanted us to meet eleven years ago. I wanted to meet my brother—my BLOOD brother. I'm sorry if that hurt your feelings because I wanted to get to know my father's side of the family. I'M SORRY!" I said upset.

"Zachariah, I didn't mea—"

"But after that day," I cut her off, "I realized that you were only trying to protect me from the inevitable. I guess some stuff you just gotta learn for yourself. I learned my lesson."

She stared at me.

"I don't want anything to do with Duane," I said. "I'm sorry he's sick and I hope he gets better, but I don't know why Angelica was trying to relay that message to me. I don't want anything to do with him. That was a choice Duane made himself. If he died tomorrow, I really wouldn't care. It's not like I know the man anyway."

"Zach," my mom said. "You are being mea—"

"That's not being mean," I cut her off., "that's being real." I stared her directly in the eyes and said, "YOU…mother…taught me that."

She said nothing else.

Upset, I looked around for the waitress.

Where was my damn check? I wanted to get the fuck out of here.

I was ready to go!

27

Zach

Wednesday, August 3, 2016

The flight attendant poured some Coca Cola into a cup and handed it to me before she moved on to the next row. I took a sip of the drink, looked out the window and exhaled. It was such a beautiful Wednesday morning.

After dinner with my mom on Saturday, images of my sperm donor has been plaguing my mind. What did I ever do to him for him to treat me like this? I thought about that letter I sent my grandmother eleven years ago where I spoke about my frustrations with my mom, other members of my family, but most importantly, my birth father.

After my grandma read the letter, she reached out to my Uncle Maurice to find my sperm donor. My uncle located my sperm donor and told him that I wanted to see him. I didn't find this out until I was home for an extended weekend back in the fall of 2005.

I remembered that day like it was yesterday:

It was Friday, October 7, 2005. Symon rode with me back to Orlando and I had just dropped him off at home. My grandmother was expecting me, and I was excited to see her. My mom was at my grandma's house, too. After about an hour of relaxing and catching up with my grandma and my mom, I headed back to my room to watch TV. My Uncle Maurice arrived soon thereafter.

While I was watching TV, Uncle Maurice headed into my room. He asked, "What are you doing?"

"Just watching TV."

"Oh," he looked at the TV for a second.

"What's up?" I asked, wondering why he was standing in the room.

"I heard that you wanted to see Duane."

"Yeah."

"Mama told me to find him for you."

I cut my eyes to him.

"He should be paying you a visit today or tomorrow," he added.

"Really?"

"Yeah. If you wanna see your dad, you should be able to see your dad."

"How did you manage to do that?" I asked.

He smiled and said, "I have my ways, but that ain't for you to worry about. Just let me know if he doesn't show up."

"Ok," I said as he turned around and walked out of the room.

I sat in the room and waited for nearly another hour or two before my grandma called me to the living room. My birth father was standing there when I arrived.

My first reaction was to look to my mom. She had a major attitude on her face. She acted as if he didn't even exist. My grandma, on the other hand, was cordial. She talked to him. He would occasionally say, "Yes ma'am, Ms. Carrie."

The entire time I stood there, my body was frozen. I couldn't believe he was actually here. I could probably count on both hands how many times I've seen him since I was at an age where I could remember shit.

When my grandma finished talking to him, she said, "Well, I know you ain't come here to talk to me. So y'all can gone outside."

"Ok, Ms. Carrie. I'll see you later," he said.

"Duane, don't lie to me," my grandma said. "Just gone out there and talk to your son."

"Yes, ma'am," he replied. He turned to my mom and said, "Nice seeing you again, Paula."

She never replied.

As he picked his face off the ground, he looked to me and then followed me outside. The sun was starting to set. When the door closed, I leaned against my grandmother's car; he leaned against the Kelly green painted wall. The vibe was awkward. Nobody really knew what to say.

He cleared his throat and said, "It's good to see you again. You've really grown up."

"Yeah, that's what happens over time—you grow up."

He stared at me.

"What?" I asked.

"You've got a mouth just like your mom, huh?"

"She had a hand in raising me," I rolled my eyes.

"So she poisoned you, too?" he asked.

I looked at him and said, "Don't talk about my mother like that, ok?"

"Sorry."

There was silence.

He exhaled and asked, "So you hate me, too?"

I shook my head and said, "Duane, I know it sounds crazy, but I don't hate you."

"Yes, you do," he said as I could see his eyes getting watery. "I've never been there for you. I've never done shit for you. You have every right to hate me and I can't be mad at you for that. I was a horrible father. You're my first born and I don't even know you. I don't know anything about you. You are the oldest grandkid in my family and nobody really knows you."

I just looked at him.

"So just say it," he begged. "Just say so we can get it over with. Just say you hate me."

"Duane, I don't hate you. I am not my mother."

He wiped his face.

I continued, "Yes, you haven't been there, but we all know that. That's the past. That's not why I wanted to meet you. I don't care about my mama's feelings. I don't. This is about me, Duane. This is about Zach. I'm a grown man now. I am very capable of making my own decisions. I don't care about the past. I don't know what happened between you and my mom when I was a baby. I don't care. I don't. I don't care that you missed my graduation from high school. I don't care that you missed the most important things in my life. I'm past that. We're past that. I'm looking forward to the future. I want a relationship with my father. I have a father figure in my life. He's been there ever since I could remember, but he isn't you, Duane. I don't look like him. I look like you. Look at me, Duane. I'm a spitting image of you. I want a relationship with you, Duane. I want a relationship with my father. I want to get to know you. I want you to get to know me. This is what I want. The only thing I ask of you is to be honest with me. You tell me right now if this is what you want. Let me know, Duane. If you don't want that, it's cool. It is what it is. I'm not vindictive. I will not throw the past back in your face. I just want a relationship with my father. That's you, Duane. I just put myself out there for you. I just laid it out on the line, Duane. Now you just let me know if you want a relationship with me. ME, Duane. Not Paula, but Zach. ME! I forgive you, Duane. I forgive you. I just wanna know you—my father."

He reached over and pulled me into him. He cried, "You don't know how long I've waited to hear those words. I want a relationship with you too, Zach. I want a relationship with you, too."

As I felt my father's grip on me, I released myself into his arms. Years of anger and frustration released itself from my body. We were getting a new start.

When we broke, I wiped my face; he wiped his face. We stood there and talked. He brought me up to speed about the thing going on his life. He was happy to know that I was off in college at FAMU. That really made him smile. We exchanged numbers and vowed to stay in contact. Before he left, he said, "You know what—what are you doing Sunday?"

"Nothing that I know of," I replied. "Why?"

"I want you to meet someone."

"Who?" I asked.

"Dorian."

"Who's that?"

"That's your brother."

My body froze.

"What's wrong?" he asked.

"I have a brother?" I quizzed.

"Yeah," he smiled. "You have a bother. He's two years younger than you."

"Are you serious?" I asked not knowing how to control my excitement.

"Yeah. He'll be in town on Sunday and we're supposed to get up and play basketball."

"ARE YOU SERIOUS? I LOVE BASKETBALL!"

He chuckled and said, "Yeah and I want you to come if you're not busy. I want you to meet your brother. We can play a game or two, grab something to eat, bond and get to know each other. What do you think about that?"

"We can do that," I smiled as I was overjoyed with excitement "Yeah, we can do that!"

"Ok. We were getting up around 1 or 2, but I'll call you so we can meet up somewhere."

"Ok… ok!" I smiled. "That'll work."

He looked at me, smiled and then said, "I appreciate this."

"I'm happy you came. I really mean that," I smiled.

"But let me get going," he gave me another hug. "I'll call you on Sunday."

And then he left. When I went back into the house, I explained to my mom and grandma what happened. My mom said, "Don't fall for that mess. He ain't coming."

I got upset. She was always so fucking negative. I wanted to give him a chance. He just told me that we were starting over. He told me that he wanted to start over with me. So I was going to hold him to his word. And I held him to his word.

I looked out the plane window and exhaled. I wiped my eyes. I never saw him again.

Never.

It's been exactly 564 Sundays and 4,148 days since the last time I saw my sperm donor.

I'm still waiting on that phone call.

I'm still waiting to play a game of basketball with my brother.

28

Dray

New York, New York

I answered the phone, smiled and said, "I was just thinking about you."

"Oh, really?" said my old high school friend and current business partner, Phoenix Cummings.

"Yeah," I walked into my home office sipping on a bottle of water. "You back in Chicago?"

"Yeah, I'm here. I'm actually surprised you answered the phone. I thought you might be at work or something."

"I am. I'm just working from home."

"Must be nice."

"It really is," I replied sitting at my desk.

I thought about Zach. I needed someone to talk to. I knew Phoenix used to mess around when we were in high school, but I don't know if he still does. I knew I needed to put this out in the open, but I didn't want to embarrass myself.

"You straight?" Phoenix asked.

"Yeah, just thinking."

"About?"

"Something I need to get off my chest."

"What's wrong?"

"Man, Phoenix, I guess I just need to say it."

"Say what?" he asked with suspicion.

"Since we're going to be working really close together on this project, and I don't want any issues, I just need to put it on the table that I'm in a relationship with a dude."

"Ok."

"Ok?"

"Yeah. Ok," he said as if he didn't care.

"Can I ask you a question?"

"Hit me up," Phoenix said.

"Do you still… you know?"

He chuckled, "Dray, we're in our own fraternity. With the position you hold at Rolling Stone and me being in the NBA, I believe that I can trust you. I'm not attracted to women. Never really have been."

"Don't you have a son?"

"Yeah, Giovanni. I love my lil boy, but I only fucked that chick for my rep. One of my hating ass teammates when I was on the Kings told one of the dudes on the team that I was cool with that he thought I was gay. I was young, Dray. I was scared. My career was just starting. I couldn't have that shit on my back. So I hooked up with one of the dancers and we had a lot of sex. And secretly, I've never told anyone this, but I tried to impregnate her."

"Why?" I asked.

"Because after getting to know her I knew she would be a great mother. And I wanted at least one kid and that shit wasn't happening fucking with dudes. So I took advantage of the situation. I make sure my baby moms and my kid are well taken care of. I'm a damn good father!"

"I believe you," I thought about my son.

Phoenix said, "But back to the topic. I'm not attracted to women. I don't fuck women. I only fuck with men. Black men. It's usually other professional athletes, actors, rappers, musicians—people like you, the behind the scenes people. But point being, we all have something to lose, feel me?"

"I feel you," I exhaled. It felt good to get that out in the open.

He said, "So going back to the other night when I called you and you were in Atlanta, were you mad at your dude or something?"

I chuckled and said, "Yeah, man. It's just been a lot going on. It's been so crazy that I really haven't been able to sleep lately."

"Damn, it's that bad?"

"Shit is getting crazy. Since Zach and I have been going through a lot of these tests lately, I can't sleep. I've been focusing my attention solely on my work. Since I can't sleep, I've been in the home office working, grinding it out. Lately, at nights and early morning is when I've been the most creative I've been in a long time. It's like I've found a way to channel the anger into my work."

"Wow, it's that bad?"

"I may be exaggerating a bit, but we've hit a rough patch."

"How long have y'all been together?"

"A couple of months will make eight years," I smiled.

"Wow! That's rare in this lifestyle. I haven't seen much longevity in male-on-male relationships, at least in the black people I know anyway."

"We've been lucky. That's why I want to work it out. I really do love him. We've both made mistakes, Phoenix. We both have. I just want to get through this and move on."

"I feel you."

"Are you seeing someone?"

"Not right now. I'm just doing me," he laughed. "I got a quick question though. How does your bosses handle you working from home?"

"The environment is really laid bad. My immediate supervisor is cool as shit. I go into the corporate office when I want to. I work from home when I want. I'm the same way with the team I'm over. My boss doesn't care where the work gets done, as long as it's done by the deadline. Matter fact, I spoke to my superiors today and informed them about the move to Atlanta."

"What did they say?" Phoenix asked.

"Surprisingly, they were ok with it as long as my team production doesn't drop off. But I have to be in the corporate office every Monday for the mandatory production meeting. I'm so excited right now because I was just officially offered the job at Clark yesterday."

"Damn. You're gonna be flying to New York every Monday, working on the community project for the kids back home in Miami and teach classes at Clark Atlanta?"

"Yep."

"Wow. Speaking of Clark Atlanta, my homeboy, CJ, little brother goes to school there. But I know you're gonna be dog tired, Dray."

"I know, but I'm hustling right now. My philosophy is work hard now, live easier later. Phoenix, when I turn 40, I ain't working for nobody. It's my goal to have my publishing house and TV network then. I'm working now for my future."

"So how exactly is the school thing gonna work in relation to Rolling Stone and what we're planning to do?"

"It actually all works out. On Monday, I fly to New York for Rolling Stone. On Tuesday's and Thursday's, I'll be teaching at Clark Atlanta. Wednesday's will be dedicated to the project back in Miami. I'll have the weekends to spend with my dude."

"Besides the jet lag, seems like you got everything worked out, huh?" he asked.

"Pretty much," I smiled. "But I'm used to the traveling, so it's nothing."

He started rambling about something but I cut him off, as it all hit me like a ton of bricks.

"What?" he said, as I stopped him mid-sentence.

"Something strange happened when we were at the bar on Friday."

"What happened?" Phoenix asked.

"When I came back to the table, I apologized for taking so long to return, but I mentioned that I was talking to Phoenix about this project. Our homeboy said your name in a manner, suggesting he knew you personally or something. And then he asked if I was talking about the NBA player, Phoenix Cummings."

"I have lots of fans," Phoenix laughed.

"I see," I smiled and shook my head. "Anyway, so I asked him did he know you and he said he went to school with you at UCF. He seen you around campus a lot but he really didn't know you like that, or something along those lines."

"Oh," Phoenix's said. "How do you know him?"

"He's really good friends with my dude."

"What's his name?" Phoenix asked.

"Keston."

The phone went silent.

"Hello?" I asked.

"Yeah, what up?" he cleared his throat.

"You know him?"

"The name sounds familiar," he replied as I heard a beep alerting me that I had a call on hold.

"Phoenix."

"What up?"

"Hold on one sec, I gotta take this call."

"Ight," he said as I clicked over.

*****

Dorian

Atlanta, Georgia

Every single time we come here, this place is packed. Sometimes the lines are wrapped around the corner but that's the result of some good southern food.

Once a week, usually on Wednesday's, Brandon and I take turns treating each other to lunch. This week was my treat and the place of choice was Busy Bee's Cafe. It was a little drive from the job, but it was well worth it.

Brandon decided on the beef stew and I picked the fried chicken. As we ate, Brandon talked about his weekend getaway with his dude, Micah. I was listening to him, but my mind was on this Douglas character. I guess Brandon could sense that I wasn't really paying attention, so he said, "DK, what's going on?"

"What are you talking about?"

"Something serious is running in that head of yours. I can see it all over your face," he said as he dipped a piece of his cornbread into some cane syrup and then stuck it into his mouth.

I exhaled and said, "Ok, I met this dude."

"REALLY?" he said shocked.

"Yeah, really," I rolled my eyes.

"What does he look like?"

"I haven't met him in person yet. We were talking on Jack'd about four days ago and then we talked on the phone."

"Jack'd?" Brandon said shocked. "You're getting on social media and apps and shit now?"

I just stared at him. He was trying to be funny.

He continued, "I'm just saying you know how you are. Hell, you still don't have a Facebook. Everyone has a Facebook."

"Social media isn't my thing," I said. "Anyway, we were supposed to meet up for breakfast when he got off work, but I fucked it up."

"How?"

"I tried to stay up so I could meet him but I guess I eventually fell asleep. I set my alarm just in case I fell asleep, but I mistakenly did it for 5:15 p.m. instead of 5:15 a.m."

"Damn, what time does he get off work?"

"Six."

"Oh," he replied.

"When I woke up, it was almost ten."

"Did you hit him up when you got up?"

"Yeah, but he never replied, so I just left it alone."

"He never contacted you back?" Brandon asked, sipping on his drink.

"Naw and I really don't know what to do. I don't wanna seem like a lil bitch, but something about him intrigued me. Most dudes don't impress me."

"Yeah, we know," he laughed out loud.

I just stared at him and then said, "I find a lot of dudes attractive, but just because you're attractive doesn't mean that I wanna get to know or fuck you, nah'mean?"

"I know what you mean."

"Now I really don't know what to do. Do I hit him up again or do I just let it go?"

"Hit him up one more time," he said. "He was probably asleep or something and may have forgotten to hit you back up."

"Maybe," I took a sip of my drink.

"You just gotta try. He might be what you need to get your mind off Morgan."

"Yeah, you gotta point," I stated as I saw a group of Spelman women walk inside proudly displaying their school t-shirts.

"So hit him up."

"I will."

"Nah, I know you. I need you to do it now," he stared at me. "Pick up the phone and call the dude, whatever his name is."

"Douglas," I said as I grabbed my phone.

My heart was beating so hard, I felt like it was going to pop out of my chest. As I dialed his number, I tried to think of something to say. I looked at Brandon and he had put his focus back to eating his food. A few rings later, he said, "Hello?"

"Yo? Doug?"

"Aye, what up Dorian?" he replied.

I smiled. He remembered my name. "How's it going?" I asked as Brandon cut his eyes back to me.

"Everything is everything," Doug stated. "What's up with you?"

"At lunch. Just hitting you up."

He said, "Cool. I meant to hit you back up the other day but I got swamped with work and some other stuff and I never got back around to it. What happened to you though?"

"I tried to wait up and I fell asleep."

He laughed and said, 'That's cute. You tried to wait up for me?"

"Whatever," I smiled. "What are you doing tonight? Let's get up for dinner or something."

"I'm actually out of town on business," he replied.

"Oh," I sighed.

"But I'll be back in Atlanta tomorrow. Maybe we can get up then."

"That's cool," I replied. "You should hit me up when you get back in town."

"I can do that," he said. "But I gotta get off the phone. Someone is on the other line. I'll hit you up tomorrow."

"Ight, take care," I hung up the phone.

Brandon was staring me directly in the eyes. He asked, "So, what's the result?"

I smiled and said, "We're gonna get up tomorrow."

Brandon said, "Now that's what's up and you know I wanna know all the details."

"Whatever, Brandon," I stood up.

We needed to get back over to our job.

29

Zach

New York, New York

As the taxi driver arrived at my condo, I exhaled. My mini-vacation was over. It was back to reality.

I guess Dwight is still pissed at me because I haven't heard from him in four days. I hoped Dray wasn't home because I really didn't feel like dealing with his shit, either. I could still hear that argument when Dray said, *"Fuck you and that bitch ass nigga!"*

I just gotta get through these next couple of weeks and then I will be in Atlanta for good.

I paid and tipped the taxi before grabbing my luggage and heading into my building. I spoke to the doorman, entered the empty elevator and headed up to my floor. I walked in the condo and heard some music playing softly. I exhaled. He was home.

As I walked past his home office, he said, "Hey, babe."

In a cold tone, I said, "Hi," as I continued onto our room. I could hear him walking behind me.

I placed the luggage on the bed and popped it open. As I started to put things away, he stepped into the doorway. I ignored his presence.

I could feel him staring at me before he finally asked, "How was the flight?"

"It was fine," I said as I kept about my duties.

"How's your mom?"

"She's fine," I replied without looking in his direction.

"Did you enjoy yourself?"

"Yes."

"I got the job at Clark," he said.

"Congratulations," I said as I walked into the bathroom to put away my toiletries.

I looked at myself in the mirror and exhaled. Why won't he just leave me the fuck alone? When I came back out, he said, "Are you ok?"

"I'm fine," I said keeping busy.

He stood in the doorway and said, "I have to fly back to Atlanta for a meeting tomorrow. I'll spend the night at our place down there and then fly back up Friday morning."

"Oh, ok," I replied nonchalantly. "Do you, sir."

"WHAT THE FUCK, ZACH?"

I faced him and said, "And who exactly are you raising your voice to?"

"We need to talk!" Dray demanded.

I looked at him for a second before I turned around and continued putting away my clothes.

"So you're just gonna act like I'm not here?" he asked.

I turned to him and said, "Now you want to talk? NOW YOU WANT TO TALK? I've tried talking to you for two days. I tried calling you. I tried texting and you never replied to none of my fucking messages, but now you want to talk?"

"I was with Nolan when you tried to reach me."

"Dray, do I have stupid written across my forehead? Nolan is so convenient for you now, huh? So when we move to Atlanta, is everything going to be about Nolan? Dray, it doesn't take much to send a text to say I'm with Nolan. It's not hard. It's not chemistry. It's not physics. It's not differential equations. It's not trigonometry. It's a fucking text message!"

He calmly said, "Zach, you're really pushing my buttons. You're pushing my last nerve. I'm trying to talk to you and all you are giving is attitude. This attitude of yours needs to go. IT NEEDS TO GO!"

I stared him in the eyes and said, "So, again, everything is on your terms. We move when Dray says move. When Dray says lets have sex, we have sex. When Dray says let's go eat, we go eat. When Dray says call him at this time, you better call him at this time. Nigga, you're controlling and you need to check that shit really quickly!"

He just stared at me.

I continued, "Dray, I'm not going to continue to put up with your bullshit. You keep doing all this traveling to avoid dealing with our issues at home. You ain't slick. You can't run forever. You can't! Did you ever think on why Dwight brought that issue up, about you traveling? DID YOU EVER THINK TO ASK YOURSELF WHY THE FUCK HE BROUGHT THAT UP? You travel to fucking much to be in a relationship—"

"I have to make money," he cut me off. "I'm making moves for our future."

"Money doesn't make me happy, Dray. Money doesn't rule me. I went to school to become a fucking teacher. Obviously, money is nothing to me!"

"I GIVE YOU EVERYTHING, ZACH! I GIVE YOU THE WORLD AND ALL YOU DO IS COMPLAIN! YOU COMPLAIN LIKE A FUCKING BITCH!"

"Dray, you travel to much," I shook my head. "I get lonely, Dray. I do. You're never here. All those nights that you ain't here, I feel like I'm in a relationship with myself. The only thing that keeps us here is sex. We can fuck each other without having to look for random fucks two or three nights a week. So, do we have a title on this because of sex? What gives Dray?"

"You're so over dramatic," he rolled his eyes.

"Am I really? But that still has nothing to do with the fact that you're controlling!"

"No, I am not," he said.

"So when I decide I want to spend some time at school, to do my work, it's a problem. Right? Do you remember that Dray? Do you know why it is a problem? Huh?"

He didn't reply.

"It's a problem because I'm not there at your call. It's a problem because you wanted to have sex that night and I wasn't there. Because you decided to actually go to bed and not do work at three in the morning, it's a problem. So because I decided to stay at school and do my work, you threw an attitude. You threw an attitude because I didn't do what you said to do. You are controlling, Dray. But when you get ready to do something, I just better accept it, because that's just the way it is, right?"

He stared at me with fire in his eyes.

I said, "Talking to my mom made me realize something. You know what—fuck all the other shit, Dray. I'm just gonna put it out there."

"What?" he said with attitude.

"Do you want to really be with me? Do you want to make this move to Atlanta? Dray, I've never forced you to do anything and I will not force you or run game on you or use a guilt trip tactic to make you move with me to Atlanta. If you still want to be in this relationship, going 50/50, and not Dray's way is the only way, then you need to let me know right now."

He stared at me.

"Dray, I love you, but I'm not going to continue to just eat your words and act like that shit doesn't bother me. I'm at a point in my life where I'm over everything. I'm tired. My body is tired. I can't take this anymore. I can't. I'm tired of being stressed. I'm tired of the constant arguments. I'm tired. So you need to let me know what you're going to do. So what is it going to be Dray? What are you doing to do?"

As he slowly began to open his mouth, I cut him off and said, "Regardless of what you may say, and if you say it's over, you know it may hurt for a little bit, but being with my mom made me realize that I am strong, Dray. I am still me. I am still Zachariah. I may have lost myself in the process, but I'm still here. I've never been one to bite my tongue. I started doing that shit when I started dealing with you. You changed me, some for the good and some for the bad. I'm telling you Dray that I'm not going to do that anymore. I'm going to return to being me. So if you leave me today, it'll hurt, but I'll adjust. Just like I told Dwight the other day, the key word here is respect. Just like he needs to respect you, you need to respect him."

"REPSECT?" he yelled. "THAT NIGGA DOESN'T RESPECT ME! FUCK, YOU DON'T RESPECT ME, EITHER!"

I stared at him.

He stared at me.

"Dray, Dwight is my best friend. He has been there for me when nobody else has."

"I bet he has," he cut.

I looked at him. He was fuming. I said, "Dwight has had my back through thick and thin. Dwight isn't perfect. I'm not perfect. Dwight is my friend and I don't know where I'd be right now if it wasn't for Dwight. I said some shit to Dwight on Saturday that was hard. I put my friendship on the line because of you, Dray. YOU! So you need to understand that the both of you are the most important men in my life and I can't have this bickering back and forth. I will not take this drama to Atlanta. I will not. So you need to make a decision.

What is it going to be? Are we going to work this out, or is this it? The ball is in your court. What will it be, Dray?"

I looked at him, waiting for an answer. He mumbled something under his breath that I couldn't make out.

He stared at me as if he wanted me dead. He mumbled something again.

"What was that?" I asked.

"Did you fuck him?"

I looked him directly in the eyes, taken aback by his question.

He stared me in my eyes and in a cold, cutting tone, said, "Zach, did you fuck him? Did you fuck Dwight?"

30

Dwight

I felt a series of soft taps hitting me on my shoulders. I squeezed my eyes tight before opening them. Lexi was standing in front of me smiling. I looked around the room trying to figure out what was her issue.

"Good morning, baby," she said, continuing to smile.

I sat up in bed with a curious look on my face.

"Why are you looking at me like that?" Lexi asked.

"What the fuck is going on? Why are you smiling at me?"

"Boy, stop playing," she playfully hit me on the arm. "I made you breakfast."

"You did what?"

"I made breakfast, silly," she laughed. "Now gone and get up, clean up and come on down for breakfast. The food is almost done."

She smiled at me and walked out of the room. I slapped myself in the face as hard as I could to make sure this wasn't a dream. *This wasn't a dream.*

After I brushed my teeth, washed my face and pissed, I threw on some basketball shorts and walked down stairs. I must say, it smelled damn good.

Above that, as I walked into the living room, I was taken aback at how nice and neat the house looked. She actually cleaned up in here.

She brought the plates to the dining room table and said, "Just go sit down. I'll get the orange juice."

There were no dishes in the sink. I looked around the room. Something wasn't right. She was up to something.

I cautiously sat at the table. She pranced over to me and said, "Here's a drink for my King." She placed a kiss on my cheek.

"Lexi, what's going on?"

"Nothing is going on," she replied as she sat across from me.

I stared down at the food, looking to see if there were any signs of foul play. After she said a quick prayer, she immediately began to eat. I just looked at the food.

"Don't eat it all at once," she replied.

I looked at her.

"Your food is going to get cold, Dwight."

"Did you poison this? Are you trying to kill me?"

She stared at me like I was crazy.

I stared at her. I was dead ass serious.

"Dwight, eat the damn food!" she said with attitude. "Here I am trying to show my husband some love and you're talking about poisoning your food. Dwight, I know I have some problems, but I don't want you dead."

Cautiously, I ate a piece of bacon. She couldn't fuck that up.

She continued to eat and said, "Dwight, I really want to apologize for the way I've been acting the past couple of months."

I ate a spoonful of grits.

She said, "I know I've been out of control and I just want to make this marriage work. I love you." She paused and said, "With the kids gone to my mom's for the next couple of weeks until school starts back up, I'd figure we'd take this time to rekindle our relationship. Maybe you can take a few days off work or something and we can go to St. Thomas or St. Croix and we can have a little vacation. You know we can lay in the sun all day and make love like we used to all night. Doesn't that sound relaxing?"

"I'll look into it," I forced a smile.

The truth was I had no aspirations in making this trip a reality. I have a meeting next week with a divorce attorney. I need to figure out what legal options are available to me.

After listening to her, I realized the food wasn't poisoned and I continued to eat more.

She said, "Since you're off today, I was thinking maybe we can catch a movie. Grab lunch. Do a little shopping. Make love to each other. I really want to spend the day with you. I really miss you, Dwight. I miss us."

I cleared my throat and said, "I've already made plans for the day."

"Well cancel them," she demanded as I could hear that attitude arriving in her voice.

"I'm afraid that isn't possible," I replied.

She exhaled. She was quiet for a few moments, before she refocused and came back in a different direction by saying, "Well, I want to go. Let me tag along. I won't be a bother."

"Naw," I shook my head. "Not today."

She stared at me.

I placed the fork down, took a sip of my orange juice, stood up and then said, "Thanks for breakfast, but I'm stuffed."

"You barely even touched your food!"

"I'm full, Lexi," I replied as I started to walk out of the dining room.

"FUCK YOU, DWIGHT! FUCK YOU!"

I smiled as I made my way back upstairs. Now that's the Lexi I know.

*****

TJ

Today was *the* day. I was so excited once Daddy and Ray left for work. I jumped in the shower and jacked off so I wouldn't cum to fast. Some good head will do a nigga in real quick. I told Elijah to ask the hoe could we fuck, but he was like she was like, "Hell naw, I'll suck y'all up and that's that."

I ain't picky right now. Head is head. I just hope this hoe ain't busted or no shit like that.

I was trying to get Elijah to get her to come over earlier in the week, but this was supposedly the first day that she could come. My dick was getting hard again just thinking about that shit.

I sat in the living room and waited. Elijah said he had to wait until his mama, Ms. Genevieve, was gone before he could come over because she had him doing shit around the house. A few minutes after one, the doorbell started to ring. I jumped up and headed to the front door. I looked out the peephole and saw that it was my buddy.

When I opened the door, he smiled and said, "You ready?"

"I was born ready, nigga," I closed and locked the door. As we walked into the living room, I said, "So where is the hoe?"

"She just text me a few minutes ago. She said she was on the bus," he showed me his phone. "She said she was really close."

Elijah headed into the kitchen and grabbed something to drink. He seemed nervous to me. He was smiling like he usually does, but he seemed a bit *different* today.

When he came back into the living room with a glass of red Kool-Aid that I made last night for dinner, I said, "You straight?"

"Yeah, I'm good."

"Nigga, what's wrong?" I asked.

"Ain't nothing wrong, shawty."

I just stared at him.

"Ok," he sighed. "I ain't trying to get caught."

"You ain't gonna get caught," I replied. "Stop being a bitch. Live a little."

He just stared at me.

"Loosen up fool. Daddy and Ray are at work and will be at work until at least four. We got like three hours. We gonna be straight."

"Ok," he said as his phone started to ring. He looked at it and said, "This shawty calling right now."

I listened as he gave her directions on how to get to the house from the bus stop. When he was off the phone, he looked at me and smiled. I just stared at him. What the hell was he looking and smiling at me for?

His phone started to ring again. He looked at it and said, "Hey, this is Nolan."

"See if that nigga wanna get some, too," I suggested.

When Elijah answered, he put it on speaker and said, "What up Nolan?"

"Nothing. What you up to?" Nolan asked.

"Chillin at TJ's crib."

"That's the new kid, right?" Nolan asked.

"Yeah. He lives a couple houses down from me," Eli said.

"Cool. What y'all boyz getting into today?"

"Bout to get some head," Eli stated.

"FROM WHO?" Nolan asked.

"Samara," Eli answered.

"Oh, I guess," Nolan said.

"You should come through," Eli added.

Nolan laughed and said, "Y'all on that faggot shit. I ain't bout to get my dick sucked with two other niggas. I'll pass."

"Whatever," Elijah replied as he looked at me and shook his head.

Nolan got me fucked up. I ain't on no faggot shit.

"Get at me when y'all done," Nolan said.

"Ight," Eli hung up the phone.

As soon as he hung up, it started to ring again. He looked at the phone, answered and said, "Hello?" He paused and then said, "Ok...yeah that's it... just come up to the front door... it'll be open... yeah... ight." He looked at me and said, "Showtime."

I followed behind him as he went over and unlocked the front door. Moments later, the knob turned and the door opened. She walked inside and said, "Hey."

"What up, shawty?" Elijah replied.

"Sup?" I said.

"He cute," she smiled as she looked at me.

She wasn't that bad herself.

"Samara, this is TJ. Like I said, he'll be going to school with us."

She waved her hands and said, "Look, we gotta hurry up because I gotta get back home before my mama start calling me."

"Shit, let's go then," I replied as I locked the door and then motioned for them to follow behind me to my bedroom.

Once we got inside, she stood at the door and looked around. Elijah looked at me.

"What?" I asked.

"Nothing," he said.

"We need to hurry up," she said again. "Take off y'all clothes." As we started to undress, she said, "Don't get no nut on my clothes either."

My dick was so hard, it hurt. When I was out of all my clothes, I walked over and sat down on the bed. She looked at my dick and smiled.

Elijah's back was to me and he was still coming out of his clothes. When he was undressed, he turned around and I saw him stare at my dick.

I mean he stared just a lil too long. He stopped when she said, "Y'all ready? Who's first?"

"He's first," Elijah said as he continued to stand up.

She walked over to me, got on her knees and started to go to work.

Shit felt really good. This wasn't her first time.

I closed my eyes and started to play with my nipples. Shit was feeling really good. When I opened my eyes, Elijah was standing there rubbing his dick, looking at me. He looked like he was getting turned on and I instantly got turned the fuck off. I could feel my dick getting soft.

I stopped her and said, "I'm straight. You do him now."

She looked at me strangely and said, "You sure?"

"Yeah, I'm straight," I replied as I stood up and started putting back on my clothes.

When I looked back at him, she was sucking him off, but he looked nervous again. It was like he was scared to look at me now.

I shook my head and walked to the door. Before I walked out, I said, "Y'all need to hurry up."

I closed the door and headed downstairs.

31

Dray

Chicago, Illinois
Friday, August 5, 2016

Phoenix was standing outside his front door, waiting for me as I pulled into his driveway. I parked my rental car next to a black Cadillac Escalade, turned off the GPS and smiled. I got out of the car, pointed to the Escalade and said to Phoenix, "Damn, this your ride?"

Phoenix chuckled, "Naw, that's my homeboy ride."

We dapped each other up and exchanged brotherly hugs before we headed inside and I must say it felt like heaven compared to that midday heat.

"So, yeah, this my shit," Phoenix said as he started to show me around his mansion.

I was amazed at how he had put together this huge house.

"Did you decorate this yourself?" I asked.

He laughed and said, "Hell naw." He pointed to a picture and continued, "She had fun doing this. I wanted to hire an interior designer, but she really wanted to do it, so I let it be."

"Who is that?" I stared at the picture.

"My older sister."

"Oh, ok. She's very pretty."

He laughed and shook his head.

"What?"

"You don't even want to know," he sighed as we continued on the tour of his house.

When we finally got to the living room, I said, "You said that was your homeboy's Cadillac out front. Where is he?"

"Oh, he went down to speak to D. Rose."

"Derrick Rose?"

"Yeah," Phoenix said nonchalantly. "He lives a couple houses down."

"Cool."

"I'm still mad he got traded to New York. I didn't sign in Chicago to do this shit by myself. I've got to get the fuck out of here. But that's neither here nor there. Just one more year and I'm out!"

I just stared at him. I wasn't a sports person. I knew about all the sports current events because of Zach.

As we headed back into the family room, Phoenix sighed and said, "I hope you don't get mad."

"Why?"

"Well, just to let you know but my homeboy gets down, too. I know you came to chill. He's been here visiting, so I just laid it on the table so we can really talk and shit. Don't get me wrong, I'm very discreet and very private about my shit."

"So you're saying that he knows about me?"

"Yeah," he said.

I just stared at Phoenix.

Phoenix said, "He can help you, especially giving the shit you're going through. He's been through a lot. He's cool as shit and he has just as much to lose as the two of us, so the secret is safe. I promise you that. You're not mad are you?"

"Naw. I trust you, Phoenix."

He smiled.

"Y'all fucking?" I asked.

He chuckled and said, "He's just my homeboy."

"Yeah, y'all fucking," I said.

"I didn't say that," he smirked.

"Whatever," I laughed. "But seriously why are you living in this big ass house? And it's just you living here?"

"Yeah, it's just me. I don't know why I chose this house. I fell in love with it the moment I saw it. It just fits me."

Phoenix said, "I'll be right back."

I walked around and admired some of the fine art. I didn't get far as I heard voices and then the door closed.

"We're gonna get a game in tomorrow," the unfamiliar, but familiar voice said.

"Where?" Phoenix asked, as they got louder as they approached the living room.

"He said at the Bulls practice facility," the unfamiliar, but familiar voice said.

"Cool."

When Phoenix's friend walked into the living room, he lifted his head and said, "What's up?"

"What's up," I replied.

I couldn't believe *he* was standing here in front of me. I couldn't believe that *he* got down with dudes. *Wow.*

Phoenix said, "Dray, this my homeboy, CJ. CJ, this is Dray, my homeboy I was telling you about earlier."

"Nice to meet you," CJ said as he walked over to me.

"Nice to meet you, too," I replied as we exchanged handshakes.

The first person I thought about was Zach as he taught me everything about this dude.

Clinton Wendell Wright Jr, better known as CJ Wright, is one of Zach's favorite basketball players, especially when he played for Zach's home town team, the Orlando Magic. CJ Wright just finished his ninth season in the NBA. He has appeared in seven NBA All-Star games and is a two-time NBA Champion with the Miami HEAT.

CJ was drafted by the Atlanta Hawks in 2007, but was traded to the Houston Rockets on the same night. In 2009, he was traded from Houston to the Orlando Magic. In January 2011, tragedy hit the Magic. People have speculated, but no one knows what exactly happened that January day, but it's clear that CJ was definitely affected by those events. It's been five and a half years since that happened and CJ has yet to speak publicly about that day. The only thing we've heard from people close to CJ was that it was just *Incidental Contact* gone wrong—whatever that means. Based off what Zach told me, CJ soon left the Magic and signed a three-year contract with the Miami HEAT. When his contract was up and after winning two NBA championships with Miami, CJ surprised everyone and signed with the team who originally drafted him, the Atlanta Hawks.

"CJ, can I ask you an honest question?" I asked, as we all sat down.

"Sure."

"My dude is a huge fan. And as you know the entire sports world was taken aback at your decision to leave the Miami and join the

Hawks. I know I was. I'm from Miami and I loved when you played for my team. You've never answered the question publicly, and I know we've just met and I don't deserve any explanations from you, but why did you leave my hometown team?"

He laughed, turned to Phoenix and said, "Do you want to answer?"

Phoenix looked at me and said, "He left Miami because of his brother."

"I don't follow," I stated.

CJ said, "My little brother moved to Atlanta for college. If you didn't know, I'm originally from Chicago. Anyway, my brother wanted me close by. I know it may sound strange, but we're very close. Short answer, that's why I decided to play with the Hawks. I wanted to be close to my brother. I mean hell, this was going to be my last *big* contract. I've won at every level. I won in high school. I won the NCAA championship in college. I've won NBA championships with Miami. I've been on several All-Star teams and I've won a gold metal on the 2012 Olympic team. Why not be close to family again?"

"Speaking of the Olympics, why are y'all not playing this year?" I asked.

CJ said, "We needed a break. We've been playing basketball non-stop. It's time to let some of these young dudes take over the league."

"I cosign," Phoenix added.

CJ said, "I'm actually having fun again. The Hawks aren't the best but I enjoy playing basketball again and given everything that has happened in my life over the last five years, happiness is what I desire most."

I listened as CJ and Phoenix talked about some basketball related shit. I had other issues on my mind, mainly Zach, even though I came here to relax for a few days and to clear my mind.

When they finished their conversation, Phoenix turned to me and said, "So what's the deal with you and your love back home?"

"Man, it's so much," I replied as I brought them up to speed.

CJ and Phoenix stared at me as I told them my story.

"What happens when they cheat?" I asked. "What do you do? Logic says leave, but your heart says stay. We've been together for eight years. Do you really just wanna give that up? These are the questions I battle internally."

"Did he actually admit to cheating on you?" CJ asked.

I told him my answer.

I couldn't believe I was talking to someone about my private life. I've never done this before, but it felt so free talking to these two dudes.

"Wow," Phoenix said.

"Yeah," I exhaled. "I love this dude so much. He's the love of my life. I'd give anything for him to be happy. I want him to have the world. I just don't know if he feels the same way about me."

CJ added, "Speaking from personal experience, true love will stand the test of time. I know it's very cliché, but I am a witness. In my situation, even though things happened that we had no control over, he was the love of my life. And before everything went to hell, we found our way back to each other. So, I say all of that to say if you love him the way you profess, stick it out. Our situations have some different variables, but if you love him, stay with it. I know it hurts. I know. But if it's supposed to be, it will be."

Phoenix interjected, "I saw this dude in the café when I was in college. It was something about him that touched me. I saw him again at a bus stop a few months later. It was something about him that instantly captivated me. Long story short, we finally met and I was in love. Being with him changed me for the better. I know people say that love at first sight is crazy, but it happened to me. I believe in that shit. I knew from the time I saw him, it was something about him that I had to get to know. When we finally got together, I felt like everything in my life was perfect. I made some mistakes not being transparent with him up front, but he just dropped me. I mean just dropped me. That was one of the hardest things to get through. I spent months hoping and praying that he would call me or pop up at my door. It never happened. And then I realized he really wasn't coming back. So I said fuck love. I tried to do the right thing and life still fucked me over. I claim some responsibility in what happened but damn man. When I got to the NBA, I went back to being the old me. I didn't give a fuck about nobody. I was back to my destructive ways. Then one day in Sacramento, I thought about him. He wouldn't be proud to know I was hoeing around. That day I told myself that I was going to do right because being him with matured me. I couldn't go back to being who I was before we met. You're supposed to learn something from each relationship. CJ knows that I've prayed that dude and I would come back in contact with each other. Nothing happened and I just put it out of my mind.

Dray, it's been years since I've even thought of him. And then God starts working. You have no idea why people enter your life when they do. You think it's for one thing, but it is really for another. That all became clear to me the other day."

Phoenix turned and looked at me.

"What happened the other day?" CJ asked.

"It's not important," Phoenix said. "However, I just know if it's supposed to be, it'll be."

I looked at Phoenix.

I thought about Keston's reply to my mentioning Phoenix's name; I thought about Phoenix's reply to my mentioning Keston's name.

He had to be talking about Keston.

He's saying that God is using me to connect the two of them.

Wow, this is crazy.

Fucking crazy!

32

Tony

Today was extremely long. I just wanted to go home and relax. But since Raidon made plans for the family to go out to dinner tonight, I had to suck it up. Raidon said he was on the way and would be home soon.

I turned on our street and saw TJ's friend, Elijah, dribbling the basketball on the side of the road. He waved. I blew my horn before parking in the garage. As I got out of my SUV, I saw Raidon pulling into the driveway. I smiled.

When he was out of his car, he said, "Baby, I'm starving. I hope TJ is dressed."

"I tried calling him but his phone kept going to voicemail."

"I wonder what he's been up to," Raidon said as we entered the house.

Once inside, I gave Raidon a kiss. TJ was sitting in the living room with the look of death of his face. Surprisingly, he wasn't listening to his music, but just staring at the wall.

"We're about to go get something to eat," I said. "Go get ready."

He just looked at us for a second and then turned and continued to stare at the wall.

"What the fuck is wrong with your face?" I said getting upset. "You're too young to be making a face like that."

He turned to me and said, "This is *my* face and I can make whatever face I want!"

"Who the fuck you talking to?" I asked. "You done lost your God damn mind, boy!"

TJ looked at me and then at Raidon before staring at the wall again.

Not wanting to get into it with him and ready to just forget what happened, I said, "So like I just said, we're about to go get something to eat. Go upstairs and put on some clothes and come on. You've got fifteen minutes."

"I ain't going nowhere with y'all," he spat.

"What do you mean you're not going anywhere with us?" I asked.

"It's either/or but not the both," he said. "Y'all my parents and I love y'all, but I don't want the world to know y'all gay."

"Boy, go put on some damn clothes and bring your ass on!" I replied. "I don't got time for this shit!"

He stood up, looked me in the eyes and said, "Daddy, I ain't stutter. I ain't going nowhere with y'all!"

"WHAT THE FUCK DID YOU JUST SAY TO ME?" I made my way over to him. "WHAT THE FUCK DID YOU JUST SAY?"

In a panic like voice, Raidon said, "TONY, TONY, TONY, TONY, TONY!" as he pulled me away from TJ and into the direction of the door. "Come on let's go. Let's go, Tony."

"THAT BOY DONE LOST HIS FUCKING MIND! HE THINK HE A MAN! I WILL SHOW HIS ASS A MAN!"

"Baby, let's go. Let's go. Calm down," Raidon pleaded. As we walked outside, Raidon yelled, "TJ, WE'LL GET YOU SOMETHING TO EAT!"

"I'm tired of this blatant disrespect, Raidon. I'm tired of this shit!"

"Get in the passenger seat," Raidon said. "I'll drive."

I couldn't believe that he stepped to me like that. He is really trying me. Once we left the house, Raidon said, "Baby, you really need to chill out."

"I NEED TO CHILL OUT? YOU GOT THIS FUCKED UP. I AM THE ADULT!"

"Yes, you are and he is a teenager. Key word—teenager. I don't think he has a problem with us per say, but he's troubled. TJ loves us. I believe that in all my heart. I believe it when he says it. But you have to keep in mind that he's a teenager. Tony, TJ is your child. Like I've said plenty of times before, he acts just like you. He has that hot temper just like you. He acts first and then thinks second, just like you. Y'all are just alike, Tony. He's his father's son."

"I am still the adult in that house," I said.

"True but think about where this boy is coming from. Our

situation is not orthodox. We've never had a conversation with him in regards to how HE felt about our situation. Not once. TJ really doesn't bring people home. Do you think it's because he doesn't have friends? It is because he's scared? It's like we're a big secret. Teenagers already really don't wanna be seen in public with their parents and I don't know if you've forgotten but WE ARE GAY! Put yourself in his shoes for a second and honestly think about how you would feel."

"It still doesn't give him a right to talk to me anyway he pleases. He needs to learn some respect."

"And I agree and you can check him on that. But let's not forget where this anger is stemming from. TJ is a good kid. He makes good grades. He doesn't get into any trouble. He loves you, Tony. He loves me. But speaking truthfully, I don't think that boy is gay. I don't get that vibe from him. So this has to be hard for him to deal with. You've got to learn how to talk to that boy without raising your voice and using aggression."

I exhaled then said, "Well this is how my daddy raised me. This is what I know."

"But does that make it right? There is more than one way to parenting."

I just stared out of the window.

"I want to talk to him about this to see how he feels," he said.

"I can talk to him," I said.

"No, I'll talk to him. I'm the leveled headed one. I've been dealing with kids all my adult life. Besides, I think he'll be more honest with me than you about whatever is bothering him."

I turned to Raidon and said, "Fuck you."

He smiled and said, "I can't wait."

*****

Zach

Atlanta, Georgia

Dwight escorted me on a shopping trip today to decorate the home Dray and I purchased seven months ago. Being that I'll be in Atlanta for good in a few days, I wanted to put the finishing touches on the house so it'll finally have that warm, inviting, "homey" feeling.

It was great to spend the entire day with Dwight, especially after everything that has happened over the past few weeks.

As I was searching for something to eat online, I could hear our conversation from earlier:

Dwight drove the car and said, "That stuff you said to me last week really pissed me off. I mean really pissed me off. Maybe I needed to hear some of it, but none of that matters because I love you, man. I mean that shit, Zach. I love you." He glanced at me for a second, turned his attention back to the road and continued, "We've been through too much shit for it to end like this. I'll never let anyone or anything come in between our relationship for as long as I live. Do you understand what I'm saying to you?"

I nodded my head.

"Zach, you mean too much to me for some bullshit to fuck it up. I mean that. You hear me shawty. I mean that shit. You mean too much to me. I love you, Zach."

"I love you, too, Dwight."

I came back into reality and submitted my online pizza order. I had about a forty-minute wait. I closed the laptop and exhaled. I took a moment and thought about everything that's happening in my life. As successful as my professional life is, I feel like my personal life is on a downward spiral. The more successful I become, the worse my personal life gets.

I closed my eyes. An image of Dray appeared. Where did we go so wrong? Is this really my fault?

I started to cry at our situation. What would even make him think I cheated on him?

I felt my phone vibrating. I looked at the name. It was Dray. I wiped my tears, cleared my throat and tried to answer as cheerfully as I could.

"How are you doing?" he asked.

"I'm ok," I replied.

"I was just calling to see how everything is going."

"It's ok. I just ordered some pizza. How is Chicago?"

"It's been pretty amazing so far. I met one of your favorite NBA players today."

"Who?"

"CJ Wright."

"Seriously?" I asked.

"Yeah, seriously," he chuckled. "I met him at Phoenix's place. They're very good friends. I found out they have the same agent and that's how they became so close. Besides that, you'd love him. He's so sweet, a really cool person. He's down to earth."

"I'm jealous."

"You should be," he laughed. "But CJ's mom is cooking dinner for us, so we're about to go over there. I'll call you later, ight?"

"Ok," I exhaled. "I'll wait up."

"I miss you and I love you."

"I miss you and I love you, too, Dray," I hung up the phone.

33

Zach

I felt a tapping on my arms. I heard, "Wake up, child. Wake up." When I turned over, my eyes got wide and I instantly smiled. She smiled, too. She looked so young and elegant.

"What are you doing here?" I asked.

"You want me to leave, Zachie?" she asked.

"No ma'am," I sat up in the bed.

"I didn't think so," my grandmother stated as she walked over and pulled out a chair. She sat down and started to look around the room. "I like the new place. You've got good taste."

"Grandma?"

"Yes," she turned and looked at me. She had on a white summer dress.

"How did you know where I was at?"

"Zachie, I know everything. I know I've been away for a long time but I still keep up. I know what's going on."

"What are you talking about?" I asked.

"Don't play stupid. You know exactly what I'm talking about."

I just looked at her.

"You know those looks didn't work when you were growing up and it won't work now."

"Grandma," I sighed.

"Now, I don't have much time," she said. "I'm having breakfast with my mother later but I'd figure I'd stop in for a few minutes while I was free. Again, you know exactly why I'm here."

I just stared at her.

She said, "Well, since you want to play dumb, I'll tell you. He knows, Zachie. He knows everything. Tell that boy the truth."

"That's impossible," I replied. "There's no way he could possibly know."

"He knows!" she said with authority in her voice. "You don't have to take my advice. It is what it is. You mortals don't listen. I'm used to it. That's why I just stay far away and mind my own business." She stood up.

"Grandma, the only people who know what happened would be Dwight and me. I know I haven't told anyone and Dwight hasn't told anyone, either. Dray couldn't possibly know."

"You are incorrect," she said. "Three people know. You, Dwight and Drayton."

"That's impossible. I know Dwight didn't tell him."

"I know he didn't. He still knows." She exhaled and said, "Can't say I didn't warn you. Anyway, enough of that mess. Another thing before I go."

"Yes?"

"Someone is coming to visit," she said.

"Who?"

"You know you ask a lot of questions," she said. "This is your life and you have to live it, Dr. Finley. You'll find out when you need to. But the way I see things right now, trouble is looming."

"Is this 'guest' bringing the trouble?"

"Maybe… maybe not," she said as she started to walk towards the bedroom door. "Maybe the trouble is you! Let that marinate for a moment. Just don't forget your faith, Zachariah. Don't forget the things you were raised with. Don't forget your values. I must run now. I don't wanna be late."

"You can't stay a little longer? I have some questions for you."

"No. I've said everything that needed to be said right now," she turned the doorknob. "Oh, yeah, before I forget."

"Yes ma'am?"

"Tell your mother to answer the phone! That phone call that she keeps ignoring is important to you."

"What phone call? Who is it?"

She smiled and then she was gone.

"GRANDMA!" I yelled. "GRANDMA, COME BACK!"

I jumped up from the bed and turned on the lamp light.

"I've got to get used to this new house," I said as reality hit that we were in Atlanta for good now.

I turned my head and Dray wasn't in bed. I exhaled. I know I'm not going crazy. I know we're both in Atlanta. He's not in New York. I know he was here when I went to bed last night. I looked at the alarm clock. It was a little after three am on an early Thursday morning.

Maybe he went to do some work or something. I thought about the words my grandmother told me. I knew I needed to tell him. This shit has been eating at my conscience for years and it needs to be put on the table. I exhaled and got out of bed.

Dressed only in my turquoise boxer briefs, I stepped into my slides and headed out of the room. I walked down the hall to the room Dray designated as his home office. My office was next to his. I opened the door but no one was there besides some papers on his desk.

"Where the hell is he?" I asked myself as I closed the door and checked the other rooms. Realizing that he wasn't upstairs, I headed downstairs.

It was pitch black. I turned on the hall light. *I've got to get used to this house.*

As I approached the living room, I heard the garage door opening. I looked at the wall clock. It read 3:16 a.m. I sat down on the couch. I heard the side door opening. Dray was laughing as he entered the house. *Where the fuck is he coming from this time of morning. And better yet, who the fuck is he talking to?*

His voice got louder as he arrived in the living room. He looked at me and then smiled as he started to laugh again. I tried not to show my anger.

"Man, get some rest and I'll call you back later," Dray said. He laughed again. "Yeah…do that…ight… yep because you got a long day tomorrow and your day starts before mine." He chuckled. "Ight… yep. Later." He hung up the phone.

I stared at him.

"What are you doing up?" Dray asked.

"Where the hell are you coming from? It's three in the morning!"

"Calm down, boy," he smiled. "I went out for a drive. I couldn't sleep. I got up and started doing some work, got tired of that and just went for a drive."

"Who the hell are you talking to this time of morning?"

"Damn, it was just Phoenix," he said.

"Phoenix? Really?"

"Umm, yeah," he looked at me like I was stupid.

I stared at him, shook my head and then jumped up from the couch.

I looked at him again, shook my head as I turned around and started to head back to the bed.

"What—you mad now?" he asked as I climbed the stairs.

I never replied.

34

Raidon Harris

Atlanta, Georgia
Thursday, August 11, 2016

It was a little after seven when I walked into the kitchen. Tony had just taken his pills for the morning. He smiled when he saw me.

"You're leaving early," I said.

"Yeah, I've got a lot to do today," Tony replied. "I need to get in earlier and get started before my phone goes crazy."

"I spoke to Zach yesterday," I stated.

"What for?" he asked.

"This thing with TJ. I've thought about it and figured it would be good to use Zach since he has the Ph.D. in Counseling Psychology. I want him to pick TJ's head before I talk to him."

"It's been a week, Raidon. You should have just let me handle it my way."

"I had to wait until Zach was in town for good. TJ won't even know he's being interviewed."

"This shit better work."

"It will," I replied. "But I don't wanna hold you up. Did you eat breakfast?"

"I'll pick something up on the way. It's some fast food by the job." He kissed me and said, "I love you and I'll call you later."

"I love you, too," I replied as he headed out of the house.

I looked at the time and marched upstairs. When I got to TJ's room, I knocked on the door and waited. He didn't reply.

"TJ," I said as I knocked again.

No reply. I turned the knob and entered. His head was under the covers. His ass heard me knocking the first time.

"TJ," I said walking over to him and pulling down the covers. "Get up!"

"Whhhyyyyyyy?" he moaned.

"Get up and get dressed."

"But whyyyyyyyyyy?" he pouted.

"Because you're coming with me today."

"Wherrrreeeeeeee?" he moaned.

"I'm not going to repeat myself," I stated. "Get up, shower and get dressed. You've got thirty minutes to get ready and meet me downstairs. Don't try me. The time starts now!"

I walked out of the room and closed the door.

*****

Dwight

I felt hands on my chest. I felt hands on my stomach. I felt a kiss on my neck. Then there was a kiss on my chest. I felt those same hands touching my dick. I opened my eyes and Lexi was getting ready to kiss my stomach.

"WHAT THE HELL ARE YOU DOING?" I yelled as I pushed her off me.

"I'm trying to get my husband in the mood," she said. "You had a long night at work and I wanted to relax you a little."

"Lexi, sleep is relaxing," I replied. "And I was doing that until you woke me up."

"You can just lay there and let me ride it," she said seductively as she started to play with my dick.

"GET THE FUCK OFF ME!" I yelled.

She looked at me like I was crazy.

I just got home from work an hour ago and here she goes fucking up my sleep. We are not cool anymore. She must not realize that this shit is over.

"Are you pregnant or something?" I asked.

"What?" she said with attitude.

"Are you pregnant and trying to fuck me so you can frame the baby as mine?"

"Fuck you, Dwight!" she yelled as she jumped out of the bed. "YOU MAKE ME SICK!"

"I guess that makes two of us," I replied as I jerked the cover and turned on my side so I could get back to sleep.

35

Zach

With my mind coupled with my grandma's visit and Dray's late night arrival back into the house, I didn't get much sleep. He never returned to the room.

I had to put all that shit out of my head. Today was my first day on the new job.

I looked at myself in the mirror one last time. I checked my tie then grabbed my bag, cell phone and wallet and headed out of the room.

When I got downstairs, I stopped and looked at Dray. He was asleep on the couch with the laptop on his lap. I shook my head and walked past him.

After I grabbed a bottle of water from the fridge, I headed for the side door to take me to the garage. Right before I stepped out, Dray said, "I love you."

I stood there for a moment and then said, "Whatever." I closed the door and walked to my car.

Before I got on the interstate, I stopped by McDonald's and picked up a sausage biscuit. As I drove south headed for downtown Atlanta, I listened to my gospel mix. While listening, I could hear my grandmother's words. "He knows," she said. "He knows."

I exhaled.

My conscience is mind-fucking me because it ain't no way in hell he could possibly know I had sex with Dwight.

I could see that scene from a few weeks ago in New York playing in my head:

"REPSECT?" I heard Dray yell. "THAT NIGGA DOESN'T

RESPECT ME! FUCK, YOU DON'T RESPECT ME, EITHER!"

"Dray, Dwight is my best friend. He has been there for me when nobody else has."

"I bet he has," he cut, staring me in the eyes. "Did you fuck him? Did you fuck Dwight?"

I stared at him. Did he really just ask me did I fuck Dwight?

My heart was beating a mile a minute. Where the hell did that come from? This isn't gonna end well.

Before I could even speak, he shook his head and said, "You know what, I'm tripping. I'm tripping. You wouldn't cheat on me. I know you wouldn't. I'm tripping. Just forget I even brought that stupid shit up."

"Dray," I said.

"Zach, I don't wanna hear it," he walked out of the room. "I don't wanna hear it."

I stood there not knowing how to react. I just dodged a major bullet.

A few moments later, he returned and said, "Zach, I love you. I heard everything you just said today. I didn't know you viewed me as controlling. I didn't know you felt that way. I love you and we're going to make this work. I'm going to work on changing some of those things. I don't ever want you to think that I'm controlling or I'm controlling your life. I love you and I would never intentionally do that. Do you love me?"

"Yes, I love you," I replied.

He smiled then said, "I apologize for not returning your calls and acting like a total bitch. You forgive me?"

"Yeah," I smiled.

"Good because I wanna hear all about your trip with your mom."

I exhaled. I should have told him then. That was the perfect opportunity.

I've got to tell him the truth.

Problem is that shit is easier said than done.

*****

Dorian

There was a knock on my office door. I said, "Come in!"

Brandon walked in and said, "You've really gotta get a bigger office. This shit is small."

"Who you telling," I replied. "But at least I'm not at a cubicle like how we used to be."

"That is true," he smiled. "One of these days you'll get on my level and get a bigger office like me."

"Whatever," I yawned.

"You look tired, DK. The day just started."

"Shit, I'm tired," I replied.

"You didn't get any sleep last night?"

"I did at first and then Doug called because he wanted to come by on his lunch break."

"What time was the break?"

"I don't remember. 1:30 or 2. He left around 2:45, 2:50."

"This morning?" Brandon asked.

"Yeah," I yawned. "We talked on the phone until he got back to work. Then we were texting and stuff until around four this morning when I eventually fell back to sleep. Then I had to get up two hours later to come here. So yeah I feel like a zombie right now."

"Have y'all had sex yet?" Brandon whispered.

"Naw, not yet," I replied. "But it's getting close. I can tell. I really like him, so it is what it is."

"I wanna meet this Doug character," he said.

I laughed and said, "We'll see about that."

He chuckled and said, "Let's do lunch in a few hours. My treat."

"Ight, Brandon," I replied as he walked out of my office.

36

TJ

As soon as we got out of Ray's car, I grabbed my laptop bag that housed my computer and iPod and said, "Why did you bring me here?"

"To get you out of the house," he replied as we started walking towards some building.

I saw two females walking and talking. As we walked, I followed them with my head. *Damn, they are fine as fuck.*

When I turned back around, Raidon was saying, "I think being in that house is messing with your brain cells, especially after that incident last week with your father."

"I'll be out the house soon. School is about to start."

"True enough," Ray said. "But I just wanted to tag you along with me today."

A few moments later, we walked inside an office.

"Good morning," Ray said to a lady.

"Good morning, Dr. Harris," the woman said as she looked at me. "And who is this you've brought along?"

"Oh, this is my son, TJ," Ray said looking at me.

"I didn't know you had kids, Dr. Harris," the woman said.

Ray smiled and said, "Well now you do."

She looked at me, smiled and said, "He's cute."

I smiled back.

"Please stop, Cynthia," Ray replied, as he grabbed the mail that she handed him. "That's only gonna go to his head."

She chuckled and then the phone started to ring. I followed behind him as he inserted his key and we entered his office.

Ray placed his things down and said, "Make yourself at home."

"This is your office, Ray?"

"Yep. This is where I do most of my work."

"I like this. It's big."

He smiled and sat down at his desk.

"Who was that out front?" I asked.

"Cynthia. She's the office secretary."

I sat down at the small circular table on the other side of the room and asked, "Are you gonna take me home on your lunch break?"

"Nope. You're here all day with me."

I exhaled.

"But while you're here, you're free to explore the campus," he opened the blinds.

There was a knock on the door.

"It's open," Ray said.

"Yo, good morning, Dr. Harris!" some dude burst into the office.

"Good morning, Renzo," Ray said.

The Renzo dude looked at me and said, "Sup?"

I lifted my head before turning on my Mac.

"I need you to sign these papers," Renzo hurried over to Ray's desk.

I tuned them out and logged on the internet. I was brought back in the conversation when I glanced up and saw Ray staring at me with a grin on his face.

Ray looked at Renzo and said, "I've got a quick question for you."

"What's up?"

"Are you looking for any extra volunteer hours, because if you are, I have the perfect job for you."

"Actually I do need a few more for graduation," Renzo replied.

"Great!" Ray smiled and looked at me.

"What?" I said.

Ray handed him some papers and said, "We'll talk about it later."

"Ight. Good looking out. Just get at me," Renzo said as he left the office.

I rolled my eyes and resumed on my laptop.

*****

Zach

I arrived on campus and hurried off to Raidon's office. I know he wanted me to talk to TJ today, but I was really looking forward to stepping into my new office. As soon as I approached the dean's office, the door opened and Renzo walked out.

"Hey, Dr. Finley! What's up?" he asked as he gripped me up.

I smiled and said, "Good morning, Renzo. How are you?"

"I'm doing great!" he replied. "I had a great night last night."

"Umm, TMI!" I laughed.

"Just keeping it real, Doc!" he smiled. "But are you here for good now?"

"Yes. I'm moving into my office today."

"That's what's up. I got class in a few minutes, but if you need me to help or anything, I can stop by when class is over."

"I appreciate it but I think I'll be ok for now."

"Ight. I don't wanna be late, so I'll holla at you. Happy to have you here at Clark Atlanta."

"I'm happy to be here, Renzo."

He smiled and rushed off.

As I entered the office, I smiled and said, "Good morning, Mrs. Yarbrough."

"Good morning, Dr. Finley," she smiled back. "It's great to have you on board. And for the last time please call me Cynthia. I prefer Cynthia."

"Has Dr. Harris made it in yet?" I asked.

"Yes, he's in his office. I know he's expecting you. You can go on back."

I arrived at Raidon's door and knocked.

"COME IN!" he yelled.

As soon as I walked in the room and closed the door, I saw TJ, on my right, sitting at a small circular table. He looked up and his eyes got wide.

"UNCLE ZACH!" TJ yelled as he jumped up and rushed to me. "UNCLE ZACH!"

I looked at Raidon as he smiled.

"What's up, TJ," I smiled as I hugged him.

"Uncle Zach, what are you doing here?" he asked with

excitement.

"Today is my first official day on the job."

"But don't you live in New York?" he asked confused.

"I just moved to Atlanta a few days ago."

"FA REAL?"

"Yeah, man!"

"Awe man, this is great!" he said excited. "Ray, Uncle Zach is here in Atlanta, too!"

"I know," Raidon smiled as he looked at me. "Did you get all that parking stuff situated?"

"Yeah, I did it yesterday."

"Ok, cool," he said, as he walked towards the door. "Let me get your key."

I turned and looked at TJ.

"You just made my day, Uncle Zach. Can I go with you today?" he asked.

"I don't care, just make sure you ask Raidon. Besides, what are you doing here anyway?" I asked as if I didn't know what was going on.

"I don't know," he shrugged his shoulders. "Ray woke me up and told me I was coming with him today. I really didn't have a say in the matter."

Raidon walked in the room and handed me the key. "You are on the second floor, first door on the left."

"Thanks, Raidon."

"No problem," he looked at me. "Thank you for everything."

"It's nothing," I smiled as I looked at TJ.

"Yo, Ray, can I chill with Uncle Zach today?" TJ asked.

"Yeah," I added playing along. "I've got to move my stuff into the office and I could use TJ's help."

"That's fine," Raidon said. "Don't cause any trouble, TJ."

"I WON'T!" he said excited as started to turn off his computer.

I turned and smiled at Raidon. He exhaled as he sat down at his desk.

TJ had no idea he was just set up. Hopefully, I'll be able to get to some of the issues that are plaguing him.

Hopefully.

37

Dray

The phone was ringing. I sighed as I reached over and grabbed it. I was finally getting some sleep and the phone is ringing. Go figure. I was taken aback by the Tallahassee area code flashing on the screen. *Who the hell is calling me from Tallahassee?*

I cleared my throat and answered. Some woman said, "Mr. Wescott?"

"Speaking."

"Hold one moment. Governor Reed would like to speak to you."

And then there was music. I smiled. *J. Nehemiah Reed, II.*

Mr. Reed is a close friend of mine and is currently the sitting governor of Florida. Nehemiah is not only the first African-American governor of Florida, but the youngest elected governor in state history.

I met Nehemiah – whose first name is actually Justin, but since he is the second, he just goes by Nehemiah – when I was at FAMU. He was a few years older than me but I worked directly under him my freshman year when he was the student government president. I worked on his reelection campaign when he was in graduate school. We've been good friends ever since.

He graduated from FAMU and headed off to Harvard Law School. When he returned to Florida, he immediately began working as a community organizer in Miami, while teaching as an adjunct professor at Florida International University, also located in Miami. That launched his quick rise in Florida politics. He ran for the Florida state senate and won. He served in the Florida senate for a few years before being tapped to run as governor. No one thought he had a chance, but here he is today, the current sitting governor of Florida.

"DRAY!" Nehemiah said, voice full of excitement.

"Mr. Governor," I smiled. "What a pleasure."

"Please, Dray, I told you to fuck all that governor shit. I'm still Nehemiah, fool!"

I laughed and said, "What's up, man. I haven't heard from you in a minute."

"I've been pretty busy, as you can imagine."

"God be with you. I know that is a tough job."

"That it is," he replied. "But listen. I can't talk long, but I just wanted to warn you."

"What's up?" I asked.

"I trust you, Dray. You know some of my darkest secrets, so I know you can keep this one to the vest."

"You're scaring me," I replied. "What's going on Nehemiah?"

"I'm in the top two of potential candidates to be Senator Fitzgerald's vice president."

"GET THE FUCK OUT OF HERE!" I yelled as I stood up in excitement. "VICE PRESIDENT OF THE UNITED STATES OF AMERICA?"

"Yeah," he replied.

"The senator's campaign team has kept this very private so the media has no idea that I'm in the running. They're doing an extensive search on me and checking into a lot of my relationships. I say that to say they might contact you, since you are one of my good friends. Tell Zach, too. How is he, by-the-way?"

"He's fine," I replied.

"Cool. Whatever you do Dray, do *not* let them know my secret."

"I'll never repeat that to anyone, Nehemiah. Never."

He exhaled and said, "Thanks, buddy. I've got to get going, but I'll be in touch. We've got to do dinner before I'm selected and my schedule gets crazy."

"You're pretty confident that Senator Fitzgerald will select you as her running mate, huh?"

"I know she will," he replied. "I'll be in touch."

"Ight, Nehemiah. Good luck."

I hung up the phone. My nigga is in the running to become the next Vice President of the United States.

Wow. This is amazing. J. Nehemiah Reed, II could become the next Vice President of the United States. Man, if he gets it, I've got to put Nehemiah on the cover of Rolling Stone.

This shit has to be a dream. It has to be.

After I did my morning duties, I headed into the kitchen to make breakfast. I was stopped when I heard the doorbell.

"Who the hell is at my door?" I asked myself.

As I got closer to the door, it rang again. I looked out the peephole.

What the fuck was he doing here?

I opened the door and looked at him.

"Can we talk?" he asked.

I just stared at him.

"Can I come inside or are you gonna keep me standing out here?" he asked.

"Zach isn't here," I replied.

"I know," Dwight said. "I came to talk to you."

I stared at him.

"So, can I come inside?"

*****

Dwight

Dray moved out of the way and said, "Sure." I walked inside. He closed the door and said, "You were the last person I expected to see standing here."

"I know," I walked over to the living room.

"Can I offer you something to drink? I was just about to make something to eat. You are welcome to something."

I looked at him. He knows damn well he doesn't want me eating his fucking food.

"Naw, I'm not hungry," I replied forcing a smile. "I actually didn't come to stay. I just needed to get something off my chest."

"Is there something I can help you with?" he asked.

"I figured I'd be the bigger man."

He just looked at me.

"Listen," I added. "I don't know if Zach told you, but we got into a huge disagreement after that night at the bar. He really went off on me in your defense. I didn't like it, but I eventually respected it. He made some very important points and I now understand where he was coming from. So I just want to bury the hatchet between the two of us. We both love Zach in our own ways and we don't need to be fighting like this. It isn't healthy for any of our relationships with Zach. We are professional men and I think we need to draw some common ground."

He just looked at me. I wish I knew what he was thinking.

"You know Dray," I continued. "If I can be honest."

"By all means, please do," he said.

"I remember the first time I met you. I was taken aback at the way you approached me. You were very direct and stern. None of Zach's boy toys had ever stepped to me like that. I instantly had a newfound respect for you. It was that night that you quickly grew on me and that is saying a lot because I've never liked or respected any of Zach's boy toys. You were different. Even to this day, you are different and as crazy as it is, I respect that. I knew that Zach would be in good hands as long as you were in the picture. I remember how torn Zach was because you wanted him to go to New York and he didn't want to go. I remember encouraging Zach to go to New York and try it out. I did that for a number of reasons, but mainly because

I felt that y'all deserved each other. I know how much my word means to Zach and I didn't want him to regret not seeing where that thing with you could go."

His face was unreadable as he stared me directly in my eyes.

"Again, like I said, I didn't come to stay. I just hoped that we could move past whatever it was that was causing the friction between us. I just wanted to be the bigger man."

"Dwight, you more than anyone know my qualms," Dray said with his eyes still planted on mine. "But that's water under the bridge."

What exactly was that supposed to mean? Was he trying to say that he knew about my encounter with Zach? Naw, that is impossible. I know Zach didn't tell anyone, much less Dray.

Dray continued, "Y'all have been friends longer than he and I have been together. We are both grown men. You have a family. I have a son and I have Zach. I just hope you, as a man, can respect me. As a man, I've only given you the utmost respect. Respect—that's the key word. Dwight, I don't want to do anything to jeopardize what I have with Zach. I think you know how much I love him and he loves me. If we're all gonna be here in Atlanta, the least we can do is respect each other as men."

"I agree," I said as I started to make my way back to the front door. He followed behind me. "I appreciate you taking the time to hear me out."

"I appreciate you coming over to talk to me."

"Just one last thing," I said looking at him.

"What's up?"

"Don't tell Zach that I came by. I just want this to be between you and I."

"Here's that respect word again," Dray said. "Listen Dwight, I respect you and all but I don't like keeping secrets from my dude. How about this—I'll just let him know that we buried the hatchet."

I stared at him.

"Is there something else you would like to tell me?" Dray asked.

"Naw, that's it," I opened the door. "I'll see you around."

38

Zach

TJ helped me move into my new office. Although the summer session was ending, I couldn't wait for the fall semester to start. Once we were settled, I grabbed him a soda from the vending machine. He opened the soda, took a sip and said, "Thank God for the A.C. I feel like Kunta Kinte."

"Boy, you a mess," I laughed. "Besides, what do you know about Roots and Kunta Kinte?"

"Ray made me watch that long behind movie," he shook his head. "He said I needed to know my history."

"You do need to know your history," I laughed. "So how has the move been?"

"It's been cool, I guess."

"What do you mean, you guess?" I asked.

He took a sip of his drink. "Daddy and Ray be doing too much."

"What do you mean?" I started to unpack one of my boxes.

"I mean… well… it's like this… I understand that daddy is gay and ain't nothing wrong with that Uncle Zach. Do I treat you differently?"

"What do you mean?" I stopped and looked at him.

"I know you're gay, but has that messed with our relationship?"

"Not that I know of," I replied.

"Exactly. I don't care that Daddy and Ray are gay. That doesn't bother me. I'm happy that they're happy."

"So what's the issue?" I asked.

"The issue is all the gay stuff."

"What gay stuff?"

"They be making me go places with them and stuff, like it's cool to be gay or something. That shit ain't cool."

I stared at him.

"Sorry, Uncle Zach," he said ruefully. "But it's like they don't care about my feelings. They can be all lovey-dovey at home. I don't care. But when we're in public, I just don't want to be around them together. Can you understand what I'm saying?"

"You're afraid of what someone will think? Are you afraid that you may see one of your classmates out in public and they'll know that your parents are gay? Is that what bothers you the most?"

"Basically. It's like they don't understand. Well, I think Ray understands, but it's daddy. He's the problem, forcing me to go places with them and stuff and then he gets mad when I don't wanna go. He's always yelling and cursing. I don't wanna hear that mess. All he gotta do is talk to me. Ray talks to me like I'm a person. He doesn't talk down to me. He doesn't yell at me. He just talks to me. Daddy doesn't do that. He's just angry all the time and ready to give me a whooping. I'm so used to them now that it doesn't even bother me anymore. My body is numb to it. I wish daddy were more like Ray. I know when Ray is joking and when he is serious. Like this morning—"

"What happened this morning?" I asked.

"Ray woke me up and told me to get dressed. Even though I pouted and didn't want to get out of the bed, I could tell in Raidon's voice that he meant business. So I got up and got dressed. If that was daddy, he would've been yelling and cursing and I don't wanna hear that. He be pissing me off. Sometimes I just wanna punch him in the face and I was about to do it the other day. What did I do to him? I ain't never done nothing to him for him to be talking to me like that. I just don't understand daddy sometimes. But Uncle Zach, all that gay stuff, didn't they think about how this was going to affect me before I was born? They don't ever think about me. The only nice thing daddy has done for me since we've been here in Atlanta was give me money to go buy some school clothes, but other than that he's been mean and everything is gay, gay, gay. Then one time Uncle Morgan came over for dinner and all they talked about was gay stuff. I'm like dang—"

"You do know, TJ," I cut him off, "just because your dads are gay doesn't mean that you are gay."

"I...I...I...I ain't worried about that," he stuttered. "I ain't gay, no disrespect."

"None taken. I'm happy that you didn't punch your father. TJ, that could have turned out very badly. It sounds as if the both of you have some anger issues. Is your father's tone of voice the only reason why you're upset?"

He just looked at me.

"You can talk to me TJ. What's going on?"

Gravely, he said, "I wish my mom was here. I wish I knew my mother. Why does all the crazy stuff have to happen to me? My mom died of AIDS and my daddy is gay. Do you understand how messed up that is? I listen to all my friends talk about their moms and it makes me mad because I don't have a mother to go home to. Sometimes I just want to cry. I don't know what having a mother feels like. Why did God pick on me?"

"You know something TJ, my grandmother used to tell me that God works in mysterious ways. Truth is TJ, I don't know why God took your mother away from you. I don't know why your parents are gay. Hell, I don't know why I am gay. Point is, this is the reality that we live in. This is it, TJ. We never know why certain things are put into our lives. Even through all your issues, you are still blessed. Even though Tony pisses you off at times, you are still blessed. As crazy as it is, even when you become an adult, your parents will always seem like they are doing something to piss you off. That's just how parents are. Trust me… I know," I smiled.

He smiled.

"TJ, I love you and I want you to be the best person you can be. I want to challenge you to start looking outside yourself. Life isn't about you. Life shouldn't be about what they can do for me. Life should be about what you can do to help someone else. You may not know any better because this life is all you know, but your parents give you a life that many kids only wish for. You don't understand how blessed you are. You have a life of privilege that most kids can't have. I'm not saying that money is everything, but you have two parents that love you unconditionally, where some kids only have one, if they even have that. Some kids live in foster homes; other kids are homeless. Some kids only eat one meal a day and that is lunch at school; other kids live in houses where there is no lights and hot water. Your issues are nothing compared to some of the things other kids deal with. Having gay parents is not the end of the world. Just think about it this way, if your friends can't accept the fact that you have gay parents, are they really your friends to begin with? Tony loves you, TJ. I remember when you were born. I remember the sacrifices he made so you could have a good life. Nobody is perfect, but your father loves you. He really does."

We changed the subject and started talking about sports and then we started to talk about girls.

I knew this boy wasn't gay. I have a pretty good gaydar. TJ isn't gay. He is about as straight as they come.

"I remember when you were a little kid," I smiled.

"What happened?" he asked with excitement.

"All the ladies would look at you and say you were going to break some hearts. You were so cute."

"I'm still cute," he smiled.

"I know you like girls and I know they're gonna start coming at you because you've got your dad's personality. Girls are drawn to confident people and you are very confident. I must warn you, all that glitters ain't gold. I know you are hitting that stage where sex is on your mind."

"UNCLE ZACH!"

"Naw," I shook my head. "We're gonna keep it real. I was a teenager. Your daddy was a teenager. Ray was a teenager. We all went through this stuff. Gay or not, we all were there. Just be careful, TJ. And since you're in Atlanta, you've gotta be careful around some of these dudes, too."

"I've noticed," he replied.

"Where is that coming from?"

He said, "It's nothing. But is that why daddy and Ray wanted to come to Atlanta so they can be gay like everyone else?"

"Actually, your parents liked where you were. I know Tony loved Charlotte and he really didn't want to move here at first. You've got to understand, TJ, that this was an opportunity for your parents to advance in their careers. This was an opportunity in where all of you guys can succeed. I think you will really come to like Atlanta."

"I hope so," he replied.

"I think you will," I stood up and motioned for him to follow behind me. "I learned in life that you've got to take each thing, each opportunity, each situation as a learning experience. If you do, you'd be a better man because of it. You hungry?"

"I'm starving."

"Good," I said as I locked the office. "Let's go grab some lunch."

39

Phoenix Cummings

Chicago, Illinois

CJ and I had just left his mom's house. She had made us a late lunch. I loved visiting Mrs. Wright because she always took good care of me. She loves CJ's friends and I'm happy that I was one of his closest friends.

We were in his black Escalade heading back to my place when he said, "So I've been thinking."

"About?"

"Your friend, Dray."

"What about him?" I asked.

"He's very attractive," CJ said. "He's successful. He's got a good head on his shoulders. Whoever his dude is must be out of his mind to let Dray go. If I was with Dray, I wouldn't let him go."

"You're talking as if you like him or something," I looked at him.

"I said he was attractive, successful and he's got a good head on his shoulders."

"Ummm, have you forgotten?" I asked.

"Forgotten what?" he looked to me and then put his focus back on the road.

"You're in a relationship with a very powerful man. Y'all have been together what three or four years now?"

"Four," CJ replied. "And I haven't forgotten about him. I am very happy—thank you very much. I do have eyes. I can look. Just because I look doesn't mean I'll touch."

"Umm, hmm," I said. "I know you, CJ. Don't do anything to fuck up that relationship. That man you're dating is on his way to the top. Don't fuck that up."

"I hear you, Phoenix. I wish Keon was here."

"Good ole, Keon Douglass," I replied, as I thought about my friend and fellow NBA All-Star who was now playing for the Brooklyn Nets. Like me, Keon also has an off season/summer home in Atlanta. "Have you talked to Keon lately? Tell K-Doug to come on up here and chill with us."

"I talked to him a few days ago," CJ replied. "He was getting ready for a family reunion."

"Oh," I sighed as I changed subjects. "You know what though. My mind has been fucked."

"How?"

"Thinking about Keston. I really want to call my sister and get his number, but I'm scared. What if he's in a relationship or something? What if he isn't gay anymore? I don't know anything about Keston anymore. I haven't seen him in nine years."

"Well, if it's something I learned dealing with Dedrick and that is time waits for no one. I think you should just call the man. If Keston meant that much to you, and for whatever reason, memories of your time with him has been flooding your mind lately, I think you should just get the number and call him. What harm can it cause? Seriously, what harm can it cause?"

*****

Zach

I enjoyed my time spent with TJ. I love that little boy as if he was my own. At times, he is the closest thing I will have to a child.

I sighed as I approached a red light. I was excited for dinner. Keston wanted to meet up at Maggiano's, an Italian-American restaurant over in Buckhead.

I was excited for the opportunity being at Clark Atlanta can offer me. I'm excited to be at my new job. I already feel like I can make a difference.

I love my relationship with Renzo. I just love the atmosphere of being at a black college. Something in the air is different. I knew I made the right decision to come down here. I know I did. I haven't felt this excited about work in a very long time.

As I approached the intersection leading into the entrance of the restaurant, my phone started to ring. I looked at the battery and it was about to die.

"Hello," I answered as I searched for my car charger.

"Hey, Zach," my mom said.

"Hi, how are you?" I asked.

"I'm ok," she replied. "I was just thinking about you."

"I'm doing ok. Just got in Atlanta for good a couple of days ago. I moved into my office at work today. Got a lot accomplished. Now I'm off to dinner with a close friend to top off a pretty good day."

"I'm happy that you're happy," she said. "I don't want to interrupt your dinner; I was just calling to send my greetings, as you would say."

I laughed and said, "Before this phone dies, I just wanted to say that grandma came to visit me this morning."

"Really?"

"Yeah and she told me to tell you to answer the phone."

"Answer the phone?" my mom said. "What is that supposed to mean?"

"I don't know," I shrugged my shoulders as the light changed. "Have you been avoiding a call? Well, if you have, I think you should answer it. She was very direct. I'm just letting you know. But let me go. I love you and I'll talk to you later."

"Ok," she said a little stunned. "I love you, too."

When I got off the phone, I looked at the battery bar and it was blinking. I couldn't find the charger. It was probably in the house or something. As I parked my car, the phone started to ring again. It was Kris! I answered full of excitement.

"What up?" he said. "How are you?"

"I'm doing good," I said. "But listen, can I call you back? My phone is about to die. I don't have my charger and I've got to make a very important call."

"Yeah that's cool. I just got one question."

"What's up?"

"Are you in Atlanta?" he asked.

"Yep."

"Are you here for good now?"

"Yep," I smiled.

"That's what's up," he said excited. "I'm back in town from all my business trips. I've been traveling like crazy with this job, working all kinds of crazy hours. We've got to get up for drinks soon. We have so much to talk about. But call me when you get some free time."

"Ight, Kris. I will do," I replied as I hung up the phone.

Before the battery was completely gone, I phoned Keston. He was five minutes away. Once I ended the call, the phone died.

40

Dray

I had been on the phone with my son for almost thirty minutes. I loved talking to Nolan. I don't know what life would be like if he wasn't here.

"Dad," Nolan said.

"Sup?" I asked as I walked into the kitchen to start dinner.

"Can I be real with you?"

"I always want you to be real with me. You know that."

"Since you're living in Atlanta, I think you and mom should try and be a family. I would be so happy if you and mom got back together. She still loves you."

"Nolan, I love you and I don't have to live in the same house as your mother for you to know that."

"Do you have a girlfriend or something?" he asked.

"Nolan, your mom and I aren't meant to be together."

"How do you know? You won't even give her a chance."

"Nolan."

"Dad, can I come spend the night at your place?"

"Tonight?" I asked, immediately thinking about Zach.

"No, not tonight. Mom is making my favorite dinner. But sometime soon before school starts."

"Yeah," I said with an uneasy feeling in the pit of my stomach. "That can be arranged."

"YES!" he said. "I can't wait! But I wanna go play the game now before mom gets done cooking."

"Tasha is home?" I asked.

"Yeah, she's in the kitchen," he replied. "I love you, dad. I'll call you later."

"Ok, Nolan. I love you, too."

I exhaled. I knew this shit was coming.

I can't let Tasha and Nolan find out about my sexuality. Nolan is very smart and if he comes here and sees Zach, he's going to start to wonder.

When we were in New York, I told Nolan that Zach was my roommate. Most times when Nolan came to town, Zach got lost. Zach knew how much keeping my sexuality away from Nolan meant to me, but being in Atlanta is a different story. Zach just can't get lost for a weekend. Nolan can pop up whenever he feels like it.

I exhaled and then picked up the phone to call Zach. I wanted to see what he had a taste for dinner.

The phone went to voicemail.

I waited a few more minutes and then called him again. Maybe he was in a bad area or something. But again, the phone went to voicemail.

Not wanting to waste any more time, I grabbed some chicken breasts out of the freezer. Hopefully, he was on the way home.

*****

Zach

We arrived at the restaurant and was greeted by the maître d'. Once we were seated, the waitress came over and took our drinks and order.

I listened to Keston as he talked about his day with some of the Falcons players. I don't know if I could be in a position like his. He works around all those fine ass, hard bodied professional athletes. *Jesus take the wheel!* I don't know where he finds the inner strength to keep everything professional. God knows he's better than me.

As Keston talked, my eyes were drawn to the front door. I knew he saw me too when he started to smile. He was with some chick though.

Once the female was seated, he immediately came over to our table. Sy dapped Keston up, looked at me and asked, "What are you doing here?"

"I just moved here," I replied.

"You live in Atlanta now?" Sy asked, shocked.

"Yeah. I got a job at Clark Atlanta."

"That's what's up," Sy said excited. "Keli would love to see you."

"Where is he anyway? And who is that chick?" I asked.

Sy laughed and said, "Trust, it's not what you think. She's just a co-worker and she invited me to dinner. Keli is out of town at some national teaching conference they have every year in Cincinnati. But, Zach, text me your number."

"My phone is dead, but take mine."

After I spit the digits, he said, "I'll send you a text. Save the number and hit me up. We've got to get up."

"Ight."

"Good seeing you again, Kes," Sy said as he walked away.

Kes said, "Symon has always been cute in his own way."

I smiled as the waitress brought over our drinks. When she left, I said, "I love Sy. He's always been down to earth and very straightforward."

I took a sip of my drink.

"So," Kes replied. "It's something I really want to say, but I don't really know how to say it."

"What's up?" I asked.

"I've never told anyone before," Kes replied as I saw a look of worry on his face.

"Kes, what's going on? Are you ok? Are you sick?" I whispered.

"Sick?" he asked confused. "What do you mean?"

"You know; do you have HIV or something?"

He shook his head in disagreement and said, "You are wayyyyyyyyyy off base. No, I am not sick."

"Well, what's the issue? You're worrying me."

"Well, some years ago I was put in a situation." He stopped and took a deep breath. When he opened his mouth again, he said, "On second thought, now is not the right time."

Concerned, I replied, "Well, you know I'm here for you whenever you need to talk."

"I appreciate that Zach," he stated. "I really do."

He took another sip of his drink then said, "On another topic, you know I've been sleeping with LaRon Copeland."

"And what a lucky man you are," I nodded my head. "God, that man is FINE!"

Kes smiled and whispered, "And the dick is lethal."

LaRon Copeland was the star wide receiver for the Carolina Panthers. He was tall, muscular and had Hershey brown skin. He was like the Idris Elba of football. LaRon, along with star quarterback Cam Newton, was a force to be reckoned with.

"But seriously," he continued. "LaRon is talking about getting serious with me."

"WHOA!" I replied. "Are you serious?"

"Yeah," Kes stated. "He said he wanted to make this official."

"Wow. That's what's up!"

"Naw, it ain't," he shook his head in disagreement.

"What's wrong with it?" I asked. "LaRon is fine, successful, and as far as we know, loyal. What's the issue, other than the fact he lives four hours away? He spent damn near his entire off season here with you."

Kes said, "The problem is that I can only think about my real first love. He's been on my mind heavily the last few weeks. I know LaRon is a good dude, but my mind is in such disarray."

Keston's phone started to vibrate. He looked at it and said, "Hold on. This is my cousin, Qier."

*****

Dray

Where the fuck was he? The food is damn near done and he isn't home yet. I know he isn't still on that damn campus.

I phoned him again. Voicemail. The phone keeps going to voicemail. All I wanted to do was apologize for this morning and have dinner with him.

I waited a few minutes and called him one last time. Voicemail again. I walked away from the kitchen island. When I reached the breakfast bar, I pulled out the barstool and took a seat.

As images of Dwight and Zach filled my mind, my body started to become filled with rage. I could see Zach riding Dwight's dick. I could see Zach bent over on all fours, throwing that phat ass back on Dwight's dick. I could see them kissing, loving, embracing each other.

And this nigga had the audacity to come to my house and spit all that bullshit about respect and shit, but yet we ain't been in this city a good two days and they're already fucking.

Was that conversation with Dwight this morning supposed to make me feel any better about him? I don't think so! That nigga is a snake. And snakes can't be trusted!

He was talking about he encouraged Zach to go to New York and try it out with me, because he felt that we deserved each other.

He did it for a number of reasons alright, but was that before or after he fucked my man?

I don't even know why I bother sometimes. Why am I still in this relationship? Why am I doing this to myself?

Wait, I'm tripping. *You're tripping, Dray*! I need to trust my dude. I've got to trust Zach.

I picked up the phone to call him again, but it went to voicemail like the times before.

You know what… FUCK THAT! I don't trust no nigga. And I damn sure don't trust no nigga who will stand there and lie in my face...

Part Four:

What Webs We Weave...

41

Zach

The server placed a plate down in front of Keston and said, "The Eggplant Parmesan for you, sir." He placed my plate down and said, "And the Chicken and Spinach Manicotti for you." It looked so good.

"Thanks," Keston replied.

"I hope you enjoy," the attractive dude said before walking away.

After a few bites, I looked at Kes and said, "So back to this first love."

"Yeah?"

"Why haven't you mentioned him before?"

"Never had a reason to I guess," he shrugged his shoulders.

"So who is he? Who is this man that swept you off your feet?"

After Kes took a sip of his drink, he said, "I really don't wanna repeat his name."

"Do I know him or something?"

"He's very famous," Kes said. "Even though he wasn't famous when we met."

"Interesting," I replied.

"You know, LaRon is different. But I don't wanna put my first love out there. He may not even get down with dudes anymore."

"How is LaRon different?"

Kes sighed, "He just is. I had to tell someone about him. I trusted you not to tell anyone and you didn't. But I just don't feel comfortable putting the name of my first real love out there."

I ate a piece of my food and then said, "Keston, I want to confide in you."

"About what?"

"My real first love."

"I thought that was Dray."

"Not quite," I stated. "About ten years ago I confided in someone who I thought was a real friend. I told him some very personal stuff about me and my first real love. I would have never thought those words would come back to bite me in the ass."

Kes stared at me.

"Several years after I confided in my so-called friend, turns out, he went back and told all of my stories to my first love's fiancée."

"Are you serious?"

"Dead ass. My real first love was pissed off at me, but thankfully, he didn't hold it against me. After that day, I promised myself that I would never tell another soul about the things that transpired between the two of us." I took a deep breath and said, "Kes, I've wanted to tell you for a long time, but I couldn't out of fear that you would open your mouth. You and I have been friends almost nine years now. I know I can trust you. Besides, I have to get this shit off my chest or I'm gonna go insane! I've been holding this secret inside for seven years."

He placed his fork down and said, "What's up, Zach?"

"My real first love is Dwight."

His mouth dropped.

I swallowed my spit.

"Zach, tell me you are lying."

"No, I'm not and there is more."

I gave Keston a detailed history lesson on my relationship with Dwight, explaining every intricate detail from the moment we met at FAMU's Summer Band Camp, up until today. I did omit what happened the night before Dwight's wedding.

"Wow," Keston said in shock. "So what happened seven years ago? You said, you've been keeping this secret for seven years."

I stared at Kes.

"What?" he said.

"You can't tell a soul. Keston, you have to take this to your grave."

"I won't tell anyone," he stuck out his pinky finger.

After our pinkies connected, I took a deep breath and said, "The night before Dwight's wedding, we had sex."

"You've got to be fucking kidding me!" he said in disbelief. "This has to be a joke or a game or something."

"This is not a game, Keston. This is the truth."

"Wait—weren't you and Dray together then?"

"Yes."

He took a deep breath and said, "Wow. Does Dray know?"

"No. You are the third person to know behind Dwight and myself."

"Wow."

"I'm not done," I said.

"There's more?" he asked.

"About three years or four years ago—"

"Don't tell me y'all had sex again," he cut.

"No," I shook my head. "But Dwight started telling me how he wanted to make us work."

"Us—as in you and Dwight?"

"Yes."

"But he's married," Kes said. "Married with kids."

"Dwight wants out of that marriage," I said. "He's been talking about it for years. Kes, Dwight has asked me eight separate times over the past few years to come be with him. He wants me to leave Dray and come live a life with him."

"What do you say to him?"

"I reject his advances. I fucked up once; I can't fuck up again."

"Oh, my God," Kes said. "It all makes sense now."

"What?"

"Dwight and Dray at the bar a few weeks back. Their attitudes towards each other. Man, this is crazy."

"Yeah. Now, I'm torn."

"How?"

"Something is missing with Dray. I don't know what it is, but something is missing. I love Dray, but at times I feel like we're together out of obligation. It's like we don't connect anymore."

"Wow."

"Can I be a little more honest?"

"What is it, Zach?"

I exhaled and said, "I still love Dwight. I know I do. I never stopped loving him. I never did. I just suppressed those feelings. I've been quite the professional with hiding shit these days, hiding shit from myself and shit from others. I love Dwight but I'm scared."

"Of what?"

"Keston, Dwight played me for years. I put up with so much of Dwight's bullshit. Through it all, I still love him. My insides still tingle at the sight of him. I never stopped loving him. That night we had sex was more than sex. We connected. That was love, Kes. I've never felt anything like that in my life. I've never felt anything like that since. I just know we can't be together."

"So you've kept Dray around because you know you couldn't be with Dwight?"

"I love Dray," I replied.

"That's not what I said," Keston replied. "I said you've kept Dray around because you couldn't be with Dwight. Am I correct?"

"Keston, don't do this to me."

"Answer the question, Zach. Stop lying. Stop beating behind the bush. Man up and face the truth. You said you wanted to be honest, so be honest."

I could feel tears starting to fall from my eyes.

"Am I correct?" he asked, staring me in my eyes. "Is that why you've kept Dray around? He was the next best thing since Dwight didn't work out?"

"I love Dray," I pleaded.

"If you loved Dray, you would've told him you cheated on him with Dwight."

"He didn't tell me about Nolan until he was caught," I said trying to justify myself.

"True enough. But those are totally different circumstances and you know it. While Dray kept his son in the dark, his son was born years before y'all met. As far as we know, Dray has never cheated on you."

"He is now," I replied. "Sneaking back in the house at three in morning."

"Let's not divert," Kes said. "This is about you, not Dray."

I exhaled.

"You're playing a dangerous game and it needs to stop, Zach. You're my friend and I'm only going to give it to you the way I see it."

"I know, Keston."

"Zach, this is your life and no one can live it but you. With that being said, even if you aren't honest with me, you've got to be honest with yourself. You've got to be true to yourself."

I wiped my eyes.

"Zach, you've got to do the right thing. It's not fair to Dray if you're feeling your best friend, if you're in love with your best friend. Dray doesn't deserve that. You don't deserve that. Stop living a lie and man up. You've got to do the right thing."

I looked at Kes and said, "What's the right thing?"

He shook his head and replied, "Only you can answer that question, Zach. Only you."

42

TJ

Daddy gave me these pictures of my mom a few years ago. Now I was laying in the bed, listening to some music, looking at these pictures and wishing she were here. I cherish these pictures like they were a piece of gold that could make me a very rich man.

I studied each picture intensely as if I was studying for an exam at school. I know every mark in her face, every curve in her body. I feel like I know her better than she knew herself.

I didn't want to get emotional, so I put the pictures down, got out of bed and headed off to use the bathroom. As soon as I stepped out into the hallway, my stomach dropped. I heard baby making music and moaning coming from Daddy and Ray's room.

"They're always fucking," I shook my head as I went on into the bathroom.

When I was done, I ran down the stairs as fast as I could so I wouldn't have to hear them. I opened the fridge and grabbed a peach and a bottled water.

Embracing what was to come, I took a deep breath and ran back up the stairs and to my room as fast as I could, hoping not to hear them.

I laid back down on the bed and bit into the peach. This was my favorite fruit.

I looked at my mom's pictures again. I closed my eyes and exhaled. I wish my mother was alive. I wish I knew her.

*****

Zach

I had spent more time at the restaurant with Keston than planned. It was getting late, but we needed to have that conversation. I needed to get that stuff off my chest before I arrived back home with Dray. The couple of hours spent at the restaurant took me away from reality.

Now, it is back to Dray. Now, it is back to the shit I left this morning when I went to work. Now, it is time to face Dray. It will be very interesting to see how he tries to spin that shit from this morning.

I know I'm not perfect, but what am I supposed to think when you mysteriously get out of bed in the wee hours of the morning, leave the house to go for a ride, but when you come back home you're on the phone with some nigga. When I question him about it, he tries to put it off on his NBA friend, Phoenix.

Really, Dray? Really?

Besides, I can't tell you the last time we've had sex. I know Dray's body and he needs it consistently. Either he's jacking off, which I seriously doubt, or he's getting it from someone else.

I wouldn't be surprised if his baby mama, Natasha, was still sitting on his dick.

I guess in my mind, if he admits he was out cheating, then I could admit my faults. Somewhere in that, I guess we could move past everything.

Yeah, right.

I hope I made the right decision to tell Keston. I know Keston isn't going to say anything to anyone, but Dwight would kill me if he knew someone knew of our secret.

I know one thing is for certain and that's I don't want any drama when I get home. I hope that Dray is asleep, or in his office doing work. It would be perfect if he wasn't home at all. I really don't want to deal with him right now. I just want to take a nice long shower, release some stress and get my ass in the bed.

Chances of that working out the way I like are slim to none, but we shall see.

*****

Phoenix

Chicago, Illinois

CJ sat across from me and said, "I'm not leaving here until you make the call."

"It's late," I said.

"Nigga, we're in Chicago. Seattle is two hours behind us. Pick up the phone and make the damn call! You're starting to piss me off, Phoenix."

I exhaled. It was just a phone call. I'll make the call and get the number so he can get the fuck out of my house.

"I'm waiting," CJ said.

I exhaled again.

He said, "Phoenix, I'm doing this for your benefit. I don't want you to be in the situation I was in regarding Dedrick. Just pick up the phone and call your sister."

So he could just shut up already, I grabbed the cell and phoned my oldest sibling. Within moments, she answered, "Hey P.C."

Kookie was the only person in the world who called me by my initials, P.C.

"Hey, how are you doing?" I asked.

"I'm ok. What's going on?" she said.

"Are you busy? I've got a quick question for you."

"No, I'm not busy. I just ate dinner. Qier and Germaine went to some teammate's birthday party. What's up?"

"Ok," I said as I looked to CJ. He was staring me dead in my mouth. I stood up and started to walk around the room. "I need you to promise me that you won't tell Qier."

"Why? What have you done?"

"I haven't done anything," I said. "Can you promise me that first? Can you promise me you won't tell Qier?"

"I promise. What's up?"

"I need Keston's number."

"Why?"

"I need to get in contact with him."

She held the phone for a few moments and then said, "P.C., where is this coming from?"

"Are you gonna give me the number or not? I really don't have time for the interrogation."

She exhaled then said, "Yeah… hold on."

I heard her typing in her phone and then she said the ten digits. I saved the number in my phone and said, "Thanks. Please don't tell Qier."

"I won't say anything, but what do you need Keston's number for?"

"I'll explain later. Thanks, sis."

"No problem, I guess."

"I love you…talk to you later," I hung up the phone.

I sighed.

I looked to CJ and said, "There. I made the call. Now you're more than welcome to dismiss yourself."

"You aren't done," CJ said.

"Yes, I am," I replied. "I did what you told me to do. I got the number."

"Yeah, you got it, now it's time to use it. Make the call, Phoenix."

I stared at him.

He stared back and repeated, "Make… the call!"

43

Keston

As I walked into my condo, I listened to my current fuck buddy, LaRon, talk about his day at the Carolina Panthers training camp. While I listened to LaRon, my mind was really focused on Zach. Our conversation from dinner was still lingering in my head. I'm still shocked at his revelation. I can't believe he and Dwight had sex.

"Kes, baby, are you listening?" LaRon asked as I took off my shoes.

"What… ummm yeah I'm listening," I replied.

"What's the last thing I said?" LaRon asked.

"You were talking about the pass you caught from Cam Newton and how everyone went crazy."

"Oh, ok," he said. "Just checking."

LaRon Copeland was the 29-year-old star wide receiver for the Carolina Panthers. He grew up in Greenville, South Carolina and was the youngest of four kids. I first met LaRon when I was a trainer during my graduate school days at the University of Georgia.

Being a new trainer to the Georgia Bulldog team, I learned from my previous stints at the University of Central Florida for undergrad and my first grad school experience down at FAMU, that it's best to get the new players. It is good to build a rapport with the new kids, as those relationships can carry you a very long way. That's how my relationship with LaRon developed. Not only was I a student trainer for the football team, I was his paid tutor.

During his sophomore year, we developed a very good friendship that extended through the duration of his junior year. I always thought LaRon was attractive, and in the back of my mind, I pondered over the idea of if he got down. LaRon was different from the other footballers on that team. He was always about his business and I really never seen LaRon around females. All his friends were dudes. I knew those were some of the tale-tale signs and despite the fact I wanted to have one night with him, I knew that sexual relationships with players were off limits. That was the forbidden "NO" in the world of sports.

During his senior year, I landed the job with the Falcons. He was sad to see me go, but we kept in contact. Slowly, as time passed, our communications stopped.

When I tried to call him one day, his number had changed. LaRon didn't do the social media stuff so it wasn't as if I could find him on the internet.

Just so happen, about a year ago, I was invited to a party by one of the DL dudes on the Falcons. It was a private, high security, invite only party at a ranch he rented out in San Antonio, Texas. It was at that party, when I ran into LaRon. Germaine, who is my cousin's, Qier, best friend, was there, along with Kameron "Killa" Davis from the San Francisco 49ers. There were about fifty dudes there in total, with majority of them stemming from the NBA and NFL.

LaRon and I started talking and reconnected that night. We've been talking ever since. A few months later, we started having sex and it has been no turning back.

"So Kes, bae, what's up?" LaRon said.

"What do you mean?" I asked.

"When are we gonna make this official? You know how much I like you. I liked you when I was playing ball at Georgia. I ain't never been about games and you know that, Kes. You know how much I like you. I know you have reason to doubt. I'm a NFL player. I can have anyone I want, but I don't fuck around like that. I wasn't raised like that. I know I live in Charlotte, but we can make this work. It's only a four-hour drive. We can make it work. I want more than just sex. Think about that, ight. Think about that."

"Ight, LaRon."

"I'm not trying to rush you into anything, but I really like you and I wanna make you mine."

"I know, LaRon," I smiled. "I know."

"I'll call you in the morning on the way to practice, ight?"

"Ight," I smiled. "Later."

I grabbed my phone and placed it on the charger. I needed to get in the shower and get my behind in the bed. I had another long day at training camp tomorrow.

I rushed over to the bathroom and started to run the shower water. While that got heated, I undressed before I started to brush my teeth.

In the midst of brushing, I heard my phone ringing. I tried to finish as fast as I could. Once my mouth was rinsed, I rushed out of the bathroom, dick slinging from side-to-side as I yelled, "I'm coming!"

As soon as I got to the phone, it stopped ringing. I grabbed my iPhone and stared at the unknown number. It didn't ring a bell.

I looked back at the bathroom.

I shrugged my shoulders and said, "If it is important enough, whoever it is will call back. This shower is calling my name."

*****

Zach

Once the car was parked, I took a deep breath. It was clear Dray was home because his car was parked in his spot in the garage. Before I got out of my ride, said a quick prayer and headed for the side door.

The house was pitch black and I couldn't see shit, but a pleasant aroma immediately filled my nostrils.

"Dray must have cooked," I said to myself as I fumbled around the wall for the light switch.

Once the light was on, I turned my head to the right and there was Dray sitting in the living room, staring at me while rubbing two tension balls together.

It instantly reminded me of the scene from the movie *Boyz in da Hood* where Laurence Fishburne's character, Furious Styles, sat in the house rubbing two tension balls and waited for his son, Tre, to return home.

"Was it good?" Dray asked.

"What?"

"You heard me," he said as he stopped rubbing the balls and stood up. "Was it good?"

"Dray, what the hell are you talking about?"

"So, now you're gonna stand there and play stupid, like you don't know what the fuck I'm talking about."

"I really don't know what you're talking about," I shook my head as I walked in the kitchen to grab a bottle of water. I plugged my phone in to the wall charger to get some juice.

"I've been trying to call you all night," he said, walking closer to me. "Like all fucking night! You know what I get? Voicemail. Since about six this afternoon, I've gotten nothing but voicemail. You know what that tells me, Zach?"

"And what exactly does that tell you, Dray?" I asked staring at him. "Huh? What does it tell you?"

He just stared at me.

I grabbed my phone, shoved it in his face and said, "My phone died! Look at it—it's dead, nigga! DEAD!"

"WHERE THE FUCK YOU BEEN, ZACH?"

"I had dinner with Keston," I said as I walked away.

"Dinner with Keston," he laughed. "Yeah, right."

"Do you need to see the receipt, Daddy?" I sarcastically stated.

"Don't no fucking dinner take four damn hours!"

"What are you implying?" I asked.

"You're fucking him, Zach. Just admit it!"

"Dude, Keston is my friend. Stop tripping!"

"I AIN'T TALKING ABOUT KESTON AND YOU DAMN WELL KNOW IT!"

I stared at him and said, "Well, who the fuck are you talking about?"

He didn't reply.

"Dray, please," I said disgusted. "You need to be the last motherfucker talking about cheating when your ass is sneaking out the house and coming home at three in the morning, talking to some nigga. Please spare me, ok."

"I told you that was Phoenix. If you would have just heard me out this morning, instead of acting like a bitch and throwing a hissy fit, you would have known that."

"Whatever, Dray," I shook my head. "Whatever."

"I couldn't sleep so I went for a ride. I couldn't sleep because my mind is too fucked up over you and this relationship! I know this relationship is in trouble. I called Phoenix to let him know that I still wanted to help with the project back home, but I couldn't be as hands on as I wanted to be. I know I have to be here for you and this relationship. I was letting him know that I would be on the Board of Trustees, but I had to salvage this relationship. Doing more traveling wasn't going to help that."

"Oh, ok," I nonchalantly replied as I swallowed some of my water. I rolled my eyes.

"I'm telling you the truth, Zach."

"Yeah, Dray. Sure."

"YOU MADE ME MOVE DOWN HERE AND YOU KNEW I DIDN'T WANT TO BE HERE, ZACH! YOU MADE ME MOVE DOWN HERE TO LOOK LIKE A FUCKING FOOL!"

"I didn't make you do shit," I cut. "Don't start with me, Dray. I don't have time for this."

"Nolan is down here and I gotta figure out what I'm gonna do about him and Tasha not finding out about us. Here I am worried about us, and you're out FUCKING THAT NIGGA! Here I am trying to have dinner with my man and he's out FUCKING THAT NIGGA! Here I am trying to make this work and here you are

FUCKING THAT NIGGA!"

"DRAY, YOU SOUND SO FUCKING STUPID RIGHT NOW!"

"Do I really? Hell, we don't communicate anymore. When we do, it's like this. We sleep in the same bed, I try to hold you and you pull away. We're not lovers, we're roommates. When is the last time you kissed me, Zach? I DIDN'T MOVE DOWN HERE TO BE YOUR FUCKING ROOMMATE! If you didn't want to be with me, maybe you should have told me that shit before I up and changed my life to move down here with you. You're so fucking selfish! You wanna talk about my shortcomings but you never sit and think about the shit you do wrong. You never think about how your actions affect me!"

"Dray, you're acting fucking crazy," I placed my water down.

"YOU'RE MAKING ME FUCKIN' CRAZY, ZACH! YOU'RE DOING THIS SHIT! YOU! YOU KNOW I DON'T LIKE DOING ALL THIS YELLING AND SHIT!"

I stared at him and calmly said, "Then stop fuckin' yelling."

"How can I when you're standing here talking about I'm cheating on you. Really Zach? Cheating? I love you. I would never cheat on you. Why would I cheat on you when you're everything I want? I just told your ass I couldn't sleep so I went for a ride. Damn, do you fucking listen? If anything, you should know I'm too afraid to catch something from somebody to talk about me cheating on you. If you believe that shit you're thinking in your head, you're stupid."

"Oh, so now I'm stupid, Dray?"

"We haven't had sex in four months, Zach. FOUR FUCKING MONTHS! I haven't jacked off so much since I was in college. YOU AIN'T FUCKING ME, SO YOU'RE FUCKIN' SOMEBODY. YOU'RE FUCKING THAT NIGGA!"

"I ain't fucking nobody, Dray."

"I'M NOT STUPID, ZACH! I'M NOT STUPID! JUST ADMIT YOU'RE FUCKING HIM!"

"I AM NOT FUCKING DWIGHT!" I yelled. "I AM NOT FUCKING DWIGHT!"

"DAMN, ZACH, STOP FUCKING LYING! JUST STOP LYING! YOU ARE FUCKING HIM. JUST STOP LYING AND ADMIT IT!"

I said, "I am not having sex with Dwight. In how many fucking languages do I need to say that to get shit in your thick ass skull?"

"I know that nigga been inside of you, Zach. I know he has."

"Fuck this!" I said. "I ain't gotta deal with this shit. I'm out!"

"We don't even fuckin' talk no more. What the fuck you mean you out?"

"I'M OUT!" I yelled, as I snatched my keys off the counter.

"WHERE THE FUCK YOU GOING?" he yelled. "WE'RE NOT DONE!"

"You can argue with yourself, I'm done and I'm out!"

With a shocking move, Dray reached out and grabbed my arms, locking me into place. With his grip and fingernails digging into my skin, he said, "You're staying here! I won't allow you to run, Zach. We need to work this out."

I stared him in his eyes and slowly said, "You've got one second to get your fucking hands off me."

We intensely stared each other in the eyes before he suddenly released his grip and ruefully said, "Sorry."

"Who the fuck *are* you?" I asked as I stared him in his eyes. "WHO THE FUCK ARE YOU?"

He exhaled and said, "I should ask you the same question. Who are you?"

I shook my head, grabbed my phone, brushed past him and rushed out the side door. I slammed the door on my way out.

All of my emotions started to pour out inside my car. I had enough tears in my eyes to fill the Gulf of Mexico.

Not knowing what to do or where to go, I drove and I cried. And cried. And cried.

While on the interstate, I grabbed my phone. Within moments he said, "Hey, Big Z. What's up?"

"I need you," I cried. "I need you right now, Dwight."

In a worried like tone, Dwight said, "Zach, what's wrong? What's going on?"

"I…need… you," I forced out.

"I'm on the way," he said. "Where are you?"

I wiped my face and said, "I'm going to a hotel."

"A hotel, why?" he asked.

"I'll be at the Marriott Marquis…downtown."

"Zach, what the fuck is going on? Did he hurt you?"

Frustrated, angry and upset, I cut, "Dwight, are you coming or not?"

He exhaled and said, "I'm on the way. I'll be right there."

44

Zach

Friday, August 12, 2016

I felt the first of his blows connect with the side of my face. He said, "Talk that shit now you faggot ass nigga! Talk that shit now!"

I shook my head to erase those memories of that fight with Kyran out of my mind. As much as I tried to forget, the pain and the anguish and the fear I felt that day, seven years ago, was now so real and vivid in my mind.

I shook my head again. I just wanted it to leave. I closed my eyes and opened them.

"Jesus take the wheel," I replied.

I exhaled.

Kyran Barr. That bitch ass nigga. He invaded me seven years ago and now it feels like it was yesterday.

Whom do I have to thank for those memories? Dray.

All that shit flooded my mind when Dray put his hands on me last night. In the hotel bed early this morning, I had a dream that Kyran was in the room and he was trying to kill me. Luckily, Dwight was there to knock some sense into me.

I exhaled and I looked around my small office. I needed some fresh air. I walked out of the building and looked at the view of the campus of Clark Atlanta University. It was nice but it had nothing on my alma mater, Florida A&M University.

I thought about last night and exhaled. What the fuck got into Dray?

Instead of going home this morning, I got up early and purchased a new outfit for work and some toiletries for the hotel room. I just wasn't in the mood to deal with Dray and I wanted to avoid him at all costs.

Once Dwight got to the hotel last night, I turned my phone off and I haven't turned it back on. I'm sure Dray has been blowing up my phone, but I just need to do me right now. I just didn't want to be bothered.

After standing outside for a few minutes, breathing in the fresh air, I headed back to my office. While I thought of Dray, an image of Kyran re-appeared before me.

Being a little curious, I opened my laptop and clicked on my Firefox browser. I did a Google search. I entered Kyran Barr, Florida Mugshot.

I shook my head as images of my former roommate appeared. I randomly clicked on one site. On that site, he had four different mugshots. I felt my stomach sink.

Aggravated Battery with a deadly weapon. Assault and Battery. Criminal Mischief $1000 or more. Dealing in Stolen Property. Fugitive from Arkansas.

Shocked, I refreshed the last page again.

I wasn't tripping.

"Fugitive from Arkansas," I said aloud.

Going back to Google, I typed in Kyran Barr, Arkansas mugshot.

There he was again. I clicked on the first site. I shook my head as I read his charges.

Robbery. Violation of probation.

At least it wasn't just me. That motherfucker was crazy—robbery, aggravated battery with a deadly weapon, dealing in stolen property.

I'm thankful that God allowed me to get myself out of that situation before it got worse.

I scrolled down. His release date from the Arkansas penitentiary was September 23, 2016.

"You've got to be fucking kidding me," I said in disbelief.

This bastard is being released from prison, next month, on my fucking birthday?

He had been locked up since 2010.

I exhaled.

After I rubbed my hands over my face a few times, I picked up my phone and turned it back on. Within moments, it began to vibrate. There were text messages and voicemails.

I looked at the text messages first. They all were from Dray. I skimmed over them and then listened to my voicemail.

"Hey, Bae, give me a call. I'm worried about you. I love you."

Delete.

"Hey, Zach, it's me again. Call me and let me know you're safe."

Delete.

"Zach, this Dray. Come home. Damn, man. Just come home!"

Delete.

I went through about five more of Dray's messages and deleted them all.

There was one from Dwight that said, "Big Z, I'm just checking on you to make sure you made it safe to school. Sorry I had to leave this morning but I have an appointment. Call me when you get this, ight. Oh, yeah, you were tripping hard last night with that dream. You scared the shit out of me. What's up with that? Call me, ight? I love you, shawty. Later."

Saved.

I listened to the first few words of Dray's next message and then ended the call. I called Dwight and he immediately answered, "What up Big Z?"

"Just got your message."

"Cool. You made it to the office safely?"

"Yeah, I'm here. I'm not gonna be here too long. Probably gonna head home in a lil bit before Dray kills himself."

"You talked to him?" he asked.

"Naw. He left a zillion messages. It's kinda cute."

Dwight didn't reply.

"How did your appointment go?" I asked.

"I'm actually heading there now. I will call you later, ight?"

"Ok, Dwight."

"You need me to go home with you?" he asked.

"Naw," I exhaled. "I think I can do it myself. I think I can manage."

"You sure? I'll go with you if you want me to."

"Naw, it'll only make matters worse if you come."

"Are you sure you're ready to do this?"

"I need to," I said. "I have to."

"Ight. Well, you know I'm here for you, so just get at me if you need me."

"Ok. You got the keycard to the hotel room, right?" I asked.

"Yeah. I'll stop by when I'm done here."

"Ok. What about Lexi though?" I asked.

"What about her?" he said. "She'll be alright. Let me take care of this and I will get at you."

"Ight, Dwight. Thanks for everything last night."

"It was nothing, Zach. It was nothing," he hung up the phone.

As soon as I placed the phone down, there was a knock on my office door. I said, It's open."

I smiled as soon as the door opened. Renzo closed the door, smiled and said, "What's up, Doc?"

"How are you?" I asked.

"I'm doing very good, Doc. Very good," Renzo said as he walked over and sat down in one of the seats placed in front of my desk. "I was just stopping by to see if you needed me to do anything."

"Naw," I shook my head. "I think I got everything handled."

"You sure?"

"Yeah, I think so."

"That's what's up," he said. "I'm really excited."

"Why is that?"

"Today is the last day of classes for the summer session. My brother is flying back into town tomorrow and then we're going on vacation for a week."

"You and your brother?" I asked.

"Yes."

"Is he older or younger?"

"About ten years older. It's just us two and he's the best brother in the world. Are you and your brother close like that?"

"I'm actually an only child."

"Really?" he asked.

"Yeah, it's just me. My birth father had another kid, but I don't know who he is. I'm my mother's only child, so in my eyes, it's just me. I have stepbrothers but they don't count."

"Wow. I don't know what I would do without my brother."

"Where are y'all going for the vacation?" I asked.

"Jamaica," he smiled. "We're going back home to Chicago to chill out before the fall semester starts once we get back."

"Wow, that's what's up," I said. I knew his brother had to have some money.

"Yeah, when I was a teenager, I tried to go to Jamaica with him but my mom wouldn't let me go. However, she can't stop me now. I'm a grown man who makes my own decisions."

I laughed.

"What, Doc?" he replied. "I'm just saying."

"Nothing, Renzo," I shook my head. "I just remember those days when I used to think like that. Are you from Chicago?"

"Yes, sir. That's where I was born and raised until I came down here for college. But let me get going, Doc."

"Ight, Renzo. Enjoy your trip."

"All those beautiful, Ebony, sexy bodies. Ummm… Jamaica," he smiled. "I am most definitely going to enjoy myself."

"Be safe, Renzo, protect yourself," I seriously said.

"Most def, Doc. I don't want no babies."

I smiled as he walked towards the door.

"Oh, yeah," he said as he opened the door.

"What's up?"

"I registered for one of your classes," he smiled. "See you in a couple of weeks."

I smiled as he turned around and exited.

*****

Dwight

When I hung up the phone with Zach, I reached over and turned up the radio. A few moments later, she reached over and turned it down. As I drove on the interstate, I cut my eyes to her.

"You know, you *are* making the right decision," my mom said.

"I hope so, Ma. I hope so."

"You are," she said again. "You're only going to see what your legal options are. You need to know what's available to you under Georgia law."

I exhaled.

"You shouldn't have married that girl in the first place," my mom ranted. "I told you not to marry her. You don't listen. You're just hardheaded! Just hardheaded!"

"MA!" I cut as I turned and looked at her. "NOT TODAY, OK. NOT TODAY!"

She placed her hand over her heart, rolled her eyes then turned to look out the window. I turned up the radio.

This situation with Zach has me bugging. I exhaled.

I saw her hands reaching over and turning down the radio. When I turned my head to face her, she said, "What is going on Dwight?"

"Nothing, Ma."

"Bullshit and you know it! Do I need to call Maury and give yo' ass a lie detector test? You know I got him on speed dial."

"Ma, it's nothing."

"Dwight, you don't seem like yourself. As soon as you arrived at my house this morning, I noticed it. At first, I thought it was just the pressures of going to see the attorney. But I just heard you talking to Zach. Is that what's wrong? Is something wrong with Zach? You said he was in town for good the other day. Why is he at a hotel? Why do you have a keycard to his room? Did something happen between you and Zach?"

"Ma, stop worrying about nothing."

"Umm, hmm," she said, "The truth shall set you free, child."

"Ma, I ain't trying to hear your speculations today."

She exhaled then said, "I just want you to be happy, Dwight. That's all. I just want my baby to be happy."

45

Dray

Frustrated, I walked in the house after a very long jog around the neighborhood. I don't know what got into me last night and now Zach won't even turn on his damn phone. It's been off since he left last night.

What the fuck was I thinking, putting my hands on him? I would never hit Zach. I know dudes always say that shit, but I wouldn't. I had no intent on hitting him. I grabbed his arm because I wanted us to finish our conversation. Damn, I keep fucking up.

Zach hasn't been here in the relationship for some time now and that shit scares me. I would let this go before I ever hurt him. I wanna fight for us, for this relationship, but if it needs to end, then I might as well let it go. It'll hurt more if we force it. When Zach is ready to talk, we'll talk. Maybe I've been trying too hard. I know I've been trying too hard.

This shit is just so confusing. Did I misinterpret what I think I know? Is my mind playing tricks on me?

Maybe Zach and Dwight never had sex. I know Zach would have said something to me by now.

I just don't know what to do. What gives?

I walked into the kitchen and grabbed a bottled water out of the refrigerator. I walked upstairs to the linen closet and grabbed a towel to wipe off my body.

Heading into the bedroom, I silently prayed that Zach had returned my call. When I grabbed the phone, there was nothing. I sighed.

On the nightstand was a picture that I took of the two of us. We were both smiling and in love. You could tell by the look in our eyes that we were in love. I grabbed the picture and held it close to my heart. Damn, I love this dude.

I know every relationship has problems, but when will this storm pass? I don't want to give up. I want to fight for Zach. I want this to work.

When I placed the picture back down, I grabbed the remote and flipped on the television.

I smiled as the channel was on MSNBC. It was just like Zach to leave it placed on this channel. I don't watch politics much less TV. I don't have time for it.

Just before I flipped to one of the music stations, I saw an image of my good friend, the Governor, flash across the screen.

"Could Governor Reed be a possible running rate for Senator Fitzgerald?" the anchor, Dominique Grant, said. "Stay tuned for more. We'll be right back."

Dominique was beautiful. She was once married to NBA star, Dedrick Grant.

As the politics show went to a commercial break, I grabbed my cell phone and dialed the personal cell number of my friend, J. Nehemiah Reed, II.

Within a few rings, he answered, "What pleasure do I owe this call?"

"Shit, I'm surprised you answered," I replied. "It's hard to catch up with you, Governor."

"Dray, please," he said. "I've told you time and time again, please stop calling me that. I am still Nehemiah."

"Ight, Justin," I laughed in reference to his first name that only his mom calls him.

"Watch it," he joked. "What's up though? I only got a few minutes."

"How do you do it?"

"What are you talking about?" Nehemiah asked.

"How do you balance everything? You know, keeping your private life private. How do you deal with your dad, the Bishop? How do you deal with your mom, your son, Jocelyn, your dude and then on top of that, you're in charge of one of the biggest states in the union! How do you do it all when you are such a public figure?"

"A lot of sleepless nights," he laughed. "Dray, I knew what I was getting myself into when I decided to run for the governorship of

Florida. I knew that. My family knew that. My dude knew that. I've learned that sometimes you've got to make some sacrifices for the better good." He paused and then said, "Where is this coming from? Are you and Zach having some issues?"

"Yeah, we are," I replied as I started to explain the recent past to Nehemiah. He listened intently, asking a few questions when he saw fit.

Once I was done, he said, "I'm just going to put it out there."

"What?"

"I know us colored folk don't think too much of it, but the shit works. Dray, y'all need counseling. Real talk."

"Counseling? Man, I don't know about that. I don't think Zach will be down for that."

"The shit works," he said. "It really does. Listen, I've got to run. I've got to make another phone call before this meeting starts, but I can text you the name and number of someone I highly recommend, if you want it."

Feeling a bit uneasy about the counseling thing, I said, "Yeah, do that."

"Ight. I'll call you later though. Let me make this call."

I smiled and said, "Ight, Mr. Vice President."

Nehemiah laughed and said, "Naw, not yet. She hasn't even confirmed me yet, so don't jinx me."

I chuckled and replied, "She'll pick you. I can tell."

"Bye, Dray."

"Later, Mr. Governor."

I hung up the phone and looked around the room. Maybe I should treat myself out to a day of luxury?

Yeah, I think I'll do that. I got another two weeks before I have to report to Clark Atlanta, so I should enjoy the little free time I got and it'll help me get my mind off this shit with Zach.

Why the hell did Zach start work so damn early? Their summer session ends today.

"Whatever," I nodded my head as I picked up the phone to dial Nolan.

I'm sure my son would love to spend the day with me.

Yeah, that'll be great!

*****

Dorian

I was at work but my mind was elsewhere. I couldn't wait to spend some more time with Doug. I can't wait to run my hands across that hard ass body, suck on those nipples and play with his dick.

"Stop, Dorian," I told myself.

I could feel my dick starting to react.

I looked at the laptop on my desk. I needed to focus. The deadline for this project was just a week away.

"Ight, Dorian, get your head in the game."

Just as I started to look through some of the documents related to the project, my cell phone started to vibrate. I reached over and grabbed it. My eyes got wide when I saw the number. She was returning my call. Ms. Paula was returning my call!

Before I could answer the call, I was startled by a knock on my door. In walked my boss, Thomas Whitehead, and another younger looking black dude with a huge smile on his face.

Damn, the young dude was sexy as hell. Who the fuck is he?

My boss, Mr. Whitehead, was an older white man with a mustache. He was a little chubby with a bald spot in the center of his head. I really liked working for him, as he was a really good boss.

"Mr. Kierce," my boss said as he made his way over to my desk.

"Yes sir, Mr. Whitehead," I stood up.

"I have a new task for you," he replied.

I looked at him, over to the black dude, and then finally back to Mr. Whitehead.

The black dude was sexy! He was tall, brown skin and athletic with a low cut and clean shaven face. He had a killer smile with stupid swag. Even his dress code was on point.

My boss said, "This here is our newest hire. Mr. Matthews just moved to Atlanta and I am happy to have him on the team. I personally chose you, Dorian, to train Mr. Matthews. Is this something you can handle? I understand that you still have the other deadline. Will you be able to take care of both?"

I looked at the sexy black dude and then turned to Mr. Whitehead and said, "Yes, sir. I can handle both."

"Good," he smiled. "That's what I expected to hear from one of my top workers. Well, get acquainted. Please ask plenty of questions.

I'll be in touch."

Mr. Whitehead patted the black dude on the back and then walked out of the room.

Once he was gone, the black dude said, "He's something else."

I was taken aback at his Louisiana Cajun English. That shit sounded sexy as fuck! He was definitely from the New Orleans area. That accent was heavy!

"Yeah, that's just Mr. Whitehead," I smiled as I extended my hands. "I'm Dorian Kierce."

"It's nice to meet you, Dorian," he shook my hand. "I'm Kory. Kory Matthews."

46

Phoenix

Since today was CJ's last day in Chicago, he decided he was going to treat me for lunch. He was going on vacation tomorrow to Jamaica with this younger brother, Renzo.

While we were grabbing our food, we signed a couple of autographs and took some pictures with the fans. It was really a beautiful day, clear blue skies and not a trace of rain.

After everything died down, we grabbed our food and got back in CJ's car. We headed south on South Shore Drive and ended up at the South Shore Cultural Center. The Culture Center houses youth and teen programs, community art classes, dance studios, music practice rooms, and a visual arts studio. There are banquet facilities for rent for weddings, receptions, and meetings. There is a golf course that's still in operation, and is open to the public, as are the beach, picnic areas, gardens, and a nature center. This building was a treasure in South Side Chicago.

Thankfully, that many people weren't out as we sat down on one of the benches and began to eat. That breeze coming in from Lake Michigan was feeling good as fuck.

"Damn, you hungry like that?" I asked as he tore into his gyro.

After he swallowed, he said, "I ain't ate shit all morning. I told you I was starving when we left your house."

"Yeah, I see," I replied, taking a bite of my Philly Cheesesteak.

Our lunch was interrupted as CJ's phone started to ring. He looked at his phone and said, "Hold on one sec, this is Nehemiah."

"Ight," I replied as I sipped on my banana milkshake. I was just getting ready to talk about Keston. I sighed.

While CJ talked to his boyfriend, I turned my head to the left and watched the police patrol this center on horseback. I spotted another couple hold hands as they headed closer to the beach. They kissed before placing their towel down on the sand.

I sighed and thought about Keston. I thought about all the good times we had together. I thought about that trip to Daytona Beach when we were in college. I remembered taking him for a ride on the jet ski. I remembered that Keston was scared out of his mind, but he trusted me. He sat behind me on the motorbike and held onto my torso as if he was holding on for his life.

We raced with the wind. We had to be going at least 40mph on the motorbike. Kes screamed and held on tighter as I made sharp turns. I screamed in excitement as I was having too much fun. At times, the water was hitting my body with such force, it hurt. My heart was pumping faster than it should, but that was good. That was a good rush of adrenaline. We had so much fun that day. I'll never forget that trip for as long as I live.

As I came back to reality, I smiled and I blinked my eyes a few times. I turned to look at CJ. He was still caking with Nehemiah.

I never realized how much I still love Keston. That time spent with him was one of the best of my life. *What is Keston doing to me?*

I exhaled and looked over at CJ. He smiled as he talked to his dude. Another image of Keston appeared. There hasn't been anyone like him since him.

I cut my eyes to CJ; he was happy. I deserve to be happy, too. I deserve happiness. Above that, I deserve closure from that situation with Keston. What the fuck happened to our relationship?

I picked up my phone and scrolled down until I reached the number that my sister gave me last night. Without thinking too hard, I pressed the button to place the call. There was no dial tone. His phone was turned off.

His voicemail said, "You've reached Keston. I'm not at my phone. Leave me a message and I'll get back with you. God Bless."

As I prepared the words to say, I was stopped when the automated voice said, "The person you're trying to reach, mailbox is full. Please try back later. Goodbye."

I hung up, exhaled and took another sip of my milkshake. *Maybe next time*, I thought as I waited for CJ to finish his conversation.

*****

Zach

I was so happy that Dray wasn't home. I just wanted to get in and get out without seeing him. I looked around the closet for any other immediate stuff I might need. My mind was such in a rush. I knew I was forgetting something.

Once I grabbed the last few items, I placed them in the suitcase and made my way downstairs. I grabbed my keys off the counter and popped the trunk open. As I walked into the garage, I reminded myself that I had to do this.

After I placed the suitcase in the trunk, I realized I didn't have my phone. I closed the trunk and ran back in the house, upstairs to the bedroom. I grabbed the phone off the nightstand and cut my eyes to a picture on the nightstand. We looked so happy back then. We were happy back then.

I sighed and said, "I have to do this. I have to."

I turned around and headed out of the room. As I closed the room door, I stopped. "Oh, fucking great," I exhaled. I heard the side door leading to the garage close. Dray was home. I took a deep breath, exhaled and headed downstairs. When I walked into the living room, Dray was sitting on the couch looking at some mail. I said, "Hi."

"How are you?" he asked, cutting his eyes to me.

"I'm good."

He stared at me then said, "I want to apologize for last night. I was wrong. I should not have put my hands on you. I would never hit you, Zach. I had no intent on hitting you. I just wanted to get my point across. I just lost myself for a moment."

"Dray, can I tell you a story?"

"Please, take a seat."

"No, it won't take long."

He just stared at me.

"Remember when I met you, I had this roommate named Kyran."

"Yeah, I remember the dude who kept fucking with you."

"Well, I never told you this but, one night when you were up in New York for your Rolling Stone internship during Spring Break, he attacked me. Kyran knocked on my door. When I opened it, he started calling me faggot a million times then he starting hitting me. We got into a huge altercation. Our other roommate, Anthony, broke it up. My face was all fucked up."

"Why didn't you ever tell me this before?" he asked upset.

"Because you would have killed him, Dray. It's as simple as that."

He didn't reply.

"Anyway," I continued. "After that fight happened, I called Dwight and he helped me get out of that situation. Remember when you came back to Tallahassee, I moved in with you shortly thereafter."

He nodded his head in agreement.

"Dray, when you put your hands on me last night, all that shit came rushing back to my mind. All those memories that I had flushed out of my head, all the rage, all the hurt, all of it was back. That was one of the reasons why I left. I had to get out of here. I know that wasn't your fault and I'm not blaming my leaving last night on you, but I had to get away. When I tried to sleep last night, I had nightmares that this dude was trying to kill me. When I got to work today, I Googled him only to find out that he is in prison for a number of charges ranging from robbery to aggravated battery with a deadly weapon. He is due to be released next month, on my birthday."

"He is not going to hurt you, Zach. He probably doesn't even remember you."

"Nonetheless," I continued. "I just need to go away for a few days."

"Where are you going?"

"I need to spend some time alone to evaluate my life, evaluate this relationship and figure out the next step I'm supposed to take."

"Zach, you don't have to do that. We can work this out together."

"Dray, this isn't about you anymore. This is about me. This is about me getting myself together. If this thing we have," I said pointing back and forth at the both of us, "is going to work, I need to figure this out. I need to do this alone."

"Zach, don't do this," he pleaded. "You know where this is going to go if you leave."

"That's not true," I said.

"Yes, it is and you know it."

"Dray," I stared him in his eyes. "Regardless of how you feel, I've got to do this. I've got to do this for me."

I walked over and kissed him on the cheek.

"Where are you going? Will Dwight be there?"

"I'm going to a hotel, Dray," I said as I made my way towards the side door.

He said, "Zach, we can get counseling. Don't leave. I love you." When I got to the side door, he called out my name. I turned to him and he said, "Zach, do you hear me? I love you!"

I paused as I let the words marinate into my brain. I stared at him for a few seconds and then said, "Dray, I'll call you."

I headed out of the door.

I felt a little bit more liberated with each step. I knew I was making the right decision.

As the garage door opened and I backed out of the driveway, I took a deep breath and exhaled.

I have to do this for me.

I have too...

47

Zach

Stretched out on the plush hotel bed, I reached over and grabbed my cell phone to check the time. Hopefully, Dwight will be here any moment now. I don't want to be late. I know he said he had to take his mom back to Macon so he was probably stuck in the I-75 traffic.

Tired of watching this Olympic swimming shit in Rio de Janeiro, I grabbed the remote and stared to flip through the channels. Somehow, I ended up on MSNBC. I smiled and shook my head as I thought of Dray.

I could hear Dray saying, *"I don't see how you follow this political shit. "It's the same shit over and over and over again."*

The image of J. Nehemiah Reed, II – a fellow FAMU Rattler Alum, a Harvard law school graduate and the incumbent governor of my home state of Florida – was positioned on the screen.

"We have breaking news," the anchor said. "Senator Fitzgerald's campaign team has leaked her top three short list of potential vice presidential candidates. From what we understand, Governor Reed is at the top of the list. Can anyone say they are honestly surprised about this?"

"He has high rewards but he has high risks, too," a pundit said.

"Quite frankly, I think he is too young and will eventually get overlooked," added another.

"Well," the anchor cut. "The governor is of legal age to run for president, so technically he isn't too young."

"No disrespect to the governor," a different republican pundit interjected, "but I don't think he is politically ready to possibly be the next Vice President of the United States, or God forbid, President. This is Sarah Palin all over again. Frankly put, Senator Fitzgerald only has him on the short list because he can rally up the African-American vote."

The anchor said, "I think that's a dumb statement because as a whole, African-Americans generally vote democratic so that doesn't help the senator. Governor Reed is on the short list because having him on the ticket can help get the younger voters to come out and vote and more importantly, having Reed on the ticket puts the state of Georgia into play for the democrats. Reed grew up in Atlanta and his father is—"

"YOOOO BIG Z!" I heard Dwight yell as he burst through the hotel door.

I cleared my throat and jumped off the bed to greet him.

"What are you in here doing?" he asked.

"Watching this stuff on Nehemiah," I flipped off the TV.

"Yeah, I heard he could be vice president," Dwight said. "Do you know how crazy that would be? A Rattler in the White House?"

"I know," I shook my head at the possibility. "It doesn't even seem real."

"Oh, it's real," Dwight said as he looked at his phone.

I sat down on the bed.

After he replied to his text message, Dwight said, "Do you really want to go? You don't have to go. They'll understand. We can get something to eat, some drinks and just chill out in the hotel like old times."

I can think of a time of when I was in a hotel with Dwight and liquor was involved, we had sex.

Naw, I won't be doing that.

"What?" Dwight asked. "Why are you looking at me like that?"

"Nothing," I stood up to put on my shoes. "Yeah, I want to go. I can use a few drinks to clear my mind. I just want to get out for a little."

"Ight then," Dwight said as he sent another text. "We can do that." After he put his phone down, he said, "How did everything go with Dray?"

"It went," I sighed.

"You got everything you needed from the house?"

"We're not breaking up, Dwight. I just need a few days to clear my mind."

"I know," he said stood up and grabbed his keys.

"Dray was upset but we'll get through this."

"You know if you were with me, you wouldn't be going through all this stuff with Dray."

Before I opened the door, I turned to Dwight and said, "But you've cheated on everyone you've supposedly loved. Naw, I think I'll pass on that."

He just stared at me.

"Well, c'mon, Dwight," I said as I walked out of the hotel room, "Let's go."

*****

Keston

I was on the interstate talking to my other best friend, Raheim Tyms, who was also Zach and Dwight's band brother. Raheim was now on the FAMU band staff.

"Are you ready for the new football and band season?" I asked.

"You just don't know how excited I am," Raheim replied. "It's been a long summer."

"I can imagine."

"We're expecting a nice freshman band class this season," he said. "We've really put the hours in and did some major recruiting. Kes, I can't tell you how many homes I've sat in to explain to concerned parents that their child will be safe at Florida A&M University. You know after Robert passed, everything changed. All the parents ask the same questions, too. I get so tired of explaining everything we've done to ensure what happened to Robert never happens here again."

"Wow."

"Yeah, man," he sighed. "But at least things are finally starting to get back to normal after Robert's death. Can you believe this November will mark five years?"

"Time waits for no one," I added in disbelief that the five year anniversary of his death is months away.

"Ain't that the truth," he said. "It's been rough but things are working itself out."

"I can't wait to see the band, Raheim."

"I can't wait to get started. Just three more days until we get this thing kicked off. But enough about this stuff, how is everything going with LaRon?"

"He's trying to settle down with me."

"WOW! That's major. I told you I liked him," Raheim said.

"Yeah, he's cool," I sighed.

"Hold up. What's wrong? I can hear it in your voice."

"I've been thinking about Phoenix. I can't get my mind off Phoenix."

"Kes, that shit was damn near a decade ago."

"It was nine years not ten—"

"I said damn near a decade," he replied.

"Same difference," I said. "But I can't get my mind off Phoenix. I fucked up, Raheim. I fucked up big time."

He said, "Well, Phoenix is a thing of the past. Chances are Phoenix has another life now, so you can sit there and ponder over what could have been with Phoenix, or you can get serious with LaRon Copeland, one of the top wide receivers in the NFL. The choice seems pretty easy to me. I'm just saying."

"I know," I sighed. "I like LaRon and all and he is really a good guy, but something is missing. I can't put my fingers on it, but something is missing. I had a dream about Phoenix a few nights ago. I don't know why but I get this feeling that we will cross paths soon."

"If you say so, Keston," Raheim said in a suspicions tone. "I'm all for true love, but don't let this good man pass you by because you're worried about some shit that happened damn near ten years ago. Why did y'all break up anyway—and don't give me that DT shit. There has to be more to it than that."

"It's not important," I replied as I arrived at the restaurant. "Let me get at you later.."

"Ight, Kes. I miss you, I love you and I can't wait to see you again."

"I miss you, I love you and I can't wait to see you again, too. Take care buddy."

"Call LaRon," Raheim got in before he hung up the phone. "Bye!"

48

Dray

Taking a page out of Zach's playbook, I decided that if he can do it, I could do it too. I should get away for a few days to clear my mind and reevaluate this relationship, reevaluate my position in this relationship. He's doing it, why can't I?

I love Zach but I can't continue to get strung along with his games. So, with that in mind, this is exactly why I'm here.

After I rang the doorbell for the second time, I received a text message. While I was replying to the message, the door flew open.

"Dray, what are you doing here?" she asked.

I smiled. She just stared at me. I said, "Are you going to let me inside or are you going to keep me standing out here?"

"Sorry," she smiled. "Come inside."

As soon as I walked inside, she said, "I ordered a pizza for dinner. You are welcome to stay for dinner."

"Thanks, but I'm ok," I looked around. "Where's my son?"

We walked into the living room and she yelled, "NOLAN! COME DOWNSTAIRS!"

As I waited for Nolan, I replied to another text message. A few seconds later, I heard his footsteps. When I turned my head, he was running across the hall. As soon as he saw me he yelled, "DAD!"

We embraced with a hug. I looked over at Natasha and she was smiling.

"Dad, what are you doing here?" he asked.

"I got a surprise for you."

"REALLY? WHAT IS IT?"

"It's a surprise," I said.

"Dray, what's going on?" Tasha asked.

"Nolan, go pack your bags."

"Ok. Where are were going?" he asked.

"Just go pack your bags," I smiled.

"OK!" he yelled as he ran up the stairs.

As soon as he was out of the picture, with an attitude, Tasha said, "Where the hell are you taking my son?"

"On a trip," I said as I read and replied to my text message.

"Where and when are you coming back?"

"Sometime next week."

"SOMETIME NEXT WEEK? ARE YOU CRAZY?" she yelled.

My phone went off again. I looked at the message. I laughed in response to the message and somewhat Tasha's reaction. I said, "Calm down. We're only going to New York. I miss my home."

Relieved, she said, "Oh, ok. You miss New York already? You just left."

"DAD!" Nolan yelled as he leaned over the rail. "How much clothes should I pack?"

"Enough for at least five days," I said.

"OK!" he ran off.

Tasha turned to me and said, "You're not thinking about moving back to New York are you?"

I shrugged my shoulders. My phone was vibrating again.

As I read the message, she said, "OH, MY GOD, DRAY! WHO ARE YOU TEXTING? That is rude as hell, texting while you are trying to hold a conversation with someone else."

I turned to her and chuckled.

"What's so funny?" she asked. "I asked you a question."

"You're funny," I shook my head. "If I told you who I was texting, you wouldn't believe me anyway. So, in my mind, it's useless."

"Whatever," she rolled her eyes.

This was the Tasha I knew—full of attitude. "On that cue," I said. "I'll go back to the car."

"That's not necessary."

"Yes, it is," I replied. "Tell Nolan to hurry up. We've got to catch our flight."

"What about dinner?" she asked. "I already ordered pizza."

"Tasha, I'll get him something on the way," I cut as I reached into my pocket and pulled out a twenty and handed it to her. "This is for your troubles. I'm sorry for the short notice and I'm sorry you've already ordered dinner. That should compensate you for dinner. Tell Nolan to hurry up. I'll be in the car."

I turned around and headed out.

"Dray?"

"Bye, Tasha."

*****

Dorian

I placed my phone down on the counter and smiled. I loved talking to Doug even if it was via text message. I really like this dude.

Realizing that I needed to finish dressing, I walked into my room and grabbed my shirt. I looked at myself in the mirror and smiled. Tonight was going to be very interesting.

The vibrating phone caught my attention. I saw the name and answered, "Sup Brandon?"

"What are you doing?" he asked.

"Finishing up," I replied.

"I bet my last dollar, yo' ass is standing in the mirror," Brandon said.

"No, I'm not," I replied, as I looked at myself one last time in the mirror.

"Nigga, you're lying," he laughed. "You're always in somebody's mirror."

"Whatever Brandon," I walked out of the bathroom looking as fresh as ever. "What time are you heading over there?"

"In a second," he replied. "I just got to give Micah something first, so I'm waiting on him to get home. He said he was around the corner right before I called you."

"Y'all not about to fuck are you?" I asked. "Because if that's the case, I can chill out a lil bit longer at my spot."

"No," he laughed. "We're not about to fuck."

I shook my head as I sat down on my bed.

"So do you think *he's* coming?" Brandon asked.

"We shall see. I extended the invitation this afternoon and he said he'll stop by, so only time will tell."

"He's kinda sexy though."

"Kinda? He is sexy," I replied.

"Ain't you supposed to be talking to Doug or whatever his name is? You can't be looking at the new boy."

"I just got finished texting Doug," I replied. "We ain't official so I can look at whoever I want."

"You're a mess," he laughed.

"I get this vibe that Kory gets down," I said.

"What makes you say that?"

"Intuition. You know what else? I've seen him before."

"Sure you have," Brandon joked. "Let you tell it, you've always seen someone before."

"I'm serious," I replied. "I'm good with faces. If my memory serves me correctly, when I was at school at Cookman, we went up to Jacksonville one night to go to the gay bar."

"Let me guess, you saw him in there, right?" he sarcastically replied.

"Ummm, yeah," I said. "I'm not crazy. We had a conversation. He was with some other dude with dreads. I'm not crazy. I don't go to the gay bar often, so I think I can remember when I've met someone. This shit has been bugging me all day, ever since I started talking to him at work. I'm not crazy, Brandon."

"You are aware we were in college some seven, eight, nine years ago, and I'm supposed to believe that of all the people you encounter on a day-to-day basis, you remember him?"

"I ain't crazy," I said.

"Yeah, whatever, DK," Brandon said. "Micah just walked in the house. I'll text you when I'm leaving."

"Ight," I hung up the phone.

I ain't crazy. I know I saw him at the gay bar.

*****

Zach

The ride to the bar was pretty silent. I can imagine Dwight was still stunned over my statement at the hotel. I don't regret what I said; I meant it. The truth of the matter is that he has cheated on all of his lovers.

I looked over to Dwight. I've seen that look—the look of deep thought— planted on Dwight's face a lot over the years.

As we edged closer to the bar, Dwight turned down the radio and said, "So that's how you feel?"

"Dwight, what are you talking about?"

"Your statement at the hotel. That's how you feel?"

I exhaled.

He continued, "So you won't be with me because you think I'm gonna cheat on you?"

"Actions speak louder than words, Dwight. And your actions over fourteen years says a lot."

"But isn't Dray cheating on you now?" Dwight asked. "So it's ok for him to do it but you scorn me for it, even though I would never cheat on you."

"I was upset, Dwight. When I told you that last night about Dray, my feelings were all over the place. I've had a lot of time today to sit and think. Dray wouldn't cheat on me. He wouldn't do it. I came to the conclusion that I figured he was guilty because I was guilty. You do remember it was me who cheated on him with you."

"Zach that was a long time ago."

"But does it make it right?" I asked.

"So if Dray is the upstanding citizen as you are painting him to be, why are you sleeping at a hotel? Why aren't you at home with your man?"

I just stared at him.

"You don't have to answer," he said. "We both know why you're at that hotel."

We arrived at the bar moments later. As soon as he parked the car, I exhaled.

"What Zach?" Dwight asked.

I turned to him and in a matter-of-a-fact tone, said, "I'm going to tell Dray."

"Tell Dray what?"

"What the fuck do you think, Dwight? This secret is killing my relationship. I can't do it anymore."

"You know you can't do that, Zach."

"Why can't I?" I asked. "This is my life and my relationship with the man I love is hanging on by a string and a lot of it is my fault. Yes, he has something to do with it too, but this is on me, Dwight. That one night with you has haunted me for a long time. I have to tell Dray. He already suspects we're fucking anyway."

"I'm working on getting a divorce from Lexi. I can't have that shit coming back up to fuck me over. Besides, Zach, that was our secret. That was something shared between me and you—no one else."

I thought about Keston. Dwight would kill me if he knew Keston knows about our night of passion. I exhaled.

"Just come be with me, Zach. We can build a life together, me and you, the way it is supposed to be."

I looked at my phone. Kes had just sent a text saying what table he was at in the bar. I turned back to Dwight and said, "Dwight, let's enjoy our night, ight. Kes is waiting."

Before we got out of the car, he said, "You know I love you."

"I love you, too, Dwight. You know that."

He smiled.

Moments after we entered, we were escorted off to the left and towards the back over to the booth with Keston.

"Hey, y'all," Kes said as he placed the menu down.

"Hey, Kes," I sat down.

Dwight greeted him and then sat down next to me.

After we placed our drink orders, Kes and Dwight began to engage in a conversation about college football. I looked over the menu trying to decide on what I wanted to eat.

"OH SHIT!" I heard that familiar voice say. "HE'S REALLY HERE!"

I looked up and smiled. I pushed Dwight out the way so I could embrace Kris. After we gave each other a brotherly hug, we took our seats.

"Hey, Kes," Kris said.

"How are you, Kris?" Kes replied.

"Freshman bruh," Dwight smiled. "What's up?"

"You know how it is, just trying to make it," Kris said.

This is why I wanted to move to Atlanta. Words can't describe how it felt to be around my three closest friends. Even though it's only been a few minutes, I haven't felt this good in a very long time.

Dwight said to no one in particular, "This is much better without the husband, wouldn't you agree?"

I sighed.

"Dray was here?" Kris asked.

"The last time we came here, Zach invited him to tag along," Dwight said.

"Wow. I know that was awkward," Kris laughed. "It probably didn't turn out very well."

"It sure didn't," Kes said as he looked at Dwight and then over to me. "He and Dray got into it a little bit."

"Enough about Dray," I interjected. "Please."

Kris turned to Kes and said, "Something's never change."

"Ain't that the truth," Kes replied as the waiter came over with Dwight's pitcher of beer and my Blue MotherFucker cocktail.

49

Dorian

Brandon can't be on time for anything. I swear he is going to be late to his own funeral. That stems from that upbringing he got in the FAMU Marching '100' band. They are so undisciplined and just ratchet. That's half the reason why their band got in all that trouble when that boy died. That director had no control. I'm so thankful my college band director didn't allow that mess. We knew the importance of being disciplined and it showed in our half time shows.

Damn, I miss my band. I miss being a drum major for the great Bethune-Cookman University. Those were some of the best years of my life.

A few minutes later, I saw Brandon pull up. As he approached me, I said, "You're a member of the '100' through and through. Just undisciplined and can't ever be on time. Just ratchet."

"Hold up, nigga," he stared at me. "Don't do it to yourself. Didn't you want to be a part of my band, too, but settled for Cookman? Don't do it to yourself. Don't hate on us because our directors allowed us to have fun. Don't hate on us because our directors treated us like adults. Don't hate on us because our directors gave us freedom."

"Umm, hmm," I said as we approached the entrance door. "That same freedom that you speak of is what got the blood of that boy permanently stained on your program. That same freedom is what got y'all asses in trouble. Your band program is forever tainted."

With an attitude, Brandon turned to me and said, "Don't go there, ok. Let's just enjoy our night."

We were escorted over to the right side of the restaurant. The waitress came and took our drinks.

"I see yo' boy ain't here," Brandon said.

"Give him some time. He'll show up."

Right on cue, my phone started to vibrate. I smiled.

"What?" Brandon asked.

"This is him calling. I answered, "Hello?"

"What up Dorian, this is Kory. I just parked and I'm about to head inside. Is Brandon there?"

"Yep," I said as I told him where we were sitting.

"Cool. See you in a sec," Kory hung up.

*****

Zach

While we sipped our drinks, the boys spent a lot of time talking about sports. I was listening, but I was thinking about Dray.

Was I making the right move? If I tell Dray what transpired between Dwight and me, things will never be the same. Some stuff is better left unsaid. Maybe I should just keep quiet. I seem to be good at doing shit like that anyways.

When I zoomed back in on the conversation, Dwight said, "So, yeah, I went and saw the attorney today."

"WHAT?" Kris said.

Kes and I looked at each other and then turned our eyes to Dwight.

"Yeah," Dwight said. "Lexi has no idea that I'm thinking about this divorce."

"Man, Rozi and I have had some rough moments, but I never thought about divorce," Kris said.

"I can't do it anymore," Dwight said. "I've had enough of her and her tactics. If I would have listened to a couple important people in my life, I wouldn't have married her in the first place."

"Excuse me for butting in," Kes said. "So why did you marry her?"

"He married her because she was the mother of his child," I cut.

Kes looked to Dwight for approval.

"Basically," Dwight said. "I thought I loved her. I thought by doing this I could erase certain feelings that I had inside of me. I thought marrying her would heal me, but it didn't work. The only positive thing that came from the marriage was my three kids. The day I married her, I did right by her. I tried my best to be the best husband and father I could be. Lexi and I just don't mesh. She knows it and I know it. Then this thing that she's got going on is a deal breaker. Not many people know about it, but I can't have that on my conscience. I won't have it on my conscience."

If what Dwight told me was true, Lexi does have a serious issue that needs to be addressed immediately.

"What does she have going on?" Kris asked.

"It's not important," Dwight replied. "But just know that today was the first day of the rest of my life. So what's going on with you, Kris? How are Rozi and the kids?"

"Everything is going well," Kris said. "The twins are getting big as hell. They're bad, too. Damn, I hope I wasn't that bad when I was a kid."

We all laughed.

"You have a beautiful family," Kes said.

"Thanks, Kes," Kris replied. "When I was flying back to Atlanta earlier this week from one of my business trips, I had the craziest memory."

"What?" Dwight said.

Kris turned to me and said, "Do you remember our freshman year, after our first game of the season down in Miami."

"Yeah," I said.

"Do you remember what happened when we got back to Tally?" Kris asked.

"No," I shook my head.

He laughed and said, "Even though I didn't know you were the roommate, you were supposed to be gone."

"OH SHIT!" I burst out in laughter realizing the story.

"I think I know where you're going," Dwight said.

"Hell, I want to know," Kes eagerly stated.

Kris laughed and said, "Well, it was this dude I was talking to on the DL. We had been messing around and shit. Anyway after the first game, he said that his roommate was gone for the night."

"And I was," I cut. "That was until Chaz had to go to hospital because Xavier was sick."

Kes continued, "Anyway, so I'm in the room with the dude,

getting some ass when the door opens. The light flips on and Zach is standing right there. Zach turned out to be the roommate."

"WOW," Kes said in amazement. "Zach caught you fucking his roommate?"

"Yep," Kris laughed.

"And then here comes Dwight's eavesdropping ass at practice the next day," I shook my head.

"Dwight was good for doing shit like that," Kris said. "Dwight, you were nosey as fuck!"

"Whatever," Dwight added. "But speaking of that, I saw Micah a few weeks ago at Walmart."

"Micah was the roommate?" Kes asked.

"Yep," Kris said. "He ended up being my boyfriend. Those were good days."

"They were the good days," I added. "Life was so easier back then."

"Ain't that the truth," Kris added.

"Wait," Kes said. "Excuse me for being slow, but Zach, isn't Micah the dude you told me about that had the drug problem that almost got y'all evicted?"

"Yep," I shook my head. "That's him."

"And that was your boyfriend?" Kes asked Kris.

"Yep," Kris replied. "You know what else?"

"What?" Kes asked.

"The person Micah cheated on me with when we were together is the mother of my children and the woman I'm married to now," Kris said.

"Wow," Kes said.

"Crazy ain't it," Kris laughed as our main dishes arrived at the table.

"Crazy doesn't begin to describe it," I sighed.

*****

Dorian

It felt good to have Kory join us tonight. He really fit right in. We immediately jumped on the topic of sports. We left that topic and started to talk about the job. The more we sat and talked, the more I realized that Kory was the dude I saw in the club. I ain't crazy.

"So," Brandon said as he sipped on his drink. "Tell us more about you, Mr. Kory."

Kory smiled and said, "What do you wanna know?"

"What are you advertising?" Brandon asked.

Kory chuckled and sipped on his drink.

"How did you get to Atlanta?" I asked.

"Well, I'm from Baton Rouge."

"Did you go to Southern University?" Brandon asked. "That's one of our good rivals."

"HELL NAW!" Kory said. "I had to get away from Louisiana."

"Where did you go?" I asked.

"I played football in high school and college. I ended up going to UCF."

"The University of Central Florida in Orlando?" I asked as I looked at Brandon.

"It's only one UCF that I know of," Kory laughed.

"So tell me this," I said looking to Kory.

"What's that?"

"While you were down in Orlando, did travel around the state?"

"Yeah," he smiled. "Those were great times. My frat brother and I was all over the place."

"You ever go to Jacksonville?" I asked.

"Yeah, a few times," he said as he stared at me. "Why?"

"Just wondering," I replied as I smiled internally.

Kory looked to Brandon and said, "You said Southern University was one of y'all rivals. What school did y'all go to? Jackson State? Grambling?"

"You got life FUCKED UP," Brandon said. "I went to FAMU!"

Kory laughed and said, "Oh, ok."

"DK went to Bethune-Cookman," Brandon said.

"Over in Daytona, right?" Kory asked.

"Yeah," I nodded my head as I stared at him.

"Why you keep looking at me like that?" Kory asked me.

"Just thinking."

"About?" he asked.

"I'm from Orlando and I feel like I've seen you before. That's all."

"Oh," he smiled.

"When did you graduate from UCF?" Brandon asked.

"I actually didn't finish there," Kory said. "I left there in 2007 and went back home. I took some time off but ended up finishing my degree at LSU."

"Why did you leave UCF?"

"Some personal stuff, family stuff, you know how it is," he replied. "I worked a few years as a teacher and then went back to school for my MBA. I left Louisiana and moved to Dallas. I had a job back in Dallas but got tired of it, so once I secured the job here in Atlanta, I packed up and moved."

"How long have you been in Atlanta?" Brandon asked.

"A little over a week now."

"You got kids?" I asked.

"Naw," he laughed. "It's just me."

"You married?" Brandon asked.

"Naw," he laughed again. "It's just me. Are y'all this inquisitive with everyone you meet? Or is it just me?" He took a sip of his drink.

"It's just you," Brandon joked.

Kory chuckled and said, "I see."

Soon after, our food arrived. I was happy because I was ready to eat!

I was also happy because I knew he was he dude from Jacksonville. I know I ain't crazy.

This nigga is gay.

50

Keston

This night was very interesting. I've been observing the interaction between Zach and Dwight. I was so oblivious in the past, but now everything makes perfect sense.

I can't believe their relationship went over my head all these years. Here I was thinking they were just really close best friends, but there is really something there.

I look at Dwight and I see the way he looks at Zach. I look at Zach and I see the way he looks at Dwight.

Zach is in some deep shit. Zach explained the situation he and Dray is in now and how Zach is taking some time to "clear his mind."

Poor Dray.

I don't know how he deals with this, knowing that the best friend has feelings for your lover. Man, this is crazy.

If this was a perfect world, then I guess Zach and Dwight would be together, but the world isn't perfect.

I know one thing—Zach better fix this shit before more people get hurt. Zach is playing a very dangerous game and if he isn't careful, it will have some dire consequences.

Very dire.

This is exactly why I suggested Zach come to my condo. He doesn't need to be in that hotel with Dwight. Nothing good can come of that.

Nothing.

*****

Dwight

I'm very observant and Keston knows something. It's just the way he has replied to certain things I've stated. It's the way he looks at Zach. It's the way he's been looking at me. It's the way he basically made Zach agree to come to his condo instead of going back to the hotel. It's like the pieces of the puzzle finally came together for him tonight.

I don't know what Zach has told him, but I hope it wasn't our secret.

If Zach told Keston our secret…

You know what, I'm not gonna even think that shit. Zach wouldn't do that.

He fucked up once by telling Will. He wouldn't do it again.

I know he wouldn't.

I'm tripping. I know I am.

*****

Zach

While we ate our food, they continued to engage in conversation. As much as I wanted to get my mind off Dray, I couldn't.

My phone started to vibrate and it was Dray sending me a text. He sent, "I'm on my way to NY. I guess I'll be back sometime soon."

I stared at the message.

New York? What the fuck?

"Something wrong?" Kris asked as he looked at me.

"Huh?" I looked over to him.

"Seemed like something shocked you," he said. "Everything ok?"

"Yeah," I forced a smile. "Everything is cool."

I took a sip of my drink and Kris said, "I can't wait to see the band."

Dwight ate more of his food and then looked at Keston.

"I was thinking," Kris said.

"About?" Dwight asked.

"I was thinking maybe we all can go down together for the homecoming weekend."

"That sounds good to me," Dwight smiled.

"That's cool," I said.

Kes said, "Homecoming falls on our bye week this year, so I'm down. The only other game I'll be able to attend is the first home game and the game in Mobile."

"Well, you know I'm always down for a trip to Tally," Dwight stated as the waiter came to check on us. "Just give me the dates so I can make arrangements."

"Me too," Kris interjected.

"Since you mention that," Kes said. "I spoke to Raheim right before I came here."

"Really?" I said. "How is he?"

"He's doing well. He's really excited about the season."

"That's what's up," Kris said. "I'm so happy for him. When we were freshmen, I always knew he was going to be something special. His talent on that saxophone is amazing."

"Did he finish his doctoral stuff yet?" Dwight asked.

"He said he's in the final stages of writing his dissertation. So he hopefully successfully defends it and graduates in December."

"That's what's up," I said. "Tell him to hit me up if he needs any pointers. I know how stressful that process is."

"That's right, Dr. Finley," Kris smiled. "Help your fellow brother."

"Whatever, Kris," I smiled as I shook my head. "But I can't wait to see the band too. Pre-drill should be staring soon."

"Yeah," Kes replied. "Raheim said that it starts in a few days. He says they are expecting a huge freshman class this year."

Kris shook his head.

"What's wrong with you?" Dwight asked Kris.

"Just thinking about how that night changed everything. The night of November 19, 2011 changed everything! Who could have imagined something like that happening?"

Dwight exhaled.

"Yeah, I'll never forget when I found out," I said. I pointed to Dwight and said, "We had just talked to Rob earlier that day before the game. We saw him outside the stadium. He looked so happy. I was happy for him. After all these years he was finally a FAMU drum major. Who would have thought that was the last time we would see him alive?"

Dwight shook his head.

I continued, "I remember the first time I met Rob."

I paused as all the memories flooded my mind.

"What happened?" Kes asked in relation to our fallen drum major.

"It was spring 2004. I had stopped by Keli's room to get something from him and Rob was in there. Keli introduced us and said that Rob had just transferred from Clark Atlanta and was coming to Pre-drill to join the band in the fall." The waiter returned with our drinks. When he was gone, I said, "There were a few people in the room and after Keli introduced us, we immediately hit it off. We began talking like we were old friends. He told me then, in that initial conversation, that he wanted to be a FAMU drum major. I asked him what instrument he played and he said clarinet. I laughed and told him that if he wanted to be a drum major in our band, he needed to drop the clarinet and pick up the saxophone or something."

"Why?" Kes asked.

"Because our director had it out for the clarinets. They were always on his hit list."

"Ain't that the truth," Kris laughed. "They were always getting kicked out the band. Doc didn't have it with those clarinets. Our clarinets were of a different breed. Before I joined the FAMU band, I always thought of clarinet players as some weak ass, fat ass, sorry ass, lazy ass women. Not at FAMU. Those chicks, and dudes, were on some other type shit. I don't know what cloth they were cut from, but you just knew not to fuck with the clarinets. You always prayed for their freshmen. The clarinets didn't play that shit. They're crazy I tell ya'. They were crazy!"

I laughed and I continued, "I kindly explained that to Robert and he told me that he was going to be a drum major and he was going to make it playing the clarinet. I wished him luck, but in the back of my mind I knew it was never going to happen."

"Obviously, you were wrong," Kes said.

"I know right," I laughed. "He worked his way up the ranks of the band until he finally got the position."

"He was one determined dude," Kris added.

Dwight didn't say anything.

"That day in Keli's room was the start of a really good

friendship," I said. "We talked about a lot of shit. I really miss him."

"So how did you find out about his death?" Kes asked.

"After the Florida Classic game against Bethune-Cookman, Dwight and I went to get something to eat and drink. We went back to the hotel and got fucked up. I needed that release because that doctoral shit was kicking my ass. Early that Sunday morning, my phone kept ringing. I was pissed off because I was trying to enjoy the rest of my sleep. After the phone wouldn't stop, I finally answered and it was Jared:

"Are you sitting down?" Jared said.

"It's seven in the morning, what do you want?" I asked with attitude.

"I'm serious," he replied. "This is serious, Zach."

"What's up?" I sat up in the bed.

"Robert died last night."

"Robert who?" I asked as I was immediately awake. There was only one Robert that I knew and it couldn't be that Robert.

"Robert Champion, the drum major."

"Don't play with me," I said as I started to pace around the room. Dwight had awoken.

"I'm not playing. Omar called me. It's all over twitter and it's on Facebook. Champion is dead."

"Don't play, Jared," I said as Dwight started to look at his messages. After he read the first couple of messages, he looked at me with wide eyes open.

"I ain't playing, Zach. They fucked up. The band fucked up big time."

"Don't tell me he died from some hazing shit," I pleaded. "Please don't tell me that, Jared."

"He died doing The Bus."

"Oh, my God," I panicked. "Don't say that. Please don't say that. Don't tell me he was trying to cross Bus C."

"I ain't lying, Zach. That shit is all over. Everybody 'bout to get fired. His family 'bout to get paid. Somebodies children are about to go prison. We done, man! The band is history...toast... a thing of the past. Nigga, we're done! They went too far. They went too fucking far this time!"

"Jared, let me call you back," I said. I couldn't take that dramatic shit right now, much less any speculations. I'll wait for the truth to come out.

"Ight, man. Pray, Zach. Pray for everybody. God bless Robert Champion and God bless Florida A&M University," he hung up the phone.

I looked at Kes and said, "I called you when I got off the phone."

"Yeah, I remember that," he said. "When I first heard that a drum major died, we were in the club early that morning, but I thought that shit was a joke or something so I didn't take it serious until you called me. I had no idea it was hazing related."

"That entire ordeal bothered me for a long time," Kris said.

"In regards to what?" I asked.

"The media," Kris said. "I am not condoning hazing, but why did we have to be the image of hazing? There were two other hazing deaths in 2011 before Robert passed. One was at Indiana and the other was at Cornell. That was the fifth death—count 'em…the FIFTH person to die in Cornell's school history because of hazing. Why wasn't their president asked to resign? Why wasn't Cornell on CNN every fucking night? People wanna act like this was the first time this has happened in this country. Get real. Again, I'm not condoning what happened, but my God, get off our dick. I understand he died and I am sorry about that, but the school didn't kill him."

"No, the school didn't kill him," Kes said. "But let's be real, the administration knew it was a serious problem."

Kris said, "You can't watch grown folk twenty-hour hours a day. How many times had Doc spoke to us when we were in the band about hazing? What is he supposed to do? When he finds out you are participating in that shit, he kicked your ass out—point, blank, period. End of discussion. You were guilty until proven innocent. It ain't like the shit happened on campus in the middle of practice. Hazing typically happened off campus in the wee hours of the morning. The band staff can't monitor you at your house. In this case, the band was dismissed for the night. They were supposed to be eating dinner and enjoying the last night of the football season, not crossing kids on a damn bus! Hell, the buses should have been locked. How did they even get back on the bus?"

"This is exactly why I don't speak on the subject," Dwight said.

"Why?" Kes asked.

"Because I speak in reality. My stance is very unpopular," Dwight stated. "No disrespect Keston, but Kris, Zach and myself were in the band and we know how the shit goes. Maybe the media and the general public didn't know, or doesn't know how it happens, but we all know better."

I took a sip of my drink as Dwight said, "Not diverting the blame because the people who did it are in some serious trouble, but my issue with that entire fiasco was when exactly was Robert going to take some of the blame in that shit? His parents were painting him as a victim. I understand he isn't with us anymore, but he was no victim. He was a participant. I know it's harsh, but it's the truth. He was a participant. There is a difference. For example, if a group of people broke into your home to rob you and they killed you in the process, you are a victim. On the other hand, if you are part of the group of people who broke into someone home and the homeowner ended up killing your ass, you are a participant in the crime. Let us not forget, hazing is a crime and what they all did was illegal, which is why criminal charges were filed and punishments were handed out against those who aided in his death. His parents irked my nerves talking about 'my son would never do something like that. That wasn't Robert.' I wanted to be like 'ma'am, I guess you don't really know your son.' That wasn't the first time he got his ass beat to be part of something. Crossing Bus C was not his first illegal organization, so please spare me." Dwight shook his head and said, "This is what I don't understand about him. He was 26. If he was 17, 18, 19, my stance might be a little different. But we all know how it is when you're a freshman in the band and you want to be a part so bad, you'll do anything. But Robert was no freshman. He was 26 and a drum major."

I said, "It's easier for us to think like that now because we're older, Dwight. You don't know what kind of pressure he was under."

"Because we're older?" Dwight replied. "And he wasn't older? C'mon, Zach, that's bullshit and you know it. Even if the freshmen didn't know better, he knew better. At 26, you know what is right and what is wrong. What the fuck you doing letting some pussy ass niggas in the band put their hands on you, especially when those same pussy ass niggas wouldn't dare step to you in your face on the street. I was a drum major in the band and you got life FUCKED UP if you think a motherfucker was gonna try to cross me to say I can ride a bus. Get the fuck out of here with that bullshit! Nigga, I own these buses. You ride if I say you can ride. I'm the drum major. I run shit in this band, not some bitch at the bottom of the totem pole. And then to find out these other motherfuckers on that damn drum major squad had crossed that shit, too, was a disgrace to the legacy of the past FAMU drum majors and I was deeply hurt. What the fuck are they doing? My question is when the fuck did this start happening? When did drum majors start allowing some random niggas in the band to put their hands on you? Nigga, you're a drum major. You stand at the top. I just don't get it. When I was a drum major we didn't play that shit. I think about the drum major squad when we were freshman with Chaz, Ian and the other seven of them. Y'all know I didn't like Chaz personally, but he was damn good drum major. They demanded their respect. You just knew better. You just knew not to fuck with them. They had that killer mentality, no pun intended. You saw those niggas and you got intimidated. That was like the drum major squad I was a part of. When did shit go wrong? When did random niggas start running the band? Why submit to these fools? I don't get it. I just don't understand."

"Maybe he did it because he wanted the respect of his peers," Kes added. "Maybe that was really important to him. You never know what people would do when their back is against the wall."

"FUCK THAT!" Dwight said. "RESPECT? If they didn't respect your authority before, what the hell make you think they gonna respect yo' ass now? What logic does that make? They got a free ass whopping at your expense and they still gonna fuck with you. This shit is so stupid."

"C'mon, Dwight," I said. "Don't act brand new. Don't forget we got our ass beat to be a part of our section."

"Yeah, we did," he nodded his head. "We were stupid lil 18 and 19-year-old kids, too. After that shit was done, you quickly realized how stupid you were and you didn't submit to that bullshit again."

"That is true," I said.

"That's the other thing," Kris said. "People laugh at me when I say there is no hazing to be a part of the FAMU Marching 100."

"Kris, someone is dead," Kes said.

"I'm aware of that," he said. "But my statement is true. The only thing required to be a part of the band is to finish pre-drill, come to practice, earn a spot, march your games and when you march off the field at the Florida Classic, you are in the 100. Nobody is hazed, physically anyway, to be a part of the band. All the hazing comes from the extra shit you choose to do. Nobody forces you to do anything you don't want to do. Everybody has a choice. Everybody. Look at Randy."

"Wow," I said as I thought about our long lost freshman brother.

Kris continued, "If you remember, from day one of pre-drill, Randy showed that he wasn't down with that shit. Remember we didn't want to be late to the field so we left the café without eating breakfast. He stayed and ate. When we got to the field our section leader, Quinton, fucked with him for a few minutes and then pretended like he was kicking him off the field, but only to tell him to come back. When we were in Cincinnati and we were offered our first drink of alcohol, Randy didn't take a shot. What happened to him? Nothing. When Randy said he wasn't giving up his money, what happened? Nothing. When Randy said he didn't want to go through none of that extra shit, what happened to him? Nothing. ABSOLUTELY NOTHING! Yeah, we may have argued with him and he and Dwight even got into a fight in Cincinnati, but what families don't argue and fight? Yeah, he was alienated from the rest of us, but that was the choice he made. Ultimately, what happened to Randy? Nothing. Not a Goddamn thing. He marched his games and he was a member of the '100' just like you, me and everybody else who wore the Orange and the Green. For whatever reason, we chose to make that decision to submit to our upperclassmen. Nobody forced us to do anything. Even then, we knew that shit was wrong, but we did it anyway. Doc always peached against it. But we still did it anyway. University officials told us what could happen—hospitalization, expulsion from the university, jail time, lawsuits, even death—but we chose to get in those cars and go to those off campus houses and get beat. We made that decision, the exact same way Robert walked into the hotel, changed out of his uniform into regular clothes, had a conversation with his roommate, who was first year drum major like him, walked out of that hotel and made his way to that bus. He did he because he wanted to, for whatever reason he wanted to cross that bus."

"Not to mention that none of that stuff is sanctioned by the university," Dwight said. "All of it is illegal."

"Ok, yeah he got on the bus with intentions to cross, but he didn't deserve to die though," I cut.

"I didn't say he did," Kris said. "That's not what I'm saying."

"Well, I think all of it is wrong and it's sad that someone had to die because of that shit," Kes said. "The dirty little secret of the '100' has been exposed. My mama used always said nothing will stay in the dark forever. EVERYTHING eventually comes to the light."

Kes looked at me and then to Dwight.

Dwight said, "Well, what I'm saying is supposedly he was supposed to be this great anti-hazer. My question is, if he knew what was going on that bus, why did he watch two other people cross the bus before he started his process? He watched that girl and fellow drum major roommate cross the shit. C'mon now. Spare me. If he was so against hazing why didn't he tell someone? Why wasn't Dr. Hunter or Dr. Burton informed? If he was really about stopping the hazing, as his mother claimed a million times on TV, he would have told Doc. That's what he would have done and this shit could have been avoided."

"So why didn't we stop it? I asked. "We all knew what happens in the band and we all turned a blind eye to it. Why didn't we do something about it?"

Kris said, "Because as wrong as it is, it was just the way it was. That's just the way it was. As alumni, you know what you went through and you know what the new kids were going through. It was those traditions that tied us all together. Even though each section is different and had their own rituals, we were tied through that stuff. It's the band we came into and it's the band we left."

"It was going to happen to someone," I said. "If Robert stopped it, ok, it spared his life. But someone was eventually going to die and I'm just being real. Doc had just kicked 30 people out of the band before the classic for hazing, and yet even after the threats from the administration two days before said dooms day, people still participated."

"Would you say the band was out of control?" Kes asked.

"That's a good question," Kris said. "I don't know, but I do know I feel bad."

"Why?" Kes asked.

Kris said, "I feel bad because, like Randy, everyone in the band doesn't partake in those illegal activities, but everybody in the band got a bad rap for it. The entire band got suspended for the actions of a few. What about the people who did the right things? What about the people who followed the rules?"

Kes added, "Not to mention the university president lost his job. The band director was basically forced to retire, or he was going to be fired. Other band staff members lost their jobs. The band was gutted and after the suspension, basically forced to start over from nothing. People have criminal records and one person is in prison. The school was placed on probation from our accrediting agency. Although not the sole factor, but the hazing contributed to the enrollment decline. Morale at the school was low. The school took a beating in the national press. I'm not even gonna talk about the coverage in Florida. The governor's office stepped in and did investigations. The Florida Department of Law Enforcement did investigations. The school got sued by his parents. Everything got messed up because of the actions of a few. But through it all, we were still ranked with the best colleges in this nation. We were still ranked as one of the top HBCU's. We've rebounded. It's been five years and we still have work to do, but things are turning around."

I turned to Dwight and said, "You said a lot about Rob's mother tonight, but what if that was Brennan or Dominic or God forbid your precious Chloe who was lying in a casket, to a hazing ritual gone wrong. How would you feel if that was your child?"

Dwight said, "It is my responsibility as a parent to teach my children right from wrong. As a parent, it is my responsibility to let my children know and understand that they are loved unconditionally. As a parent, it is my responsibility to let my children know that they don't have to submit to peer pressure, they can still do things the right way and get respect. With that being said, I can't control my children when they're not in my presence. I can only hope that the values I've instilled in them will carry them through life. If my child died from hazing, I would be upset, but because I know what hazing is, I know better. Don't get me wrong, I'd be very upset but still, I would have to come to the realization that no one is kidnapped to be hazed. No one is forced at gunpoint to be hazed. That's exactly why I hate the word hazing. It has such a negative connotation. It comes across very one sided, when in fact there are two sides to hazing. When something happens it is always the hazer who gets in trouble, but when is the hazee, the person who submits to the shit, gonna get in trouble? Hazing is a two-way street."

Kris said, "If hazing is going to stop, we're going to have to raise strong kids that understand the importance of saying no. It's as simple as that. As long as someone is willing to submit to the pain, someone will be willing to administer it."

"Maybe if Nehemiah gets to the White House, he can somehow get the federal government to pass a national hazing law. Right now the shit is a joke with each state having their own laws on the topic," Kes said. "Nehemiah is a Rattler and Robert's death had to touch him in some way."

"Wow, that's interesting," I said. "I'll ask Dray to speak to Nehemiah about that."

"This question is to all of you," Kes said. "If you were given the opportunity to redo your band experience, taking Robert's death out of the equation, would you do the stuff you did your first time around?"

"No," Kris said.

"Hell no," I replied.

"You got life fucked up," Dwight said. "I would be a fool to do that shit again."

*****

Keston

We talked a few more minutes on the subject and then Kris said, "I love y'all, but I'm a married man and I've got to get home to my family."

We paid for our meals. Before we all departed, I excused myself from the table. I had to use the restroom.

I see why Dwight never said anything on the subject of Robert's death. He publicly voiced tonight, what many people I knew thought internally, but was always afraid to say because it was an unpopular opinion and the man was dead.

I walked into the restroom and passed an older white male. Before I walked to the urinal, I checked out the bathroom. It is a bad habit of mine to do a quick glance to see how many people were in there. I could see two pairs of shoes in two different stalls. One was peeing and the other was shitting.

As I finished at my urinal, I zipped up and walked to the sink to wash my hands. I soon heard a toilet flush. I looked in the mirror to check the shoes and the person who was shitting was still in the stall. As the door unlocked, I stepped away and pulled down a paper towel to dry my hands.

When I looked back in the mirror, everything stopped. Our eyes locked and the memories and pain from that night filled my thoughts and the very fiber of my being.

I can't believe this. *Why the fuck was he here. Why the fuck can't I move?* We both stood there unable to move. I felt like I had no control over my body. In my head, I screamed, "Move Keston, MOVE!"

But nothing happened.

The last person I wanted to see was standing right there.

Kory Matthews was back.

51

Keston

As I stared into the restroom mirror, I suddenly felt like all the air was being sucked out of the room. My body was frozen. I couldn't move. I couldn't think. I couldn't do shit. I just stared at him in the mirror.

That couldn't be him. There was no way in hell Kory Matthews was taking up the same space as me.

We just looked at each other in the mirror.

I needed to go. I wanted to go. I couldn't go.

"Move, shit, move, Keston," I told myself.

Nothing happened.

"Move, move, move," I said again to myself.

My body was stuck to the ground.

Maybe it wasn't Kory. Maybe my eyes were playing tricks on me.

"Keston," he said.

"Oh, fuck it really is him," I thought.

He started to approach me.

With a face as hard as a bag of rocks, I said, "What the fuck are you doing in Atlanta? Why the fuck are you in my space?"

The room felt as cold as death as he killed a part of me that I could never get back.

"Keston, can we talk?"

"Don't fucking come near me," I cut.

"Hey, is everything ok?" the person taking a shit yelled from his stall.

"Keston," Kory stuttered. "I, I, I just want to talk." He kept creeping closer to me. "Can we talk?"

"Get the fuck away from me," I said as I started to back away. "Stay the fuck away from me!"

"I'm not gonna hurt you," he said.

"HEY, WHAT'S GOING ON OUT THERE?" the strange dude yelled as I heard the toilet flush.

"You're fucking crazy and I don't want shit to do with you! I can't believe you're fucking here," I reiterated. "Just, just stay the fuck away from me. Leave me the fuck alone."

I backed myself into the door, turned around, forced it open and started to walk as quickly as I could over to the table. As soon as I saw Zach, Dwight and Kris, I grabbed my keys, stared at Zach and with coldness in my voice said, "Let's go, Zach!"

"Is something wrong, Kes?" Dwight asked.

"I SAID LET'S GO!" I yelled, "LET'S GO RIGHT NOW! FUCK!"

I rushed out of the restaurant. I know people were looking at me as if I was crazy, but I didn't give a fuck. I had to get the hell out of there.

*****

Zach

As Keston walked away, I turned to Dwight. Both he and Kris looked at me with the same look of confusion planted on their faces.

"What the hell happened in the bathroom?" Kris asked as we started to leave the table.

"I've never seen Keston act like that, much less raise his voice," Dwight replied as everyone on our side of the sports bar looked at us.

"I don't know but I guess I'm about to find out," I added.

When we got outside, Kris pointed and said, "I parked over here. I'll get at y'all later."

"Ight, man," Dwight said as we started to walk in our separate directions.

Knowing that something was wrong with Kes, we sped walked.

While walking very quickly, I saw Kes' car lights turn on, followed by the white light indicating that he had put the car in reverse.

"Yo, I think if you're staying with Kes, you better hurry up before he leaves you," Dwight stated.

"Yeah," I said as I started to jog. "I'll call you."

"LET ME KNOW WHAT'S WRONG WITH HIM!" Dwight yelled.

"IGHT!"

Just as Kes was starting to back out of the parking space, I made it to his car. He stopped when I knocked on the window. I heard the door unlock and I quickly got inside.

As soon as I was seated, he backed out and left the parking lot. Within a few minutes, we were merging onto coming traffic on I-20.

"Kes, what's wrong?" I asked.

He never replied. He just looked straight ahead as he drove faster.

"KES!" I yelled, starting to get nervous. "WHAT THE FUCK?"

He was driving like a bat out of hell.

Trying a different approach, I said, "You know Dray sent me a text that he went back to New York tonight."

Nothing.

No reaction.

It was as if he was in a trance. He never turned my way. He just looked straight ahead. I slowly reached over and grabbed my seatbelt.

If this were a suicide mission, hopefully I wouldn't fly out the window when we crash, because the way he's driving, we were definitely gonna crash.

52

Keston

I could hear Kory's voice. I could see that night from nine years ago. It was as vivid as if it just happened:

"You know, I never quite understood niggas like you," Kory said.

"Niggas like me?" I said, offended, over the music that was playing in the background of the apartment.

"Yeah, all y'all uppity ass niggas. Girly men. That's all Phoenix is attracted to. Girly men. What he needs to start doing is fucking with some real men!"

"Like you?"

"Yeah, like me," he admitted.

"So, that's it," I said. "We finally get to the root of the matter."

"What the fuck are you talking about?" Kory asked.

I said, "You like your best friend. That's where this is coming from. You like Phoenix sexually and he doesn't like you back. Yep. It makes sense now."

"WHAT? HELL NAW! DA FUCK WRONG WITH YOU?"

I said, "So, you're hating on the dudes he likes because he doesn't wanna fuck with you? So, you're fucking other niggas with Phoenix so you can see him in the nude, so you can be intimate with him even if it is with another dude in the middle. Kory, you are sick! So, you're trying to ruin your best friend's rep to me so you can fuck with him. Typical. And you have the nerve to call me a faggot—well, excuse me—me a girly man."

He stood up and said, "You're way off base, homeboy!"

"I ain't ya homeboy, muh'fucker," I said upset, as he walked into the kitchen and fixed another drink. "Don't get it twisted!"

"So, why are you fucking with Phoenix? That nigga doesn't look better than me!"

"I don't fuck with people like you," I replied.

"People like me? Da fuck that's supposed to mean?" he asked, appearing around the corner.

"Arrogant ass niggas like you! Trust and believe you ain't my type—and I say that shit with a straight fucking face. Looks ain't everything dude! And in my eyes, Phoenix is way more attractive than you, inside and out!"

"So, that's why you never fell for my advances, huh? I wasn't good enough for you? I wasn't sexy enough for you? I wasn't your type? I hate niggas like you. You think you're better than everybody else. Niggas like you who grew up privileged. Hell, yo' cousin 'round here driving a motherfucking BMW. Where they do that at?"

"Privileged? Kory, you're a fucking joke," I said, as I looked at my phone.

He said, "You walk around the training room like you run shit! All the niggas be at yo' table and shit. You fucking them niggas? You're just like her. You act all good and shit for the public eye, acting like you're innocent. Nigga, you ain't innocent! I guess I was wrong about you from the start. You're probably sucking off all the niggas from the team. That's why you ain't mad at Phoenix. Y'all are just alike!"

"You are out of line!"

"No, what's out of line is your faggot ass tipping off Cheyenne that I fuck with niggas! I know it was you who did that shit! I know punks like you. That's what y'all do. Always trying to out a nigga."

"You are so far off from the truth, it's sad. But ummm, you've got one more time to disrespect me bruh, calling me a faggot and a punk and shit."

He walked over to me and said, "OR WHAT? NIGGA YOU AIN'T GONNA DO SHIT! Yo' bitch ass cousin ain't here to fight your battles this time, nigga. You're a bitch! He's a bitch! Bitchassness must run in your family. And after all this time, you still ain't answered my MOTHERFUCKING QUESTION FROM THAT GOD DAMN PLANE! HOW WELL DO YOU SUCK DICK, NIGGA? NO—HOW WELL CAN YOU TAKE SOME DICK, NIGGA?"

I jumped up off the couch. I had that strange feeling in the pit of my stomach again. Time was up.

"Where the fuck you think going?" he asked, placing his cup down on an end table.

"The fuck away from here," I said.

"NAW, NIGGA! WE'RE NOT DONE TALKING!" he yelled.

"YOU'RE TALKING. I'M FINISHED!" I stated, as I reached for my keys.

"I SAID WE'RE NOT DONE," he yelled again, as he gripped me up.

"GET YOUR FUCKING HANDS OFF ME!" I yelled over the

music that was still playing as I kicked him in the nuts.

He yelled, as his grip loosened. As soon as I started to run, he ran, too. I didn't get very far as he grabbed me. He turned me around and I punched him in the face.

"YOU FUCKING FAGGOT!" he yelled, as he began to attack me back. I threw up the fighting stance that my daddy had taught Mario and me when we were kids. He threw a punch; I threw one back. I may be small, but I'm not a bitch by any means.

He threw another punch. I dodged it and snuck one into his stomach. The next thing I knew I felt his hands come across my face with such force it made me stumble.

I could feel the warm blood oozing down the side of my face.

I don't know where I got the strength, but I kept punching him back. He punched me, I punched him.

He was yelling. I couldn't make it all out. I could hear bits and pieces of profanity.

I was so mad, I cried. I was breathing hard. I was running out of breath. He was in a rage.

We were going around and around in the room.

Punch after punch after punch.

He was going to know I wasn't a wimp. I could defend myself.

And then things changed.

He hit me so hard that it knocked me to the ground. He reached down and grabbed me by the neck and then yanked me up against the side of the wall.

"YOU PISSED ME OFF!" he yelled in my ear.

"LET ME DOWN!" I yelled. I don't know where he got the strength to hold me up like this.

"Yeah, nigga," he said, as he kicked me in my nuts. "Talk that shit now! Got my face all fucked up and shit!"

"OUCH!" I screamed in pain. "LET ME DOWN! HELP! HELP!"

"I wanna see what got Phoenix so hooked," he said, staring me in the eyes.

"GET THE FUCK OFF ME!" I yelled. It wasn't like anyone could hear because the music was still playing.

He punched me again and then threw me to the ground.

The last thing I remembered was my body going towards the wooden coffee table.

When I came to my senses, he was—

53

Zach

By the grace of God, we arrived safely at Keston's condominium. He still hadn't said anything but I saw tears falling down his face.

"Maybe someone died," I thought. *"Maybe that's what happened."*

While we were on the elevator, I sent a text to Dwight that we made it safely. He asked what was wrong with Kes and I replied, "I have no idea."

When we entered the house, Kes said, "The guest room is yours." He placed his keys down on the kitchen counter. He went into his room, closed and locked the door.

I stood there for a moment, not really sure what to do. I felt like a kid scared to ask my mother for some money, afraid of what she would say.

After taking a deep breath, I knocked on the door and said, "Kes, you want to talk about it?"

He didn't reply.

"I'm worried about you. Talk to me, Kes."

I heard him crying.

"Kes? What is going on?"

With his voice cracking, he said, "It's some basketball shorts in the drawer you can use."

I stood there not sure of what to do. What I did know was he wasn't in the talking mood. We were supposed to stop by the hotel to get my car and clothes. I guess that is out of the game plan for tonight.

It was clear that Kes couldn't be alone tonight. I got ready to knock on the door to try to talk to him again, but something inside told me to just let him be.

We all need our alone time. I hope his mother didn't pass away.

I walked out to the kitchen and grabbed his keys. There was no way in hell he was going to drive that car again tonight.

While in the kitchen, I grabbed my phone and typed Dwight's name into it. Within a few rings, he said, "What up, Big Z?"

"You made it home yet?" I asked.

"No, why what's up? Is everything ok with Kes?"

"I don't know but I need a huge favor," I sighed. "Really huge."

"Sure, what is it?" he asked.

After I got off the phone with Dwight, I walked back over to Keston's door. He was still crying. Worried about him, I tried getting him to say something...anything...so I said, "I can't believe Dray went to New York. I just hope he knows because he left this isn't over."

Nothing.

Trying to get a response out of him, I posed, "What do you think?"

Still, there was nothing, just him sobbing and shit.

"Keston, this is the shit I'm talking about," I continued. "How does he just up and decide to go to New York and we have all this shit going on? Do you think this is a subtle way of him trying to control the situation? You know I told you he was very controlling."

I sighed.

Still there was nothing, so I said to myself as I slid down to the floor, *"I hope it's nothing crazy going on with Kes."*

I knew I wasn't gonna get a good night's rest. I knew it. This Friday night was done.

I sighed again.

Hopefully, it wouldn't take Dwight to long.

*****

Dray

New York, New York
Saturday, August 13, 2016

Nolan walked into the kitchen and said, "Dad, it smells really good in here. It woke me up. I love Saturday mornings, don't you?"

I smiled as I looked at my only child.

His shirt was off and he had on some red University of Georgia Bulldog basketball shorts.

"Did you get all cleaned up?" I asked.

"Yes sir," he replied.

"You woke up right on time then," I replied as I flipped the last pancake. "Breakfast is served. Get the jug of orange juice out of the fridge."

"Ight," he stated as he headed over to the refrigerator. "I really like New York. I think I might move here."

I looked at my son out of the corner of my eye. He was really growing up and his body was maturing right on time as well. I smiled to myself. My body matured at a very young age, too.

Nolan is one of the good things about being in Atlanta. I'm happy that I'll be there to help him when he needs help. I'm happy that I'll be there to take him to the gym, to play a game of basketball or to throw a football.

I'm happy, that, unlike myself, my son will have an active father in his life. I'm happy, that, unlike myself, my son will never have to want for anything.

My mom damn near killed herself working hard to make sure that I never went without. My mom laid the foundations on which I live today. I'm happy that I'm only miles away for whenever my son will need me.

"Mama sent me a text this morning," Nolan said as he placed the gallon of orange juice on the counter. "Asking did I get there safely, what we were doing, how she missed me. You know how she." He exhaled and shook his head.

I smiled.

He sat down at the breakfast bar and said, "Dad, I swear she is so overprotective. I love her but dang, she's got to loosen up some."

He shook his head. I forced a smile.

"She needs to let me grow up a lil," he replied. "You know, I'll be a grown man soon. What is she gonna do then, you know when I get married and have kids and stuff?"

"It's a good thing you got a very long time before that happens, huh," I smiled as I handed him his plate.

He smiled and then said grace for the both of us. When he finished grace, he began talking about school.

I stared at Nolan, amazed at how fast time flies.

I remember when Natasha had him. I remember how upset my mom was when she found out Natasha was pregnant. I remember how pissed off Natasha was when my mom and sisters wanted a paternity test for Nolan.

From the second I saw him, I knew he was my child. There was no doubt in my mind and the paternity test only confirmed that.

These are things Nolan will never know. There is no way in hell I'll let him find out that my mother and his aunts wanted a paternity test done on him. How would that make him feel if he ever found out the truth?

That's why when I look at shows like Maury, I can only shake my head. While it's very entertaining for us while we are watching, I've always wondered what kind of effect would it have on those kids when they are of age and they see their parents denying them on national television. That has to have some kind immediate effect on the child if they ever run across a rerun of the show or a clip of it on YouTube.

"Dad, why are you looking like that? What's wrong?" Nolan asked.

"Huh?" I stared at him.

"What's on your mind?" he asked after he took a sip of his orange juice.

"Just thinking about when you were a baby," I smiled.

"What about it?" he asked with eager emotions.

"Just how lucky I was that you were a part of me. I'm really the luckiest man in the world because you are my son. I love you, Nolan, and I'm really proud of you."

"I love you too, dad," he smiled.

There was an awkward moment of silence.

I started to eat my eggs and then he said, "What would you do if you have gay friends?"

"What?" I asked as that came out of the blue. "Where is that coming from?"

"I think one of my classmates is gay."

"What gives you that impression?" I asked.

"Just the way he looks at other dudes. Then we got a new guy that is starting school with us this year that I met at the mall and my old classmate who I think is gay, Elijah, is already friends with him. They're doing stuff that is very questionable. I don't know, dad, but I just know that something isn't right."

"So you think the old guy and the new guy is messing around?"

"Yep," he nodded his head. "That's disgusting and it ain't natural. How you gonna be 'round here messing with dudes and stuff and all these girls running 'round here. I'm happy I ain't gay and they better not bring that mess around me."

"So you have a problem with gay people?" I asked.

"I don't like it," he stated in a very strong tone.

"Why not?" I asked as I started to get nervous feeling in the pit of my stomach.

"I just don't. It ain't right. My mama has been telling me that stuff since I was a kid. When we go to church, Bishop Reed says the exact same thing. I'm very smart, dad. I pay attention and I listen to everything. I don't wanna go to hell and burn for all of eternity. Bishop Reed says being gay is the first way to get to hell."

"Are you done with your food?" I asked.

"Yep," he stood up. "Thanks dad, it was really good."

"I do what I can," I forced a smile.

He smiled back and said, "Well, I'll wash the dishes."

"You don't have to do that," I stated.

"Mama makes me do it back home. She cooks and I do the cleaning."

I smiled and said, "I'll take care of it today. You just go ahead and get dressed."

"Ok," he smiled as he ran off.

I stared at the empty plate and shook my head.

My son's dislike of gay dudes was to be expected, but how exactly do I deal with this? How do I make this right in his eyes?

First Zach, now this. Could my week get any worse?

54

Zach

Just like I imagined, I didn't get a good night's rest. After Dwight dropped off some of my clothes and toiletries, I fell asleep in front of Keston's door only to wake up in the middle of the night and headed over to the guest bedroom. My mind has been working overtime trying to balance this issue with Dray and now hoping that I can help my best friend through whatever it is he is going through.

My grandma taught me a good trick when I was younger. She used to say if you want people to get up on a Saturday morning, start cooking breakfast. People will try to ignore it but before long, the aroma of the good food will have everyone in the house getting out bed and making their way to the kitchen. This was my plan today.

Hopefully, Kes will come and talk to me about what happened last night from the time he left the table to go to the bathroom and came back pissed the fuck off.

After I showered and cleaned up, I headed over to the kitchen to start preparing breakfast. I know he will like this because Keston does not cook. Truth be told, I was very shocked to see that he actually had some food in here to cook. I did look at the expiration dates though.

He'll get in the kitchen every once in a while, but he hates standing over a stove. He'd rather spend his money eating out somewhere. That eating out stuff is cool but that shit is a drain on your pocket.

I wanted to talk to Kes about Dray, but I know that is really not an option now as he has his own thing to deal with—whatever that may be.

While I prepared breakfast, Keston joined me.

"Good morning, Zach," he said as he pulled up a chair at the island.

"Mornin' Kes," I replied. "How are you doing?"

"Much better than last night," he sighed. "You know you don't have to be in here making breakfast."

"I know I don't have to but I want to. There is a difference," I winked my left eye.

He smiled.

Seeing him smile felt really good.

"I'm sorry about last night," he said. "I really want to apologize for my actions."

"It's cool, but do you mind telling me what happened?"

He exhaled and said, "Is breakfast almost done?"

"Yep, I'm finishing up now."

When breakfast was done and the plates were fixed, we sat down at the dining table and Keston started to open up to me.

"Zach, last night I saw someone who I never expected to see ever again in life."

"Who?"

"A guy named Kory Matthews."

"How does he affect you? Was he an ex-lover or something?"

"No," he took another deep breath.

"Kes, what's wrong?"

"Zach, I need your word that whatever I tell you will stay between the two of us."

"You got it," I replied.

He took a deep breath then said, "First, I want to say that you are the first person in the world to know this information."

"The first?" I asked.

"The first and the only besides me," he said. "Qier doesn't know. Raheim doesn't know. My old best friend, Izzy, doesn't know. My brother, Mario, doesn't know. My parents don't know. I've held onto this information for nine years. And seeing Kory Matthews last night unleashed all those emotions I had buried deep inside of me. While I laid in bed last night, I asked myself if I wanted to tell you or continue to keep the information a secret. I decided that for my own sake and sanity, I needed to tell at least one person. And while you trusted me with your darkest secrets as it dealt with Dwight, I know I can entrust in you the darkest moment of my life."

"Keston, you're scaring me. What's going on?"

He ate a piece of his ham and cheese omelet, took a sip of his apple juice and then said, "Ok. This is my story."

*****

Dorian

I slept in later than usual today, but it was needed after last night. I had a blast with Brandon and Kory at the bar.

After the bar, Kory invited himself back to my place and we got fucked up even more. I don't know what happened last night but he suddenly was ready to drink himself into a coma. He followed me to the liquor store, purchased another bottle of Patron and then proceeded to get royally fucked up.

Something was wrong. I could tell he was drinking away his problems. I didn't mind though. He was sexy and that body of his was on point.

He left this morning and went back home. He said he would give me a call later to hang out if I wanted too, as he was looking for some new friends to kick it with in Atlanta.

Brandon sent me a text asking what happened, but nothing happened other than us drinking, talking about our lives and eventually going to sleep.

He slept in the guest bedroom.

Normally, I wouldn't let a strange dude in my house, but it is something about Kory that just makes my dick hard. There's something about him that made me defy all sense of logic.

Whatever.

Now, it was damn near one in the afternoon and I hadn't done anything productive. I hadn't heard from Doug today either and that was strange. Something about him is still a mystery to me. I can't put my finger on it, but it keeps me on my toes.

After I got cleaned up, I fixed something to eat to help cure this mild headache.

While sitting on the couch eating my sandwich, I saw a picture of my father and me.

I needed to get to Orlando to go visit him before it is too late. I looked at my cell phone. I know I needed to return that phone call, as she finally did call me yesterday when I was at work.

I grabbed the phone and held it in my hand. I exhaled.

I don't understand why my dad can't do this shit himself. He fucked up his relationship with Zachary, Zachariah, Zach, or whatever the fuck his name is. I didn't fuck up that relationship, he did, so why is he putting me in the middle of this mess?

Don't get me wrong, I would love to meet the dude, but I didn't mess up, my dad did. This is what I don't like about him. He always gets other people to do his dirty work.

"Whatever, Dorian," I sighed as I stared at the phone. "I guess I'll just wing it," I told myself as I placed the call.

Deep down inside, I hoped she didn't answer. I didn't want to talk to her.

Those fears were magnified when the phone stopped ringing and I heard an alto female voice say, "Hello?"

"Ummm, hi," I cleared my throat. "May I please speak to Mrs. Paula Finley?"

"Speaking?" she said with attitude, trying to figure out who was on the other end of the telephone. "How may I help you?"

55

Zach

It has been hours since Keston revealed his secret to me, and I've been floored ever since. How do you respond to something like that? What do you say?

As Keston explained how he and his ex-boyfriend broke up, I thought about my relationship with Dray. And while our situations are different, I realized that I don't want to end up like Keston. He still loves that ex-boyfriend, whoever he may be. And while I don't like the fact that Keston ended the relationship the way he did, I understand why he did it.

I know I have to fight for my relationship with Dray. I have too. I can't just let it end like this.

I do love Dray. I've always loved Dray. I love Dwight, too, but Dray is the man in my life and I know it needs to remain that way.

Kes dropped me off at the hotel to get the rest of my things, check out and get my car. Once I was done, I told him I would head right back over to his place.

While he seemed a little better on the outside, I know he was still hurting on the inside. And after what happened to him all those years ago, and having that dude just rise up from the dead last night, I want to be there so Keston wouldn't hurt himself. That was a very tragic situation and I don't want him to think he has to do something drastic to get those memories that he'd suppressed for so long out of his head.

When I was in the car, I took a deep breath and phoned Dray.

Within a few rings, he said, "Hello."

"Dray, how are you?"

In a mono like tone, he replied, "I'm ok."

"Why did you go back to New York?" I asked, cutting straight to the heart of the matter.

"Why did you leave the house?" he asked.

"Dray."

He sighed and said, "I left for the same reason you left, to clear my mind, to re-evaluate myself in this relationship. More importantly, I left to spend some alone time with my son. Speaking of that, he's here in the house now. Is there anything I can help you with?"

He sounded very agitated.

"Dray, listen," I replied. "I know you're busy and I don't want to keep you away from Nolan."

"What's up Zach?" he asked.

"I thought about what you said and I want to take you up on your offer for us to get counseling. I want our relationship to work."

"Zach, if you aren't going to be completely honest then we will only be wasting our time. I don't have time to waste, Zach, as I've wasted much of this year trying to read and understand you and your motives. I'm telling you, I'm tired Zach. I'm fed up and truth be told, at times I don't want to fight for this thing we have anymore. You've killed all the fight I have left."

"Dray, I'm sorry," I pleaded. "And I will be honest. I can promise you that. I will be honest. I want to make this work."

"Yeah, I hear you, Zach," he said. "Actions speak louder than words."

"I'm serious Dray and I'm sorry for all the pain I've put you through lately."

He held the phone.

"When are you coming back to Atlanta?" I asked.

"I want to spend some quality time with Nolan before his school year starts. I'll be back sometime within the week."

"Oh, ok."

"Have you returned home?" Dray asked. "Or are you still in the hotel?"

"I'm actually gonna stay with Kes for a few days to make sure he is ok."

"What's wrong with Kes?" Dray asked concerned. That was the first change of tone in his voice the entire conversation.

"I really can't talk about it Dray, but just pray for him. He really needs all our prayers right now."

"Damn, it sounds serious," Dray said.

"It really is."

"HEY, DAD!" I heard Nolan say. "WHERE YOU AT? I GOTTA QUESTION."

"Zach, I gotta go. I'll call you," he whispered. "I love you."

"I love you, too, Dray."

*****

TJ

I don't know why I waited until mid-afternoon to leave but now was better than never. Because of some special event at his company, daddy had to go to work today. He never goes to work on Saturday's but I guess there's always a first time for everything.

After I grabbed my headphones, I made my way downstairs. Ray was in his study looking over some papers. Even though the door was open, I knocked on it, catching him off guard.

"Hey TJ," he smiled. "What's up?"

"Ray, I'm about to go to the convenience store and probably walk around or something. I just need to get out of the house."

"Ok," he smiled. "Don't get into any trouble."

"I won't," I smiled as he put his attention back to his work. I stood there for a second and then said, "Hey, Ray?"

He looked up and said, "Yes, TJ?"

"I love you," I smiled.

He smiled really hard and said, "I love you, too."

As I headed down the road, I realized that Elijah and his family were back from their vacation. Elijah's mom, Ms. Genevieve is a teacher and they have to go back to work on Monday. The only sad part about that is that we only have one week left in our summer vacation and then it's back to school for us, too. I sighed.

I wasn't ready to go back to school. I liked having my days free with nothing to do. I liked chilling about the house without having to worry about doing homework or waking up early to go to school. I enjoyed sleeping in late. I was not looking forward to going to school, especially since I was gonna be the new kid.

As I continued onto the convenience store, I thought about my last encounter with Elijah and that girl. He was foul for that shit. He knew he was, looking at my dick and shit. We were supposed to be getting some head, not sneaking peaks at my body. That shit was a major turnoff.

In a number of ways, I'm kinda happy that they went out of town right afterwards. It allowed me to cool off. But still Elijah was wrong for that and he knows it.

After I got my bag of chips and a Gatorade, I headed back towards the house. As I edged closer to our place, I could see Elijah bouncing the basketball in the middle of the road. He had the goal up, too.

I shook my head as I was reminded that this was how I met him a month ago, playing basketball in front of his house. I saw him starting to smile as I got closer to him.

"WHAT UP, TJ!" he said with excitement in his voice. He embraced me with a dap like we were long lost friends.

"Sup?" I asked as I looked around.

"Nothing. Got back early this morning. My mom said that she wanted to get a few days of rest before she has to go back to work dealing with people's bad ass kids."

I shook my head as I took a sip of my Gatorade.

"But what's up with you though?" he asked. "You wanna get in a game right quick?"

"Sure," I replied as I sat my things down and engaged him in a game of basketball. Like I knew I would, I beat him 21-9.

"You always getting lucky," Elijah said.

"Boy, you gonna learn that ain't luck," I shook my head as I sat down on the curb. "That is all skill."

"So I talked to that girl again," Elijah said looking down at me as he dribbled the basketball from side-to-side. "She said she wanna get up with us again."

I looked around to make sure no one was around and then said, "Are you gay?"

"WHAT?"

"Nigga, you heard me," I replied. "You staring at my dick and shit when ole girl was sucking me up. Real niggas don't do shit like that."

"You got me fucked up!" Elijah said. "You got life fucked up!"

"Answer my question, nigga. Are you a fucking punk?"

"Whoa, shawty," he said taken aback. "Ain't yo' daddies two punks?"

I stood up in his face and then said, "What nigga? What was that? What?"

"You heard me," he said. "Callin' me a punk. You got two daddies who fuck each other in the ass. They the pu—"

Next thing I knew, my fist connected with the side of his face, then again and again until his ass was down on the ground.

"We ain't talking about them, we talking about you," I said as I stood over him. "And I better not ever hear you open your motherfucking mouth and call my two dad's punks again, you sissy ass, sorry ass, punk ass faggot!" I kicked him in the ribs and yelled, "Bitch ass nigga!"

And then I grabbed my shit and walked away unbothered.

Bitch ass nigga!

Part Five:

Getting Acquainted

56

Zach

Thursday, August 18, 2016

The campus was very quiet, but it was expected since no one was here. All the freshmen and new students were to arrive next week.

I kept coming to my office because it allowed me time to focus on this book I'm writing. This seems to be the only place in the world where I can concentrate.

I worked on the book for another hour or so before taking a break. I turned and looked out the window. And out of nowhere, an image of my ex-boyfriend, Eric McDaniel, appeared before me. Eric was also Chaz's cousin. Eric's sister, Rozi, is Kris' wife and the mother of his children. I swear these circles are too small.

The last time I saw Eric was about three or four years ago and he was in the last year of his residency. I remember I had to make a stop in Chicago to visit with my publisher. After the meeting was over, I had the rest of the day to myself so I decided to stop by a mall to do a little shopping and grab a bite to eat. While eating in the food court, I heard my name:

"ZACH?"

I looked around confused because nobody knows me in Chicago. And then I saw his face. And then I saw his new body.

"That can't be," I said to myself as I shook my head in disbelief.

"ZACH!" he smiled, as he stood in front of me. "Don't look like you've seen a ghost."

"Eric, what the hell happened to you?" I asked.

"You like the new look?" he smiled. "I've been working hard on this body."

I stared at his body. He was no longer the skinny, twenty-one-year-old dude I met back in 2003. This was a grown ass man, with muscles and shit. He was definitely on his grown and sexy vibe.

I swallowed on my spit.

Taking a page out of the LL Cool J playbook, Eric licked his lips then said, "What are you doing in Chicago?"

"I had a business meeting," I said, motioning him to take a seat. "What are you doing here and when did you get this body?"

He laughed and said, "I've been playing in the gym. But seriously, I'm doing my residency at a Chicago hospital."

We sat there and talked for at least another thirty minutes. Since my flight didn't leave until the next morning, and he was off for a few days, we decided to catch dinner and a movie that night. It felt great to spend some time with Eric and play catch up with our respective lives. Eric has always been the perfect gentlemen and that time in Chicago was no different.

We made a vow to keep in touch with each other but like most things in life, that died down. I thought about him earlier this year and when I tried to contact him, he had changed his number. I went looking for him on the various social media sites but it was to no avail.

I thought about asking Kris to get the number from Rozi but then I thought about Dray and what he would think if he knew I was going through all those hoops to get the phone number of my ex-boyfriend.

I realized it wasn't a good look, so I left it alone. If Eric and I were meant to talk on a continual basis, God would find some way for us to come back in contact with each other.

Sometimes I sit and wonder what could have been if Eric and I continued our relationship. What would life be like? That was a long time ago though. A very long time ago.

I walked back over to my desk and grabbed my phone. Dray had been gone for five days and we really haven't spoken other than through text message because Nolan is with him. I know Dray has to return soon because Nolan starts school on Monday.

Above all, I just know he better hurry up and get these counseling sessions started before I change my mind.

And that's on some real shit!

57

Tony

I sat in my car and looked at the sign. I ran my hands through my hair. I loved my hair. Did I really want to do this?

I grabbed my hair again. It was so long, so healthy, so beautiful. My hair was my pride and joy. I sighed and looked at the time. My appointment was now.

Ight, Tony. You can do this.

I wanted to cry, but I gathered myself and headed towards the shop. I walked inside and men were laughing and talking about sports. My eyes cut to the TV and SportsCenter was playing. I headed over to the main desk and told the receptionist, "I've got an appointment with Amanuel."

The petite young black woman typed something on her computer and then said, "Tony?"

"Yes," I smiled.

"Just go take a seat and he'll be with you shortly."

Raidon recommended this shop because this is where he comes for his haircuts. He's taken TJ a few times as well since we've been here in Atlanta.

I knew the dude in front of me was Amanuel based off the way Raidon had described him. He looked young, but he was sexy.

He reminded me of rapper T.I., although Amanuel's body had muscles. Amanuel had tatts all over him. He sported a Caesar cut and had a toothpick hanging on the side of his mouth.

I looked around the establishment and this shit was nice. One side was for the barbers and the other was a salon, with an option for a manicure and pedicure.

Once Amanuel was done with his client, he pointed to me and said, "You're Tony?"

"Yes," I replied.

"Ight. C'mon, Shawty," he stated in that heavy Atlanta dialect as he cleaned the seat of any excess hair. Some little kid came and swept up the hair from the floor.

I sat down and he extended his hands and said, "I'm Amanuel, nice to meet you."

"Same here," I said. "Someone told me you were the best in town, so I had to try you out."

He smiled and said, "I do what I can. But what can I do for you today? You getting a tape up?"

I exhaled and said, "Naw. I'm ready to cut it off."

In a nervous laugh, he asked, "You're going to cut off your hair?"

"Yeah," I said as I thought it through one last time.

"Ight. What kind of cut you want?"

"Brush cut."

"You want me to save your hair?"

"Yeah."

He chuckled and said, "Ight."

A few moments later, I realized there was no turning back as I felt the vibration of the hot clippers slicing through my hair like a knife to a stick of butter. I could cry.

"Why are you cutting off your hair?" he asked.

"It's just time."

"Feel ya," he said as he moved to the side.

The real reason deals with my job. With this new position comes a higher level of responsibility. I see how people look at me in my new job in the regional office. Even though my hair is always neat and in the best condition possible, I don't want or need anything that may cause *the white man* to demote me. I've learned that in corporate America, you've got to play the game by *their* rules.

I haven't told Raidon or TJ of my decision to remove my hair, so I'm looking forward to their reaction.

"How did you hear of me?" Amanuel asked.

"My homeboy brings my son over to get his hair cut."

"Who's your son?" he asked, as he looked at me. "I know all my clients."

"His name is TJ."

He stopped cutting my hair and stared at me and then a few

moments later said, "Oh, you do look like him. I can see it now. That's where I know you from. When you walked in, I was like I know that dude from somewhere, but ok, it makes sense now. TJ was telling me that y'all just moved down here."

"Yeah."

"Where'd you come from?" he asked, as he started back on my hair.

"Charlotte."

"Is that where you grew up?"

"Naw. I'm from Orlando."

"How'd you get to Charlotte?"

"I played football at FSU and then a few years after graduation I moved to Charlotte with a better job."

He cut off his clippers and stared at me again.

"What?" I asked, nervous.

"You played football at Florida State?" he asked.

"Yeah," I nodded my head. "Why?"

"HOLD UP, HOLD UP, HOLD UP!" he stared at me.

"What?"

"I knew I knew you," he said. "It wasn't from TJ, you're Tony Shaw. Man, that's wild, Shawty! The world too small!"

"You know me?" I asked.

"Not really," he said. "I know of you."

"Oh," I chuckled.

"I was down in school in Tallahassee when you got paralyzed in that game, only to find out that you had a heart condition and couldn't play football anymore," he shook his head as he begin working on my facial hair. "Man, you were on your way and then that shit happened. That was a biggest story in Tally for a long time."

"Yeah," I sighed. "That was a long time ago. Are you from Tallahassee?"

"Naw, Shawty," he looked at me in the mirror to check his work and then resumed on my face. "I'm from Atlanta. I went to FAMU for a few years and played snare drum in the band. I didn't finish because I ran out of money. Those out-of-state fees ain't no joke. Anyway, I came back home, got certified and got a job at a barber shop. Been here making good money ever since."

"You said you were in the band at FAMU?" I asked.

"Yeah for two years. The 2004-2005 school year and 2005-2006 school year."

"My homeboy was in the band."

"What was his name?" Amanuel asked.

"Zach."

"Finley?" he asked.

I smiled and said, "Yeah, that's him."

"Yeah, I know Zach. Well, I didn't know him personally, but I remember him."

As he walked around me, I said, "You look kinda young."

He laughed and said, "Good genes, Shawty. I just turned thirty last month."

"How long have you been cutting hair?"

"I started when I was fourteen. Then I started cutting hair in my dorm when I was at FAMU, you know, hustling, making that money. When I left school, I came back up here and got certified and got a job at a shop over in Decatur. Saved my money, shawty. Saved hard and then I got a loan. My sister could always do hair, but she went to school and got a business degree from Georgia State. And me and my sister got together and came up with the concept and opened this shop."

"This is your shop?" I said amazed.

"Yeah… well half of it is mine," he said. "My sister takes care of the salon portion of it."

"Man, that's what's up. Congrats, Amanuel."

"Thanks, Shawty."

As another barber came over to ask Amanuel a question, I looked at myself in the mirror and then put my head down in disbelief. It was really gone. My hair was gone!

After Amanuel put his finishing touches on my face and hair, we exchanged numbers.

"You can hit me up directly," he replied. "You know… to schedule you for your next appointment."

"Ight," I stated as I looked at the haircut.

It was looking good. He then gave me some pointers for my head now that my hair was a thing of the past. After he gave me my bag of hair, we exchanged daps, I gave him a tip and then paid my tab at the front desk.

As I walked out the shop, I exhaled.

This was the new me and I must admit it felt damn good!

*****

TJ

I felt bad, very bad. I haven't heard from Elijah since I punched him on Saturday. He usually calls or text me every day.

I really fucked up. I lost my temper.

I didn't mean to hit him, but he made me so mad that I wasn't thinking clearly.

Every day this week, I've been hoping that he would knock on the door or send me a text, but it's been nothing. With each passing day, I know that I need to go and apologize but I just can't get myself to walk out of the door to go do it.

I've been pacing around my bedroom all day trying to convince myself to just go apologize. I don't want to start school on Monday and not have any friends. Hopefully he'll still want to be my friend.

He just has to learn that the one thing I don't play about is my family. Say what you want about me, but don't talk about my family especially when they haven't done anything to you. Finally, after another hour or so of pacing, I took a deep breath and prepared to head out of the house.

As I walked down the road, I felt like I was walking into my death. Luckily, I didn't see any of his parent's cars in the driveway. When I stood at the front door, I took a deep breath and rang the doorbell.

"WHO IS IT?" I heard Elijah yell.

"It's me, TJ," I replied.

There was nothing.

"Elijah, man, open the door."

Nothing.

"Please?" I begged.

A few seconds later, he opened the door, looked at me and said, "What?"

"Can we talk? Please?"

"I can't leave. My sister is sick and taking a nap. What do you want?" he said agitated.

I exhaled and said, "Man, Elijah. I'm sorry about Saturday. I don't know what came over me, but I'm sorry. I really mean that."

He stepped out of the house, closed the door and said, "That shit was foul, TJ, and you know it."

"I know and I'm sorry. I want to be your friend and I don't want to fuck it up. I just lost my cool when you started talking about my parents. I don't play about my family. I love them too much to just let someone talk about them."

"I understand," he said. "And I'm sorry for calling them punks. You were calling me a punk and stuff and I just blurted it out."

"So we cool?" I asked.

"Yeah, man, we cool," he smiled.

I reached over hugged him and said, "Thanks, man." When the hug broke, I said, "You're cool, Elijah, and I like chilling with you."

"I like chilling with you, too."

"Man, I'm just being honest, bruh. I ain't gay. Yeah, my parents are but I ain't gay. If you like dudes, Elijah, I don't care. My parents are gay. I just want your friendship. I shouldn't have called you a punk, but you can be real with me. Ain't nobody but me and you and I ain't gonna judge you."

He just stared at me.

"I know what I saw that day," I stated. "You were looking at my dick. So what's up? You fuck with niggas?"

He stared at me, opened the front door looked around and then closed it back. I stared at him and then he nodded his head in agreement.

"Do you like girls?" I whispered.

"Naw," he nodded.

"Did you like me or something?"

"You ain't gonna hit me or nothing are you?" he asked.

"Naw, bruh. I just wanna know."

"Yeah. I'm feeling you," he said shyly.

"I ain't gay."

He said, "I know that now, so it's cool."

"I got some questions for you," I said. "Maybe you can help me understand my parents."

He chuckled.

"Do your parents know about you?" I asked.

"HELL NAW! Are you crazy?"

"Just asking. So have you messed with a dude before?"

"Yeah," he replied.

"Who?" I asked.

"You don't know him," he stated.

"Y'all had sex or just oral?" I asked.

"Sex."

"Wow," I said. "Man, let's go back to my place. I got questions for you."

"I can't," he said. "I told you my baby sister is sick and I gotta stay here until my mama or her husband gets back from work."

"Oh."

"You better be happy I lied for you," he said.

"What do you mean?"

"My mom was asking about my face and I told her I fell playing basketball. If she knew we got into a fight, she would have been at your house raising hell with your parents. I was mad, but I didn't want you to get in trouble. I was hoping that you'll apologize and you did, so we cool."

He smiled. I smiled.

"Let me get back in here before my sister wakes up. I'll get at you later, ight," Elijah replied.

"Ight, buddy," I smiled as we dapped each other up. "Thanks for not holding it against me and still being my friend."

He smiled and said, "I'll get at you."

"Ight," I stated as I headed back to my house, happier than ever that I finally got that conversation over.

It felt like a ton of bricks had been released from my shoulders.

58

Dray

Atlanta, Georgia

I was beyond pissed. I couldn't miss this dinner. I had already rescheduled once before and I couldn't reschedule again. If things were as planned, we would have been in Atlanta, but that damn weather fucked everything up.

Nolan and I were stuck at the airport in New York for hours because of bad weather. I am really cutting it close.

"Looks like mama is home," Nolan said. "I guess you gotta ask her now."

"I guess so," I stated as we pulled up in the driveway.

"I enjoyed myself," Nolan stated as I cut off the car. "Thanks for the trip."

"I enjoyed myself, too," I smiled as we got out of the car.

When Natasha opened the door, she embraced Nolan like he had been away for years. *Damn, it was only a week.*

"Thank you for bringing my baby back safely," Tasha said as Nolan looked at me and said, "Good luck, Dad." He carried his bags off into the house.

"Good luck for what?" Tasha asked. "What's going on?"

"Tasha, I need a huge favor."

"What?" she asked.

"I have a very important dinner that I have to attend in a few minutes. We were supposed to be back in Atlanta hours ago, but nasty weather messed up our flight."

"Ok, so what are you asking me?" she quizzed.

"I can't reschedule this dinner again and if I go all the way home,

I'll be late. The restaurant is about fifteen minutes from your home."

She just stared at me.

"I really need to use your shower and get ready here or I'll be late."

"Oh," she shrugged her shoulders. "I guess. I thought it was something serious. We have a guest bathroom that you can use. Do you need an iron or anything?"

"Yes," I nodded my head.

"Ok, I'll grab it. You can get your stuff and I'll have Nolan show you to the bathroom."

"Thanks, Tasha. You're a lifesaver."

*****

Dorian

I was listening to K. Michelle as I got ready for my date. The song was entitled, *These Men.* She was singing her heart out and she was speaking directly to me.

She sang, *"You see these men. They don't know nothing about love. One woman ain't never enough. What am I to do? You see, these men. Sho' do be messing around. Wifing all of these hoes around town. But I can't play fool. They don't know nothin', 'bout nothin', 'bout love. Pain, it's life. Oh, every time I try to find somebody to love me, I end up hurting."*

Tonight was the night. Even after almost a month of talking, Doug was still a mystery to me. If this thing we have was going to go any further, I needed some truth from him tonight.

I stopped and sang along with K. Michelle. *"They always on IG doing something, you know? They tryna get with her, they tryna get with him, hell, fuck all of them. You know cause at the end of the day, if it ain't gone go my way, I don't want to play no more."*

Over dinner, I planned to ask him some important questions. His response tonight, or lack thereof, was going to tell me if this would be our last meeting.

I think he is married, or at least in a relationship.

I'm not stupid.

I've tried to ignore it, but I'm not stupid. I know how the game works. Like K. Michelle said, *I can't be played fool.*

All the late nights/early morning meetings, the canceled or rescheduled dinner dates, his secretiveness, something has to give.

There is one thing I don't do and that is married men. I don't fuck up homes—whether if it's a gay home or straight home. Dorian doesn't do that.

I believe in that thing called Karma, and she will not come back to bite me in the ass. No sir, she will not!

I don't have time for men who want him, him and her, too. I'm too old for that shit.

So, tonight it is.

Either we'll continue on, or this will be our last outing.

*****

Dwight

I stepped out of the shower and exhaled. These were the final days of peace and quiet in this house. With school starting on Monday, Lexi left this morning for Savannah to go get the kids from her mother's home.

I looked at the time. I was cutting it close. I had to be at the restaurant soon. I was looking forward to this dinner. As I ironed my clothes, my phone started to vibrate. It was my brother. I answered and Ced said, "What are you doing?"

"Ironing some clothes, getting ready for dinner."

"I'm surprised you answered. I figured you'd be getting some sleep for work tonight."

"Naw, I'm off this week."

"You on vacation?" he asked.

"Naw, I told you that we started this new program at my job. We work seven days straight and then we're off for seven. We just recently started, but I like it so far. It only takes a day or two to recoup from the week, then the other five days or so are yours. It's like a vacation every other week."

"That's what's up," he said. "Who are you going to dinner with because Michelle said Lexi was going to Savannah to get my niece and nephews."

"I'm going to dinner with a friend."

"Zach?" Ced quizzed.

"Naw. Just a friend. A co-worker. It's nothing serious."

Ced said, "I talked to mama the other day and she said you went and saw the lawyer. Are you gonna get the divorce?"

"That's the plan," I turned the iron off. "Ced, let me call you right back."

"Why?" he asked.

"I'll tell you in a second," I hung up.

After I put on my basketball shorts and slid into my flip-flops, I grabbed my phone and ran downstairs. I got inside of my car and turned it on. Once I was comfortable, I phoned Ced.

"Ight," I said when he answered.

"Was that your friend calling?"

"No," I replied. "Nobody called. Is Michelle around you?"

"No," he said. "She took the boys to the park."

"You're not telling Michelle about my plans to divorce Lexi are you?"

"No, what would I do that for?"

"Your wife and Lexi are very good friends. Women have ways of getting information out of men."

"We don't talk about you, Dwight. Michelle knows better than to ask me anything about you as it concerns Lexi. I drew that line in the sand way back when y'all got married."

"Ight, just checking. But I had to call you back because I had to go get in my car."

"Why?"

"I don't trust Lexi. She could have the house wired or something. Women are far from stupid and Lexi knows something is up. I can tell. So I stopped talking on the phone at home about personal stuff. As far as I'm concerned, she could have her own lawyer, trying to set me up or something. I don't trust her as far as I can see her and I can't see her."

"Why are you really getting the divorce? It is because of her ways or is it something or someone else. I hear Zach is back in town."

"Ced, Zach is driving me insane," I confessed. "I love him so much, it's killing me."

"WHOA, THERE BUDDY! You're admitting it now? You love him now?"

"I admitted it seven years ago," I sighed. Images from our night together started to flash in my mind.

"You admitted it to Zach?" Ced asked.

"Yeah."

"Wow."

"Ced, I've got to get this off my chest. It's killing me."

"What's up?" he said.

"I don't know who I am."

"What do you mean?" he asked.

"This is part of the reason for the divorce, too. Yeah, I'm not happy with Lexi, but I don't know who I am. Who am I?"

"You're losing me, big bruh," Ced interjected.

"Ced, I'm about to tell you something and you can't tell a soul."

"You know what we talk about is our business."

I took a breath and said, "Zach and I had sex."

"Say what? Run that through me again!"

"You heard me."

"When was this?" Ced asked.

"Seven years ago."

"Wait… you got married seven years ago." He paused then said, "Wait a minute. The night of your bachelor dinner at the restaurant, you and Zach went back to the hotel afterwards. You didn't want a party, just a dinner. Did it happen then?"

"Yes, it did and I'm fucked in the head!"

"Y'all finally did it. Wow," he said in disbelief.

"Ced, that shit is the past. My mind fucked is fucked *now*! I don't know what to do."

"About what?"

"I don't know if it's just Zach, or am I really attracted to men. I don't know. Something inside of me wants to see what it's like to sex another dude not named Zach. Maybe then I can answer the question. But if I feel like if I have sex with another dude, I'd be cheating on Zach."

"Isn't Zach in a relationship?"

"Yeah."

"Do you think he's thinking about you when he's having sex with that dude?" Ced asked.

"I'd rather not think about him having sex with Dray."

"DAMN BRUH," Ced said shocked. "Zach got yo' ass whipped! He gave yo' ass one taste of some male-on-male sex seven years ago and your mind is all fucked up." He started laughing.

"Ced, this isn't funny. This is my life and I don't know who, what… never mind. Ced, I'll get at you. I've got to finish getting ready for my dinner."

"Hold up," Ced stated. "This dinner you keep talking about—is this with some other nigga? Is this dude a possible candidate? Are you trying to fuck him to satisfy your curiosity about your sexuality?"

"First off, I never said it was a dude, you did. I said it was a co-worker and I'll leave it at that."

"Umm, hmm," he chuckled. "Whatever, Dwight. I know you better than you know yourself."

"Bye, Ced," I hung up the phone.

When I got out of my car, I headed back into the house to finish getting ready for my dinner.

It was just a co-worker.

Damn.

59

Zach

The doorbell was sounding. I rushed over to the door and opened it. I smiled and let him inside. He dapped me up and I said, "You made it right on time. I just took the dinner out of the oven."

"It smells good in here," Keston replied, as we walked through the foyer. He said, "I know I told you a thousand times, but I really, really like this place."

We got washed up and I fixed our plates and brought them over to the dinner table. After a small lead-in conversation, I asked, "How has everything been?"

He said, "I still think about that night nine years ago, but I'm ok."

"Are you sure?"

"Yeah. I'm at a different place in my life now than I was nine years ago. I'm ok."

"So what happens if you see him again? What was his name?"

"Kory," Kes stated.

"Yeah, Kory. What happens if you run into him again? If you saw him at the bar, chances are he probably lives in Atlanta."

He ate some of his Caesar salad and said, "I've thought about it a few times, but I really don't know what I'd do. I think I reacted so strongly last week because it was so unexpected and it just brought all those emotions out of me. But being that I know he's around, I don't know what I'd do. I have no idea." He sighed and said, "That's old news. What's going on with you? When is Dray coming back?"

"I don't know," I shrugged my shoulders. "Sometime soon. I tried calling him earlier and his phone was turned off. Maybe he took

Nolan to a theme park or something. He really loves that boy, so I don't get upset when they're spending time together. It does make me jealous though."

"Why?"

I took a sip of my wine and said, "Because it makes me wish I had my father, Duane, in my life when I was a child."

"Is this related to that void you used to speak of?" Kes asked.

"Yeah. The one thing I've always wanted was a brother or a sister, and to know that I have one on my father's side of the family, and don't even know who it is bothers me. It's like the one thing I want most is somewhere on this earth and I have no way of getting in touch with him."

"What about your dad?"

"What about him?" I asked.

"Would you want a relationship with him?"

"I want a relationship with my brother. I just want to get to know him, at least meet the dude."

"Have you ever prayed on it?"

"I have," I sighed. "I pray every night that I'll meet my brother. I've been praying for ten years and I've gotten nothing. Sometimes I ask myself why do it. Why? But I can hear my grandmother saying that God works on his own time, things will happen when they are supposed to. So I just pray and leave it in his hands. I know that one of these days my prayers will be answered. That's how I was raised. That's what my grandma taught me."

"I wish I could have met your grandmother. She seemed like an awesome woman."

I smiled and said, "She was. I miss her so much, Keston. Not a day goes by when I don't think about her."

Our conversation was interrupted by the vibration of my phone. I looked at the name and shook my head.

"Is it Dray?" he asked.

"No, my mother," I motioned for him to hold on. I answered and she asked, "Are you busy?"

"A little. What's up? Is everything alright?"

She said, "I've been going back and forth for the past few days, trying to decide if I wanted to tell you."

"Ma, what's going on?" I stared at Keston.

"Long story short, a few days ago I got a phone call from someone who was trying to get in contact with you."

"Who?"

"I wasn't going to tell you because you don't need that drama in your life, but my husband made me realize that you're grown and capable to make your own decisions. And I agree. This is your decision to make."

"What's going on?" I asked agitated.

"You got a pen and paper handy?" she asked.

I walked into the kitchen, grabbed the pen and paper and said, "Yes."

"Take this number down."

When she finished, I said, "Whose number is this?"

"Dorian."

"Dorian?" I asked trying to figure out who was that. "Who is Dorian and how does he know me? I don't know anyone named Dorian."

She cleared her throat and in a stern voice said, "Dorian Kierce."

My body froze.

"Zach? Are you there?"

"Ma, don't play with me. This is Duane's son's phone number?"

She exhaled and said, "Yes. He wants to get in touch with you. I told him that I'd give you the number. If you want to call, call him. If you don't, just throw the number away. It's your decision. Personally, I don't think you need to be getting involved in that mess. You don't know who that boy is or what kind of game he's running. You can't trust people anymore. If I were you, I wouldn't waste my time. I feel like you are about to invite some trouble into your life, trouble you don't need. But that's your decision. You're a grown man, so proceed with caution. Let me go. I'll talk to you later."

I hung up the phone and stared at the paper. Keston came into the kitchen and said, "Is everything ok?"

I handed the paper to Keston and exhaled.

"Whose number is this?" he stared at me strangely.

"Dorian."

"Who is Dorian?" he asked.

"My brother."

His eyes got wide. I exhaled.

"This is amazing," Kes said. "We were just talking about this and look at that, God answered your prayers. Wow. Just wow."

*****

Dorian

I stared at Doug. Damn, he was sexy. I engaged him in conversation over dinner but in the back of my head, I was trying to build up the courage to start asking the important questions.

We had been here for about forty minutes and were well into our meal. His phone vibrated a few times during dinner but he quickly sent the calls to voicemail.

Again, caution flags were being thrown in my face.

"Why are you staring at me like that?" Doug asked. "It's like you're here but your mind is elsewhere. Is something going on?"

"Doug, who are you?" I asked.

"Excuse me?"

"Something about you isn't adding up. Is there anything you need to tell me?"

"No," he shook his head.

"Seriously, pretend to be me for a second," I said. "It's obvious you have a very nice job, but yet you work overnight. When you come visit, you're on your lunch break or on your way home when you get off work. Logic tells me that it's easy for you keep me on the side since I'm just a pit stop on your way home. Your lover wouldn't think anything of it. Then there are the constant canceled or postponed dinners and dates. Something about you just doesn't add up. Am I wrong? Tell me what I'm missing."

He started laughing.

"What's funny?" I asked.

"Are you done?" he quizzed.

"No, I'm not."

"Well, continue," he sipped on his drink.

"Doug, be real with me, are you married?"

"No."

"Are you married but separated?"

"No, I'm not married."

"Do you have a girlfriend?"

"No."

"Do you have a guy friend?"

"No."

"Are you in a relationship with anyone?"

"Besides God, no."

"Do you have children?" I asked.

"No. Is there anything else?" he asked.

"I'm confused. Either you're lying or you're lying. Somewhere in here is a lie. Something isn't adding up, Doug. I have two college degrees. I'm far from dumb."

"I have a couple of degrees myself," he smiled.

"Doug, I'm serious. I really want to see where this can go. I like vibing with you, but I don't want to enter into something built on lies. The worst thing you can do is lie to me. Is there anything I need to know about you that you haven't disclosed?"

He stared at me for a second and then took another sip of his drink. He exhaled and said, "Yes, there is something you should know about me."

"You weren't born a woman were you?"

"WHAT? God no," he laughed as he shook his head.

"Hell, I've gotta ask. We are in Atlanta."

He cleared his throat and said, "All that stuff about me is true. I'm not married. I don't have children. I don't have a significant other. That is all true. However, my name isn't Douglas."

"I kinda figured that much," I replied.

"Well, technically, it is, but it isn't my first name. Because of my profession, and in contrast, my sexual orientation, I have to keep my identity as private as possible. There is a lot on the line."

"So who are you?" I asked. "And what the hell do you do?"

"My name is Eric," he said. "Dr. Eric Douglas McDaniel."

60

Zach

Saturday, August 20, 2016

Since Dray has gotten back into town, things in the house have been really good. There hasn't been any arguments, no slick comments, no distance from each other. Maybe the few days we spent apart to *re-evaluate* our part in the relationship did some good. Maybe spending some time with Keston did some good. Maybe Dray going back to New York with his son did some good. All I know is right now, things are good and I like it that way.

On Monday, the first day of public schools start, and all the college instructors have to report to campus. Our first day of classes aren't until the following Monday.

Dray has been excited about teaching his first class. He's been asking me a lot of questions in regards to the teaching profession. Happy that he is happy, I've given him my honest opinions.

Since today was a Saturday and neither one of us didn't have anything to do on the agenda, we've both been lying on the couch watching movies. Laying inside of Dray's arms reminded me of the good days we shared in New York. We spent a lot of lazy Saturday's enjoying each other company. I miss those days. I miss them a lot. I sighed.

As the movie drew to a close, Dray removed himself from under me and said, "I'm thirsty. Babe, you want something to drink?"

"Naw," I smiled. "I'm ok."

He kissed me on the cheek and then made his way over into the kitchen. Damn, I love this dude so much. While in the kitchen, he said, "My sister said she wants to bring my mom over to see the new house."

"When?" I asked.

"I'm not sure," he replied as I heard the refrigerator close. "We gotta get our schedules worked out."

"Oh," I thought about the conversation with my mother the other night.

When Dray walked back into the living room, he took the old movie out of the Blu-ray player. As he grabbed the new movie, he looked at me and said, "Babe, what's wrong?"

"Nothing," I shook my head.

"Zach, what's going on?"

"It's nothing, Dray," I forced a smile.

He stared at me for a few seconds then said, "Does this have something to do with that phone call from your mom?"

"Yeah."

He walked over to me and said, "So what are you going to do?"

I sat up on the couch and said, "It's so strange, Dray."

"What's that?"

"I finally get the number to the man I've wanted to get in contact with for the longest and now it's just like what do you do? I don't know what to do. My mom and I don't always see eye-to-eye, but I do take her advice to heart. I know my mom doesn't want to see me get hurt. I know that. As she was telling me the other night about the phone call, I could hear the pain and worry in her voice. What if my mom is right? What if this dude is out to scam me or something? What if he has done his research and figured out that I have money? Why now? Why contact me now? What does he have to gain from this? Thinking about what my mom said, something about this does seem strange. How did he get my mom's number in the first place? It's so many questions."

"Personally," Dray said as he walked over and sat next to me, "I understand your concern and I understand your mother's concern. But look at it this way. As long as I've known you, you've always wanted to get to know your brother. You've prayed on it, you've cried over it, you've searched for him. Now, he's here. Maybe he is running a game, trying to scam you. Or maybe he's just like you. Maybe he's tried to get in contact with you. Maybe he's wanted to know his older brother. Maybe he wants a relationship with you. I understand your concern, Zach, but I think you should step out on a leap of faith and take that chance. That's what your grandma would tell you to do, right. Have faith the size of a mustard seed. Go out and take a leap of faith. The least you can do is meet the man and then try to make a decision. If you don't, you will beat yourself up over the missed opportunity. I think you should call the man. At the end of the day, it's your decision to make. Do you listen to your mom and stay far away from Dorian, or do you follow your heart and take the chance to call the man? No one can make that decision but you, Zach. No one but you. I know how much this means to you, so if it means anything, I think you should make the call. What's the worst that can happen?"

*****

Dorian

As soon as I walked inside of Brandon and Micah's place, I was taken aback by the aroma coming from the kitchen. When Brandon closed the door, he said, "You came just in time. Micah is making lunch."

"That's what's up," I smiled as I've always enjoyed Micah's cooking. I peeped my head into the kitchen and said, "What's up, Micah?"

He turned to me, smiled and said, "Hey, Dorian. What's up?"

I smiled and replied, "Hoping that you're making me a plate, too."

"You know I got ya," he said. "I'm making some Philly Cheesesteak Subs and fries, so I can add you in, too."

"I appreciate it Micah."

"It's nothing to it but to do it," he winked as he put his attention back to the task at hand.

The TV was playing in the living room and that's where I joined Brandon. He was watching some band DVD's of his time as a drum major in the FAMU Band.

"Must you look at that foolishness?" I jokingly asked. "What you need to be watching is my band."

"You got life fucked up if you think I'm gonna sit here and look at that robotic ass band from Bethune-Cookman. Naw, I'll pass."

"Whatever, Brandon," I shook my head.

As close of friends as we are, we always get into an argument when it comes to our respective bands, especially when November hits and the Florida Classic is in the air.

"I still got it," he laughed as he jumped up and starting marching to the beat and sound of the band. "Once you learn the concept, you never forget it."

"Boy, sit yo' country ass down somewhere," I chuckled.

"Country? Nigga, I'm from Jersey. You better recognize, fool."

"Yeah, but you went to college in country ass Tallahassee."

"I can't argue that shit," he laughed as he lowered the volume on the TV. "That motherfucker is country as hell!"

While Micah cooked lunch, Brandon sat down and said, "So tell me the news about Doug. I was overwhelmed in work yesterday and we couldn't talk. So, did you get to the bottom of the matter? Did you ask the important questions?"

"Yes, I did."

"He's married, isn't he?" Brandon asked.

"Naw, not married. No kids. And he says he isn't in a relationship with anyone."

"That doesn't make any sense. Based on the shit you've been telling me, something isn't adding up."

"Douglas is his middle name. Eric is his first name. And catch this shit—"

"What?" Brandon asked.

"Eric is a doctor."

"A doctor? Like a medical doctor or a professor?"

"A medical doctor."

"Yeah, right," Brandon replied. "You believe that shit? Dude is a con-artist."

"Yeah, I do believe it. After dinner the other night, he invited me back to his place. His house and the neighborhood he lives in says that either he is a doctor or he is a big time drug dealer."

"Umm, hmm."

"Anyway, we get to his house and he showed me his degrees. He got a bachelor degree in biology from Florida State."

"Florida State?" Brandon said. "He was in my neck of the woods in Tallahassee?"

"Yeah, but he had graduated a year before you came to Tally. He went to medical school at Howard. He showed me some of the plaques and trophies he's earned, so I don't think he's lying. It makes sense why he had all the canceled dinners and late nights."

"I guess," Brandon said. "So, did y'all have sex?"

"No, not yet."

"You know, I'm not hating or anything like that, and as your friend, I'm only looking out for you."

"Ok?" I replied.

"Even though Eric is a doctor, I think you and Dr. Eric should get an HIV test before y'all move to that stage in the relationship."

Before I could reply to Brandon's statement, my phone started to ring. I looked at the number. It had a 917 area code. Who the fuck was this?

I turned to Brandon and stuck up my index finger motioning him to hold on. A moment later, I pressed talk and said, "Hello?"

61

Zach

When I heard his voice for the first time, I paused. I couldn't believe he was on the other side of the phone. He said something but I didn't make it out. He raised his voice and said, "Hello? Who's there?"

"Umm," I cleared my throat. "May I speak with Dorian?"

"Speaking. Who is this and how can I help you?"

"Dorian, you called my mother about a week ago and asked to get in touch with me. This is Zach."

"Oh, wow," he said nervously. "Ummm, wow. I really wasn't expecting to hear from you." There was an awkward moment of silence on the phone.

"So, what can I do for you?" I asked. "My mom said you were trying to get in contact with me."

"This was so unexpected," he laughed nervously. "Do you know who I am?"

"Yes, you are Duane's son."

"Yeah," he replied. "Ummm, wow." After he collected himself, he said, "What area code is that?"

"New York. Manhattan."

"You're in New York?" he said disappointed. "Man, I wanted to meet you and hang out. Get to know you. I'm all the way down in Atlanta."

"I actually just moved from New York to Atlanta a few weeks back," I stated.

Excited, he said, "Yo, are you serious?"

Hearing him get excited made me excited. "Yeah, I'm serious."

"Listen," he said, "I know you don't know me or anything, but I just want to get a chance to know you. We come from the same blood and I just want to get to know you, if that's cool."

"That's what's up," I smiled. "I want to get to know you, too."

"Are you in Atlanta now?" he asked.

"Yeah."

"Can we meet up tomorrow or is that too early?" he asked.

"No, tomorrow over lunch is fine."

"Cool. Do you have somewhere in particular you'd like to go?"

"No. You can pick the place."

"How about Marlow's Tavern on West Peachtree."

"Ight, that'll work," I smiled as I made a mental note to get the directions. "Will noon do?"

"That'll be just fine," he said. "Tomorrow at noon."

"Tomorrow at noon it is. I'll see you then, Dorian."

"No doubt. And Zach, thanks for returning the call. It really means a lot."

"I'm happy I did," I smiled. "I can't wait to meet you."

"I can't wait to meet you, too."

When the call ended, I ran around the room like a little kid. I had so much energy inside of me; I had to release it in some way. When I stopped, I sat down on the bed and smiled. I'm so happy I made the phone call. So happy.

Now if Dray will hurry up and come back with lunch, I'll really be excited.

I'm about to meet my brother for the first time.

I looked to God and said, "Thank you. Thank you so much!"

*****

Dwight

I pulled into the parking lot and shook my head. There were a lot of cars here. "Thank God for appointments," I said, as I parked and headed towards the entrance door.

As soon as I walked inside of the building, I saw the receptionist/cashier and said, "Good afternoon, Tina."

"Hey, Dwight," she smiled and then continued to look at her fingernails as if they were the most important thing in the world.

I walked over to the main floor and, as usual, the men were watching and talking football. As soon as I sat down next to this light skinned brother, Amanuel said, "What's up, Dwight?"

"You know how it is," I replied as he stopped cutting the dude's hair. Amanuel looked at his watch and said, "Dwight, I'm almost done. I ran a little over time."

"Take your time. I'm not in a rush."

"Yooo, buddy," Amanuel said as he pointed to the light-skinned dude next to me.

"What up?" the dude said.

"I'm gonna get you after Dwight. He had an appointment. I know this is your first time in my shop, but just be patient shawty and I promise I'll get to you."

The dude sitting next to me nodded his head.

Amanuel looked at him again and said, "Yo, what's your name again?"

The light skinned dude sitting next to me cleared his throat and said, "Kory."

"Ight, Kory," Amanuel said as he returned to the dude sitting in the chair. "I'll be with you shortly."

As Amanuel resumed cutting the dude's hair, he looked at me and said, "Dwight, how is Ced and the family?"

"They're ok. I talked to him a few days ago."

"That's what's up. Tell him I said hey."

"Ight," I replied as I looked at Amanuel cut the dude's hair.

If I were to fuck with another dude, it would have to be someone who looks and acts like Amanuel. Shit, if the opportunity presented itself now, truthfully, I don't know what I'd do. Amanuel is sexy. No one can deny that shit.

Jaxon Grant

I've known Amanuel Wallace for a very long time, as we both graduated from the same Atlanta high school. I became really good friends with Amanuel through Ced. Amanuel and my baby brother were best friends through high school. When they graduated in 2004, they both came to FAMU. It was at FAMU where Amanuel and Ced started to split. They tried to remain close, but sometimes you just grow apart. Ced meeting Michelle probably didn't help, either. Amanuel eventually moved back home because of his monetary issues. It was just a bad situation.

I never thought of Amanuel as a DL dude until he came to FAMU in 2004. Being around Zach and Kris did a lot for me as far as awareness in that game goes. Zach taught me many lessons on the ins and outs of the DL lifestyle. He taught me what to look for when targeting a certain type of dude. He taught me the keys of knowing when a dude is checking you out or hitting on you.

One day in practice after I made drum major, I was standing off observing the percussion section going through one of their cadences. For some reason, I zoomed in on Amanuel and it was at that point when I began to watch him very closely.

Hanging around Zach and Kris, I knew of some of the other DL dudes in the band, and coincidently, Amanuel hung out with them, too.

I focused in on Amanuel without him even noticing. I watched him look at dudes with lust in his eyes. I watched his interaction with other dudes in the band. I was sold. He got down, too.

Now that we're older and every time I come to his shop, I still wonder does he mess with dudes. I would think some dudes grow out of it, or at least find a way to suppress the feelings.

Look at him. He is very attractive. He has that *swag* that a lot of dudes look for. He's successful. He has no kids, and as far as I know, he doesn't have a girlfriend, either. Every time someone asks him about a girlfriend, he says, "I'm just doing me, enjoying life, not trying to be tied down in a relationship."

Naw, nigga, you gay.

I grabbed my phone to send Zach a text to check on him. Before I could type anything, the dude sitting next to me, Kory, said, "Is it always busy like this in here?"

"Yeah, but man it's worth it. Amanuel will take care of you. Best thing to do is make an appointment. He actually prefers appointments."

"True. I just moved to Atlanta two weeks ago so I'm trying to find a permanent barber. I can't have everyone messing in my head."

"I understand," I replied as I looked at him.

He was kinda sexy. His skin...flawless. His lips...perfect. His body...nice. As he talked, I zoomed in on his lips. He would run his tongue over them on occasion and then bite his bottom lip for a quick second.

I caught myself. I need to get it together. This was a nigga.

He laughed; I laughed too.

I had no idea why I was laughing because I had no idea what he was talking about. So not to make myself look guilty for checking him out, I laughed and played along.

"So, like I said," he continued. "I just moved here and I'm looking for a workout buddy, too, trying to make some friends, feel me?"

Was he hitting on me? Was this one of the *rules* to the game that Zach taught me?

Deciding to see where it goes, I said, "Yeah, that's cool. We can do that. I hit up the gym about four times a week."

"Well, listen," he said, as stared me in the eyes while he ran his tongue over his lips. "Text me yo' number and I'll store it in. Then we can get up and do something, nah'mean."

I nodded my head. And then he spit his ten digits.

After I sent Kory the text, Amanuel called my name. He was finished with his client.

62

Phoenix

Sacramento, California

As soon as I arrived back in my hotel, I started to pack my bags. I had another long ass flight tomorrow, but I've got to make my rounds before training camp starts up.

When CJ left Chicago to take his baby brother, Renzo, to Jamaica, I flew over to Seattle to spend some time with my sister. After I left Seattle, I flew down to Sacramento to spend some time with my only son. Giovanni just turned six.

For Giovanni's birthday, I took him to Disney Land and we just got back yesterday. Sometimes it's hard to believe that I have my own offspring. Having a child was the greatest gift God has ever bestowed upon me. Now, as I pack my bags again, it's time to make that cross-country flight to Atlanta. Realizing who was in Atlanta, I grabbed my phone. Within moments, he answered, "Sup?"

"Chilling in Sacramento," I said.

"What are you doing over there?" Dray asked.

"Spending some time with my son."

"Oh, yeah. I forgot about that. How is everything?"

"Everything is good. Really good. So check this."

"What's up?" Dray asked.

"Do you have anything on the agenda for tomorrow?"

"Not that I know of. Why, what's up?"

"I'll be in Atlanta tomorrow, so make some plans for us."

"I can do that."

I said, "I have a meeting with my agent tomorrow around three and then another appointment after that. I should be free around six.

Can we do dinner or something?"

"That's fine, Phoenix. I'll take care of everything, just let me know when you're in town."

"Ight, I'll get at you. And while I'm in town, I want to meet this Zach dude."

Dray laughed and replied, "We can make that work."

"What's funny?" I asked.

"Nothing, Phoenix," he replied. "I'll take care of dinner. Just let me know when you arrive."

*****

Zach

After lunch with Dray this afternoon, I headed off to the room to take a nap. I had a headache earlier but now I'm feeling much better.

I must admit that I'm excited, but nervous about meeting with Dorian tomorrow. I can only hope that Dorian isn't running game and is only trying to start a brotherly relationship.

While I was looking at some videos on YouTube, Dray walked in the room with a devilish smirk on his face.

I looked at him and said, "What are you smirking about?"

"Nothing, boy," he replied as he sat down on the bed.

Out of my peripheral vision, I could see him staring at the wall. While sitting next to him on the bed, I turned and looked to face him. He was in deep thought about something. I asked, "Is everything ok, Dray?"

"Yeah," he scratched his head. He stared a little longer at the wall in front of him.

Not ready to believe him, I said, "What has you in such deep thought?"

He turned to me and said, "Look, I've put two and two together."

My body started to tense up. We were starting to get back on good terms. I don't need any Dwight issues right now.

He continued, "And I need your help getting this shit on the road."

Confused, I asked, "Dray, what are you talking about?"

"Phoenix will be in town tomorrow."

"Ok?" I replied. "What do I have to do with Phoenix? He's your friend."

"What do you have to do with Phoenix?" Dray snickered. "More than you can ever imagine."

I just stared at Dray.

"Will you help me?" he asked.

"I don't even know what I'm helping you do. What is this about?"

Dray planted that devilish smirk on his face and said, "Listen, this is my plan."

*****

TJ

I followed Elijah out of the neighborhood and into an area of trees. As we walked through the woods, I said, "You ain't trying to get me killed are you?"

"What? No, TJ," he laughed. "We'll be there in a second."

When we arrived, he sat down on the ground and said, "Sit."

I looked at the ground, over to Eli and finally back to the ground. I know he don't expect me to sit there.

"The dirt wipes off, ole prissy ass," Eli shook his head.

Deciding to play along, I sat down on the ground. He grabbed a rock and threw it into the small pond.

"This is the place I go to clear my mind," Elijah said as I looked at the tree infested area. The pond was the center of this dead piece of undeveloped land. "This is my spot away from the world. You're the first person I've told about this place."

"So why did you choose me?" I asked. "If this is so important and private to you, why you bring me out here?"

"So we can talk," he stated. "With your parent's home and my parent's home, we can't talk at your house and we can't talk at my house, so why not. Ain't no cars, no buses, no parents. Ain't nobody out here but us, a few squirrels and nature."

"How did you find this spot?" I asked as he threw another rock into the small body of water.

"Bored, walking, exploring shit like I always do. It's so quiet out here, man. I come here and talk to God. I talk to my dad, Chaz and older brother, Xavier."

"I thought you said you don't remember them."

"I don't, but they're still part of me," Eli said. "I see the pictures and it's not like they didn't exist. They walked the earth, they just ain't here anymore. So, the other day you wanted to ask me some questions. What's up?"

I turned around to make sure no one was behind us and said, "How did you know you were gay?"

"Truthfully, I don't know," he shrugged his shoulders. "I just know I like dudes."

"How do you know you don't like females if you never tried it?"

"Females just don't do it for me. I don't look at females the way I look at dudes. I just don't. I don't know why God made me this way. I just know what I like."

"Were you molested or something like that?"

"No," he shook his head. "Everyone who is gay wasn't molested or raped."

"So how is it?"

"How is what?" Elijah looked at me.

"You know… sexing with a dude. Is it like a female?"

"I've never had sex with a female so I don't know what that is like."

"What do you do when you're with a dude?"

"I like getting my dick sucked; I like sucking dick, too."

"Oh, fa' real?" I asked.

"Yeah. I mean that shit feels good and I like making other dudes feel good, too."

I stared at Elijah. He stared at me. I could feel my dick flinch.

Breaking the awkward moment, he grabbed another rock and threw it into the pond. When it splashed, I said, "So, I can hear my dad's fucking and shit and I can tell who is doing what. So what you do?"

"What'cha mean?"

"When you're sexing with a nigga, you fuck him or does he fuck you?"

"Well, I only had sex twice."

"So what happened?"

"One time, my friend did me. He was fifteen. The other time, I did him, but he ended up doing me."

"Did it hurt?"

"Yeah at first, but you get used to it. It feels good."

"I guess," I shook my head. "So, it's only been one dude?"

"Yeah, this guy at my church. Now, I've gotten head and stuff from another guy and I sucked him off, too."

"So do you like to be the giver or the receiver?"

"The top or the bottom?" Elijah said.

"What's that?" I asked.

"The top does the fucking. The bottom is kinda like the woman, but all bottoms don't act like women. They're just the receivers like women. Understand?"

"Yeah. How you know all this stuff?" I asked.

"The internet and my friend from church teaches me a lot."

"So what made you like me?"

"I don't know," he shrugged his shoulders. "You have a natural confidence about you that I like. I don't know."

"So what did you think when you saw my dick? You were looking at it kinda hard."

Elijah just stared at me.

"Answer the question, boy."

"It was straight," he shrugged his shoulders.

"It was straight?" I asked offended.

"It was bigger than the dude I be having sex with and he fifteen."

"Oh."

"Maybe I shouldn't say this," Elijah said.

"Say it. I ain't gonna hit you or nothing."

"When I went home afterwards, after the day we got our dicks sucked at your house, I had an image of your dick in my head, and I jacked off to it."

Seizing the opportunity, I asked, "You wanna see it again?"

He looked at me.

"It's just us out here, right?" I asked. "You can touch it if you want." I put my hands on the button of my jeans to execute my point. "This offer ain't gonna stand for long."

"Yeah, I wanna see," he replied.

I stood up, looked around to make sure nobody was looking, then unbuttoned and unzipped my jeans. I placed my hands inside of my boxers.

I looked at Elijah with lust in his eyes. I could see a tent starting to form in his basketball shorts. He was still looking for my approval, so I removed my hand and said, "Take my dick out and suck it."

He looked around and then looked at me.

"Suck my dick!" I said again with more force.

He stood up, walked over to me, kneeled back down into the dick sucking position and began to grab for my dick. As soon as he reached his hand over to touch my dick, I jerked back and laughed while I zipped and buttoned my jeans back up.

"I ain't gay," I laughed. "I told you that shit, ole gullible ass!"

He stared at me. I was still laughing. He didn't find it funny, but it was funny as hell to me.

"That shit ain't cool, TJ," he said pissed off as he jumped up and headed towards the trees.

"DAMN, HOLD UP," I yelled. "IT WAS A JOKE, MAN! IT WAS JUST A JOKE!"

"You play too damn much," he said as I caught up to him.

"It was just a joke, damn," I said as I stepped in front of him, abruptly stopping his walk.

"Get out of my way, TJ," he pouted as I moved in every direction he moved making him stand there and talk to me.

"You forgive me?" I asked, licking my lips.

"Move, TJ!"

I moved in closer. Our noses damn near touched. Staring him in the eye, I softly repeated, "You forgive me, right?"

He stared at me and stepped in closer. And then in a sudden and unexpected move, he quickly kissed me on the lips then kneed me in the nuts.

"OH, FUCK!" I yelled, grabbing my balls as he ran away laughing. "THAT'S FUCKED UP ELIJAH!"

"YEAH, I FORGIVE YOU!" he laughed as he continued to run. "I FORGIVE YOU!"

63

Tony

Sunday, August 21, 2016

After I showered, I headed out into the kitchen to make a quick breakfast. TJ was already sitting at the breakfast bar eating some Cinnamon Toast Crunch cereal and listening to his music.

"Good morning," I said.

He looked at me and as he removed the headphones from his ear, he said, "Huh?"

"I said good morning," I stared at him.

"Hey," he replied coldly.

"I'm about to make breakfast, you want something?"

"I'm already eating," he cut as he put the headphones over his ears.

I looked at him for a second, shook my head and proceeded to continue with breakfast. It wasn't even worth the hassle this Sunday morning.

A few seconds later, I saw TJ grab the bowl of cereal and head out of the kitchen. I exhaled and started to grab the pots and pans I needed to make our breakfast.

When I finished cooking some cheese grits, bacon, scrambled eggs and toast, I fixed my plate and Raidon's plate, two glasses of orange juice, placed everything on the tray and headed upstairs. TJ was back in his room as was evident by the music playing over his surround sound stereo system.

Once inside our room, Raidon was stepping out of the master bathroom.

"Smells good," he said, as he grabbed his plate and juice.

I forced a smile and sat down on the bed.

"Did you make TJ a plate?" he asked.

"He said he didn't want any."

Raidon ate some of his grits and stared at me.

"What?" I looked over to him.

"What's on your mind?"

"Nothing really."

"Stop lying," he said. "I can see right through you."

I exhaled, took a sip of my juice and said, "For the life of me, I just don't understand that boy. He's so fucking rude."

"He gets it from you," Raidon said. "He's a younger version of you. I've said it time and time again that y'all are just alike."

"Whatever," I bit into my bacon.

"Speaking of that," Raidon said. "You know I had Zach talk to TJ."

"Yeah, whatever happened with that?"

"Turns out your son wants to punch the fuck out of you."

"EXCUSE ME?"

"You heard me, Tony," he said. "I didn't tell you that to get you all rowdy, I said that to make you aware of the way he sees you. The two of y'all have major issues that y'all need to work out."

"I'm the adult, he's the kid. That's that."

"Hell, that's half the damn problem."

"WHAT? Half the problem? I clothe him. I feed him. I provide shelter for him. What the fuck is he complaining about?"

"Clothes, food and shelter are your responsibility as the parent. That's what you are supposed to do. Tony, the era in which you were raised has passed. Times have changed. For Christ's sake, you still beat the boy! There are other ways to discipline and raise our son without going back to the times in which our parents were children. This is 2016. Get with the times, Tony."

"Well, if he doesn't like the way I do shit in my house, then he can go take care of himself for a few days and watch his ass come crawling back."

"You act as if TJ is a bad kid," Raidon said upset. "TJ is good kid, a great kid. He doesn't get into any trouble. He makes good grades. He's clean and respectful. I swear for the life of me I just don't understand, Tony. I don't understand why you treat him the way you do. When TJ was younger, he was your everything. Now, it's like you hate looking at him. He can see that shit, Tony. He can sense it as well. You need to change your ways around him. This boy is a teenager. If you don't stop your ways, you're only going to create a monster. Based on the things that Zach was telling me, TJ has so much anger built up towards you and it has nothing to do with your homosexuality. He just doesn't like you as a person. So, Tony, you tell me what the issue is. Make me understand. What the fuck is the problem?"

I didn't have an appetite anymore. I placed the food down on the nightstand, stood up and said, "You want to know what the problem is? You want to know what the fuck the problem is? The problem is every time I see him, I see April! She fucked up my life, Raidon. I'm a walking dead man because of her. I am HIV positive because of her. That boy is a product of her. She had HIV for years and never let me know that I could have been infected. She dropped him off at my doorstep one day and never returned. I had to drop everything to become a single father. I had to give up my playing career to take care of him. So, forgive me if I have some fucking issues as it deals with TJ. Maybe I'm still learning how to deal with the shit!"

"You should be ashamed of yourself," he said. "ASHAMED!"

"You asked me what the problem is and I told you. Now I should be ashamed?"

"First off, you need to stop blaming your mishaps in life on everyone else. You know what Tony, I have HIV, too. I trusted someone and they passed the shit onto me. Was I upset with Phil? Yes, the fuck I was. It's a natural reaction. But, you do know it takes two to tango. I had just as much of a role in the transferring of that disease as he did. Nobody forced you to fuck her raw! You did that! You made the decision to go in without protection. And don't give me that story that you were in high school. Bullshit. Yes, you were in high school but you were also the star quarterback. You also had sex education classes. You knew to strap up. YOU KNEW IT. And then, after all those years, you never once... NOT ONCE... got an HIV test? Tony, that's your fuck up. If that girl never told you, you could be dead right now. DEAD, TONY! You can't blame her for you contracting the fucking disease. Stop blaming everybody else for your Goddamn problems and man the fuck up for once! Be a fucking man, Tony. You better be grateful that boy didn't contract the virus. Yeah, you didn't make it to the NFL. I'm sorry but that shit is life. It just wasn't for you! And you have to nerve to take the blame out on your son? YOUR SON? That boy has done nothing but love you. He has loved you from the day he was born. You're all he knows. YOU, TONY! How would you think it'll make him feel to hear you, HIS FUCKING FATHER, say the things you just said? HOW THE FUCK WOULD THAT MAKE HIM FEEL? If you heard your father say that to you, how the fuck would you feel? You know what, I'm ashamed. I'm ashamed of you right now. I can't believe you just said that shit."

I sighed.

He stared at me and then said, "Let me get out of here before I say something I regret."

He opened the door, looked back at me, shook his head and then slammed the door as hard as he could.

*****

Dwight

I didn't get a good night's rest. Lexi and the kids will be home sometime today. I was looking forward to seeing my kids, but I could do without Lexi.

I was sitting in the living room looking at my phone. The encounter at the barbershop yesterday has my mind all fucked up. Somewhere inside of me, I was hoping that Kory would send me a text. But there was nothing.

Did I read the signs wrong? Does he not fuck around with dudes? Or is he playing the game too?

Something inside of me is telling me not to do it because it will fuck with Zach. I know he'll be so pissed at me if he knew I was talking to another dude. And then I think about what Ced told me. Zach hasn't left Dray. In fact, Zach has told me *no* numerous times in regards to us being something more than just best friends.

My curiosity wants to see what happens with Kory. I ain't trying to marry the man, I just want to see what he is about.

I looked back at the phone. I exhaled, pulled his name up and sent a text that read, "What up man...this Dwight from the barbershop yesterday."

A few seconds later, Kory replied, "Aye… what up bruh? What you up 2?"

"Shit...at the house...bored," I sent.

"Me too. I was gonna go 2 church but then didn't feel like moving out da bed. God know my heart though LOL."

"LOL... u a mess," I replied.

"LOL... I know...lol...but what you got on the agenda?" he asked.

"Nothing really. I gotta do some stuff later."

"So you free now?" he sent.

"Yep."

"Shit... come by da house... come chill with a nigga for a sec. I live by myself and I'm bored as da fuck!"

I stared at the text message for a few minutes. Did I really want to do this? If I was going to go, I better go before Lexi gets home.

I took another deep breath and replied, "Ight... send me your address and I'll be on my way."

64

Zach

After Dray and I got back from early morning church service, I took a quick nap to pass the time before meeting the infamous, Dorian.

When I arrived at Marlow's, I took a moment to collect myself. I was finally about to meet my brother. Words can't describe how jubilating this feels.

I looked at the time. It was a little after noon. I grabbed my phone and dialed him to see if he had arrived. He answered and said he was standing outside the front door.

I got out of my car and headed for the building. As I turned the corner, I saw a tall, light brown dude standing at the door looking down at his phone. I instantly knew it was him. I knew that was my brother!

I had a nervous feeling in the pit of my stomach. When he looked up, he smiled. I could tell he instantly knew I was the man he was looking for. I smiled. He started to walk towards me. When we meet, he reached out and gave me the biggest embrace.

In that instance, every worry I had was suddenly erased. I knew it was a genuine gesture; this was my brother. The people around looked at us as if we were crazy, but I didn't care. My brother was standing right here in front of me!

When we broke the hug, he said, "Man, I finally get to meet you."

I smiled and said, "The feeling is mutual."

As soon as we were seated, we just stared at each other and smiled. It was an awkward moment, not really sure what to say.

"Well," I said breaking the silence. "I'm Zach. Zachariah Tariq

Finley."

He smiled and said, "I'm Dorian. Dorian Antwan Kierce."

I stared at him and I could see my father facial features. There was no doubt about it, he was my brother.

"You're two years younger than me right?" I asked.

"I was born in 85," he said. "October 3rd."

"Wow, we're both Libras," I said.

"Really, when is your birthday?"

"September 23 of 83."

"So, tell me this, big bruh—if you don't mind me saying that...big bruh."

I smiled. It felt good to hear those words come from my baby brother. *Damn, I've got a baby brother.*

"What's up?" I asked.

"Where did you grow up and how did you get to New York, and now here in Atlanta?"

"I grew up in Orlando and went to school at FAMU. I received both my bachelors and masters in Tallahassee. I moved to New York to get my Ph.D."

"You have a Ph.D.?" he said shocked.

"Yes, sir," I replied as the waitress brought over our drinks.

"Wow," he said. "So you're Dr. Zachariah Tariq Finley."

"Yeah, I guess so," I smiled. "Anyway, I lived in New York for about seven years and I finally moved back down south earlier this month."

"So you're a professor or something?" he asked.

"Yeah, I taught at Columbia but I'm over at Clark Atlanta now."

"What did you study in school?" he asked.

"I received my bachelors in English Education. For my masters, I studied Counselor Education. I got my Ph.D. in Counseling Psychology."

"Wow, that's what's up," he took a sip of his drink.

"What about you?"

"Well," he cleared his throat. "I don't have a Ph.D., but I can hold my own."

"Look," I said stopping him. "I'm not here to compare my life to yours or anything like that. I just want to get to know you."

He smiled and replied, "Well, I was born in Orlando but moved to Jacksonville. I lived most of my life there with my mom and my younger brother until my grandma got sick. When she couldn't take care of herself anymore, we moved back to Orlando. I graduated from Jones High School."

"I graduated from W. P. Foster," I cut.

"Are you serious?" he asked.

"Dead ass," I replied. We went to rival high schools.

"Wow," he continued. "After graduation, I ended up going to Bethune-Cookman."

My face dropped.

He laughed and said, "What?"

"You went to Cookman? Yuck!"

"Don't hate," he laughed. "I was in the band at Cookman. I played trombone for two years and was a drum major for a few years."

"You were in the band at Cookman and you were a drum major?" I asked in disbelief.

"Yeah, why?"

"Dorian, I was in the band at FAMU."

"Word?" he smiled. "Damn, we're closer than I could've ever imagined."

"Yeah, man. That's crazy."

"What class are you?" he asked.

"2002."

"I'm 2004," he said. "So that means we marched against each other in high school and in college."

"Pretty much."

"The world is so small, Zach," he shook his head. "Anyway, you know what else is crazy? I almost went to FAMU, but they kept losing my paperwork and stuff, so I accepted the offer from Bethune on the last day possible. Best decision I ever made."

I stared at him. As he talked, I noticed his eyes kept wondering off to someone behind me. Not wanting to make it obvious, but I knew I had to turn around and see who was behind me.

He said, "I graduated from Cookman and got my masters from UCF. After my mom died, I got a job in Atlanta and I've been here ever since."

"Sorry to hear about your mom," I said.

"It's cool."

"So what do you do? How do you like it in Atlanta?" I asked.

"I'm a Budget Analyst for a Fortune 50 company. I like Atlanta because my daughter is here, too."

"You have children?" I asked excited.

"Just one. My lil girl, Dakota."

"Aww, I love that name."

He smiled and said, "She'll be eight in December. Zach, that's my world." He quickly looked at the table behind me and then cut his eyes to me.

"Are you and the mother together?" I asked.

"Naw," he shook his head. "We have a good relationship, so it works out for Dakota."

"Excuse me for a second," I said. "I have to use the restroom."

"Ight," he smiled. "I'll be right here."

I didn't really have to use the restroom, I just wanted to see who in the hell he kept cutting his eyes to. As soon as I stood up, it was clear. There was a fine ass nigga sitting at the table with his chick. If what my gut is telling me is correct, then my brother got down with dudes, too. This shit is crazy. *Crazy!*

The dude was facing Dorian while the chick's back was to mine. As I approached the table, the dude looked at me and lifted his head. I lifted mines back and rushed off to the bathroom. Once I returned, Dorian was sending a text.

"Sorry about that," I said.

"It's cool," he smiled as he put down the phone.

Shortly after, we received our food and we talked more about our backgrounds. Turns out we have a lot in common, from music to TV shows to drinks to sports. His favorite smoothie is strawberry banana, just like mine.

While eating, I said, "What made you hit me up? How did you even get my mom's number?"

"I got it from dad."

"You got it from *your* father?" I reiterated, with emphasis on the word, *your*.

He stared at me for a second and said, "Yeah." He nodded his head and said, "I can talk specifics another time, but he gave me the number and I put it to use. I knew you were out there, somewhere, so why not."

"How long have you known about me?" I asked.

"Since I was about seven or eight. I never really thought too much about it, not until about eleven or so years ago."

"What happened then?"

"Dad wanted us to meet. I was in my second year at Cookman

and here he was throwing this in my face. He was bragging on and on about you, about how you were doing this and you were doing that. He wanted us to meet up to play basketball or something and I wasn't feeling it. He was my dad and I wasn't about to start sharing him with some kat I didn't even know and I told him I wasn't going. He begged me to come, but I said no. That was a long time ago and I was a kid. I don't feel that way anymore and I'm sorry for thinking like that."

"So, even if you didn't want to come, why didn't he call me and tell me you couldn't make it?" I asked. "October 2005 was the last time I've ever spoken to that man."

"Well, no disrespect, Zach, but I don't want to talk about dad. Maybe another day, but right now, I want us to get to know each other. And I'm sorry for the way things went down back then."

I forced a smile. I saw him look at the dude again. I looked out the window and down the street. I remembered Keston telling me that the Daiquiri Factory was a spot that a lot of the local gay/bi/dl dudes came to unwind. He said most gay people in Atlanta knew about this place. I smiled harder.

"What?" he asked.

"Have you ever been to the Daiquiri Factory?"

"Ummm," he nervously cleared his throat. "Huh?"

I pointed and said, "You know, the Daiquiri Factory, down the street."

Nervously, he said, "I've been there once or twice."

I smiled and said, "I can tell."

"Excuse me?"

"I can tell," I said again as I cleared my throat.

He looked at me with suspicion in his eyes.

I said, "My roommate and I used to visit something similar when we were in New York."

"Your roommate?" he asked.

"Yeah... of eight years."

"Your roommate of eight years," he asked.

"Yeah."

"And you have a Ph.D.?" he asked.

"Yeah," I smiled.

"And you have a roommate... of eight years?"

"Yeah."

"Interesting," he said.

"Isn't it?" I cut.

"So, is your roommate in Atlanta, too, or are they back in New York?"

"He's here in Atlanta."

"Your roommate of eight years is a male?"

"Umm, hmm. Do you have a roommate?" I asked.

"No."

"That's not your roommate sitting behind me?" I asked.

"What?" he asked.

I smiled and said, "Or do you want him to be your roommate?"

He stared at me. I took a sip of my drink and smiled.

"Are you saying what I think you're saying?" he asked.

I smiled.

"Really?" he asked.

"Really," I stated.

"No, seriously... like really, really?" he said.

"Yeah, seriously... like really, really," I replied.

"Fa real?"

"Fa real," I replied.

"Really?" he asked again.

"Really," I smiled.

"Shit. That's what's up big bruh," he smiled. "We really *do* have a lot in common!"

"Don't we?" I chuckled.

"This is like the best news ever," he stated. "We're really gonna get along quite well."

"I think we are," I said. "I'm so happy you're in my life."

"Me too, big bruh," he smiled. "Me too."

65

Dwight

On the entire ride to Kory's house, I doubted myself. Could I really do this, I asked many times. Was this really for me?

When I got to the entry gate, I called him and he allowed me inside. A moment or two after I knocked on the door, he opened and smiled. He didn't have on a shirt and I stared at his bare chest.

Damn, he was sexy—his skin... his lips... his body—the structure of his jawbone. Damn. He had a lot of masculine traits.

"So are you just gonna stand there or are you gonna come inside?" he asked smiling.

Feeling embarrassed, I said, "Oh, my bad."

When I stepped inside, I saw a lot of boxes pushed against the wall. As he escorted me to the living room, he added, "You have to excuse my place. I told you I just moved here, and as you can see, I haven't had much time to unpack and settle into it yet."

"Naw, it's cool," I sat down on the black leather couch.

After he offered me something to drink, he flipped on the TV. ESPN was talking about LaRon Copeland from the Carolina Panthers and their upcoming NFL season.

We ragged a little bit about sports before we started to talk about each other, getting the history on how we got to Atlanta.

Kory said, "So, yesterday at the shop, I saw the wedding ring, but today, it's not there. You married?"

Taken aback by his straightforwardness, I looked at my hands, back to him and said, "Yes."

"Oh, ok," he brushed it off. "You got kids?"

"Yeah. Two boys and a girl."

"Man, I've always wanted kids."

"Why don't you have them?" I asked.

"Never got lucky enough, I guess," he shrugged his shoulders. "Time is ticking. I'm 31 and I figured I'd have a son by now."

We engaged in some more small talk but there was a clear elephant in the room. We both were avoiding the real conversation.

As we talked, I caught Kory staring at me, then looking over my body a few times. During the conversation, I still couldn't believe that I was sitting here. If Zach knew I was here, he would be so upset with me.

He went to the kitchen to refill our drinks. When he came back, he said, "So, what's the deal?"

"Huh?"

"We've been talking about a bunch of nothing all day. Why are you here?" he asked.

"I'm here because you invited me."

"Why did you hit me up this morning?"

"I don't know," I shrugged my shoulders.

"Yes, you do. What's the deal, bruh?"

"What are you expecting me to say?" I asked.

"Tell me why you're here. Tell me why you hit me up this morning. Tell me why you were checking me out when I opened my door."

After taking a moment to ponder his statement, I exhaled and replied, "I'm new to this."

"This?" he asked.

"Don't play stupid, man," I cut.

He laughed, "I'm just fucking with cha, bruh. So you've never been with a dude before?"

I just looked at him.

He continued, "The way you flirted with me on the sly at the barbershop yesterday made me think that you were deep in the game. You did that shit so smoothly."

"My best friend fucks with niggas. He's taught me a lot. So, I know a little bit, here and there."

"So you've never been with a dude before?"

"I've had one sexual encounter with a man and that was seven years ago," I said as my phone started to vibrate. It was Lexi. I motioned for Kory to hold on. I answered, "Yes, Dear?"

"Dwight, where the hell are you?" she blurted. "The kids want to see you!"

"Y'all back?"

"If I asked where the hell you were and then said the kids wanted to see you, what the fuck do you think? Yes, we're home!"

I exhaled and shook my head.

"Whose bitch house you at, Dwight?" she interrogated. "Huh?"

"Lexi, I'll be home in a little bit. Bye," I hung up the phone. I shook my head.

"Damn. I see why you trynna fuck with a nigga," he laughed. "No disrespect bruh, but she is feisty as hell. She sounds like she's something else."

"Man, you don't know the half," I shook my head. "Let me get out of here before she comes looking."

"Yeah, you do that. I don't need those problems," he said as I stood up.

As he walked me to the door, I asked, "So is my marriage gonna be a problem?"

"Naw. It's even better that way. If you're married, you ain't living here," he laughed. I didn't reply. He looked at me for a second and said, "You straight?"

"Yeah," I replied. "But ummm, just to let you know, I can't promise you that we're gonna be fucking and shit. I'm just trying to figure out if this dude thing is for me. Understand?"

"I get it. I went through that shit a long time ago, so I know how it is. We can just chill and if it happens, it happens. No pressure. No rushing. Just two niggas chilling and vibing."

"Cool," I smiled. He smiled. I said, "If something does happen, I ain't letting no nigga fuck me. It's only one dude that I'd even think about letting him do that to me and it ain't you. So if that's what you're thinking, you can drop it and we can cut ties right now."

He chuckled and said, "I do it both ways, so that's not even a problem. But that ain't nothing for us to be worried about right now, right? We're just vibing, right? Feeling each other out?"

I smiled and said, "Good point, but let me get going. My wife is a lil crazy—literally."

He laughed and said, "Ight, man. Hit me up."

We dapped each other up and I headed out, happy I made the decision to come here.

I just hope I know what I'm getting myself into.

66

Zach

Keston and I sat in the living room and talked about the encounter with my brother, Dorian. Keston seemed so happy for me. He said, "I can't believe y'all came out to each other and you were the one who pushed the topic. That was brave of you."

"Yes, it was," I said, as I heard Dray running the water in the kitchen. "There was something inside telling me that he wasn't gonna trip. It ain't like I'm ultra DL or anything like that. If someone asks me what the deal is, I'll tell 'em. I'm at a point in my life where I don't have to hide shit from anyone."

"I understand," Kes smiled. "I'm just so happy for you. Do you still think Dorian is out to scam you?"

"Not at all," I shook my head. "I think he really just wants to build a relationship. The next time we meet he said he was gonna try to bring his daughter."

"That's what's up," Kes smiled. "You went from having nothing to getting a brother and a niece in the same day. I remember when my brother brought home his son for the first time. I felt like I was the dad."

I smiled and said, "How is Mario doing anyway?" I asked in reference to his baby brother.

"He's doing very well," Kes said as his phone started to vibrate. He looked at it and said, "This is LaRon."

As Kes answered and talked to his fuck buddy and star Carolina Panther receiver, I exhaled. LaRon Copeland was trying to make Keston his for good. Dray's plans may throw a curve ball into that.

As Kes hung up the phone, he said, "Damn, he's so sexy."

I smiled as Dray walked into the living room catching our attention. "What's up?" I asked.

"Go get cleaned up. The food is almost done."

"It damn sure smells good," Kes stood up.

I smiled as he made his way to the half bath. When he was out of the vicinity, I turned to Dray and softly said, "Is he coming?"

"He'll be here in a few minutes. I just got finished texting him."

"I hope this shit works."

"It will," he replied. "I got this."

"What y'all in here talking about?" Kes asked.

"Nothing," I said. "Let me go wash up."

When I got to the half bath, I took a moment and looked in the mirror. I hope Dray knows what he's doing because I got a bad feeling this shit can blow up in his face. After I took a few moments to clear my mind, I headed out and joined them in the dining room. Once I was seated, there was a knock on the door.

"Y'all expecting someone?" Kes asked.

"Yeah, one of my friends is stopping over for dinner," Dray said.

"Oh, ok," Kes replied as he sat down at the table.

*****

Keston

Something about Zach was wrong. I couldn't put my finger on it, but he seemed nervous. Just as I was getting ready to ask Zach a question, I heard two voices. One voice clearly belonged to Dray. The other voice… I knew that voice.

They laughed as they approached the dining room. I couldn't see them because my back was to them. But I knew the voice. I knew *that* voice.

It couldn't be. *It couldn't be!*

As the voices got louder, I turned my head. *He* stopped talking the moment he saw me. *He* stared at me for a moment and then said, "Kes?"

I swallowed my spit.

"Is that really you?" Phoenix asked.

I turned my head to Zach; he was smiling. I looked at Dray; he was smiling.

I jumped out of my chair upset and said, "Did y'all set me up? DID Y'ALL SET ME UP?"

"What's going on?" Phoenix asked Dray.

"DON'T FUCKING PLAY WITH ME!" I yelled. "DID Y'ALL SET ME UP?"

"Kes, calm down," Dray replied. "Please, have a seat and calm down."

I looked at Phoenix and he was just as confused as I was.

"Kes, I will explain everything," Dray pleaded. "Just have a seat and calm down."

*****

Phoenix

Keston looked at me and took his seat. I looked at Dray and he shook his head as we entered the dining area. After I met Zach, his lover of eight years, I sat down across from Keston. Dray and Zach sat across from each other at the end of the table.

Kes stared at me and he wasn't happy. He needs to know I had nothing to do with this.

"I need some answers, right now!" Kes demanded as he looked at Dray and Zach.

"Dray, answer the man," Zach said, as he pushed the blame to Dray.

Keston turned his head to Dray.

"I thought I was doing a good deed," Dray said.

"Wait," I interjected looking to Kes. "I had nothing to do with this. I don't know what's going on, but I had nothing to do with it."

As Dray tried to plead his case to Kes, I stared at the real love of my life. Seeing him sitting here across from me feels so surreal. I want to just reach over and kiss him.

Damn, I still love this dude.

I know it's been nine years but I never realized that he still has that hold over my heart.

FUCK!

Cutting into the conversation, I turned to Dray and said, "So, you knew about my relationship with Keston?"

"I just put the pieces together," Dray said.

"How did you manage that?" I asked as Kes looked at his empty plate. No one had even touched the food.

Dray said, "One night when we were at the bar, I mentioned your name in passing and Keston's reaction to your name was strange. Remember, Kes, I asked if you knew Phoenix, and you said you remembered him from your days at UCF. You brushed it off, so I did, too. It wasn't until I was talking to you, Phoenix, a few days later, and I mentioned Keston's name in passing and you gave damn near the same reaction Keston did. When I went to your house back in Chicago, we were with CJ, and you talked about your real first love, the dude you met in college. And through the clues, I just put it together. Phoenix, when you told me yesterday that you would be in town today and wanted to meet Zach and stop in for dinner, I saw this as the golden opportunity to reunite you guys. Keston, don't be mad at Zach. He had nothing to do with this, as this was all on me."

I looked at Kes and he wouldn't even look at me. He kept his head focused down at his empty plate. This is definitely not the reaction I expected whenever I was to see Keston again. This is the way shit ended nine years ago.

"Let me tell you something," Kes said as he looked at Dray. "The last thing I need in my life is someone playing match-maker. I'm a grown ass man and I can take care of my motherfucking self. This shit wasn't cool at all Dray."

"Kes, I didn't mean any harm," Dray said.

"Don't even worry about it," Kes jumped up from the table. "I'm out."

As Keston rushed out of the dining room, Zach looked at Dray and shook his head. I saw images from our last encounters nine years ago.

"Not again," I said as I jumped up as rushed after him. "Not again!"

67

Phoenix

I yelled Keston's name as he was stepping outside. He kept walking.

"KESTON, HOLD THE FUCK UP, DAMN!" I yelled as he finally stopped walking.

"What, Phoenix?" he turned around and faced me.

"First off, calm the fuck down," I said as we stood outside Dray and Zach's front door. "Why are you acting like this?"

He stared at me.

"Kes, it's just me," I pleaded. "It's just me! I swear I didn't know anything about this. I was just coming to have dinner with Dray and Zach. But I can't lie, I can't deny the fact that seeing you tonight made me feel like the luckiest man in the world all over again. Seeing you tonight made me feel like I was back in college."

I looked at Kes and tears were starting to fall down his face.

"Bae, why are you crying?" I asked, as I reached over and wiped the tears from his eyes.

He didn't reply.

"Bae," I said. "Look at me."

He lifted his head.

"I still love you. I never stopped loving you," I said as I my tears started to fall.

He stared me dead in the eyes and exhaled.

"I've been trying to contact you," I said.

"No, you haven't," he finally said. "You're still lying after all these years."

"What the fuck do I have to lie about? I have been trying to call you but I couldn't leave a message because your voicemail is full!"

"Whatever, Phoenix."

I grabbed my phone and dialed his number. "Look at your phone, Keston."

Reluctantly, he grabbed the phone and stared at the number. His eyes got wide and said, "This is your number? You're the person who has been trying to call me?"

"Yes."

"Wow," he exhaled. "Wow, wow, wow."

"Kes, bae, I know I wasn't perfect and I made some mistakes by keeping the truth from you. But Keston, even after my mishaps we were making progress and then everything changed. Kes, tell me what happened."

"Right now in the front yard of my best friend's house isn't the best place to discuss the events of the past," he said.

"Can we do it later? I can alter my plans, Kes. I don't know what's going on in your life, but I want to get to know you again. I've missed you, Keston. I feel like this is God bringing us back together. We've both had time to learn and grow. Can we at least rejoin Dray and Zach for dinner? He put a lot of work into preparing the food for us tonight. I know you, Keston and you're a good dude. Just finish dinner."

He smiled and said, "Ight… I give…you win."

I smiled as I opened the door and walked back inside.

Once I closed the door, Kes turned to me and whispered, "I still love you, too."

He blew me an air kiss and headed back for the dining room.

I leaned against the wall, exhaled and smiled.

I looked to the heavens and said, "Thank you, God. Thank you."

68

TJ

Monday, August 22, 2016

My alarm clock was sounding. I reached over and turned it off. I looked at the time and exhaled. *Damn! Shit! Fuck!*

I stuck my head back under the cover. I took a couple of deep breaths. I just wanted to go back to sleep. Just as I was going to set my alarm to go off in twenty more minutes, I heard banging on my door.

"TJ, YOU UP?" Raidon yelled.

"YES!" I moaned, upset.

"Ight, don't be late and miss that bus. Your school is not en route to my job," he replied in his authoritative, I mean business, tone. "It's the first day of school. You can't start off on the wrong foot."

"I know," I replied.

"When I come back to this room you better be getting dressed. Summer is over," he said. I heard his footsteps edge away from my door.

I exhaled. After a few more minutes, I got out of the bed and walked across the hallway towards the bathroom.

After I finished my morning routine, I got out of the shower, I dried off, applied some lotion, wrapped the white towel around my waist and headed back to my room. While in the hallway, I could hear Anthony Brown's *Worth* playing in Daddy and Ray's room. They always listen to gospel first thing in the morning.

I heard Ray singing along: *"You thought I was worth saving, so, You came and changed my life. You thought I was worth keeping, so, You cleaned me up inside. You thought I was to die for, so, You sacrificed Your life. So, I could be free. So, I could be whole. So, I could tell everyone I know. Hallelujah. Glory to the God who changed my life. I will praise You, forever. I will worship You, forever. I will give You glory, forever. Because I am free. Because I am whole. And I will tell everyone I know."*

I headed back in my room, looked at the time and knew I needed to hurry up. I put on my new outfit and shoes for school and I looked through my book-bag to make sure I had everything I needed for the day. I threw my iPod in my bag, so I could listen to my music on the way to school.

I headed downstairs to grab breakfast. Luckily, no one was in the kitchen. I like to eat in peace.

I checked the time and poured a bowl of my favorite cereal, Cinnamon Toast Crunch. I turned on the small TV that was located on wall of the breakfast bar just in time to catch a rerun of my favorite show, The Family Guy.

While eating my cereal and watching TV, I saw daddy walk in the kitchen. He popped some pills in his mouth and downed them with some water.

What the fuck is wrong with this dude? This is the second time, in a matter of weeks, I've seen him down some pills. I shook my head and refocused my attention back to the TV.

After daddy cleared his throat, he said, "Morning, TJ."

"Hey."

"You excited about school?"

"Naw, not really," I replied staring at the TV.

"Why not?" he asked.

"Just not," I replied as I stuffed my mouth with cereal, with my eyes still purposely focused on the television. I didn't feel like being bothered with his bullshit today. Hopefully, he'll get the hint that I ain't in the mood.

It became clear that he didn't get the hint. As I took bites of my food, I could still see him staring at me.

Like really—what the fuck is wrong with this dude? He never says anything, but he just stares. It was very awkward.

While I ate my food, the show went to commercial. And then it hit me like a ton of bricks. I needed to be nice to this dude. I needed some lunch money. I have a couple of dollars to get me through today and tomorrow, but come Wednesday, I'll be shit out of luck.

A few moments later, Raidon walked into the kitchen. He kissed daddy on the cheek, smiled at me and said, "You look so nice today."

I smiled back and replied, "Thanks, Ray."

"So how does it feel to be in the eighth grade?" Raidon asked.

"I don't know but I guess we'll find out when I get there," I said.

He opened the refrigerator and grabbed the orange juice. After he took a sip, he said, "TJ, you got some money for lunch?"

"I have a couple of dollars," I said.

"How much is a couple?" Ray asked.

"About ten."

"Tony, give that boy some lunch money," Raidon said.

Daddy stared at Raidon.

Ray said, "Gone 'head and give him some money."

Daddy reached into his pocket and pulled out his wallet. He grabbed four dead presidents and said, "This is all the cash I have on me."

"Thanks," I replied as I placed the fifty dollars into my pocket.

Ray started to talk to daddy about something, but I had tuned them out with my TV show. After I finished my breakfast, I walked over to the sink and washed out my bowl. Daddy and Ray don't play about having dirty dishes in the sink. It's just become a habit to eat and then immediately wash your plate. Daddy says if you do it that way, you'll never have to worry about washing dishes because it'll never be any dishes to wash. I don't like a lot of the stuff that daddy says, but I agree with him on that point.

After I grabbed my bag, I looked at them and said, "Well, I guess I better get going. I don't want to miss the bus."

Ray smiled and said, "Have a great first day at your new school."

"Thanks, Ray."

He smiled.

"Behave yourself, TJ," Daddy stated.

"I always do," I opened the door and headed outside.

It was a nice morning. The sun was shining, but it wasn't too hot and humid yet. As soon as I started to walk towards the end of the road, I put on my headphones and began to vibe to the beats. While approaching the bus stop, I saw two other white kids standing there. I looked for Elijah but didn't see him. When I reached the intersection, I turned around and saw Elijah walking down the street. I smiled and started to walk back over to meet him. When we merged, I took off my headphones.

"What up?" Elijah said as we dapped each other up.

"Wishing I was still in my bed," I replied as we walked towards the stop.

"I know that's right," he exhaled. "I hate getting up in the mornings. We should meet up in the mornings and walk over to the bus stop together."

"That's cool."

While at the stop, Elijah introduced me to the two white kids waiting for the bus. When the introductions were over, we all went back to our respective conversations.

"I wonder what teachers you got," he said. "I hope you're on my team."

"What team?" I asked.

"Each grade has teams. The six graders have four teams, seventh grade has three and us eighth graders have two," he said as I looked down at his fresh shoes.

"What is a team?" I asked.

"Whatever team you're on determines your teachers, the lunches and all that other stuff."

"So everybody that's on the same team gets the same group of teachers?" I asked.

"Yep."

"Gotcha," I nodded my head as I saw the bus coming around the bend.

Soon after, the yellow warning lights started to flash. Moments later the bus came to a complete stop and the red lights were flashing.

As I waited my turn to get on the bus, I sighed.

"This is it," I said as edged closer to the door. "The summer is officially over."

*****

Keston

I could feel him looking at me as I massaged his inner thigh. I felt like he was staring a hole into the back of my shirt. I wasn't even concerned with that shit, no matter how sexy he was. I had other fish to fry. Mainly, Phoenix Cummings.

Seeing Phoenix at Dray and Zach's place last night took me to another universe. Phoenix was the only person who seemed to know what to say and do to keep me calm. Even after all those years, he stepped right in last night in a way that no one else could.

His manliness, the timbre of his voice, his lips, his dreads, the way he looks at me—FUCK! Why do I still love this man?

I was still shocked at the fact that Dray figured out the truth that Phoenix and I was once a couple. I felt like my heart was going to beat out of my chest. Seeing Phoenix after all this time made me realize that I have to tell him the truth. I suppressed it, but never once did I stop loving Phoenix. While daydreaming about Phoenix, I was suddenly startled by his sudden movements.

"Yo, Kes, bruh," he sat up. I turned around to face him.

In just that instance, like a light switch had just been flipped on, I could hear all the commotion in the Falcons training room that I had blocked out of my mind.

"Yes?" I asked.

"You ok?"

"Yeah, I'm fine," I replied. "Why you ask?"

"You ain't doing it right," he said disgruntled, as he moved his body to the side of the training table and planted his legs on the ground. "That ain't how you've been doing it. I can tell that something is bothering you."

I stared at the 5'10", milk chocolate, five-time Pro-Bowler running back. This season would mark his tenth in the NFL. While he was getting up there in age in NFL standards, he still had some productive years left in him. His body—which was once his greatest asset—was now becoming his biggest liability. The body that made him millions of dollars as he rushed for thousands of yards was slowly starting to deteriorate from all the years of abuse that a NFL season can provide. Injuries had taken a toll on this exceptionally talented player.

His coming to Atlanta, was in essence, in his words, a rebirth of his career. He was here to prove that he could still contribute on a NFL team.

The San Francisco 49ers traded Sergio "Serge" McNeal to the Atlanta Falcons one year ago today. Since his emergence in Atlanta, we've become really good friends. His personality easily ranks him as one of my favorite NFL players.

"So you just gonna stare at me now?" he asked.

"Ain't nothing bothering me," I said.

Serge gave me a knowing look and then stood up and said, "It's all over your face. I've never seen you look like this. You wanna go somewhere and talk about it?"

"Serge."

"Do I need to have Qier give you a call?" he asked in reference to my cousin who played for the Seattle Seahawks.

"Serge, boy you're a mess," I forced a laugh. I changed the subject by saying, "How are the wife and kids?"

"They're fine. The kids started school today," he said. Serge patted me on my back and whispered, "Talk to someone. Holding it in ain't healthy." He smiled and walked away.

I looked around the room to see if anyone caught our exchange. I exhaled and plopped down on the training table.

Serge was correct. I needed to talk to Phoenix and I needed to talk ASAP.

He deserved to know the truth.

I just hope he can handle the truth.

69

Dorian

Monday's are the worst day of the week for me. Even though my body had been at work for a couple of hours, my mind wasn't quite here. I've had to focus because I'm still training Kory. He's pretty much got everything down, but he seems to have a few questions here and there.

Kory has been using a table in my office to do his training. He's had a pretty unreadable face, but today, not so much. He has a glow about him that I haven't seen until today.

Interrupting his workflow, I said, "Why the glow?"

He looked to me and said, "Huh?"

"What are you glowing for and don't tell me it's work."

"I'm just really excited," he smiled.

"Well, do tell," I smiled.

He stared at me and said, "Well, it's clear we both know what the deal is, as it was pretty evident at the bar that night with you and Brandon."

"Yeah," I nodded.

"And I can trust you to keep your mouth shut, right?" he asked.

"Of course," I whispered.

"What about Brandon, because I know how us dudes are. We always tell someone and Brandon seems to be the person you talk to about this stuff."

"Brandon is very private and he keeps his mouth shut. We all have too much to lose."

Kory stared at me, got up and walked over to my desk. He sat down in the chair across from me. He said, "I met someone."

"Really?"

"Yeah," he smiled. "Back in my day, I don't even know why I'm telling you this, but I did a lot of hoeing around. A LOT. I'm at a point where I want to slow down. Sleeping with everyone ain't cool anymore. There isn't a thrill anymore."

"Yeah," I said wondering if this person he met is me. Kory is definitely sexy, but Eric is in my life now. Ever since that night at the bar and back at my place, I felt like Kory was feeling me.

"I'm kinda interested to see where it could go," Kory said.

"Oh, really," I smiled.

"Yeah," he smiled back. "He's gonna present a challenge though. That much I can already tell."

"How's that?"

"I just can," he stood up. "But enough about that. Let me get back to work."

"Yeah," I smiled. "You do that."

*****

TJ

I stared at the black and white the clock on the wall. This American History class was almost over.

The teacher, Mrs. Simms, was sexy as fuck though, and that ass made her look like she can be Nicki Minaj's little sister.

An ass like that can't be legal. I know her boyfriend or husband is one lucky nigga because he gets to tap that shit every night.

I sat in the back of the class. I do that in every class as I like to scope out the scene. Elijah sat in front of me and Nolan sat to the left of Elijah.

As Mrs. Simms talked about something I really didn't care about, I focused in on the back of Elijah's head. Images from Saturday with Elijah started to flash in my mind. I didn't get very far into my thoughts as the sound of the bell resonated throughout the room.

"Have a great first day!" Mrs. Simms said as everyone jumped up. "Enjoy your lunch."

I grabbed my shit and hurried out of the room.

"C'mon," Elijah said as he sped-walked to the café with Nolan in tow. "I hate standing in line."

A few moments later, we walked inside the café, joining up with the kids who had already beaten us there.

"They got the snack bar, the salad bar and the hot lunch line," Elijah said pointing to each. "I'm going to the snack bar."

"Me, too," Nolan said.

"Well, I'm following y'all," I added.

I stood behind Nolan as he and Elijah talked. As we waited in the snack bar line, I saw very quickly how long the line became. In retrospect, the hot lunch line was equally as long. I looked at the salad bar and shook my head as it was abandoned. Every few seconds we inched closer to place our order. When it was our turn, I saw a plethora of choices from pizza to chicken fingers and fries to cinnamon buns.

Nolan and Elijah both spent four dollars on two slices of pepperoni pizza. I spent three and got four chicken fingers and a side of fries. When I grabbed the bottle of fruit punch from the cooler, I paid the cashier and rushed off to sit with my two new friends.

"So how you like it so far?" Nolan asked, looking at me.

"It's school," I shrugged my shoulders.

He stared at me for a second, exhaled and took a bite of his pizza.

"I'm so happy we're all on the same team, got all the same classes for the most part," Elijah said.

"Y'all see Mrs. Simms ass though?" I blurted.

"Yeah, Shawty," Nolan smiled. "That shit big as fuck! She can teach me history all right—all night long!"

I burst out laughing. Nolan laughed. Elijah forced a smile.

While Nolan started to talk about something, my mind went back to Saturday. Elijah kissed me and I didn't trip. Like…he really placed his lips on top of mine and I didn't stop him.

I know it happened so fast and then he ran off, but why didn't I trip? Why didn't I get mad? What the fuck is wrong with me?

I ain't gay. He may be, my daddy may be, Ray may be, but I ain't gay.

I wonder if he thinks about it. He hasn't said anything about Saturday. I know it's only been two days since it happened, but still.

Why didn't I trip? Why didn't I get mad? Why ain't I mad now?

Once school was over and we got off the bus, I said goodbye to Elijah and headed onto my house. My stomach dropped when I saw daddy's car parked in the driveway.

He isn't supposed to be home already. It's only 3:30. He ain't supposed to be home for at least another hour, hour and a half.

I sighed. I don't feel like dealing with him today.

Before I turned my key to enter from the side door, I took a deep breath. Maybe he was in his room or something. But he was sitting right there at the dining room table looking at some papers. He cut his eyes to me and said, "Hey, TJ."

"Hi," I replied as I closed and locked the door.

"How did your first day at the new school go?" he asked with excitement.

With a cold tone, I said, "Fine," as I walked past him.

"That's it?" he asked. "Just fine?"

"Yeah," I said as I walked out of the dining area headed for my room. "Fine."

*****

Zach

After I finished my orientation at Clark Atlanta, I was done for the rest of the day. I had a taste for Popeyes. I stopped and grabbed a two piece and a biscuit and then headed home. That should hold me over until dinner. As I edged closer to the home I shared with Dray, I saw a moving truck unloading some furniture off the truck and into the house next door to us. I turned into our driveway and ultimately into the garage without seeing who the was new neighbor.

Dray wasn't home, so he still must be in the orientation meeting with his department on campus. It's gonna be crazy to have Dray and I working at the same place, even if Dray is only there two days a week.

After I got undressed, I headed back down and sat at the island to eat my food. I was dying to let my teeth sink into that moist biscuit. The enjoyment didn't last too long as my phone started to vibrate against the marble countertop. When I saw the name, I smiled, wiped my hands and quickly answered with excitement, "Hey, Dorian!"

"What's going on big bruh?"

"Just walked in the house, trying to eat some chicken."

"I ain't mean to disturb you. Go ahead and finish your meal. I just wanted to hear your voice again. I had to make sure yesterday wasn't a dream."

I laughed and replied, "I asked my partner the same thing when I woke up this morning. It's so surreal to have finally met you, Dorian."

"I'm just happy we clicked," he said. "But I'm still at work. I was just calling. Don't be a stranger. Give me a call when you get a chance, big bruh."

"I will do, Dorian. Thanks for checking up on me."

Right after I took a bite of my chicken breast, the phone started to vibrate again. I yelled in frustration as I just wanted to enjoy my meal—I was starving! I exhaled upon seeing my mother's name flash on the screen. "Yes, mother?" I answered.

"How are you?"

"I'm fine, trying to eat," I said hoping that she'll get the hint to leave me alone.

"What are you eating?" she asked.

"Popeyes."

"You don't need to be eating that mess. It's bad for your health."

"Ma."

"Well, it is. All that grease and fried food isn't good for you. That stuff will kill you."

"At least I'll die happy," I rolled my eyes and shook my head.

"Whatever," she said as I could now envision her rolling her eyes. "So, did you make a decision?"

"Decision on what?" I asked as I took a sip of my sweet tea.

"Did you call the boy?"

"Matter of a fact, I did. We had brunch yesterday."

"Oh," she said taken aback. "Is that so?"

"Yes."

"And how did it turn out?"

"Just fine," I replied. "We really connected. He has a little girl named Dakota."

In a sarcastic tone, she said, "How precious."

I exhaled and shook my head. "He's not out to get me, Ma."

"You don't know what his motives are," she said. "You've always been to trusting of people. I know you didn't get that shit from me cause I'on trust nobody. This trust thing you have is especially true when it deals with something you want, as you only see that thing you want to see."

"Ma, stop trying to stir up some trouble. Stop trying to throw doubt in my mind. I think I'm a pretty good judge of character. Dorian is a good person."

"He is his father's son," she said with attitude.

"I am my father's son, too," I replied. "So what exactly is your point? Both Dorian and I have the same blood running through our veins."

"Oh," she said upset. "So because you meet his son, Duane's your father now?"

"Ma, please stop. I don't have time for this. Whatever issues you have with Duane is your problem not mine. Dorian is not Duane. Dorian is Dorian and Zach is Zach, just as Paula is Paula. So please stop trying to play your little mind games. I'm not a little kid anymore. It won't work this go around, Paula. It won't work. I am interested in seeing where this relationship with Dorian can go. For the life of me, why can't you be happy that he's in my life? Why can't you be happy that I finally have that brother that you were too selfish to give me."

"Excuse me?" she said upset. "You must have forgotten who in the hell you're talking too. I wil—"

"Ma," I cut her off. "I don't have time for the dramatics. I'm about to go. You can argue with yourself. I'm not entertaining it today. I love you and I'll talk to you later. Bye."

~Dial tone~

70

Dorian

This was my second time in Doug's, well, Eric's place. He was making us dinner tonight. Eric was an amazing cook and seemed to like the finer things in life. He has to go back to work tomorrow and with his crazy hours at the hospital, who knows the next time I'll get to really spend some time with him.

I was in the living room watching The Rachael Maddow Show on MSNBC and the smell of the food was starting to get to me.

I was glued to the TV with Rachael Maddow talking about who Senator Fitzgerald could possibly choose for her running mate in the upcoming presidential election. I love politics as it always makes for great television.

Just as the show was going to a commercial break, Eric walked into the living room and said, "Dinner is served."

I flipped off the television, stood up and followed behind him. When I got to the table, I smiled. He had candles set up on the table and the lights were dimmed; it was very romantic. The glare of the moonlight shined in the house through the opening of the vertical blinds on the sliding glass patio door. It was so beautiful.

After I washed up, I took a seat at the table and said grace. On my plate was the T-Bone that Eric had grilled along with a baked potato, fresh corn and a Caesar salad.

"Everything looks really good," I smiled as I immediately cut into the steak. After I took a bite, I said, "And damn, it tastes good, too."

"I do what I can," he smiled.

We ate and had small talk. As I sipped on my wine, he said, "So tell me something good that's going on in your life. I love good news."

"Well," I exhaled, as I wiped my face with a napkin. "Long story short, I met my oldest brother for the first time yesterday."

"Wow," he said. "How did that go?"

"Better than I could have ever imagined," I smiled. "We have the same father."

"Your brother is here in Atlanta?"

"Yes," I replied. "Eric, it was the greatest feeling in the world to finally meet him. When I was younger, my dad wanted us to meet but I was immature back then and wasn't ready for that. Now, that I'm an adult, things are different. We have so much in common it's crazy. When I saw him for the first time, I just knew he was my brother. I'm so happy right now. I want him to meet my daughter but I wanna feel him out some more first before I bring Dakota into the mix."

"I'm happy for you," Eric said.

"Thanks," I smiled. "He's handsome, he's educated. He's very well off."

"If he wasn't *well off,* would it have made a difference?" Eric asked.

"I don't know," I sighed. "I know with my brother having his own money means that he has no reason to try and come ask me for mine. Even though we took different paths in life, we both ended up in the same city and we're both are doing very well for ourselves."

"What does your brother do?" Eric asked.

"He's a professor at Clark Atlanta."

"Cool," he took a bite of his salad. "Not to bring down the mood or anything, and I am really happy for you meeting your brother, but I wish I had that connection with my brother that I once shared."

"What happened?" I asked looking Eric dead in the eyes.

"Man, it was so long ago," Eric sighed. "When I was in college at Florida State, I met this dude. We instantly clicked but the problem was he was dating my male cousin and neither one of us knew it at the time. My relationship with him was very platonic at first, until he and my cousin broke up. I know it sounds crazy that I ended up dating my cousin's ex-boyfriend, but sometimes that's how the cookie crumbles. Besides, I loved my cousin, but he was a dog. My cousin was cheating on the dude with his baby mama. When we actually became an item, it was one of the happiest moments of my life. The only person who knew about my sexuality was my cousin."

"He went to Florida State, too?"

"No, both my cousin and the dude went to FAMU."

"Oh," I said as I thought about my brother. I wonder if Zach knew any of these people.

"Anyway, my dude and I built something very special and things were really going well for us until one-night Black popped up and changed everything."

"Who is Black?"

"Black is my brother," Eric said.

"Did Black live in Tallahassee, too?"

"No, he lived in Orlando. But he showed up at my house unexpected, put a gun to my head and basically told me to give up the gay shit or he was going to expose me to the family."

"WHAT?" I said in shock. "He put a gun to your head? How did your brother know?"

I listened in shock as Eric explained in great detail how RJ entered into his brother's life. This seemed like some shit you'll see in the movies.

"So turns out your brother was gay, too," I said.

"Yeah and now he lives his life with RJ."

"Wow."

"I love my brother," Eric said, "always have, always will, but ever since that night things haven't been the same between us."

"So I take it you broke up with the dude?"

"Yeah," Eric said. "I was twenty-one. I was scared. I didn't know what to do. I couldn't risk being put out by Black. My family was everything to me. So, in the end, despite my better judgment, I broke it off with my dude. He wasn't happy and it was hard to do. When I realized my mistake, I tried to make things right with my dude but he was so hurt, he wasn't trying to deal with me. As time passed we eventually became friends again, but we never got back together."

"How does your cousin feel about this?"

"My cousin passed away ten years ago. While he was living, we got back on good terms and I wish he were still here with me today. In the midst of all that shit, RJ tried to tell me that my cousin was the real culprit behind everything that happened with Black."

"Do you believe him?" I asked. "In his defense, you did kinda steal the dude from under him."

"Just like I told RJ back then, my cousin is dead and cannot defend himself. Therefore, I won't even engage in that talk. I would like to keep the positive image I have of my cousin."

"I understand," I said. "And I apologize."

"No need for you to apologize."

"How did he pass away, if you don't mind me asking."

"Car accident," Eric sighed. "Both he, his oldest son and his unborn child all died in the accident."

"Wow. I'm sorry to hear that."

"It's life, Dorian," he sighed. "On a positive note, one of his kids made it out ok, so he's here to keep the legacy alive. Speaking of that, I need to pay Elijah a visit."

"He's here in Atlanta?" I asked.

"Yeah. He just turned thirteen last month and he looks just like his father."

I took a bite of my baked potato.

Eric said, "I have all the education in the world. I'm successful. I have the nice cars and I have the nice house, but I don't have the relationship that I yearn for. That's what's missing in my life. This is what I hope to achieve with you. I really like you, Dorian. You're smart, attractive, independent, have a career and a great personality. I want to build something with you."

"Do you still talk to your ex-boyfriend?" I asked.

"We're associates. I haven't spoken to him in at least three years. I was in Chicago doing my residency and we happened to cross paths at the mall. At the time he was living in New York and was in a long term relationship with his man. I haven't seen or spoken to him since a few months after that meeting in Chicago, and giving the way he loved that dude, I'm pretty sure they're making it work. So, if you're worried about me trying to reconnect with him, please stop. It's a null point. It's pretty clear that we'll be nothing more than friends. There's a reason why the past is the past and the future is the future. And Dorian, I would like for you to be a part of my future."

71

Keston

When I got home from practice this afternoon, I went back and forth in my mind for over an hour on if I wanted to call Phoenix. In the end, my heart won and he's on his way over here. I really don't know what I'm going to say to Phoenix, I just know I want him here.

A few moments later, my doorbell started to ring. I looked out the peephole, took a deep breath, opened the door and let Phoenix inside. He instantly smiled.

"I'm so happy you called," Phoenix said as I walked him over to the living room. "I told myself that I was going to let you call first. I didn't want you to think I was forcing myself on you or anything like that, so despite how much it was going to hurt, I was willing to let you decide if you wanted to see me again."

I stared at Phoenix. I thought about LaRon. I exhaled.

"So what's on your mind?" he asked. "You hungry? Wanna go grab something to eat?"

"I already ate," I replied.

The feeling in the room was awkward, neither not really sure of what to say.

In turn, Phoenix started to look around the room. Once he was done, he played with his phone for a few seconds. "How long have you been in Atlanta?" he asked.

"I moved to Atlanta in 2012. After I graduated from UCF, I attended grad school at FAMU. After I graduated from FAMU, I went to grad school at Georgia. After Georgia, I got a job in Atlanta and I've been here ever since."

"What kind of work do you do?" Phoenix asked.

"I'm a trainer with the Falcons."

"Oh, word?" he asked, surprised. "That's what's up."

"I love my job," I smiled. "I love working around the players. Each day presents a new challenge. I have the best job in the world."

"I'm happy for you," Phoenix said. "Well, as you know, or maybe you didn't, after I left UCF, I got drafted by the Sacramento Kings. They traded me to San Antonio a few years later. When my contract was up in San Antonio, I signed with the Chicago Bulls. So, I live in Chicago. That's my home."

"That's good, Phoenix."

"Did you keep up with me over the years?" he asked.

"Truthfully?" I asked.

"Yes, truthfully."

"No."

"Oh," he swallowed his spit.

"I'd see your highlights on ESPN or whatever, but I didn't go keeping tabs on you. Basketball isn't my sport anyway so trust me when I say it was no big deal."

"You know I have a son. His name is Giovanni."

"No, I didn't know that," I replied as I felt my heart sink into the bottom of my chest. This was not the news I wanted to hear. Preparing myself for the worst, I asked, "Are you with the mother?"

"No," he shook his head.

I breathed a sigh of relief.

"She was a fling I had in Sacramento to help keep my teammates from realizing that I'm gay. Trust me Keston, there is nothing there for my son's mom. We have a good working relationship as it concerns Giovanni, but that is it."

There was another awkward moment of silence.

Phoenix said, "Keston, can we stop beating around the bush? Can we get to the root of the matter here? What happened to us back in 2007? What happened?"

I exhaled.

As he stood up and walked over to me, he continued, "I know I fucked up keeping the truth about my past with DT away from you, but you and me were working on getting past that. And then it was as if you just dropped off the face of the Earth. I begged you to talk to me, to let me know what happened, to let me know what I could do to fix it. Keston, I've loved no one the way I loved you. I've tried with other dudes but no one compares. As time passed, I just put that shit out of my head, but that hurt me. I think it hurt my ability to love anyone else."

I swallowed my spit.

Phoenix sat down next to me, looked me in my eyes and said, "Keston, talk to me. Let me know what happened. Let me know, today, that I can fix it. Kes, I feel like we have a second chance at this thing. At least, I want to try us again. God put the people around us, in our lives for a reason. You ever think about that? Dray and his dude, Zach, were placed in our lives for this moment, for us to reconnect, for us to have a second chance at love. Keston, don't give up on us. If this is gonna work, we have to be transparent with each other. We have to put all the cards out on the table. Just let me know right now if I'm wasting my time. Let me know, Keston. I love you. I never stopped loving you, but I don't want to be a fool again. Tell me what happened. Let me know if I can fix it. Tell me if I have another shot at you."

"Whatever happened to Kory?" I asked, surprised I wasn't crying yet.

"I don't know," he shrugged his shoulders. "He got lost and all contact ceased. He transferred from UCF and I've never seen or heard from Kory again. Why you ask?"

"Phoenix, are you sure you want the truth?"

"Yes, Keston, please let me know the truth."

I exhaled.

Worried, Phoenix said, "Kes, baby, talk to me. What happened with us?"

"Phoenix, Kory is what happened. Your ex-best friend, Kory, is what happened to us."

*****

Phoenix

I felt my blood boiling, as Keston revealed what happened to him in my apartment nine years ago. There was so much rage built up inside of me, I wanted to kill Kory with my bare hands.

Everything made sense. EVERYTHING! From Keston's actions to Kory's disappearance, it all now made sense.

I didn't know what to say to Keston. What do you say to something like that? He seemed so strong. Not once during his revelation did he cry.

"Keston, why didn't you tell me?" I asked. "We could've gotten through this together. I could have taken care of Kory then."

"Truthfully, Phoenix, that was the straw that broke the camel's back. That was it. I couldn't take anymore. From all the shit that had been revealed about you and everything you kept from me, that incident just did it. In my mind, back then, I blamed you for everything."

"ME?" I asked dumbfounded. "I didn't do that to you!"

"Yes, you didn't do it directly, but indirectly, it all lead back to you."

"I don't follow," I said.

"Phoenix, you had Kory approach me in the first place because you weren't man enough to step to me yourself. You kept the truth about your past from me and you see how that blew up in your face. If you would have told me the truth from the get, I wouldn't have been in that apartment waiting for you. If you had never gotten Kory involved in our affairs, all this shit wouldn't have ever happened. So, back then, I blamed you. It was your fault. I couldn't stand the sight of you. You allowed your best friend to do this to me. In my mind, it was your fault. From the moment you stepped in my life, shit changed. It was always something bad. The best way for me to get over you was to leave you alone. The best way for me to get over you was to let you be."

"Keston, that's not fair and you know it," I pleaded as tears started to roll down my cheek. "Yes, I fucked up but I had nothing to do with Kory's actions."

"Phoenix," he wiped the tears off my face. "I know that now. I've grown up since then. I don't blame you for what happened."

"Why didn't you tell the police?" I asked.

"Because I loved you too much to fuck up your name. Had I told the police, the media would have started digging. It wouldn't have taken long for the media to uncover that we were a couple. It was just a tree I didn't want to climb. In addition to that, I didn't want people knowing that I was gay. That wasn't everyone's business."

"Does anyone else know what happened? Qier, Raheim, Izzy?"

"We all fell out with Izzy," Keston replied. "I haven't seen or heard from him in nine years. I never told Qier for the reason that he would have killed Kory. I never told Raheim because he would have told Qier. I never told a soul until a few weeks ago."

"You kept this secret inside of you for nine years?" I asked.

"Yes. I told Zach. Do you know why I told Zach?"

"Why?" I asked.

"Because I saw Kory."

"WHERE?" I jumped up.

"It was a few weeks ago. Zach, myself and some other friends were out to dinner and I had to use the restroom. Right before I was done drying my hands, he appeared out of the stall. Seeing him that night brought everything I had suppressed to the forefront. I had to deal with it. I had to get it off my chest. I had to tell someone."

"You saw him here in Atlanta?"

"Yes. I got the impression that he lives here now, but you never know."

"What happened in the bathroom?" I asked.

"Nothing. He tried to talk, but I didn't give him the chance."

I just stared at Keston. So many emotions were running all over my body. I didn't know whether to yell, cry, fight, scream, run, walk—I didn't know what to do.

I wanted revenge and I was going to get that shit. Kory Matthews and I were going to cross paths again. I was going to make sure of that. When you have money the way I have money, you can make mountains move.

I had no reason before to find Kory, but this changes things. This changes everything.

"But you know, Phoenix, I'm so over that. Even as I told you the story, I felt even more liberated than before. It happened and for the first time in my life since that night, I feel free. You just gave me back my freedom."

He smiled. I smiled.

"Phoenix, I have to be honest with you. I love you. I swear I do. Like you said yesterday, I want to get to know you again. I want to see where we can go."

"Let's do it then."

"There are a couple of issues."

"Which are?" I asked.

"First, I'm kinda sort of talking to someone. He really likes me."

I swallowed my spit and then with a serious look on my face said, "Drop him. He ain't me. He'll never be me. Save us all the time and let him go. What we have is real Keston. THIS SHIT IS REAL! I deserve to be happy—happy with you! Yes, I'm being selfish but I learned dealing with you to put all the cards on the table. I'm an open book, Keston. READ ME! I have nothing to hide. There are no boyfriends. There are no girlfriends. It's just me."

"Phoenix, even if I did do what you said, you live in Chicago. I live in Atlanta. It wouldn't work."

"Keston, I'll move to Atlanta if I have to."

"That's impossible," Kes said. "You're under contract with the Bulls and they are not trading you no time soon, especially being they just got rid of Derrick Rose."

"Kes, I have an early termination clause in my contract which gives me the choice to terminate my contract at the end of my third season or declare and stay with the Bulls for the last year of the deal. This upcoming basketball season will mark my third in Chicago. I'm an all-star. I have an Olympic goal medal. I have a NBA championship. Chicago is rebuilding and I don't want no parts of that. Truth is I wanted to leave the moment they traded Derrick Rose. Now, being here with you confirms that I should leave. I'd rather be happy with you than worrying about winning a championship. Being with you again will fill that hole in my heart."

"Phoenix, you'll say anything to me," he said.

"Keston, this isn't a game," I pleaded to him. "This is the truth."

I looked at him. He looked at me.

I thought about the plan that CJ, Keon Douglass and I have been thinking about. No one knew of this plan but us, our agent, and the owner and the general manager of the Atlanta Hawks. If the league found out, the Hawks could be charged with tampering so we've kept this under wraps. This is my one shot at happiness again and he needed to know how serious I am.

"Keston, the real truth is my best friend, CJ Wright, lives in

Atlanta and he plays for the Hawks. Our other friend, Keon Douglass, plays for the Brooklyn Nets. We've been talking behind closed doors about us joining forces here in Atlanta to make our own super-team. After what Miami did, and what Golden State just did, we have to join forces in order to win. No one can beat Cleveland in the east, much less talk about getting to a Finals with Golden State. Hell, Keon and I already have 'off-season' homes here in Atlanta."

"You have a home here?" Keston asked.

"Yes," I nodded. "The plan will work because we all have the same agent and he's in on the plan. It all works out because Keon's contract is up this season, too. Keon is going to tell the Nets ownership that he is walking at the end of season if he isn't traded to the Hawks. In January, I'm going to tell the Bulls management that I'm opting out of my contract to become a free agent so I can explore my options. Yes, I'm going to take a pay cut, but the endorsements my agent is lining up will take care of that."

"Interesting," he replied.

"I'm telling you this Keston to let you know that I'm serious about this. Just give me a year to end my contract with the Bulls and I'll be here in Atlanta for good. That's why I'm here now. I had a meeting with the general manager of the Hawks yesterday to confirm that we were going to do this. To him, I am the key in making this work. I am the person that will put this team over the top. Before he starts to make roster moves, he wanted to know if I'm in. Kes, I'm all in. It's gonna happen, baby. I will be in Atlanta. In the meantime, until my contract is up, I can fly to you and you can fly to me. It's only a two-hour flight. We can make this work. Just give us a chance, Keston. Just give us a chance at happiness."

Keston leaned over and stared me in the eyes. I stared him in his. I drew my face closer to his. And then our lips met. Our mouths parted. Our tongues touched.

He hands ran up and down my body.

Feeling Keston's touch was making my body weak. Electricity was shooting in my veins.

FUCK!

This is what I want to get lost in again.

This is what I've been missing.

Part Six:

Imperfect Me

72

Zach

Thursday, August 25, 2016

I was excited because I had the house to myself. It felt good to lounge around at home and not do anything. Dray was back at Clark Atlanta going through some more faculty and teacher development workshops. Luckily, my department was done for the week and I didn't plan on reporting back to campus until school starts in a couple of days. I really wanted to take this time and get my mind clear for the long semester of work ahead.

My phone started to vibrate. I read the text from Keston and it said, "Turn on the TV! It's official! It's all over the news!"

What the hell is he talking about? I grabbed the remote and flipped to MSNBC and saw the headlines: Florida Gov. J. Nehemiah Reed, II is Democratic Party VP pick. I jumped up in excitement. I couldn't believe it.

J. Nehemiah Reed is Senator Fitzgerald's vice presidential pick. A Rattler is going to the White House! As I waited for the press conference, I started to text all of my friends. This was unbelievable.

And then it hit me. Today is the first day of the rest of our lives. For the first time, today we meet the counselor that Dray's close friend, Gov. Reed suggested.

And then it was all gone. All of that excitement turned into nervousness. When we finish these meetings with the counselor, things will never be the same.

Never.

*****

Phoenix

My phone had awakened me. I grabbed it off the nightstand, looked at the name and exhaled. I said, "He better have some good news."

When I answered, he said in his distinctive voice, "Mr. Cummings?"

"Yeah, what up?" I asked as I looked over at the time.

"We've made contact with him."

I sat up in my bed.

"Are you there?" he asked.

"Don't fucking play with me, ok," I said.

"I'm not playing," he said. "We've got a match. We've found your man."

"Where is he?" I asked.

"Can you meet me?" he asked.

"Let me get dressed. Give me about twenty minutes and I'll call you."

"Ok," he hung up the phone.

*****

Dwight

I like working at night, but sometimes the overnight stuff has its drawbacks as I tend to lose a lot of sleep during the day. I regretted the fact that I couldn't sleep in as long as I wanted to, but I couldn't miss this meeting this morning.

When I woke up, Brennan and Nico were already off to school, and Lexi had dropped Chloe off at pre-school. After I got out of the shower and got dressed, I met Lexi downstairs. She was sitting on the couch gossiping on the phone. I shook my head; she rolled her eyes.

I walked into the kitchen and grabbed an apple and a bottled water. While she talked, I stood in the kitchen, raised my voice a bit so she could hear and said, "Lexi, I'm getting the kids today."

She looked at me with attitude in her face.

"Whatever," I shook my head as I headed out of the house.

I quickly jumped into my car and rushed out of the garage. I know I was about to run into some traffic but hopefully, at this time, it had died down some.

While on the interstate headed back into the city, I grabbed my phone and sent Kory a text that said, "What up? I wanna get up for drinks later. Let me know if that's cool." I looked back in my rearview mirror to make sure Lexi wasn't following me.

A few minutes later, Kory replied, "I get off work around 5. Will 7 be ok?"

After I finished making plans to get up with Kory tonight for drinks, I was at my destination. I was right on time. I walked into the building, signed in and waited until she was ready for me. A few minutes later, her secretary said, "Mr. Taylor, Miss Greene will see you now."

"Thanks," I smiled as I walked over to her office.

As soon as I entered, she smiled.

"Good to see you again, Mr. Taylor," my attorney said.

"Same here," I smiled as I sat down on the chair in front of her desk.

She immediately began to talk about the case. While she spoke, I looked around the room, but my eyes were drawn to the name plate on her desk: Natasha V. Greene.

My eyes slid over to her. Damn, she was sexy as fuck. Why couldn't someone like her be my wife? Her body is on point. She's educated. She's articulate. She has a job, and a damn good one at that. But I already know everything that glitters isn't gold. She's still a fuckin' female.

"Something wrong?" she asked, looking at me

"Huh?" I refocused my attention to her.

"I asked you a question and you didn't reply," Natasha said. "Is something wrong?"

"Umm no," I shook my head. "Forgive me."

"Mr. Taylor, if you're going to go through with this divorce, I need your undivided attention."

"I apologize," I ruefully said.

"Like I said, I've done some research on your wife. Mr. Taylor, are you sure you want to go through with this? She has some serious issues that needs to be addressed."

"Miss Greene, that is part of the reason why I want out. I don't want that stuff on my conscience."

"What about your children?" she asked.

"What about them?" I asked.

"You have three kids in the middle of this divorce. Are you sure this is something you want to do? Have you tried counseling? Have you tried separation from each other for a little while so both of you can clear your mind?"

Upset, I stood up and said, "Do I need to get another attorney to represent me? I didn't come here for you to offer me solutions on what to do with my marriage. I came here to get a divorce from my wife. Can you or can you not help me get this job done? If you can't handle my case let me know right now so I can stop wasting my God damn time!"

"Mr. Taylor, sit down," she demanded. "Your case is somewhat different than my others giving your wife issues. I'm just thinking ahead to when we get in the courtroom and the judge begins to ask some of these same questions. However, if you want to proceed with the divorce, then we can do that."

"Thank you," I replied.

She exhaled and said, "Let's get started."

73

TJ

This girl, Jodi, had caught my attention the first day of school, and now I can't seem to get her pretty face out of my head. She had long black silky hair; she was the color of honey. Jodi stood about 5'4". Nothing about her was wrong. She was perfect in my eyes.

I found myself staring at her in class all week long. I swear one time she looked back and smiled at me. Now, on the fourth day of school, I want to say something to her, but I'm not sure if it's too soon.

After we left Mrs. Simms history class, we headed over to the café. While we ate, I kept my eyes on Jodi. I tried not to make it too obvious, but guess I did.

"Who are you looking at?" Nolan asked.

"What?" I said as Elijah cut his eyes to me.

"Who you looking at?" Nolan asked again. "I see you staring at someone, question is who is it?"

"I'on know what you talking about," I replied as I looked at Elijah and shook my head.

"Umm, hmm," Nolan said as he turned around and began to scan the area. As he looked, he said, "Naw, it can't be her… naw… not her." He looked back at me and pondered for a moment. He turned back around and said, "Naw… not her… not her." He stopped and laughed.

"What?" I said.

"I know who it is," he smiled.

"Who?" Elijah eagerly asked.

"It's either Jodi or her best friend, Alison."

"Oh, I guess," Elijah said displeased.

"It's probably Jodi," Nolan said.

In embarrassment, I smiled and shook my head.

"I KNEW IT!" Nolan yelled in excitement. "You like Jodi, huh?"

"She straight," I said unbothered as I sipped on my fruit punch.

"You gonna say something to her?" Nolan asked, still excited.

"I ain't even say it was her," I replied.

"Shawty, it's Jodi," he said. "It was all over your face when I said her name."

I smiled.

Nolan looked at Elijah and said, "Da fuck wrong with you, over there looking like somebody killed ya dog."

"I'm straight," Elijah said. "Just thinking."

"What's on your mind?" I asked Eli.

"Nothing bruh," he grabbed his phone.

I looked at Nolan and he had an inquisitive look on his face.

"Whatever," I shrugged my shoulders as I put my focus back to Jodi. I don't have time for Elijah and his bitchiness.

"Shit, c'mon," Nolan jumped up.

"Where we going?" Elijah asked.

"To meet Jodi," Nolan smiled.

I looked over at Elijah and he said, "Oh."

"C'mon, TJ," Nolan said excited. I got up from my table and followed behind him. Elijah didn't come. When we got to their table, both Jodi and Alison looked at us.

"Boy, what you want?" Alison looked at Nolan.

"Not you," he replied as he put his attention to Jodi.

"Fuck you, Nolan!" Alison said with an attitude.

"When?" he looked at her.

I started to laugh.

"Anyway," Nolan replied as he looked at Jodi.

"What's up, Nolan?" Jodi asked as she looked at Nolan, then to me and back to Nolan.

"I wanted to introduce my homeboy to you."

"Why couldn't he introduce himself?" Alison said.

I looked at Alison for a second, and then focused back to Jodi.

Nolan continued, "TJ just moved here from Charlotte last month."

"Yeah," Jodi smiled. "I see you in some of my classes."

"Oh, fa real?" I asked.

"Yeah," she blushed. "I be seeing you sitting in the back."

I smiled and said, "That's what's up."

"Why won't y'all sit down," Jodi insisted.

"They don't need to be sitting over here," Alison said with an attitude.

"Alison shut up and scoot yo' ole ugly ass over," Nolan said as he sat down.

"Nigga, I ain't ugly," she said, scooting over.

He leaned over and kissed her on the cheek and said, "Now shut up, shit."

I laughed and turned around to see what Elijah was doing. He was just staring at us, not eating, not playing on his phone, just staring.

I shrugged my shoulders and sat down next to Jodi.

I wanted to learn more about her.

*****

Dwight

Chloe ran and yelled, "DADDY!" once she saw me. I smiled at her and then put my attention back to the girl working the front desk. She smiled as Chloe made her way over to me.

"Mr. Taylor," the girl said. "I can already tell that Chloe is going to be very smart. I love working with her as she is a quick learner."

"Thanks," I smiled, as I picked my baby girl up and gave her a kiss. I looked at Chloe and said, "Baby girl, you ready to go?"

"Yes, Daddy," she said excited. "BYE, MS. BROWN!"

"Bye, Chloe," the girl said. "See you tomorrow."

I placed four-year-old Chloe down on the ground and held her hand as we walked out of the preschool.

"Daddy, I color *taday*," she said.

I smiled at her pronunciation and said, "Really, baby girl? What did you color?"

"A house," she stated as we got to the car. "Then I make believe like you and mommy and Nico and BrenBren was in the house, too."

"Where is it?" I asked as I strapped her in her booster seat. "I want to see."

"Ok, Daddy, you can see," she smiled as she pulled out the sheet of paper from her book bag.

"That's beautiful, honey," I smiled as I looked at the picture. "What color is the house?"

"Ummm," she said as she looked at me. "Green?"

"Good job, Chloe," I kissed her on the cheek. "It is green."

When I got into my seat, Chloe said, "Daddy, can I have some McDonald's?"

"Ok."

She smiled really hard as I pulled out of the preschool.

Luckily for me, Nico and Brennan, who Chloe likes to call BrenBren, went to the same school and it was only a few minutes from the preschool.

I got to the school early. They still had another thirty minutes left in the day, but I didn't feel like waiting. I got Chloe and headed over to the main office. I showed my ID and signed the early release form.

"Mr. Taylor, what grades are your sons in?" the clerk asked.

"Brennan is in fourth and Dominic is in the first."

"Ok," she smiled. "Just another security measure."

She walked over to the intercom system and asked their teachers to release them from class. I stood by the door and waited for them to arrive. In the meantime, Chloe was talking about something but I really wasn't paying attention. My focus was on my meeting with my attorney, Natasha, this morning. I don't want to break up my home, but I can't continue to stay in this marriage.

"Hey, dad," Brennan said as he saw me. "Where's mommy?"

"I think she's at home."

"Oh," he said as he put his attention to Chloe.

Moments later Nico arrived and we headed over to the car. Brennan took his spot in the front while I made sure Chloe and Nico was strapped into their booster seats.

Once I pulled off, Chloe bragged, "Daddy is taking me to McDonald's."

"Daddy, I wanna go," Nico pouted.

"Me too," Brennan said.

"We're all going to McDonalds," I replied as everyone in the car was happy. "I just have to take care of a few things first, ok?"

"OK!" they all said.

Moments later, I looked in the rearview mirror and Chloe and Nico were off talking about something. Brennan, on the other hand, was looking out the window.

Brennan never said much to me as he was a mama's boy. Nico tried to play on both parents to see how far he could get, while Chloe was a daddy's girl.

I knew Lexi was going to know everything we did today because Brennan was going to tell her. That boy's mouth is like a water fountain. As best friends, Nico and Chloe are always too much into each other to pay attention to what's going on around them.

I ended up going to the bank, the post office and stopped by the gas station. About forty-five minutes later, we ended up at McDonald's.

Nico and Chloe got a happy meal while Brennan wanted chicken nuggets. He said he was too old for the happy meal, that was for little kids. I smiled. He was growing up right before my eyes. I grabbed a salad and followed them outside into the playpen area.

After they finished eating their food, all three ran over to the pen and started to play with each other. While they played, I tried to imagine how life would be for them if we got a divorce. What kind of impact would that have on my kids? More specifically, how would it affect Brennan since he is really close to his mother? I don't want my kids to hate me.

I exhaled and thought about Nehemiah. I can't believe that he is the Vice Presidential Nominee for the Democratic Party. If they win the election, he would be a heartbeat away from the presidency.

As I looked at the kids, my thoughts were interrupted by the vibration of my phone. When I saw Lexi's name, I exhaled and said, "Yes, Dear?"

"WHERE THE FUCK YOU GOT MY KIDS, DWIGHT? WHAT BITCH HOUSE DID YOU TAKE MY KIDS TO?"

"First off, you need to calm the fuck down," I said as softly as I could.

"WHY THE FUCK DIDN'T YOU TELL ME YOU WERE PICKING THEM UP? HAD ME COME ALL THE WAY OVER HERE AND YOU ALREADY GOT THEM!"

"Lexi, for the second and final time, you need to calm the fuck down and talk to me like I am your husband, not some nigga off the street."

I looked at the kids to make sure they didn't hear our conversation. I saw Brennan turn his head to see what I was doing.

As Lexi talked in a calmer tone, Brennan started walking over to the table. I shook my head. Lexi had his ass trained.

"Lexi," I said purposely when he got to the table. "I told you this morning that I was picking them up today."

"No, you didn't," she said.

"Lexi, yes I did."

Once he realized I was talking to his mom, he took a sip of his drink and headed back over to the slide. I shook my head.

"No, you didn't, Dwight."

"Yes, I did. You were talking on the phone. It's not my business you don't pay attention."

"Whatever, Dwight," she said defeated. "When are you bringing my kids home?"

"When I feel like it."

"Where are you?" she asked.

"What do I need to tell you for? That's what have got Brennan for, right?"

"Fuck you Dwight, fuck you!"

I hung up the phone.

74

Zach

I arrived at the counselors building and waited for Dray to show up. I checked the time and I was a few minutes early. Being a counselor on the collegiate level, I knew today's session wasn't going to be too bad, but just the idea of going here was making me nervous. The fact that I vowed to be completely honest with Dray during these sessions was bothersome. Well, the idea of being honest didn't bother me. The fact the Dray would know I cheated on him with Dwight is what bothered me. The entire thought of coming here has changed my mood. I'm just not in the mood for bullshit today.

The other thing about this counseling session was the fact that someone was going to know that we were gay. While I was a proud black gay man, I didn't want the world in my business. I still like to believe in discreetness and practice the idea of privacy.

I know Dray said Nehemiah suggested this counselor but I can only hope that it's some old white lady. I would most definitely feel comfortable talking to her, rather than some judgmental black female or some straight dude.

A few moments later, Dray zoomed in next to me and parked his car. When he got out, I took a deep breath and exited my car.

"You ok?" Dray asked.

"Yeah, just nervous."

"What are you nervous for, you got something to hide?" he asked.

I just stared at him.

"Complete honesty, Zach."

"Complete honesty, Drayton," I cut back.

We walked inside and both filled out some papers that the receptionist handed us. Once done, I turned mine in and sat back down and observed the huge open space. There was another couple here—white and straight—who went to see the other doctor who shared the floor with our counselor.

As the receptionist typed my information into her computer, she kept stealing glances at us as if she knew we were gay. I exhaled as her unspoken words but readable face was starting to piss me off.

A few minutes after Dray turned in his papers, the receptionist answered the phone. When she hung up, she said, "Mr. Wescott and Mr. Finley, Dr. Bynum will see you in room three."

"Doctor Finley," I mumbled as I rolled my eyes.

Dray knocked on the door and soon we heard, "Come in."

We walked in the room, and a black, fairly young, maybe in his mid-thirties, attractive black male was there. He was tall, dark and handsome. He was athletic, had a short cut and wore glasses.

I quickly glanced at his name plate located on his desk. As he came from around his desk to greet us, Dr. Bynum extended his hands and said, "Mr. Wescott and Mr. Finley, it's nice to meet you."

"Ummm… Doctor… Finley," I shook his head, putting emphasis on doctor. He's a doctor. I'm a doctor. In my eyes we're on the same level motherfucking level and you will address me as such.

"Zach?" Dray said looking at me.

"What Dray?" I cut.

"Really, Zach?"

"Pardon me," Dr. Bynum said taken aback.

Dray cleared his throat and shook his head. I cut my eyes to Dray.

"You have to excuse Zach," Dray said. "I don't know what's wrong with him today."

"It's ok," Dr. Bynum said. "A lot of people usually have some negative feelings about seeing me."

I cleared my throat.

"Please sit," Dr. Bynum said as he sat down in the chair directly across from us. He stood up, walked back to his desk and grabbed his yellow legal pad and pen. When he returned back to his seat, he said, "Well, for starters I just want to introduce myself. I'm Dr. Reginald M. Bynum. My main objective is to help you get to the root of your issues and ultimately, make you a stronger couple."

I swallowed on my spit. It felt strange being on the other side. I was always the one with the legal pad and pen.

"As you know," Dr. Bynum continued. "Gov. Reed placed a phone call to have me see you. I am extremely booked right now, but if he asked for the favor, it must be important."

"Are you from Georgia?" Dray asked.

"No, I'm from North Carolina."

"Where did you do your undergrad?" I asked.

"North Carolina Central University."

"Oh," Dray said. "So how do you know Nehemiah?"

"We attended Harvard together. It was only a few of us there," he said as he pointed to his skin. "So we all somewhat knew each other. Nehemiah and I were roommates our first year at Harvard. We instantly hit it off and have been very close friends ever since. Speaking of him, I can't believe that the senator chose him to be her running mate. Isn't that amazing?"

"Yes, it is," Dray said.

"I almost lost my mind this morning when I saw the news," I smiled.

"I wish my friend all the luck. I have no worries that they'll win the election," Dr. Bynum said.

"Me too," I smiled.

Dray smiled.

"Well, I guess we can get started," Dr. Bynum said. "I just want to reassure you that whatever we talk about in this room is confidential. I will never repeat to anyone anything that is discussed here. You have my word."

I nodded my head in agreement.

"Today's session is just a feel me out session," Dr. Bynum said. "I just want to get to know your background, how you got to where you are in your life, how you met. I don't want to get into anything to serious today. We can build up to that. Most importantly, I want you to feel comfortable talking to me. I want to build that rapport with the both of you that you can trust me and I am here to help. One of my professors back at Harvard use to say 'baby steps,'" he smiled. "Baby steps."

Dray smiled.

"Is that ok with you, Dr. Finley?" Dr. Bynum asked. "Mr. Wescott?"

We both nodded our heads.

"Ok," he crossed his legs. "So how long have you been together?"

"December will make eight years," Dray said.

"Wow," he nodded his head in amazement. "Longevity is something you don't see in the black gay community."

"I agree," Dray said.

"So," Dr. Bynum said looking at me. "Let's go back eight years. Tell me how you met."

75

Dwight

When I got back home, I never got out of the car. I dropped the kids off with Lexi and left. Like expected, she blew up my phone. Unlike the last time, I didn't answer. She sent text messages demanding that I call her. I ignored them. I didn't have time for her shit.

So, that brings me to now. I'm sitting here at the bar with Kory. We'd been here for a few hours, talking, drinking and getting to know each other.

We spent a lot of time talking about Florida Governor, J. Nehemiah Reed II, and what this vice presidential nominee pick could mean politically in eight years if the democrats win the White House in this election. We could soon have another black president.

While we sat and talked, I really learned a lot about Kory. He was from Baton Rouge, Louisiana and went to school at UCF for a few years before finishing his degree at Louisiana State. I thought about asking him if he knew Keston since they would have been on the yard at UCF around the same time, but for the sake of my privacy, along with Keston's, I kept that comment to myself.

"You ever do something you weren't proud of?" Kory asked.

"Like what?"

"Anything," he stared at me. "Anything you wish you could take back?"

"I have a few," I chuckled as my marriage with Lexi popped in my mind.

He stared at me without saying anything. He looked like he was in deep thought.

"You alright?" I asked, breaking his train of thought.

"Umm yeah," he said. "Just thinking."

"What did you do?" I asked. "What happened?"

"I rather not say," he replied. "I wasn't myself."

I looked at him with suspicion. What was he talking about?

"You know," he continued. "The past always has a way to rear its ugly head. A few weeks ago, I saw someone that I never thought I would see again in life. I wanted to apologize for my mistakes but it's some shit you can't take back, feel me? I know I fucked up that night, but the truth is I wasn't myself. I have no idea how I got to that low point in my life. I feel like old demons from my past are resurrecting. Ever since I saw him a few weeks back, I get this eerie feeling. When I'm at home, I don't sleep well. I can see the shit I did. I'm really sorry for everything," he said as tears fell down his face. "I fucked up and I have to live with it for the rest of my life. If I see him again, I don't know what will happen." He wiped his face and exhaled. "I hope I didn't turn you off. I know seeing another man cry isn't the most masculine thing in the world."

"Naw, I'm not turned off at all," I replied. "We all have a past. We can't change the past. The past is history; the future is a mystery. All we have is now. Today. Don't let your past control the rest of your life. We all make mistakes but we have to learn from them, understand? I know I've made my share and sometimes I ask myself am I making a mistake right now. Is this what I really want to do? Do I really want to divorce my wife? Do I really want to cause a rift with my children? Point is Kory, if you see whoever, just ask for forgiveness. I don't know what happened, but even if he doesn't forgive you, you have to forgive yourself and move on."

"But sometimes sorry isn't enough," he said.

I said, "True. But admit you fucked up and move on. I ain't the best person to be giving advice on this stuff as my best friend has the counseling degree, but I've learned a thing or two from him."

He smiled and said, "Thanks Dwight for understanding. I needed to get that off my chest. Maybe I'll sleep a little better tonight."

"I hope so," I checked the time. "I hate to head out, but I gotta get home and get ready for work. I've got a long night ahead of me."

After we paid our tab, we dapped each other up went in our separate directions.

*****

Phoenix

Being with Keston like this reminded me of old times back when we were in college. Now that we've reconnected, it doesn't even feel like any time has passed. The past four days have been the best four days in a very long time. I love this dude. I love being around him. I just love…HIM. I make that known every chance I get. To see his smile when I say it, makes me feel good. True love like this can't be denied. We will defy the odds. Keston and I are meant to be together, forever.

After we ate the dinner that Keston prepared, and that was special because my babe doesn't cook, we just chilled around the house. We didn't do anything special, as he was off on the internet and I was watching TV, but he fact that we were under the same roof made it all feel complete.

We haven't had sex, but even that was ok. I know how long he made me wait when we first got together and I'll wait even longer this go around if it meant we we're gonna be together forever.

My best friend, CJ, came back to town from his vacation with his brother, and moved into his new house. CJ was supposed to take me by the place so I could see it, but our times never matched up. Today, when we both finally got some free time, I wanted to go by the new place and take Kes along so he could meet CJ, but that didn't happen. CJ and his brother, Renzo, had to fly back to Chicago because their mom, Ms. Loretta, who I like to call Mama Wright, was rushed to the hospital.

My phone started to vibrate. I grabbed it off my lap and saw that CJ was calling. "Hey bruh, everything alright with Mama Wright?"

Kes looked over at me then put his attention back to his computer.

"I don't know," CJ said. "I don't know what's wrong. They can't tell us anything. They keep running tests and shit but this is getting frustrating. I don't know what I'll do without my mama, Phoenix. I need my mama," he broke down. "My mama can't die. She can't die, Phoenix!"

"CJ," I stood up and walked to the window. "Mama Wright is gonna be ok. She's gonna be ok. OK? Just make sure you stay strong for Renzo. You know how much he looks to you for your guidance and support. You hear me, CJ?"

"Yeah," he said. "Man, they got all those machines and shit hooked up to her. She ain't talking. I can't look at my mama like this. I can't take this shit. My mama ain't never did nobody wrong. She lived her life right. Why she gotta be sick?"

"Everybody gets sick, CJ."

"I know man, but still," he said. "Man, let me go. I'll call you later. I need to go check on my mama."

"Ight, CJ," I said as my phone started to beep alerting me to the fact that I had another call waiting. When I saw the name, my eyes got wide. I turned and looked at Kes and he was head first into his computer. "I'll say a prayer for you, man. Everything will be ok, CJ. I promise."

"I hope so," he hung up.

As soon as the line clicked, I said, "Yeah?"

"He's ready for you," the other caller said.

"Are you sure?" I asked.

"One hundred percent positive," he said. "He's ready for you right now."

"Ok. Is everything the same from earlier?" I asked.

"Yes," he replied. "The entry gate code is 91741."

"Ok."

"Come now."

"I am," I hung up the phone. I exhaled and turned around to face Kes.

"Everything ok with your friend?" he asked.

"Not really," I replied. "I told you earlier that his mom was rushed to the hospital. They don't know what's wrong. He's worried," I said as I grabbed my keys.

"You leaving?" Kes asked.

"Yeah. I'll be back in a few minutes. I need to run some errands, stop by the house to shower and get some clean clothes. I'll be back soon."

"Ight," he said. "I'm getting tired so I might dose off. You remember the gate code right?"

"Yeah."

"Take the spare key just in case," Kes said as he walked in his room. When he came back out, he handed me the key.

"I'll be right back," I smiled as I kissed him on the forehead.

"Ight," he smiled, as he walked me to the door. "Be safe."

76

Kory Matthews

Atlanta, Georgia

As soon as I arrived home from the bar, I undressed, ready to hop in the shower. That, however, was interrupted by the sound of my doorbell.

I wrapped the towel around my waist and walked to the door, hoping that Dwight was on the other side. When I looked out the peephole, I exhaled and said, "What the hell?"

I opened the door and forced a smile. She instantly looked down at my half naked body.

"Papi, I didn't come at a bad time did I?" she asked, as she again looked down at my towel.

The fiery hot Latina, Giselle Lopez, lived across the hall from me, and damn, she had the phattest ass I've ever seen on a woman.

"Naw," I said. "I was just about to get in the shower."

"Well," she stepped in closer to me and handed me a plate. "I made you some dinner."

I moved out of the way to let her inside. Once she was inside the condo, I closed the door.

"I already ate," I said holding the warm plate.

"It's ok, save it for lunch or something," she replied as she looked around the apartment.

I placed it down on the kitchen counter and said, "I hate to be rude, but I've got to get in the shower, Giselle."

She looked down at my towel then up to me and said, "I understand."

As we walked to the door, she said, "Please tell me if you don't like it. I really tried to make it taste good for you."

"Ok," I opened the door.

She stepped out into the hallway and said, "I made it just in time for you to get home so it could be nice and hot but you never came, so I just kept it on the warmer. I waited and waited for you to come home and I was starting to get nervous. You're usually home by seven. It's after ten."

"You're stalking me now?" I asked with a nervous laugh.

"NO, BOY!" she said as she playfully hit me on my arm. "I just happen to be walking my dog and I've seen you arrive a few times around seven that's all. But, I don't want to hold you. Let me know how it tastes, ok?"

"Ok, Giselle," I smiled. "I'm gonna go get in the shower now."

"Bye, sexy," she walked away.

I shook my head and closed the door. As I headed back to my room, my phone started to ring. It was Dwight. As soon as I answered, the sound of my doorbell resonated throughout the condo. "What's up, Dwight?"

"Nothing just heading off to work."

"I swear for the life of me, this girl won't leave me fuck alone," I exhaled as I headed back to the door.

"Who is it?" he asked.

"This chick that lives across the hall from me."

"Oh," Dwight laughed. "She wants some of that dick."

"Whatever," I laughed as the doorbell rang again.

"I'M COMING, GISELLE, DAMN!" I yelled.

"Give her that dick. It'll shut her ass up for a lil bit," Dwight laughed.

"Man, you so crazy," I laughed as I unlocked and opened the door.

Only, this time, it wasn't Giselle.

"I…I…I," I stuttered. "I gotta call you back."

I hung up the phone. I stared at Phoenix. He stared at me.

This shit had to be a dream. It had to be.

"Long time, no see, Kory Matthews."

I swallowed my spit.

As he forced his way into my condo, he said. "We've got some shit to discuss, right now."

*****

Phoenix

Kory closed and locked the door. I looked at him and shook my head.

"What are you doing here?" he asked. "How did you know where I live?"

"What am I doing here?" I replied. "Don't play stupid, ok."

Kory swallowed his spit and then said, "How did you find my place?"

"I can find any fucking thing I want." I stared at him in disgust.

"You want something to drink?" he asked.

"You think we cool, nigga?" I asked. "We ain't cool. Naw, we ain't cool!"

"Why are you in my house?"

"KORY, DON'T FUCKING INSULT MY INTELLIGENCE," I yelled as I walked up to him.

He backed back into the wall. Fear was in his eyes. We were so close together, our noses touched. I grabbed him by the neck and used my strength to slide him up the wall.

While he struggled for air, I whispered in his ear, "I can kill yo' ass with my bare hands right now and no one will ever find a bone of your got damn body. Why? Because I got enough money to take care of that shit. You'll just vanish off the face of the fucking earth, never to be seen or heard from again. But you know what," I said as I gripped his neck harder. "I'm better than that."

I released my grip and he immediately started to gasp for air.

Once he regained his composure, I said, "As much as I want to fuck yo' life up, I'm better than that, Kory. You see way back then I would have fucked your life up, but now, it ain't even worth it. I have too much to lose. Little kids look up to me. I have major endorsement deals that I can't fuck up. I have a son, Kory. I have Keston. As much as I want to show you how I feel about you, it ain't worth losing everything for a piece of shit like you. I thought you were my dawg. You were my best friend, Kory. We did so much shit together. And then you just disappeared. I can't believe you man. Why, Kory? Why would you do some shit like that? WHY? Kes ain't never did shit to you."

He didn't say anything. Tears rolled down his cheek.

"You were too much of a bitch to admit how you felt about me, so you tried to sabotage my relationship with Kes instead. You're not even my type Kory and you know it. I can't believe you, man. I lost nine years with him because of yo' fuck ass. NINE YEARS, NIGGA! He blamed me for the shit you did, Kory. YOU!"

"If," he softly said. "If I could take back everything, I would. I don't know how that shit happened, it just did. I don't know what came over me. You know me, Phoenix. You know I wouldn't do no shit like that."

"FUCK YOU, KORY! YOU DID IT! YOU DID IT. YOU!"

"I know that Phoenix and I live with it every day."

"You live with it? YOU LIVE WITH IT? NIGGA, KESTON LIVED WITH IT AND HE'LL CONTIUNE TO LIVE WITH IT UNTIL THE DAY HE DIES. You did that to him. You did it!"

He just looked at me and said, "I didn't mean for it to happen. I really didn't."

"Kory, I never thought you could stoop to such low levels," I shook my head.

He exhaled.

I said, "I don't want shit to do with you. If I see you, you better walk in the other direction. If you see Keston, you better walk in the other direction. He doesn't want to see or hear anything you have to say. If any part of our conversation from tonight is leaked, you're a dead man walking. It's not a threat. Believe that shit, nigga. I mean it. You're a dead man walking."

I looked at him and shook my head as I headed for the door.

"You're pathetic," I said as I grabbed the knob. "Why won't you do us all a favor and kill yo'self. Kill yo'self, nigga. Kill yo'self."

77

Keston

Friday, August 26, 2016

As my internal body clock went off, alerting me it was time to wake up, I felt a strong pair of arms wrapped around my body. I exhaled. Damn, this felt so good. I don't know what time Phoenix got back last night, but it was a great feeling to wake up to.

I looked at the alarm clock. I still had some time before I had to get up for work.

I didn't want to move from this position. This felt like heaven. He had me so close and tight to his body, it was like we were one.

This feels so right. I have no doubt in my mind that this is the man I'm supposed to be with for the rest of my life. This is the man God made just for me.

Yes, he made some mistakes. Yes, our past isn't perfect. But, hell, I'm not perfect either. I've made my own mistakes. I can't live in the past. I can only look towards the future and I know the future is with this man.

In the midst of my bliss, an image of LaRon popped in my mind. I exhaled.

LaRon was a good dude and I know I needed to tell LaRon what the deal is with Phoenix. So, as much as it may hurt LaRon, he needs to know where my heart resides and it's not with him.

I guess Phoenix could tell I was awake because he ran his hand across my stomach and sluggishly said, "Good morning, Bae."

I smiled and replied, "Morning." I turned around and faced him.

With those succulent brown eyes of his, he stared me in mine and smiled. He said, "I've never loved someone the way that I love you. I don't know what you do to me, but I just know this is right. This is where I'm supposed to be." Phoenix paused for a moment and then continued, "Maybe when we were younger, I didn't fully understand what it meant to be in a relationship. Maybe I didn't fully understand what honesty does for a relationship. But Keston, I'm not that young 21, 22-year-old college kid. I've grown and experienced life. And I know without a doubt, I'm ready to be that man for you. I'm ready to be that man in your life. I'm ready, Kes. I'm ready to be one hundred percent committed to you and no one else. This isn't about sex or any of that bullshit. Sex is great but I'm past just trying to bust a nut. I want companionship. I want you, Keston. From that day I first saw you in the cafe back at UCF, I knew it was something special about you, and over all these years I still feel the same way. I want to spend the rest of my life with you, Keston. You and only you."

I stared at him.

"I'm not looking for a commitment from you today or anything like that," he continued. "But I just want you to know where I stand. No fucking games, no fucking bullshit. I want you to know that this is how I feel. With my stupidity, I fucked up and lost you when we were younger; Keston, I don't want to lose you again. I mean that shit. I don't want to lose you again. Do you understand what I'm saying?"

I nodded my head and smiled.

"Good," he said. "I know my breath is probably kicking, so let me get up and get my life together."

We both got out of the bed at the same time. While Phoenix went to his suitcase, I headed directly over to the bathroom. As soon as I finished brushing my teeth and washing my face, Phoenix entered.

I needed to get in the shower, but there was no way I could undress with him standing right there. If I did, I knew we would be fucking in no time.

I hear everything Phoenix is saying, but I don't want to rush back into something. I don't want to get burned twice by him. I want to take my time and see where this goes. I love him, too, and I just want us to last this go around. I don't want there to be any mistakes.

While I sat on the bed, my phone started to vibrate. I picked it up only to see *his* name on the screen. Suddenly, my heart started to beat a bit fast. I started to feel nervous. My stomach was weak. I knew what I had to do. It was gonna hurt, but I had to do it. After a few more seconds, I answered.

"Hey, Kes," LaRon stated. "Good morning."

"Nothing much, LaRon," I replied as Phoenix walked back into the room.

"Is everything alright?' LaRon asked. "I hadn't heard from you in a few days."

I stared at Phoenix who was now looking through his suitcase for something to wear. I exhaled. I knew I had to do it. I had to do it now. "Yeah, LaRon, we need to talk."

"What's wrong?" he asked.

"I just want to be straight up and honest with you because I wish that you would do the same for me."

"Kes, what's going on?" he asked, worried.

Phoenix stared at me.

I ran my hand across my face and said, "Listen, LaRon, you are a great dude. You're a good friend. You're smart, handsome, successful. But if I'm being honest—"

He cut me off by saying, "What Keston?"

"If I'm being honest," I continued, "I'm trying to fix things with my ex, my real first love. LaRon, you did nothing wrong. And like I said, you're a great dude, but my heart is still with him. I don't think it's fair to drag you along and in the long run I don't think I can ever give you all of me knowing that I still love that man. I've tried to convince myself that being with you is the way to go, but the picture is clear. I don't want to hurt you, but I respect you too much to lie to you. I hope you can understand my plight. I'm sorry, LaRon."

"No need to apologize," he said. "The heart wants what the heart wants and it's nothing no one can do about it. I kinda felt this was coming, it was just a matter of time. No hard feelings, Keston. It was fun," he laughed nervously. "While this isn't the news I was looking forward to, I appreciate you being honest with me and I will respect your wishes."

"Thank you for understanding."

"I hope you find happiness in this dude. Be safe and I'll get at ya. Goodbye, Keston."

I hung up the phone and stared at Phoenix. He smiled and said, "You don't know how that makes me feel. You have no idea how that makes me feel. Damn, I love you."

I smiled and said, "I love you, too."

He walked over to me, kneeled down and gave me a kiss. Damn, that shit felt so good.

So good…

78

Dwight

I felt my body shaking. I could hear a distant voice. The voice was louder... and louder... and "DWIGHT WAKE UP!" Lexi yelled. "WAKE UP!"

I jumped up and said, "What, what's wrong?"

She crossed her arms right on top of her breasts and with attitude said, "We need to talk."

"Lexi, are one of my kids sick?"

"No."

"Are one of my kids in trouble?"

"No."

I shook my head and said, "I'm going back to sleep." I laid back down and pulled the cover over my head. I'm too tired for her mess this morning.

And then in an instant, I felt a cool breeze come over my body. I reached for the cover and she had snatched it off of me. When I looked at her, she said, "I SAID WE NEED TO TALK!"

"Why the fuck are you always yelling and shit?" I looked at the time and said, "Damn, it's ten in the morning. I just got home from work three hours ago. Can I please get some rest?"

"Who is the bitch, Dwight?" she asked.

"Oh, my God," I said upset. "Lexi, gone somewhere with that bullshit. I've had it up to here with you and your allegations."

"WHO THE FUCK IS SHE, DWIGHT? WHO YOU FUCKING, NIGGA?"

"Lexi, you have ten seconds to give me back my cover. I'm not playing with yo' dumb ass."

"You think I'm stupid, don't you? Nigga, I ain't stupid. My mama ain't raise no fool. I know what you're doing. I know where you be going. I know you're going to see her. Underestimate me if you want. I got something for dat ass. You think you're trying to get me? Naw, nigga, I got something for dat ass. Keep fucking with me, Dwight. Keep fucking with me."

Upset, I said, "Bitch, give me the God damn cover I paid for and get yo' stupid ass out of the motherfucking room I pay for so I can get some sleep. Today ain't the day, Lexi. You're barking up the wrong tree."

"So I'm a bitch now?" she said. "I'm a bitch?"

I stared at her and said, "Did I motherfucking stutter, bitch?"

She looked offended.

I continued, "You got five seconds to give me my cover. Five, four, three—"

"I got something for dat ass," she said as she threw the cover on the bed and stormed out of the room. "I got something for dat ass!"

I shook my head, closed my eyes and went back to sleep.

*****

Zach

When I arrived at Carrabba's Italian Grill, I was quickly escorted to my seat. While I waited for him to arrive, I went ahead and ordered my drink. He sent a text saying that he was stuck in lunch time traffic, but was only few minutes away.

I looked over the menu. The first time I ever came to this restaurant was with Dwight back in our younger days. It was our third year in college and in Tallahassee. I had never heard of the restaurant before but Dwight insisted it was good.

Hanging around Dwight opened my eyes up to a lot. He showed me that there was more to eat than Olive Garden and Red Lobster. Even though I love Red Lobster, I appreciate Dwight's lessons when we were kids. He wanted me to see the world. He wanted to try and experience new things. He was always fond of the finer things in life.

Growing up as a poor little black kid, I didn't get to try new things like that. My grandma was on a *fixed* income. There was no room for anything *extra* as every dollar in her bank account was accounted for. As a kid, we had no disposable income. It never bothered me though because it was all I knew. This was just the way life was.

It wasn't until college when I saw the manner in which my friends were brought up. Sometimes I used to say, I wish I had a life like that. But now that I'm older, I'm happy just the way it was. Every trial and tribulation my family and I went through when I was younger made me the man that I am today.

I understood what it meant to struggle. I understood what it meant to go without. I understood the sacrifices my grandma and mom made so I can have a new pair of shoes, or a new pair of jeans. My people weren't rich and we didn't live in the best neighborhood, but we survived.

"What are you doing?" I heard.

I looked up and smiled as my guest had arrived. I stood up and gave him a brotherly hug. When we broke the embrace, I asked, "When the hell did you cut your hair? I like it."

"A couple of weeks ago," Tony said as he sat down.

"Wow. I really like it."

"Thanks," he blushed. "Sorry about being late, I got stuck in traffic."

"It's no biggie, Tony," I smiled. "I'm free all day."

"Well, I'm not," he said. "I gotta get back to work in a little bit."

"How do you like the new position?"

"So far, so good. There is a lot of traveling involved, as I'm over all the human resource managers for my company in Alabama, Florida, Georgia, North Carolina and South Carolina. I haven't done much traveling yet, but I go to North and South Carolina next week for a few days."

"I know today is the five-year anniversary," I said. "How are you holding up? I know you miss them."

"Yeah, I miss them a lot," he replied as he took a moment to ponder everything. "But I'm ok. I try not to think about it too much. If I do, it just gets me down."

"I understand," I replied knowing it was time to change the subject.

After the waitress introduced herself, we both placed our orders. Tony ordered the Lobster Ravioli and I took the Chicken Parmesan. When she left, I took a sip of my drink then said, "So how is your health?"

"Everything is ok. I'm taking my meds. I see my new infectious diseases doctor in Atlanta in two weeks. Everything is going good. I work out, trying to stay on top of everything."

"That's good. Are you and Raidon ok?"

"So, so."

"What's wrong?"

"He's pissed off at me for something I said."

"What did you say?" I asked as the waitress brought over Tony's drink.

When she left, he said, "We were talking about TJ and I said some stuff I shouldn't have."

"Like?"

"He asked what was my issue with TJ and I told him the truth."

"Which is?" I asked, concerned.

"Zach, I love my son. I swear before God, I love my son. But, in that same breath, when I see TJ, I see April. I see my life. I see death. I see what she represents. This is an internal demon I'm battling."

Tears started to fall down his face. As he wiped them, he said, "I'd give my son the world, but I can't help what I see when I look at him."

"Tony, when did this happen because when he was a kid, you

loved that boy more than life itself."

"I still do love him. He's my child. He's my son. He's of my blood. I love that boy. I love him, but I see her when I see him. I don't know what to do. I don't know how to not see her face when I see him."

"Wow," I exhaled.

"You're the one with the Ph.D. You're the counselor. What do you think I should do?"

"Tony, I think I know where this is coming from."

"What is it?" he asked.

"This is fear," I said.

"Fear of what, Zach?"

"Have you told TJ about your health condition?" I asked in reference to his HIV status.

He just looked at me.

"Does TJ know about Raidon's condition?"

"No to both questions."

"I feel this is the root cause of your problems. To keep it in layman's terms, you are afraid of TJ's reaction. You are afraid that your condition will take you from your son. Instead of accepting responsibility for your actions, you're trying to throw the blame onto others and April is really the only viable target, other than yourself. Tony, TJ isn't a baby anymore. Hell, the boy is sexually active."

"WHAT?"

"Tony, if you can't see that boy is fucking, or at a minimum having oral sex, you really need to step into the real world. You need to come out of this false reality that you live in."

He exhaled.

"In my 'off the clock' professional opinion, because you ain't paying me for my advice, nigga."

He laughed; I chuckled.

"Seriously, Tony, in my professional opinion, you need to do two things and it'll help you overcome this fear that you have."

"What are they?"

"The first is to admit that you have some fault in your health condition, and I'm not talking about your heart condition that caused you to stop playing football."

"What's the second?"

"The second is to be honest. You and Raidon need to get with TJ and let him know what's going on. He needs to know that the both of you have HIV. You need to be honest with him. Raidon needs to be honest with him. Let him know how the both of you contracted the virus. Teach him the importance of sex safe. Save his life, Tony. Don't let him make the same mistakes the two of you made. When you're talking to him, you can't yell *at* him, you need to have a conversation *with* him. You need to talk *to* him. Apologize for the way things have been and be sincere with your apology. I've studied teenagers and young adults and their behavior patterns my entire collegiate career. I know what I'm talking about. Your son is at a tender age in which he can make one of two decisions—go left or go right. You don't want him to go left, Tony. Acknowledge that he's growing up. Acknowledge his young adulthood. Acknowledge his manhood. Don't just say you love him, show him you love him. And one word of advice—money isn't love."

"How do I do that, show him that I love him?"

"You're the father, Tony," I said as I saw the server walking over to the table with our plates. "You need to figure that one out."

79

TJ

Our history teacher, Mrs. Simms, walked around the class and said, "We have about twenty minutes left in the period. The *click, click, click* sound of her red high heels echoed throughout the room. "This has been, in my opinion, a very good first week of school. This is one of my favorite classes."

I looked at the clock on the wall. I was hungry and ready to go to lunch.

"Next week," she continued as she kept walking up and down the aisles, "we will start our first group assignment of the year."

I exhaled as there were other moans heard over the classroom.

"You might as well get used to it as there will be a lot of group assignments in my class. You are at the age in which you need to learn how to work together as a team," she said as she stopped walking and stared at me. She smiled, turned around and said, "There are thirty of you in this class and for this assignment, I want you to split yourself into five groups of six. You have three minutes. You may begin."

Instantly, Elijah and Nolan turned around and looked at me.

"That's three," Elijah said. "We need three more."

"YO, ALISON AND JODI!" Nolan yelled, as he motioned them to come join us.

Elijah looked at me, and then over to Nolan and said, "Why they gotta be in the group?"

"Man, stop acting like a lil girl," Nolan said to Elijah as the girls approached.

Elijah's face turned blood red.

"Hey, TJ," Jodi smiled.

"Sup, Jodi," I smiled back as she sat next to me.

"Damn, Eli," Alison said. "What's wrong with you?"

"He's acting crazy," Nolan said.

"We still need one more person," Jodi interjected.

Another one of Jodi and Alison friends, Jennifer, joined the group and we were set. While we waited for Mrs. Simms to give the next set of directions, Nolan and Alison cracked jokes on each other. Elijah still didn't say much. While his face was back to normal, it was clear that he was still upset.

Mrs. Simms said, "I'm going to give each group the opportunity to pull from the hat. Whatever topic you pull will be what your assignment will be on. After we all select topics, I want you to spend the last fifteen minutes brainstorming some ideas. I want you to take notes so when we return on Monday you won't forget what you have discussed. In addition, on Monday, I want you to come back to where you are sitting now. I want you to come back to your groups."

While Mrs. Simms brought the bucket around the room for the groups to pick their topic, Jodi playfully kicked my foot. When I looked at her, she smiled.

I smiled back and winked. Damn, I really like this girl.

*****

Zach

It was a little after nine p.m. and I was excited to meet up at Keston's house. It was my last Friday night before classes started and I wanted to get fucked up a lil. Normally, we would gather at the bar, but Keston wanted to host tonight.

I wish Dwight were here but he said he had to get some rest before work tonight. He's at the tail end of his seven days on, seven days off from work.

"Perfect timing," I said as I got out of my car. Kris was pulling into the spot next to mine. When his car was off, he got out and said, "Zach, how are you?"

"You already know," I smiled as we dapped each other up.

He walked to his trunk and pulled out a bottle of Absolut Vodka.

I smiled. He talked about his kids as we made our way up to Keston's condo.

Within moments of knocking on the door, Kes opened. After we all exchanged greetings, Kris sat down on the couch and said, "Where is Dwight?"

"He's not coming," I said. "He gotta work tonight."

"I went ahead and ordered the wings," Kes said. "They should be here soon."

Keston flipped to RuPaul's Drag Race.

"Is this a new season?" I asked, as I secretly loved this show.

"Yeah," Kes said. "It's All Stars 2."

"I don't see how y'all watch this," Kris added.

Kes and I ignored Kris' statement. I got really excited when I saw the drag queen, Roxi Andrews, step on the screen. I loved her in season five. I only hope she finally wins.

Since Kris didn't want to watch, I made a mental note to watch it OnDemand when I got home. Kes flipped off the TV and like normal, we started off the night catching up on the news for the week. We spent a large portion of the evening talking about Nehemiah and his selection to run as the Democratic Party candidate for Vice President of the United States. While we waited for our food, we sipped on our drinks and Kris started to talk about some of the things happening at his job. When the large order of wings arrived, we immediately tore into the food.

"So what's really going on?" Kris asked.

"How is the relationship with your brother going?" Kes asked.

"Yeah, how is that?" Kris asked.

"It's going well. We're trying to find some time when we both are free to get up again. I want him to meet Dray."

"How does Dray feel about it?" Kris asked.

"Dray is cool with it," I replied. "Our schedules are so hectic right now, it's kinda hard. Dorian and I talk or text at least once a day, so I'm excited."

Kris smiled.

"I still can't believe that I have a brother," I said in disbelief. "Sometimes I have to slap myself so I don't think I'm dreaming."

"How are you and Dray?" Kris asked.

I ate a piece of my buffalo lemon pepper flavored wing and said, "We started our counseling sessions yesterday."

"Wow," Kes replied as he licked his fingers. "How did it turn out?"

"It was ok," I shrugged my shoulders. "The doctor is sexy."

"Leave it to you," Kris laughed.

"Whatever," I replied as Kes smiled. "It was strange being on the other side. The first session as a whole was ok, nothing too drastic."

"So what happens when y'all really get into your problems?" Kris asked.

"I'll be honest," I said.

"I hope so," Kes said. "Dray needs to know the truth, Zach."

"What truth?" Kris asked.

"Just my past with Dwight," I said.

"Oh, I guess," Kris exhaled as he ate another one of his wings.

Kris didn't know that Dwight and I had sex.

"I have to get this off my chest," Keston said.

"What's wrong?" I asked.

"Ok, Kris," Kes said. "I need you to promise me that what I'm about to tell you stays in this room."

"Kes, you already know I don't repeat anything we talk about," Kris said.

"I'm serious, Kris. This shit is serious."

"I won't say a word."

"Ok," Kes said. "In order for you to understand the next topic, I think you need to know the back story."

"To what?" Kris asked as he looked at me.

I downed more of my drink.

"My relationship with my ex… Phoenix," Kes said.

"Phoenix?" Kris asked confused. "Who is that?"

"Phoenix Cummings," I interjected.

Kris' mouth dropped open and then he said, "The NBA Champion, Phoenix Cummings?"

"The one and only," Kes said. "Pay attention. Class is now in session."

80

Phoenix

Dray came over to my Atlanta home for dinner. As we ate, he discussed the counseling session with Zach. I was sort of paying attention, but I had a lot of shit on my mind. A part of me was happy that Mama Wright was doing better, while another slice dealt with Keston's break up with his guy friend this morning. But majority of my thoughts were dealing with last night events with Kory. Dray knew something was wrong when he said, "Phoenix, what's really going on? I can see it all over your face."

"Did Zach ever tell you what happened to Keston?"

"Naw," Dray said. "I know whatever it was, it was something serious. What happened?"

"I shouldn't tell you, but in order for you to understand, you have to know the entire story."

Starting from the first day I saw Keston in the café at UCF, to the last phone call I had with Keston, I revealed all of my past to Dray. I left no detail out. When I finished, Dray said, "What an intricate web you wove there. Wow."

"Yeah. *What Webs We Weave,* huh," I shook my head.

"So, this Kory dude just disappeared?" Dray said.

"Yeah and like I said, it bothered me at first, but as time passed I didn't even focus on it anymore. Our friendship was on shaky ground before he left anyway. But then when Kes revealed what happened that night, I had to get him back."

"Phoenix," Dray said concerned. "You didn't do anything crazy did you?"

"Dray, I can't even lie. I thought about it."

"What did you do?"

"I hired someone to track him down. My man followed Kory's every move for a few days. And then last night, we went for gold."

"Phoenix," Dray said worried.

"So much shit went through my head. I wanted him dead for what he did to Keston. I was one phone call away from making that shit a reality. My man was on standby. He was ready to take Kory out. He was just waiting for me to give him the go ahead."

"Wow."

"On my ride to his place, I thought about everything. I thought about my second chance with Keston. I thought about my life. I didn't want his death on my conscience; I didn't want his blood on my hands. I wanted a clean slate with Kes. I couldn't do it. I figured that I would kick his ass, but seeing Kory again, seeing those eyes, I realized that Kory is of a different breed. Kory is the type of nigga that'll make this shit public. He is the type of nigga that would sue me, just because he can. I thought about my career, my son, Keston, my image and I just didn't want the trouble that would come after fucking him up. Dray, it took everything inside of me not to hit him. That was the most self-restraint I've practiced in a very long time. I realized that this was bigger than him. Keston seems to be doing ok now that everything is out in the open. I guess I just wanted Kory to know that I know. I wanted him to know that we still survived. I wanted him to know that his bullshit couldn't keep us apart."

"Wow," Dray said.

"Earlier today, I realized how much God loves me, how much God made Keston just for me."

"Where is that coming from?" Dray asked.

"Seriously, think about it. Our reconnection came because of a higher power. I went to high school with you. We graduated and went our separate ways. Zach and you went to FAMU. I met Keston at UCF. You and Zach got into a relationship. Keston graduated from UCF and attended FAMU for grad school. Zach and Kes became best friends. Years later, me and you reconnect at a photo shoot. We build a good friendship. Keston lived in Atlanta. Zach got you to move to Atlanta. I wanted to meet Zach. Zach and Keston are best friends. I see Keston at y'all house. I'm telling you that this is the work of a higher power."

Dray laughed and said, "Phoenix, you got problems."

"Whatever," I took a sip of my drink.

"Quick question though," Dray said. "You said that you have a second shot with Kes and you're gonna be completely honest with him this go around."

"Yep," I nodded my head.

"Are you gonna tell him about your meeting with this Kory dude?"

"I didn't really think about it," I said.

"From knowing Keston all of these years, I don't think he's gonna be too fond of you trying to rectify the situation without his approval. Keston is pretty independent and I think you going out on your own to deal with Kory just caused an instant issue in the relationship."

"He doesn't need to know," I said. "It's for the best."

"Ok, but if you don't tell him, aren't you doing the same thing all over again—the same thing that helped break y'all up in the first place? Phoenix, I want y'all to work, but you need to be transparent with him. Don't go down that same road again. I know it's different circumstances, but the premise is exactly the same. He's needs to know."

*****

Zach

After Keston finished his story, I turned to Kris and said, "Pick your face up off the ground."

"Your reaction that night at the bar makes so much sense now," Kris said. "Wow, Kes, I'm so sorry."

"It's cool," Kes said. "Seeing him that night forced me to deal with the problem head on. I swear I'm ok now. I am okay."

I exhaled.

Kes said, "So that brings us to today. Like I told you, Dray and Zach kinda forced Phoenix and I to meet again."

"I had nothing to do with that," I cut.

"Yeah, sure," Kes said.

"I didn't," I pleaded.

"That's beside the point," Kes said. "Having Phoenix back in my life is the greatest thing ever."

"What happened to LaRon?" I asked.

"Who is LaRon?" Kris asked lost.

"LaRon Copeland," Kes said.

"You've got to be fucking kidding me," Kris said. "You're fucking the star wide receiver of the Carolina Panthers?"

"Was," Kes said so nonchalantly.

"Was?" I cut.

"You're dealing with professional athletes," Kris said in disbelief. "This can't be real."

"Oh, it's real alright," I said as I could see images of Kes and Phoenix in my house.

"How does someone get in a position to date professional athletes, of the same sex no less," Kris asked.

"Kris, you'll be surprised how many of those dudes get down," Kes said. "The hardest thing to do is get in the circle, but once you're there, you're there. After I got invited to my first DL athlete party a few years back, I kept getting invitations. That stuff isn't for me though. Trust me when I say I saw enough on my first visit to last me a lifetime."

Kris joked, "Shit, Zach, instead of being in the band when we were in college, we needed to work with the football team."

I smiled. Kes laughed then said, "But seriously I broke it off with

LaRon today."

"Wow," I replied. "How did he take it?"

"It was hard but like the standup guy that he is, he accepted it and wished me luck. I hated doing that to him. LaRon has been nothing but good to me. But having Phoenix back in my life is something I couldn't pass up. Phoenix is my real love. I love that man."

"Phoenix plays for the Chicago Bulls," I said. "Even if y'all were to get together how will that work?"

Kes smiled and said, "Phoenix has a plan. I really can't reveal it, but in the next few months, when you see it on ESPN, you'll know what I'm talking about."

"Do I smell another super team here in Atlanta?" I asked trying to gauge a reaction from Kes. His facial reaction didn't tip me one way or the other; he had on his poker face.

"I guess my question is," Kes said, "am I making the right decision to give up everything to have one last shot with Phoenix?"

"What's that shit the rapper, Drake, said a few years back?" Kris asked.

"You only live once?" I asked.

"Yes—YOLO," Kris said. "Man, do you. Go out on a limb and take that chance with happiness. If you love this man the way you say you do and he loves you the way you explained earlier, fuck what everybody else thinks. Be happy. As long as you're happy, fuck everybody else."

"Are you happy?" I asked Kris.

"What?"

"Seriously, are you happy? Yes, you have a wife and you have a lovely family, but remember Kris, you used to date dudes, too. Micah's drug addiction is what eventually led you astray. It was too hard for you, so you found solace in Rozi. After Dwight's bachelor party/dinner in Tallahassee some years ago, you and Micah reconnected and from what I understand have been close ever since. So, I ask again, are you happy?"

"I love my wife," Kris defensively said. "I love my kids. I love my family."

"That's not what I asked you," I said. "I asked you were you happy?"

Kes asked Kris, "How does that work for you, being around the one dude who has that hold over your heart?"

"Micah is in a relationship," Kris said.

"You're acting like a politician, dodging all the important questions and answering the shit you want the politically correct way," I said. "Be real, man. You know your relationship with Micah ended prematurely. When the relationship ended, y'all were still in love with each other. You cheated on him with Nate because he cheated on you with Rozi. I had plenty of issues with Micah towards the end of our friendship, but I always wished the best for you two."

"Are you with Rozi out of obligation?" Kes asked.

"I love my family," Kris said.

"Kris, just answer the question," I said. "Are you happy? Do you wish you can have one more shot on a life with Micah?"

81

TJ

I don't know what was up with daddy, but he didn't seem like himself tonight. He was smiling a lot and he actually tried to talk to me. It was strange because daddy never has anything to say, other than jumping down my back at some shit I didn't even do. Even Ray looked at him kinda funny.

We ordered Pizza Hut and watched two of the movies that Ray picked up from the Red Box. It really felt good to have some family time without all the tension. This is the way it used to be before everything changed.

I wish I could go back to when I was a little kid. Daddy used to love me then. I was the most important thing in the world to him. I don't know what changed. I don't know why he started treating me the way he does. I love my daddy. He be pissing me off at times but I love my daddy. He's all I got besides Ray and his family.

After the movie was done, I said goodnight to both Ray and daddy and then went back to my room. I grabbed my phone and laid across my bed.

As we were walking to lunch after Mrs. Simms class today, Jodi and I exchanged phone numbers. She told me that she had something to do with her family, but she would call me when she was free. I've been waiting on that phone call all damn day. I just want to hear her voice.

And then, right on cue, my phone started to vibrate. Excited, I grabbed it only to see it wasn't Jodi, it was Nolan.

"What up, Wescott?" I said in reference to his last name.

"Shit, just got finished eating with my mom's. What are you

doing?" Nolan asked.

"Waiting on a phone call."

"From who? Jodi?"

"Naw, nigga."

"I'on know why you fronting," he said. "You know you like that girl. It's as clear as day."

"Whatever, Wescott. If I like Jodi, you definitely like Alison."

"Man, I'on like dat gurl."

"Umm, hmm, yeah, whatever."

He laughed and said, "So how you liking it so far, being in Atlanta and all?"

"It's growing on me. You and Elijah are making it cool. I still miss my friends back in Charlotte and I still talk to my best friend almost every day so it's cool. Being in Atlanta ain't as bad as I thought it was gonna be. My Uncle Zach is here and Uncle Morgan is here, so it's cool."

"Can I ask you a question?" Nolan stated.

"Sure, what's up?"

"When we were at lunch today, you got sad all of a sudden. It was like your entire demeanor changed. What was up with that?"

"Just thinking," I exhaled.

"Something happen?"

"Yeah. Five years ago today, both of my grandparents died."

"Damn, man, how that happen?"

"It was a home invasion. Two men broke into their house, tied my granddaddy up and raped my grandma. After they raped my grandma, they shot her dead and then turned around and killed my granddad. They took everything important and valuable. Nobody knows who did it and why. The police came to the conclusion that it had to be a two-person job, but they have no clues or anything. It happened in the middle of the night."

"Wow, man, that's crazy," Nolan said.

"Yeah, it fucked with my dad for a long time. It fucked with me, too. I was scared that they were gonna find us in Charlotte and do the same thing to us, too. But, whatever, enough about that," I wiped the tears from my eyes.

"What's up with yo' boy?" Nolan asked.

"Who?"

"Elijah. Why he be acting bitch made lately?"

"Man, I don't even know," I said.

"You need to check him up on that shit. Y'all damn near neighbors and shit, he needs to stop that. It ain't a good look."

I didn't say anything.

"I was thinking," Nolan said.

"What?"

"Maybe next weekend or the week after you can come spend the night at my house. I know my mom wouldn't mind. What you think about it?"

I smiled and said, "I like that. I gotta ask my dad though."

"You know I never hear you talk about your mom. She doesn't live with y'all?" Nolan asked.

"My mom passed away when I was three."

"Oh, wow. Oh, damn," he said regretfully. "My bad."

"It's cool, but I'll ask my dad and I'll let you know what he says. He's really protective of me so he might wanna meet your mom and shit before he lets me go over there."

"That's cool, just let me know."

"I'm tired and about to call it a night. I'll get at you tomorrow, Nolan."

"Ight, shawty," he hung up the phone.

I put the phone on the charger and turned up the volume. I was tired but I didn't want to miss Jodi's call.

I couldn't miss Jodi's call.

*****

Dwight

I was at work, sitting at my desk, thinking over everything. I had enough of Lexi. Yes, I probably shouldn't have called her a bitch this morning but she just drives me up the wall. I'm tired of dealing with her. I guess I just had to speak to her in a way she would understand. I had to stoop down to her level.

I ran my hands over my head. Everything flashed in my mind. It was so much going on I couldn't focus in on one clear thought.

Lexi was driving me insane.

I can't continue like that. I can't.

For my own sanity, I have to do it. I have to do it tonight.

I'm gonna do it.

Yep.

I'm gonna do it!

Tonight…

82

Zach

Saturday, August 27, 2016

I squeezed my eyes really tight and then opened them. It was so dark in the room, it took a few moments for my eyes to focus and get adjusted. I reached over in the bed and Dray was gone. I turned around and zoomed in on the digital alarm clock. It was a little after six in the morning.

When I got home last night from drinking and talking to Kes and Kris, Dray had already returned from his night with Phoenix and was asleep.

Kes and I stayed and talked until a little after midnight. Like usual, Kris was the first to dip out because as he always says, *"I love y'all, but I have a family to get home to. I'll holla at y'all boyz later."*

After I took a couple of deep breaths, I got out of the bed to brush my teeth and wash my face. I needed to get some food in my system quick. As I got closer to the bathroom, I could hear the shower water running.

"Dray must have just come back from the gym," I thought as I entered the first part of the bathroom that housed the toilet and double sinks. There was another door that led to the shower. I could hear Dray humming something as he left the door leading to the shower part of the bathroom cracked open.

I shook my head and turned on the water. His ass was always singing something. After I finished brushing my teeth and washing my face, I paused.

I realized he was singing the song, *Starting All Over* by Jeremih, that he sang to me that night at the club back in Tallahassee all those years ago. I paused. I could feel the tears starting to creep down my face.

What happened to us? How did we get to this point?

I stood in the crack in the door and looked at Dray's body through the stained white shower glass door. His body was like a sculptured piece of art. The abs, the veins, the color of his skin—everything was just perfect.

Damn. I exhaled.

It's been so long since I've looked at Dray like this. It's been so long since we've been intimate with each other. I love this man…I swear I do.

I know things aren't perfect with us and I know we still have some issues that we need to work out, but I want my man. I want to love my man. I just want things to be like they were.

I can't do this anymore. I can't do this. My body needs this. I need this. We need this.

Not realizing that Dray had stopped singing, he startled me when he said, "Babe, is something wrong?"

When I focused in on him, he had his head poked out of the shower door.

"Is something wrong?" he asked again, concerned. "Why are you staring at me?"

Just going for it, I squeezed my body through the cracked door and walked over to Dray.

I stared at him dead in the eyes.

"What?" he asked again as we were face-to-face. "Did I do something wrong?"

I leaned in and kissed him.

He welcomed my kiss. My heart melted. To feel his lips around mine. *Damn.*

He broke the kiss and said, "C'mon."

I took a deep breath, exhaled and then eased out of my boxer briefs.

I needed this.

I needed this right now.

*****

Keston

I don't know if it's because I'm in an unfamiliar place, or if my mind is in overtime, but I've been in Phoenix's bed for at least five hours now and I've yet to get two consecutive hours of sleep.

Laying here with him feels go right. Having his arms wrapped around my body feels so right. Having his head placed on top of mine feels just right. This has been one of the best weeks in my life. Phoenix makes me happy; he makes me feel complete.

While in the bed, I thought about everything that Zach, Kris and I talked about. I've pondered over all the small details.

I'm not going back down that road I took when I was in college. I'm too old for that shit. I don't have time to play the games.

I know what I want and I'm not gonna lay here and lie to myself. I'm not gonna deprive myself of something good even if it was only one more day.

I can't live with anymore regrets. I've just got to do it.

Phoenix makes me happy. He's always made me happy. We've lost so much time apart over bullshit. I'm not losing another moment.

I've broken all ties with LaRon. I'm ready. I'm ready right now.

I placed a kiss on Phoenix's arm. I gently ran my tongue up and down his arm. I sucked on that same spot; that was *his* spot. That always got him. I could feel his body moving. I could feel his dick reacting to my teasing of his spot.

"Mmmm," he moaned.

I pushed my ass back into his dick.

"Kes...bae," he moaned. "What you doing?"

My dick instantly reacted to his voice and at the thought of the possibilities this moment could bring.

I turned around and faced him.

Even through the darkness, I could see his eyes from the glow of the moonlight creeping through the crack in the blinds.

We stared at each other. And then I pushed him onto his back and straddled him. I leaned over and kissed him. I was ready. I was ready right now.

I kissed his bare chest. He moaned. I looked up at him. I kissed the tip of his nose. I kissed both his cheeks. Our lips touched and became one.

Feeling Phoenix's tongue felt so damn good. We kissed longer and deeper. Our tongues played with each other. With each kiss, my dick was getting harder than the moment before.

While we kissed, Phoenix took his hands and ran them down my back. His touch was sending chills up and down my spine. My body was weak. It was wide open.

I broke the kiss. I reached back and felt his dick. I smiled. I still had it. It was so hard it was throbbing, begging to be released.

*****

Phoenix

Kes ran his tongue across the side of my face before licking down my neck. He licked around the center of my chest.

He kissed the center of my chest where my heart is located. He then licked his way over to my left nipple. He licked around my nipple before sucking on it.

"Damn, bae," I moaned as I was being pulled deeper into pleasure. "Aww shit."

He licked his way back to the center of my chest. He then licked his way over to my right nipple. He softy bit down on it causing a feeling of both pain and pleasure, a feeling I loved, a feeling that only Keston could get out of me. It hurt but it felt so damn good.

He went back to the center of my chest and then placed kisses down my body. He kissed each of my abs, making sure that each one got its own personal attention.

Keston reached back and felt my dick again. I don't know what he kept reaching back for, my dick wasn't going anywhere. It wasn't gonna get soft until it was back in familiar territory.

That was his dick; it was all there for him… and him only.

Keston looked at me and smiled. He licked around my navel before grabbing my dick through my boxer briefs. He kissed the bottom of my stomach. He pulled down my boxer briefs. My dick was standing straight at attention.

I smiled. He smiled.

It was finally time to make up for lost time.

83

Dwight

I was sitting in my chair at my desk at work, turned around with my back to the door, talking on my cellphone. I said, "Yeah, in a few minutes…ight…yeah."

When I placed the phone down, I was startled when someone said, "Dr. Taylor."

I jumped and turned around. When I saw who it was I exhaled and said, "Dr. Grier, you scared the mess out of me."

"I'm so sorry," she smiled. Dr. Raquel Grier was one of four pharmacists at the hospital.

Dr. Grier was in her mid-fifties and often reminded me of my mother. She had the same skin complexion, wore her hair the same way and to top it off, she had the same demanding, no nonsense personality like my mom. When I arrived at the hospital, Dr. Grier helped me out tremendously. I owe a lot of my early success as a new pharmacist to her.

"I didn't get much sleep last night," she said walking over to me, "so I figured I would come on in and let you leave a few minutes early."

"Thanks," I smiled as I stood up.

"I haven't heard you talk about the family much," she said. "How are Mrs. Lexi and the kids doing?"

"They're doing ok," I forced a smile.

She stared at me for a moment and then planted a fake smile on her face. She said, "Well, tell Mrs. Lexi I send my greetings."

"I will," I said as I brought her up to speed on the things she needed to know for her shift. While I spoke, it felt like Dr. Grier was looking right through me. It really made me feel uncomfortable. When I finished, I said, "Well, thanks again for coming in early. I really appreciate it Dr. Grier."

"You know you're like a son to me, Dwight?"

"Yes ma'am," I nodded.

"I have five kids of my own, all men," she continued. "My youngest, Derald, is a senior in high school. I have seven brothers. When it comes to men, I've seen it all and I've heard it all. Dwight, when I walked in here, you were talking to someone. I stood in the back not wanting to interrupt your phone call. When you finished your call, I spoke your name and by the way you reacted to my voice, I don't think it was your wife. You're a grown man and are able to live your life the way you choose, but I caution you to think about the effects your actions can have on the people closest to you in your life. Dwight, you are a very smart man and in my opinion, you are destined to go far in your career. Don't mess it all up over foolishness."

"Dr. Grier, I appreciate your concern, but you're way off base. I was speaking to my best friend."

She planted a smile on her face and said, "Ok, son. Well, enjoy your day. I know this was a long seven days. Get some rest and I'll see you next week."

"Thanks, Dr. Grier." I grabbed the rest of my belongings.

As I walked to the door, she said, "Dwight?"

"Yes?" I turned around to face her.

"Be careful, ok?"

I forced a smile and said, "Have a great week, Dr. Grier."

I headed out of the office and out of the hospital.

*****

Dray

Like two dogs in heat, I had Zach pushed up against the shower wall and we kissed each other. Something about his kisses, this time, was enticing. Something had gotten into my dude. I eagerly kissed him back with the same vigor.

He climbed up the shower wall and wrapped his legs around my waist as the water hit our bodies.

Just holding him again felt right. We haven't had sex with each other in over five months and we were way past due.

In an instance, Zach broke the kisses. He looked at me and smiled. He licked his lips.

Zach pushed me off of him, eased down the wall and then aggressively pushed me against the shower wall. Zach kissed me on my neck. That was my spot. I shivered at the feeling. Fuck, it was feeling so good. He went to the other side of my neck.

"Damn," I moaned as he kissed and licked around one of my spots. He licked on my neck before placing another kiss on my lips.

Zach sucked on my bottom lip before our tongues met. He made his way to my ear. He licked my otter earlobe before sending his tongue in circles inside of my inner ear.

Damn, he makes me feel so damn good. Fuck!

Standing under the steaming water, I wiped my eyes to get a better look at him. I looked down. He was on his knees. He looked up at me. Lust was all in his eyes as he held my dick in his hands. Water was still shooting off the top of his head and down his backside. My dick was harder than it has ever been. His dick was hard, too.

And then he took me inside of his mouth.

"Damn, baby," I moaned as he sucked me off. "Damn."

The shower was still hot, but nothing was as hot as the steam that was coming from our bodies.

84

Keston

After I finished giving Phoenix the head job of his life, he picked me up and laid me down on my stomach.

"Let me eat dat shit," Phoenix said.

Naturally, I assumed the position.

When I was on all fours, he pulled my ass closer to his face. In his typical fashion, he used one hand and forced the arch that he wanted into my back. And then he kissed and nibbled on one ass cheek and then moved over to the other. He spread my ass apart and licked around the hole.

As soon as I felt his tongue inside of me, I moaned, "Oh, shittt!"

I gripped the pillow as he buried his face deep into my ass. *Damn, it felt so good.*

He spread it apart wider and dug deeper. He was making it so wet.

Damn

Damn…

"DAMN!" I screamed in pleasure. It was feeling so good that I was pushing my ass back on his face. He kept eating my ass out. I don't know how long he was at it, but he spent a lot of time back there.

I could feel him applying pressure on my hole by pressing his thumb there. While he used his thumb to press on my hole, he kept licking and sucking around the area. It was so wet back there.

I was feeling so good.

*****

Zach

After Dray finished eating me out, he picked me up and carried me out of the shower. When he got back in the bedroom, he threw my wet body down on the bed.

Ready for the fuck of my life, I scooted to the edge of the bed and assumed the position. Dray used his spit to help lubricate my ass, which was already somewhat lubricated from the water in the shower. He lined his dick up and gently forced his way inside of me.

"FUCK!" I yelled as Dray made his entrance known.

I grinded my teeth together and tried to relax my ass muscles to receive him. It had been so long since I've been penetrated, I forgot what it felt like.

I could feel him starting to move back and forth at a slow pace, trying to allow me to get used to him.

"That's it," he said as he started to pick up the pace. I could feel him palming my ass in his hands. "Fuck this dick, nigga. Fuck this dick like you want it!"

"Shit, Dray," I moaned as the dick was starting to feel good. "Give me this dick, get deep in me."

"Naw, nigga, you fuck me," he said as he stopped moving his pelvic. "You fuck this dick."

I started to work my ass on his dick. He moaned.

After a few minutes of me fucking his dick, he grabbed me by the waist, spit, and started to fuck the dog shit out of me. The sound of Dray's thighs and my ass echoed throughout the room. Dray grunted many times telling me to, "take dis dick."

I moaned as I threw my ass back to meet his thrusts.

All the months of anger and aggression were being released in this act.

An act we both needed.

*****

Phoenix

Keston took all of me. I moaned in pleasure, "That's it. Take my dick!" We had been in this position for at least ten minutes.

I poured more lube over the magnum and placed the bottle on the side of the bed. Being inside of him again felt so good... so right... I could cry.

As I slowly worked my dick in and out of his ass, to let him enjoy every inch and savor every moment, he said, "Shit, Phoenix. You make me feel so good!"

"I love you," I said as I reached over and placed a kiss on his neck.

"I love you, too," he replied.

I knew the touch of my dreads made his body sensitive. So, while in the doggy style, I hung and shook my head to let the touch of my dreads, against his backside, take him to another place.

As I moved at a moderate tempo and shook my dreads, his breathing deepened and he moaned with a bit more intensity.

Hearing his moans and the way his body reacted to our lovemaking drove me insane.

He was so tight, I could bust right now.

But I couldn't bust.

I had to hold out for him.

I wanted to enjoy the moment.

I wanted him to get his first.

*****

Dwight

I knocked on the door and within a few seconds, he let me inside.

As soon as the door was closed, Kory said, "Is everything alright? You scared me, calling me so early in the morning."

"Yeah," I said. "I just wanted to lay with you for a few hours before I went home. I just don't feel like dealing with her shit right now."

I looked at his body and licked my lips.

"Yeah, that's cool," he motioned for me to follow behind him.

Kory got in the bed and said, "Make yourself comfortable."

As I took off my slacks, he said, "Your wife ain't gonna come popping up at my house is she? I got enough of my own damn drama. I don't need any more."

I unbuttoned my shirt and said, "Naw, we're straight here."

*****

Keston

Changing positions, Phoenix laid down and I eased my body on top of him. As I worked my ass down on his dick, I moaned. It felt so damn good going down.

Our fingers interlocked as I started to grind and rotate my ass on his dick. I reached over and we started kissing.

"Damn, bae," Phoenix moaned. "Ride this dick. Ride that shit like you like it."

I reached over and kissed him as I seductively bounced my ass on his dick.

With our hands still interlocked, and us kissing, Phoenix planted his feet and started to move his pelvic to my rhythm. It was feeling so good, I had to stop kissing and breathe.

He was moaning; I was moaning.

He wrapped his arms around my body and whispered in my ear, "Damn, I love you. I love you so much."

85

Kristopher K. Simms

Atlanta, Georgia

When I opened my eyes, I reached over to the nightstand to check the time. It was a quarter to seven. I exhaled. As much as I wanted to continue to lay here, I had to get going. He needed to get going, too. I shook him and said, "Micah, baby, get up. It's almost seven."

He exhaled and said, "What?"

"It's time for you to go back home before Brandon gets there."

He exhaled and said, "Why we gotta keep doing this? Why can't we just be honest?"

"Micah," I said as I got my naked ass out of the bed. "I don't have time for that shit this morning; it's too early for that."

"You don't ever have the time," he mumbled as he got out of the bed.

I looked at his naked body and exhaled.

"I'll go start the shower," he said as he walked over to the hotel bathroom.

While he got the shower ready, I went ahead and cleaned up the room. I picked up the two empty condom wrappers and threw them in the trash.

"You coming?" he asked as he stuck his head around the corner.

"Yeah," I smiled. "I'm coming."

*****

Dwight

As I laid in the bed next to Kory, I could sense he knew what I wanted. I knew what I wanted. I was hoping that he would just take charge. I ain't gay. He is. I exhaled. I could sense his hesitation and his nervousness.

I thought about all the times Zach and I were close to messing around, but it never happened because he was scared. I was scared, too. But like Kory, Zach was the gay person. He needed to be the one to push it there. Zach and I wasted so much time back then playing games with each other. I exhaled.

Now, here I was again, laying in the bed with another gay dude. All I wanted was some head.

I could sense Kory's hesitation, just like Zach's back in the day. I wasn't, however, going to play this game again. I wasn't! Besides, my dick was already hard.

I turned my head and looked at Kory. He was looking up at the ceiling. I took a deep breath and in a split second, I grabbed his hand. He looked at me.

I picked up his hand and placed it on top of my dick. He stared at me. I looked at him and could see the lust in his eyes. As I realized there was no turning back, I exhaled and said, "Handle that."

86

Dray

Zach and I had made our way over to the floor. He said, "Nigga, you ain't doing shit! FUCK THAT ASS, NIGGA!"

"I ain't doing shit?" I asked as I beat it up.

"DID I STUTTER?" he yelled. "FUCK THIS ASS LIKE IT'S YOURS!"

I took that as a personal challenge and went even harder on him.

"HELL YEAH," he grunted like he was in heaven. "FUCK ME, DRAY! FUCK ME!"

"Yeah," I moaned as I hit it hard, deep and fast. "Talk that shit now."

"DAMN, YOU IN THAT ASS!" Zach moaned. "YOU HITTIN' THAT SHIT! YOU HITTIN' THAT SHIT!"

On my knees, I planted one foot on the floor and gripped Zach's neck for support. Once secure, I dug deep inside that ass with such a rapid, intense pace, I felt like a jack rabbit.

Months of aggressions and mixed emotions were coming out in this fuck session. Zach was gonna know how much I loved him, but how much he has pissed me off, too.

*****

Dwight

Kory had my shit super wet. I couldn't believe I was doing this…again. It felt so fucking good. Lexi never did it like this.

Catching me off guard, Kory got off the bed and stood up. "Take off all your clothes," he said as he walked out of the room.

While he was gone, I moved to the edge of the bed and took off my wife-beater and white t-shirt. I hope he know it's just head. I ain't fucking him.

As soon as I removed my boxer briefs that were around my ankles, he walked back in the room completely naked. I was in awe as I looked at his body; he was sexy and had a big dick, like me.

He had some towels in his hands. "Stand up," he said as he placed them down. "I can't fuck up my sheets."

I smiled as his dick was rock hard. He kneeled down on the side of the bed and took my dick in his hands. I couldn't wait to feel his mouth around my shit again. He licked up and down my shaft before he placed the dick back into his mouth.

"Get it wet like you had it earlier," I said. "I like sloppy head."

I looked down and he closed his eyes. He worked my dick into the back of his mouth. The deeper he went, the wetter it felt.

"Do that shit slow," I moaned. "Slow and wet, shawty."

He followed instructions.

"Aww fuck," I moaned as I laid back and relaxed.

Kory was starting to pick up a pace. He was starting to slurp and slob on my shit. His mouth was so wet, so warm. He was deep-throatin' my dick like a motherfucking pro!

"Damn, nigga," I moaned as my body started to shake at the intense pleasure.

I leaned up to take another look at him. He looked like he was enjoying that shit. I knew I was. As he came off it, my dick was drenched in his juices.

"Hell yeah," I moaned. "You got that dick wet as fuck."

He took a deep breath and then took it back to the throat again.

"Damn, shawty. Suck that dick, nigga."

Suck that dick!

*****

Phoenix

I moved Keston to the edge of the bed. Once he was on his back, I grabbed some lube and poured it on the condom. I spread Keston legs apart and grabbed his dick as I slid my dick inside of him.

In the missionary, I was going to make him feel all of me.

I was ready to cum. I didn't want to hold back anymore but I wanted him to get his, too.

I had him right where I wanted him because as I went deeper, his eyes rolled into the back of his head.

"That's it," I moaned as I searched with my dick for that special spot. "Get into it."

I slid my dick… in and out… in and out… in and out. With each stroke, I could feel his body submitting to mine; he was in ecstasy.

"Oh, my God," he cried as tears fell down his face. "This feels so good… don't stop... please don't stop."

My stroke was long, deep and steady.

Each time I went deep, I knew I was close as his voice inched higher. His legs started to move uncontrollably. His big toe had curled up.

"Oh, my God, Phoenix," he cried. "OH, MY GOD!"

I bit my bottom lip and continued to work him.

"Damn," he moaned. "You feel so good."

Using another trick, I heightened his high by hanging my head. As soon as the first dread touched his body, he moaned louder than before.

"Don't stop," he panted. "DON'T STOP!"

I looked down at my dick.

The sight alone was gonna make me bust. My long, thick dick looked so good sliding in and out of his ass.

He was so wet. I kissed him.

His body kept shaking uncontrollably.

Tears started to fall down my face.

I was home.

I was back with the dude I was destined to spend the rest of my life with.

*****

Zach

My breathing was becoming faint. I yelled, "OH, FUCK, NIGGA! YOU HITTING DA SPOT… FUCK… RIGHT THERE… DAMN…NIGGA…. DON'T STOP… RIGHT THERE… OH, FUCK… DAMN…FUCK… DON'T STOP!"

He hit it harder.

Faster.

HARDER.

FASTER.

I yelled.

Louder and louder.

LOUDER AND LOUDER!

"DAMN, DRAY YOU GONNA MAKE ME BUST!"

"BUST IT THEN," he said. "BUST NIGGA!"

My breathing was all over the place. He was hitting the spot.

"OH, SHIT," I said. "FUCKKKKKKK, I'M CUMING!"

Dray kept hitting that spot until my nut shot out all over the bed.

I knew how to make Dray cum, and as I caught my nut, I squeezed my ass muscles as tight as they would go and gripped his dick as hard as I could. Within moments, he started to yell as he lost himself deep inside of me.

When Dray's body stopped shaking and he stopped yelling curse words, he slid out and laid down next to me.

I turned over and laid on my back.

I took a couple of deep breaths; he did too.

"You know I love you," he said.

"I love you, too."

He reached over and we kissed each other.

When the kiss broke, I turned to him and said, "You know this isn't over, right?"

"What are you talking about?" he asked.

"I want some ass, too."

He smiled and said, "Shit, take it, nigga. Come take this ass."

87

Dwight

As Kory got more into the job, I stood up, grabbed his head and started to lightly fuck his throat. He gripped my ass as he forced my dick into his mouth.

I looked down and this dude was a freak. He was enjoying that shit. Looking at him eat my dick was gonna make me cum.

My dick was extra wet. Slob was dripping from his mouth and down his chin, as my dick slid in and out of his mouth.

Behind this nut was a lot of shit. Anger. Frustration. Confusion.

Ready to let it all my problems and mixed feelings go away, I gripped his head as hard as I could and started to thrust my dick with extra force down his throat. He gripped my ass harder as he received all of me. I looked down and he was jacking his dick while he sucked me off.

My shit slid in and out, in and out of his mouth.

I closed my eyes and focused. I normally don't bust off head, but I was gonna make that shit a reality today.

The more I fed him, the closer I could feel my nut building up. Before I knew it, I was starting to moan.

I could feel his body shaking as he choked his dick at a ferocious pace.

"OH, SHIT!" I yelled. "FUCK DUDE, YOU GONNA MAKE ME CUM!"

He moaned while sucking me up. The vibration of his moans made my body shake.

"OH, FUCK, MY NIGGA!" I yelled. My legs started to shake. My voice was starting to get shaky. "FUCKKKKKKK…

FUCKKKKKKKKKK…FUCKKKKK NIGGA! I'M CUMING!"

I tried to eject my dick from his mouth before I sprayed him with my seed, but he wanted it as he pushed my pelvic deeper into his mouth.

"I'M CUMING, NIGGA!" I yelled as I shot my nut deep down his throat.

At the same time, he moaned as I felt his warm nut paste itself against my legs. I fell back on the bed and exhaled.

Now, I gotta take my ass home to deal with Lexi and her shit.

*****

Keston

I couldn't take it anymore. Phoenix had me in the missionary for God knows how long. My body was so open… wide open.

I couldn't control anything if I tried.

Despite the way he made me feel, the best thing about being in the missionary was that I could look at him and see that I was making him feel good, too. Looking at his facial expressions made this an even better experience.

As Phoenix slid in and out of my ass, I could feel that prized nut finally working itself through my body.

"FUCK, PHOENIX!" I yelled "FUCK. I'M GONNA CUM!"

"Umm, hmm," he moaned.

"YOU GONNA MAKE ME CUM!" I cried.

"Bust that nut, baby. Bust that nut. You gonna make me cum, too."

He beat it even harder.

"Get that nut for me!" he said as he grabbed me by the waist and beat me in. "Get that nut! Get that nut!"

"Damn, baby," I moaned.

"Get that nut," he repeated like a broken record.

His stroke was short and fast. It was driving me insane.

"Get that nut," he said. "Get that nut!"

"I'm…. aboooouuuttttt…. toooo bussssttttttttttttt, baeeeeeee," I moaned as he hit it harder.

"I'M ABOUT TO CUM, TOO!" he yelled.

As I felt my nut working its way up my shaft, I yelled, "OH, MY GOD. OH, MY GOD!"

"I'M CUMING," he yelled as his body started to jerk.

"I'M CUMING, TOO," I replied as my nut shot out of my dick and exploded onto my stomach.

When his body finished shaking, he fell on top of me and kissed me. He said, "I can't feel my legs," as he slid down to the floor.

After a few breaths, I stood up, only to find out that my legs were gone and I fell down, too.

"Damn," he laughed. "That was the shit."

*****

Kris

The sun was rising when I arrived back at my house. I looked at my phone and deleted the text messages from Micah.

Before I got out of the car, I checked the time. It was almost seven-thirty. The kids, twins Jadon and Jadyn, and the baby of our family, six-year-old Kayla, were probably up tearing the house apart.

I took a deep breath and entered. Upon walking into the living room, I saw my nine-year-old son, Jadon, sitting on the floor eating cereal and watching TV.

"Hey, Daddy," he said.

"Morning J.J.," I replied. "Where are your sisters?"

"Sleep," he said. He was very short.

"What are you doing up so early?" I asked.

"Not sleepy," he said as he looked at me and then faced the TV.

"Where is your mom?" I asked.

"Sleep," he exhaled. And in a tone as if I were bothering him, he said, "Daddy, I'm trying to watch TV."

I smiled and said, "Ok."

I shook my head and headed up the stairs. Before I opened the door to my room, I exhaled.

When I opened the door, Rozi was in the fetal position on her side of the bed. I closed and locked the door.

I stripped down to my boxer briefs and headed over to the bed. I wanted to get a few more hours of sleep before I start this Saturday.

As soon as she felt my presence, she turned around and in a sleepy tone said, "What time is it?"

"Around 7:30."

"You just getting home?" she asked as she wiped her eyes.

"Yeah, I feel asleep at Keston's place," I lied.

"Another long Friday night with the boyz, huh," she smiled.

"Yeah, it was very interesting," I said. "Very interesting."

"Well, I'm glad you enjoyed," she sighed.

"What Rozi?"

"I know Friday's are your night out with the boyz, but I was hoping you came back home."

"Why, what happened?"

She grabbed my hand and placed it in between her thighs. She then inserted my finger into her leaking pussy and said, "My shit is so wet, baby. So wet."

Feeling her wetness instantly made my dick hard.

"Make love to me, Kris," Rozi moaned as she reached for my throbbing dick. "Make love to me right now!"

88

TJ

Monday, August 29, 2016

I was in the kitchen eating my Cinnamon Toast Crunch and listening to J. Cole. I love his music. He puts me in another world when I'm vibing to his beats. While I listened to J. Cole spit his rhymes, I looked at a rerun of my favorite show, The Family Guy, playing on the TV in the kitchen.

It's been so peaceful with daddy being in both North and South Carolina for his job. I need him to come back though. I needed to ask him a question.

I could just ask him on the phone, but daddy always taught me when dealing with serious shit, always step to a man face-to-face. I wanted daddy to see how much going to Nolan's house meant to me. So, like a man would do, I wanted to ask him face-to-face.

I grabbed my phone to check the time. I finished my cereal and washed out my bowl. As I headed back over to the island, Ray walked into the kitchen.

"Morning, TJ," he mouthed.

I removed my headphones and said, "Good morning, Ray."

"Everything going ok?" he asked.

"Yes."

He smiled and then grabbed and started to peel the two hard boiled eggs off the stove. Before he was done, I said, "Ray, when is daddy come back from the trip?"

"At the end of the week," he replied.

"Oh, ok," I nodded my head.

"Why?" Ray asked. "Something wrong?"

"Not really. I just wanted to spend the night at my friend's house."

With a look and voice full of concern, Ray said, "On a school night?"

"No, Ray," I shook my head. "Friday and Saturday night."

Ray smiled and said, "Oh, ok. Who is it? Elijah?"

"No, sir," I shook my head. "Nolan."

"Nolan?"

"He's a friend from school," I said. "But I know daddy be tripping so I wanted to ask him to make sure it was okay. Nolan invited me last Friday for this weekend and he be asking me about it every day. I really wanna go. I guess I could call daddy, but I ain't wanna interrupt him. And you know how he is about asking stuff on the phone versus doing it in person, so it—"

"You can go," Ray cut me off.

My eyes got wide.

He smiled.

"Don't play, Ray," I said excited.

"I'm serious, you can go. I'll take care of your father."

I jumped up, ran over to him, gave him a hug and said, "Thanks, Ray, you're the best!"

He smiled and replied, "You need to go out and make some new friends anyway. Just give me the number to Nolan's parents so I can talk to them. If they say it's fine, it'll be no problem. I'll make sure you get there before your daddy gets back Friday night."

I smiled and repeated, "Thanks again, Ray. You're the best!"

I headed out of the door excited to catch that big yellow cheese wagon.

*****

Phoenix

I got out of my car, headed into the building and said, "This boy just doesn't know how good he has it." He better not do anything bad to fuck up this relationship.

This was my first time over here and I must say this shit is nice. When the elevator reached the sixteenth floor, I stepped out and made a left just like they told me. Within a few moments, I had arrived and knocked on the door, 1612.

"HEY, PHOENIX!" Renzo said, opening the door. "Sup man?"

"Ain't shit," I smiled as we dapped each other up.

"CJ said you were stopping by," he said as he closed and locked the door. "So this is your first time in my crib, huh?"

"Yeah, it is," I looked around. "This shit is nice, Renzo."

He smiled as CJ appeared from the back of the condo.

"Sup, Phoenix," CJ said.

"Nothing much," I replied as we dapped each other up.

Renzo sat down at the breakfast bar and ate his food.

"What's wrong with your place again?" I asked CJ.

"You know I just moved," he said.

"Yeah."

"I'm having an interior designer do some work on the inside of my new home. I'm giving her an entire week to make that shit nice. In the meantime, I'm staying here with my lil brother until the work is done," CJ said as he walked into the kitchen and poured a glass of cranberry juice.

"You want something to eat or drink?" Renzo asked, looking at me. "I'm just here stuffing my face 'n shit, being rude 'n shit."

I smiled and said, "Naw, man, I'm good. I ate before I came here."

Renzo turned to CJ and said, "When are you leaving for Florida again?"

"On Friday," CJ said as I knew he was going down there to see his dude while he had a few free moments.

I walked over to Renzo and said, "Man, I wish I was living like this when I was in college."

Renzo smiled and said, "I know… I got it good…really good."

"Yeah, you do," I stated as I looked at CJ.

I've always wondered if all this spoiling CJ does to Renzo is going to hurt Renzo in the long run.

I turned to Renzo and asked, "Them chicks you be fucking know you living like this?"

Renzo cleared his throat and said, "Man, I don't bring them bitches back to my house. I fuck 'em and keep it moving. Chicks ain't nothing but some gold diggers. I don't have time for that shit. I ain't giving yo' ass none of my muh'fuckin' money and you ain't 'bout to trap my ass with some fucking baby, either."

"Yeah, they will get yo' ass," I said.

"CJ taught me that shit when I was younger," he said. "You know, don't let them hoes know you got money and don't let them know my brother plays in the NBA. Bitches are trifling. When they know you got money they won't let yo' ass go. And then if you got some good dick, like I do, that shit is a wrap. I learned my lesson once. Won't do that shit again."

"What happened?" I asked.

"His ass being dumb," CJ interjected as he walked over to the couch.

"I was fucking this bitch, right," Renzo said. "So, this hoe gonna turn up pregnant 'n shit, and to top it off, the dumb bitch tried to pin the baby on me."

"Wow."

"Yeah, man," Renzo said. "Ma Dukes wasn't having that shit."

Ma Dukes was another *hood* name for mother.

I laughed and said, "I know Mama Wright wasn't. I know she got in yo' ass, Renzo."

"Hell yeah, she did," CJ laughed. "Renzo got his ass beat that night. And every time she thought about it, mama was coming for that ass."

I laughed.

"That shit ain't funny, bruh-bruh," Renzo said, looking at CJ.

"Yes, the hell it is," CJ laughed.

I nodded my head, happy that they were smiling again, happy that Mama Wright was doing a lot better now.

Renzo said, "Ma Dukes wasn't happy that I was having sex with that girl, unprotected at that, but she was determined to have a DNA test done as soon as that baby was born."

"Phoenix," CJ said. "I had to hear about that shit every fucking day."

"Of course I wasn't the daddy," Renzo said. "I was 16. What I look like being a daddy?"

"Why you fucking raw then, lil muh'fucker?" I asked. "That shit ain't safe, man. It's a whole lot more out there than just babies. You strapping up down here in Atlanta?"

"Yeah, man," Renzo said. "I learned that lesson. No mo' raw doggin' that shit for me."

CJ looked at me.

"But that's why I came all the way down here for school," Renzo said.

"Why?" I asked.

"For one, nobody knows me down here."

"Speaking of that, what made you come down to Atlanta, versus other cities for college anyway?"

Renzo said, "I only applied to black schools when I was a senior. My reasons were fucked up, but that's where I wanted to be."

I laughed, "So you can look at ass all day?"

"Basically," he chuckled. "Ass... ass, ass, ass, ass, ass... ass is everywhere. A nigga like me ain't know what to do when I first got down here!"

I laughed. CJ shook his head.

"Seriously though," Renzo continued. "I wanted to go to an HBCU. I had a teacher in high school that went to Jackson State and he always made it seem like it was fun. So, I applied to and was accepted to Howard, Hampton, FAMU, Jackson State, Morehouse and Clark Atlanta. The decision to come to Atlanta was easy."

"How so?" I asked.

"When I visited Howard's campus, I just wasn't feeling the vibe," he said. "On top of that, they didn't care too much about their sports, so it was a no-go for me. Besides, it was too much government shit up in D.C. I was straight on that. CJ took me to up to Virginia to visit Hampton. I quickly learned I wouldn't fit in there as them Hampton niggas, and bitches, was just to bougie for me. FAMU as a whole was straight, but Tallahassee was too damn country for my liking. Them kats in Mississippi was strange, so I sliced Jackson State off the list. To makes matters worse, it was more country than Tallahassee. In the end, Atlanta seemed like the perfect choice. So, it ultimately came down to Morehouse and Clark Atlanta. I didn't wanna be around a bunch of dicks all the fucking time, so that took Morehouse out of the running. All that was left was Clark and I'm happy with the decision I made. Being down here in Atlanta allowed me to get a fresh start and to top it off, I was far, far, FAR away from Ma Dukes. Phoenix, when I was growing up, my mom and I went at it all the time."

"Yeah because y'all were one of a kind," CJ laughed. "Mama was kinda hard on Renzo and she couldn't stand that I always had his back."

"She was always comparing my life to CJ's life. I love my brother and can't nobody, or anything tear us apart, but I'm my own person, feel me? I have my own feelings. I have my own beliefs. Just because CJ does something doesn't mean I have to do it too, feel me?"

"Trust me, I understand," I said.

"After that shit happened with CJ and Dedrick, it made me realize that life is short and to cherish every moment. From then on, I made an attempt to be civil with my mom. I love her so much and I'm happy that she is doing better, but I ain't moving back to Chicago. You got life fucked up if someone thinks I'm going anywhere near that city—especially with all that gun violence."

I turned to CJ and said, "What times does Keon's flight get in?"

"Around four I think," CJ said. "Keon said he'll just call us when he touches down."

"Man, speaking of K-Doug," Renzo interjected. K-Doug was Keon Douglass's nickname.

Renzo said, "Phoenix, I know you like playing for the Bulls and shit, but you need to come play with CJ down here in Atlanta. And then if y'all could get K-Doug, it'll be over for the league."

I smiled.

"The three of y'all are like best friends anyway," Renzo said. "That shit would be perfect. Hell yeah, that shit would work. And then with y'all super team, y'all could say fuck Cleveland and Golden State!"

I burst out laughing.

"Man, let me get going before I'm late to class," Renzo said as he put on his shirt that he had lying on the arm rest of the couch. "Y'all boyz be easy." He grabbed his backpack and headed for the door.

"Drive safe, Renzo," CJ said.

"I always do," he said as he opened and closed the door.

I walked over to the couch and said, "Your brother is something else."

"Who you telling?" CJ laughed as he flipped on the TV.

89

Zach

The first day of classes had finally arrived. I checked the time. I had a few minutes to go through everything before I had to head over to my first class of the semester. Just as I was going over some final notes, my cell started to ring.

I smiled and answered, "Sup Dorian?"

"Nothing much, Zach. I had a quick break so I thought to hit you up."

"I appreciate that," I smiled. "I'm getting ready to go to my first class in a little bit. I always feel nervous for some reason, even though I've been doing this for years."

"I think it's just a natural reaction," Dorian said.

"Probably so," I said.

"I ain't mean to hold you, big bruh. I know you got classes to teach and I gotta get back focused on this work. I was just calling to check on you. Holla at me when you get some free time, ight?"

"I will do, Dorian. Have a good day."

"You too, Zach."

As soon as I hung up the phone, it started to vibrate again. I saw the name and checked the time. I still had a few minutes.

"Hey, Dray," I answered.

"Sup babe," he replied. "How is it going?"

"My first class is in a few minutes, but so far, so good."

"That's cool. I'm heading out to a shoot with some of my team in a little bit. I just wanted to check in to make sure everything was ok."

"I've always dreaded first days," I said.

"I know but you'll be ok," he said. "I wish you luck and I can't wait to see you tomorrow."

"Yeah we'll see how you feel when it is your turn getting in front of the class," I laughed.

"I doubt if I'm nervous," he said.

"Whatever, Dray," I smiled. "Be safe up there in New York. Are you coming back tonight or tomorrow?"

"I'll be back late tonight."

"Ight," I stood up. "I'll see you tonight."

I took a sip of my water then gathered everything I needed for my next two classes. As I headed out, I saw the scores of students walking the campus in their new attire. It was easy to spot the freshmen.

I smiled.

As I approached the classroom, I checked the time. I was right on time.

Using a tactic that Raidon once taught me, I walked in the class and went directly over to the podium. When the students saw me, they stopped talking. I placed my things down on the desk behind the podium, turned around and headed to the dry eraser board. I wrote some notes board and then sat down at the desk.

This silence in the room always made the students uncomfortable. They didn't understand why I wasn't talking. They didn't understand what was going on.

It was all a part of the tactic.

Five minutes is a long time to sit and wait, especially when you don't know what you're waiting for. It all provided a sense of uneasiness.

The five minutes actually allowed for any late comers to arrive. It was the first day, so exceptions were made. From here on out, my rule is if you're not seated when I walk in the room and open my mouth, don't even bother to show up. The only time I make exceptions to that rule is on test day, and for those days only, I allow a five-minute grace period. People who aren't punctual, irks my last nerve. My philosophy is that college is here to prepare you for a job in the real world. If you're late to work, you're fired. One of my goals, as an educator, is to get my students to understand the importance of being punctual. In the real world, no one wants to hear the excuses for why you were late. I was always taught to leave early enough to give you time, just in case something came up in your commute to your desired destination.

When the five minutes were up, I stood up and walked to the center of the classroom. All eyes were on me.

In a very deep, attention grabbing, professional voice, I said, "You may look UP in inspiration," as I looked up to the ceiling. "You may look DOWN in desperation," as I looked down to the floor. "But never to the SIDE for information," as I turned my head to the left and to the right. "For if you do, you would have just failed my course. Greetings, I'm Dr. Zachariah T. Finley and I will be your instructor for this course… this semester."

*****

Dwight

After I finished dressing, I took a deep breath and headed downstairs. I could immediately see Lexi sitting on the couch eating some yogurt and watching television. I walked past her and headed into the kitchen.

"So you're gonna act like I'm not sitting here?" she looked at me.

I opened the fridge and grabbed a bottle of water. I closed the door and headed for the side door leading to the garage.

"Where are you going?" she asked. "I thought you needed your precious sleep."

I looked at her. She knew good and well this was my week off. I shook my head and said, "I'm going away."

"Where are you going? To that bitch house?"

Not wanting to get into it with her, I said, "Lexi, find God."

Shocked, she stared at me.

"I'll be back whenever," I replied as I headed out of the house.

I knew I had a couple of hours before his lunch time, so I just wanted to drive around and clear my mind.

I haven't seen Kory since our encounter Saturday morning. We've been sending text messages, but nothing discussing what happened in his apartment.

Truth be told, I don't know how I feel. I don't why I did what I did, but I did it.

Did I like it? Yes, I did and that scares me. Maybe it's not just

Zach. Maybe I am attracted to dudes.

Then again, it could just be Kory. He is kinda sexy. He has a lil swag about him that's hot. He's not to bitchy. He has a good job. He has his own place. He ain't down my back all the time like some bitch would be. He's a nigga.

Is this why dudes fuck with other dudes? Less hassle than dealing with a female? None of that PMS shit? Niggas don't catch feelings like females? They can't say they're pregnant?

Man, I don't know. All of this shit is so confusing to me. I don't know what the fuck is wrong with me.

Before I knew it, I ended back up in my old neighborhood. After my mom and dad got divorced, my mom took the money and moved to Macon. My dad, on the other hand, kept the house.

My dad, who just turned 75 in June, is still ripping and running the city like he was 30. I didn't see his car.

The biggest thing that concerned me was that I didn't want to end up like my father. My dad forced himself to live a straight life even though he knew he was gay. He got married and had two children, but still preferred to be in the company of men. My mom said she knew for years my dad was fucking men, but stayed with him for our sake. When Ced graduated high school and came down to FAMU, shit in the house got worse. My mom kept her mouth shut, not letting my dad know that she was building a case against him. Years later, when she had all the evidence she needed, she filed for divorce. My father was a proud man and denied the gay shit even though she had photographs of him hugging up with men.

Ced, my dad and I, have never discussed his sexual orientation. Ced and I talk about it, but never with our father. Some shit is just better left unsaid.

I know I needed to get my life in order, I didn't want to end up like my father.

I knocked on the door and rang the doorbell. No reply.

After a few minutes of nothing, I walked back to the car and phoned him. Within a few rings, he answered, "This is Dwight."

"Dad," I said. "How are you?"

"Hey, Junior," he said. "What's going on?"

"I'm at the house trying to check on you but you didn't answer the door."

"For good reason," he replied. "I'm not there."

"Where are you?" I asked as I cranked up the car and backed out of the driveway.

"In St. Louis."

"What are you doing in St. Louis?" I asked.

"I don't know. I just decided to go for a trip. I needed to get away for a little bit. I'll be back sometime tomorrow or the next day. How is your brother?"

"Ced is doing ok," I said. "I talked to him yesterday."

"And your mother?" he asked.

"She's mom."

"Yeah, we know," he exhaled.

"Well, dad, call me when you get back to Atlanta. Maybe we can do lunch or something."

"I will do, Junior. Take care of yourself and kiss my grandbabies for me, okay?"

"Ight, Dad," I hung up the phone.

When I merged back onto the interstate, I checked the time. I needed to get lunch and head on over to surprise him.

While I drove, my phone started to vibrate. I checked the name and smiled. "This can't be who I think it is," I answered the phone as I turned down the radio.

"It's me," my other best friend, Amir Knight, stated. "How have you been, Dwight?"

"Man, it's great to hear from you. I've been ok. I was just back in the old neighborhood. I miss those days."

"Yeah, life was easier back then," Amir replied.

"But enough of that, how is Chicago treating you?" I asked.

"It's Chicago," he said. "Listen, I'm coming down to visit for a few days in September. I want to get up."

"That's what's up," I said. "We can do that. How is your mom and your brother?"

"My mom is good. Dallis and his family moved to Houston a few months ago. He got a better job down there."

"So Dallis is still keeping up the 'I'm straight now' shit, huh?"

"Yeah. I hope he ain't fuckin' niggas on that girl. But you know Dallis, can't tell his ass shit. Sometimes I wish it were me in his shoes though."

"What do you mean?"

"I've always wanted a child. Fucking all them niggas back in college fucked me up. The one thing I want, I can never have, but it is what it is."

"So how are you doing, health wise?" I asked in reference to his HIV.

He paused and said, "Some days are better than others."

"Amir, is everything ok? You're not dying are you?"

"Naw man," he laughed. "At least I don't hope so."

I didn't find that funny. HIV isn't anything to play around with.

"Relax, Dwight," Amir stated. "I'm okay."

"I hope so."

"I was just thinking about you," he said. "I know we don't talk as much as we used to, but I still love you, man. Remember that, ok? I still love you."

"I love you too, Amir."

"Listen, how are the kids?" he asked. "I haven't seen them in so long."

"They're doing well," I smiled. "Chloe is in Pre-K now—"

"You love that Chloe," Amir interjected. "That girl can do no wrong. You can hear it in your voice. Every time you mention her name, it's like I can hear you smiling."

"That's my baby girl," I smiled.

"I see," Amir said. "How are Brennan and Nico doing?"

"They're ok. Brennan has a slick mouth just like his mother."

Amir laughed and said, "How is Lexi?"

"Can we change the topic please?"

"Damn, it's like that?"

"Yeah, it is," I replied as I pulled up to the sub shop.

"I'm all ears. Let me know what's going on," he said.

"Amir, let me order this food and I'll call you right back as soon as I get back in the car."

"Ight, I'm just at the house wasting time. Hit me back up, I'll be waiting."

90

Dorian

Since Kory was new to the group, we let him decide on the joint for lunch today. As suspected, he picked a national chain. Red Lobster was cool, but I like to try out the local ethnic restaurants. I'm all about putting my money back into the black families.

While we ate the cheddar bay biscuits and salads, Brandon started to talk to Kory about something at the office.

In the midst of their talking, Eric sent me a text telling me to have a good day. He had just woke up and was getting ready to head over to the hospital.

When I zoomed back in on the conversation, Brandon said, "So I was watching this show last night and the topic of discussion was cheating, so I started thinking."

"About?" Kory asked.

"Just how many people cheat or have cheated in their lifetime."

"I think majority of Americans have cheated at some point or another," Kory said.

"I agree," Brandon said.

"Have you ever cheated?" Kory asked me.

"Have I ever cheated?" I repeated.

"Yeah," he nodded his head.

"Honesty, no, I haven't. I've never cheated on anyone."

"What about you, Brandon?" Kory asked.

Brandon looked at me and exhaled. I wondered if he was going to tell the truth.

"Well, Dorian already knows the story," Brandon said. "At first,

I don't think he believed me, that was until one day when he saw the proof for himself."

I damn sure didn't believe him until I saw it for myself.

"What happened?" Kory asked. "Who was it?"

"I met my current boyfriend, Micah, when I was at FAMU back in 2008. A couple of years into our relationship, around the summer of 2010, we were having some issues and we split up. During this time, I was in graduate school and I was the head drum major for the band. That September, we were having practice here in Atlanta for our football game at the dome against Tennessee State. We had two visitors and they played professional basketball. They both were fairly young. I think they had been in the league about three or four years at that time."

"Are they still playing?" Kory asked.

"Yes," I interjected as I thought about the dudes, CJ Wright and Keon Douglass.

"Anyway, one of the dudes starting flirting with me," Brandon said. "Long story short, we exchanged numbers. Later that night, he picked me up from the band hotel. We went to a hotel that he got and we fucked."

"Just like that?" Kory asked.

"Just like that," Brandon said. "We both knew what we wanted, so why beat around the bush? So, like I said, at the time, my dude and I were split, so it was nothing. I thought it was just gonna be a one-night thing, but then a few weeks later, they had a few days off before the start of the NBA season, so he flew to Tallahassee. We fucked again. He flew me to cities where his team would be playing. He'd get me a room in a nearby hotel and before or after the game, depending on the schedule, he'd come to the room and we'd fuck. In the process of all that fucking, he paid off ALL of my student loans. Keep in mind that I'm from New Jersey, so those out-of-state fees were a bitch. He wiped out all of my debt just because he liked fucking with me. He said he liked fucking with me because I was just a regular dude. I didn't want anything from him. I didn't trip at his celebrity. Times after we fucked, we would just lay in the bed and talk. He would talk about so much in his life. In the meantime, I knew nothing with him was gonna really pop off, other than our random hookups and I was cool with that. But the problem was that my boyfriend and I decided to work out our issues."

"But you were still fucking the NBA player?" Kory said.

"It wasn't often, but whenever he called, I went. Hell, he was still paying my tuition for graduate school and he would just drop five, ten, fifteen thousand dollars in my bank account periodically. Would you let that shit go? When I would call him, he'll say he was just thinking about me, so he put some money in my account to get me over."

"So you became a male prostitute for this baller?" Kory asked.

"Naw, it wasn't anything like that," Brandon said. "I never asked him for anything. Whatever he gave, he gave because he wanted to."

"Oh, ok," Kory said.

I ate another biscuit.

Kory then said, "So you and your dude got back together, but you still continued to fuck this baller?"

"Yeah, for a little while," Brandon replied.

"So when you and your dude be fucking, he couldn't tell you were getting fucked by this baller? Was the baller's dick small or something?"

"Naw," Brandon said. "He was far from small. But, my dude is a bottom."

"So you're vers?" Kory asked.

"Yeah," Brandon shook his head.

"So your dude never knew about this?" Kory asked.

"Nope."

"When did y'all stop fucking?" Kory asked.

"A few years ago. We're still cool though. I told him that I couldn't continue to do this to Micah. He understood. He said he didn't want to break up a happy home. He had cheated in his past and he knew what it does to a relationship. Sometimes he calls me just to vent. We developed a good friendship. Whenever he comes into town, we'll get up for dinner or something like that. Nothing serious."

"But your dude doesn't know that you're friends with this baller?" Kory asked

"Nope."

"This baller—does he have dreads?" Kory asked.

"No," I interjected.

"So how do you know him?" Kory asked me.

I shook my head and said, "One night, Brandon left his phone at my house. Turns out we had the same identical phone. Anyway, he took my phone and I had his phone. The phone started to vibrate and it was a text from the dude. Brandon had already told me about the dude before, but I never believed him until that night. In the text, he said, and I quote, 'I just dropped five grand into your account. I miss you and I wanna see you. I already booked the room, but I want you to book a flight to Charlotte. We got a game there on Thursday night. I'll email you the hotel shit in a few minutes. Ight, sexy.'"

"Are you serious?" Kory asked.

"Dead ass. So, I called Brandon to make him aware that he grabbed the wrong phone. When he got back to my place, I explained to him what I read. And then he checked his account and there it was—five thousand dollars had just been transferred into his account minutes earlier. While he sat at my computer, the hotel shit came through the email. I was sold. I realized he wasn't lying."

"So, Brandon," Kory said. "How would you feel if you were the one being cheated on? What if your dude was cheating on you right now? How would that make you feel?"

"Obviously, I wouldn't like it," Brandon said. "But Micah wouldn't do that. That ain't even like him."

"So you can do it, but he can't?" Kory asked.

"That's not what I'm saying," Brandon replied. "Everyone has a past and everyone makes mistakes. Some shit is better left unsaid."

"Oh ok," Kory said as he took a sip of his drink. "Don't underestimate anyone."

"Do you know something we don't?" I asked.

"No," Kory shook his head. "I don't even know the dude, Micah or whatever his name is. I was just speaking in hypothetical terms. Don't underestimate anyone."

*****

Zach

I had just arrived back in my office from my first two classes of the day. I had one more class today in a couple of hours, but I needed to get some food in my system.

Tomorrow was going to be a light day. I only had once class scheduled and majority of the rest of my day would be dedicated for office hours.

After I decided on what I was gonna eat, there was a knock at my door.

"Come in," I said loud enough for the person on the other side of the door to hear.

When the door opened, my mouth dropped.

"How did you know where my office was?" I asked.

"I asked around," Dwight said as he closed the door. "It's not rocket science."

"Whatever," I said.

"So, yeah, I decided to bring you some lunch," he stated as he sat the brown paper bag down on the desk. "I know how much you love Firehouse, so I got your favorite, with the cherry limeade for the drink."

"Thanks, Dwight, you're the best," I said as I moved the papers off my desk to make way for our impromptu lunch.

"I know," he smiled.

"Whatever," I said as I unwrapped the sub.

As he began to eat, he said, "I so can't wait for the weekend."

"Yeah, me too," I replied. "I can't wait to get to Tallahassee. I can't wait to see the band."

"We are leaving Friday, right?" he asked.

"Yes," I stated as I thought about Kris.

I explained to Dwight what happened on Friday in relation to the question of Kris being happy. Dwight didn't comment. When I finished, I said, "Something about it just isn't sitting right. There is something more to Kris and Micah than Kris is letting on."

Dwight interjected by saying, "I think you're just over analyzing the situation. Kris is one of the good ones. He'll never step out on Rozi. He loves her and he loves his family too much to do something like that. Kris is a stand up dude."

"I hear all of that," I said. "But what I'm saying is off all the times we've hung out, Kris is always the first to leave. He always uses the excuse that, and I quote, 'I love y'all, but I have a family to get back home to.'"

"Zach, you're doing too much," Dwight said.

"But hear me out," I pleaded. "I mean think about it, Dwight."

He ate some of his sub.

I said, "It's clear, to me at least, that Rozi knows he is with the boyz. Dwight, that's a perfect opportunity for Kris and Micah to do what they do. I'm just saying, think about it. Rozi really has nothing to suspect and it's clear that she's ok with him being with us because, unlike your wife, Rozi never calls or text Kris while he's with us. Now, mind you, I've just joined these Friday night events, but you, Kris and Kes have been doing this what four or five years now?"

"Five," Dwight said. "And it's not every Friday, but at least twice a month."

I nodded my head and took a sip of my cherry limeade.

"We've done more since you've been back in town," Dwight said. "But, Zach, let it go."

"Dwight, I know what I'm talking about. I've counseled plenty of people and Kris' response and body language on Friday night told me a lot. I'll drop it for now but—."

"Good because it's a crazy accusation," Dwight interjected. "Kris and Micah fucking? C'mon Zach. Do you hear yourself?"

"But what if he is still fucking Micah?"

"Then that's his business to worry about," Dwight said. "Not yours."

"Do you know something I don't know?"

"No," Dwight replied.

"So why are you so protective of Kris? He told you something?"

"Zach, DROP IT! Don't you have your own problems to deal with?"

I stared at Dwight and said, "Like what?"

"Well…hell…my stance hasn't changed, Zach."

"Dwight, please," I replied as I took a bite of my sub.

"What? You secretly wish that you can be Kris?" Dwight asked. "You want us to get away on Friday nights and fuck before you go home to Dray?"

I stared at Dwight.

He continued, "I'm down. You let me know when you're ready.

We can get away right now if you want. What time is your next class? You know he doesn't do it like me. You know that."

"Dwight, we've had sex once."

"True, but I know that night, me and you connected. I made you feel something that he has never made you feel. You made me feel something that I've never felt before. It took me a long time to get there, but Zach, we're soul mates. You know it and I know it. I'm willing to give up everything for a life with you. I don't want to be unhappy for the rest of my life, Zach. You're the only person that makes me happy. You've made me happy for fourteen years now. Can we please stop wasting more time?"

I jumped at the sound of knocking on my door. Before I could reply, the door burst open and Renzo said, "HEY DOC! WHAT'S GOOD?"

He saw Dwight and said, "Oh... sorry... my bad... I can come back."

I looked at Dwight, then to Renzo and said, "No... please... stay. This is my best friend, Dr. Taylor. We were just eating lunch."

"Nice to meet you, Dr. Taylor," Renzo said as he headed over to Dwight.

They shook hands.

Dwight stared at me as Renzo sat down, letting me know he wasn't happy our conversation was interrupted.

I turned to Renzo, smiled and said, "Please tell me how your trip to Jamaica went."

*****

TJ

She was talking about something, but my mind was thrown. I've been staring at Jodi and then when I look at our history teacher, Mrs. Simms, I can't help but see the resemblance. I know I can't be the only person in this school that thinks they somewhat favor each other. I mean they don't look like twins, but damn, they gotta be related.

As Mrs. Simms walked the aisles talking about some shit I didn't give a fuck about, I found myself staring at her ass. Mrs. Simms is fine as fuck though. If she let me fuck, I'll hit dat shit. I wouldn't tell a soul.

She's probably a freak. Look at her.

She's always smiling and shit. She's always happy. I know she be putting that pussy down on her husband. Hell, they got three kids—one boy and two girls—as evident by the pictures on her desk, so I know they be getting it in on a regular. Damn, her husband is a lucky ass muh'fucker. Her pussy probably real pretty, too. That shit probably stay wet.

Man, I need some head… some pussy…something… and fast.

When I looked up, Mrs. Simms was smiling as she approached me. She winked her left eye and then turned around and headed back to the front of the class.

That's the second time today that she's winked at me. I know I ain't crazy. Mrs. Simms is feeling me.

I looked at Nolan who was sitting in front of me and he was scribbling something in his notebook. Elijah, who was sitting in front of Nolan, was focused on Mrs. Simms lecture.

The door opened and everyone turned their head to see who it was. When Mrs. Simms saw him, she finished her statement and smiled. She motioned for him to approach her.

I tapped Nolan on the shoulder and said, "Who is that dude?"

"The biggest faggot on this campus," Nolan whispered. "I can't stand his bitch ass."

"Oh," I said taken aback. "Ok."

"He's the eighth grade dean," Nolan said. "Dean Mitchell. He's so bitchy. His parents knew he was gonna be gay when he was a baby."

"Why you say that?" I asked.

"His first name is Keli. What nigga you know name is Keli?"

I shrugged my shoulders.

As Mrs. Simms and the dean talked, I noticed that other conversations had broken out in the room. I tapped Nolan on the shoulder and said, "You see that?"

"See what?" he asked.

"Jodi and Mrs. Simms."

"What about them?" he asked, confused.

"Don't they look alike, like they can be sisters or something."

Nolan stared then said, "Hmm, they kinda do favor a little bit. Hell, everyone has a twin though."

"Yeah, you right I guess," I said. "Yo, I spoke to my dad. He's cool with this weekend. He wanna talk to your mom though to make sure it's ok, so I just need a number I can text him so he can call her."

After he gave me his mom's cell number, I said, "What about Elijah?"

"What about him?" Nolan asked.

"You want him to come and spend the night, too?"

"Naw," Nolan said nodding his head in disagreement. "That's ok."

I just stared at Nolan, trying to read why he didn't like Elijah all of a sudden. I thought they were friends before I got here.

He said, "His mom and stepdad won't let him come. We've been down that road before."

"Oh," I said as I nodded my head and looked over at Elijah who was talking to the guy sitting next to him.

Soon after, Dean Mitchell took a seat in the back of the class. He pulled out a paper and started to jot some stuff down while Mrs. Simms resumed her lecture. While Mrs. Simms talked, I looked over at Jodi and then over to Mrs. Simms a few times.

They had to be related in some way.

Then again, I could be tripping. Yeah, I'm probably just tripping.

91

TJ

Friday, September 2, 2016

When the school bell sounded, I grabbed my shit and jumped the fuck out of my seat. I was out dis bitch!

"Have a great weekend," the language arts teacher said as there was a massive exodus towards the door.

Nolan was in front of me and Elijah was behind me. When we got into the hallway, I smiled. In just a few hours, I'll be heading over to Nolan's house for the weekend.

We walked out of the building headed for the bus ramp.

"What are you smiling for?" Elijah asked.

"Because I'm excited," I replied.

"Excited about what?"

"It's the weekend, shawty," Nolan cut. "Who wouldn't be excited?"

"Yeah and I'm going over to Nolan's crib, too," I added.

Elijah stared at me for a second and said, "Oh."

Nolan chimed in, "I ain't ask you Eli because the last time your parents was like no. I ain't in the business of wasting time, feel me, so I ain't even worry about it."

Elijah looked at me, over to Nolan, back to me and then said, "Ok."

As we edged closer to the bus ramp, I turned my head and smiled when I saw her. "I'll be right back," I said to Elijah and Nolan then headed in Jodi's direction.

"DON'T MISS THE BUS!" Elijah yelled.

I jogged over to Jodi. She started to smile as I got closer. When

I reached her, I said in my sexy voice, "Sup, Jodi?"

I licked my lips. She smiled harder and replied, "Hey, TJ."

I looked at her best friend, Alison, hoping she'll get the hint to get lost.

Three's company, bitch!

Realizing that she wasn't wanted in this conversation, in an attitude filled voice, Alison said, "Whatever you got to say to her, you can say it in front of me."

I gave her one of Daddy nasty ass, scornful looks. I cut my eyes to Jodi.

Jodi turned to Alison and said, "Girl, go save me a seat on the bus, please. I'll be right there."

"WHATEVER!" Alison stormed off.

When Alison was gone, Jodi looked at me and said, "She don't mean no harm. We're kinda like sisters."

I licked my lips and said, "Yoooo, it's cool. I just wanted to spend a lil time with you before we all leave. It's the weekend so I won't see you for a few days."

She blushed.

I reached down and ran my hand across hers and interlocked fingers. She looked up at me and smiled. We stopped walking.

I turned to her and said, "Jodi, if you can't tell by now, I like you. I know I'm new here and shit, and you probably got all the niggas in the school tryin' to holla at you, but I'm feeling you. You can ask Nolan, when I first saw you, nobody else mattered. Just give me a chance to prove to you that we should chill."

She blushed.

"I'm serious, Jodi. I ain't never seen nobody as beautiful as you before. I'm spending the weekend at Nolan's crib, but you got my cell number. Call me, girl. Just give me a chance."

She smiled and said, "I like you too. I'll call you, boy." And then, she reached up to me and placed a kiss on my cheek.

Before I could say anything, we were both startled by the loud sound coming from the bull horn that said, "NONE OF THAT LOVEY-DOVEY STUFF HERE! Y'ALL ARE TOO YOUNG FOR THAT! Y'ALL BETTER GET OUT OF HERE, CATCH THE BUS AND ENJOY YOUR WEEKEND!"

He kept walking towards us.

Jodi smiled and when he approached us, she said, "Bye, Mr. Mitchell."

The gay dude that came in our class the other day that Nolan referred to as "the biggest faggot on this campus" was standing in front of us. I think Nolan said his first name was Keli or something like that.

Jodi turned to me, winked her eye then hurried away. I tried to leave, but wasn't successful. When I tried to walk away, he said, "Hold on, son."

Hoping that I didn't get in trouble for Jodi kissing me on the cheek, I turned around and stared at him.

"What's your name?" he asked me.

"TJ," I replied.

"Is that your birth name?"

I exhaled and said, "My government name is Antonio Marquis Shaw, Jr. Everyone has been calling me TJ since I was a baby. Is there anything else, sir?"

"You don't have to call me sir," he said. "Mr. Mitchell is just fine."

I stared at him.

"Why the attitude?" he asked.

"I don't have an attitude," I cut. I exhaled as I looked to the sky for a few seconds, hoping he'd just let me leave.

"It'll be in your best interest to drop the 'tude, like yesterday," he said.

I exhaled.

"You're new here, correct?" he asked.

"Obviously."

"What grade?"

"Eighth."

"Oh, so you're one of my kids," Mr. Mitchell said. "I am your dean."

"Great," I sarcastically replied as I forced a fake ass smile.

"TJ COME ON!" Elijah yelled. "THE BUSES 'BOUT TO LEAVE!"

I turned to Mr. Mitchell and said, "I gotta go."

"Umm, hmm," he said. "I got my eyes on you. Good day."

Relieved, I ran to catch up with Elijah. I was ready to get the fuck out of here.

When the big ass cheese wagon reached our stop, I followed behind Elijah and the two white dudes that always caught the bus at this stop. As I inched closer to those coveted exit doors, I felt like I was slowly but surely regaining my freedom by the second. As soon as I stepped off the bus, I breathed a sigh of relief.

The air was so fresh. The sun was just right. The birds were chirping. Everything was perfect. It was Friday. Jodi was gonna hit me up and I was about to spend some time at my boy's crib. Daddy wasn't here to piss me off and when he gets back in town, I'll be long gone. Nothing could go wrong. Absolutely nothing.

Like every other day, Elijah regained his spot to my immediate right. As we walked down the road, I could tell that something was on his mind.

The entire bus ride home, he just looked out of the window and never mumbled a single word. That wasn't like Elijah. He always had something to say. He was always smiling.

Now, it was just a straight face—no emotion, no nothing. We were just two strangers walking side-by-side.

A part of me wanted to ignore him and act like nothing was wrong, but this is my friend. He was the first person I met down here, so that wouldn't be right of me to act like it was nothing. I'm better than that.

As I was bracing myself for what was to come, I saw a car heading in our direction. Once the 2016 Nissan Maxima passed, I took a deep breath and said, "Eli, what's up with you?"

He looked to me and said, "Nothing."

"Man, it's all on your face," I said as I slowed the pace of our walk. "What's going on, bruh?"

He took a deep breath and said, "Just let me know straight up."

"Let you know what?" I asked as we stopped in front of his house.

"Are we still cool?" he asked.

I stared at him like he was crazy and said, "Yeah, we're still cool. Why in the hell would you ask something like that?"

"I'm just saying. You always hanging with Nolan and shit and he always saying something slick to me. It's like once you started chilling with him, you stopped talking to me, you know other than when we going to and from school."

"Eli, I don't know what's up with Nolan and you, but me and you are still cool. You my homie...shawty."

He smiled and said, "Look at you trying to talk like you from Atlanta, talking about some shawty."

I smiled and said, "I did that just for you."

He smiled then said, "So what are you gonna do at Nolan's crib?"

"I don't know, just play video games or whatever. I really don't know. I'm just excited to get out of the house, nah'mean?"

"Yeah, I feel you. But let me get going, us standing out here talking looks kinda...gay... and you ain't gay, right?"

I shook my head, smiled and said, "Yeah, you better head on inside your crib. I'll get at you."

"Ight," he smiled as he ran up his driveway and to his front door.

*****

Kris

I could hear Micah's voice saying, "*Why we gotta keep doing this? Why can't we just be honest?*"

I stared down at the papers in front of me. I wasn't up to this shit today. I hadn't been up to it all fucking week!

That statement from Micah has been on repeat in my head all week, ever since he said it Saturday morning.

"Mr. Simms," one of the interns said as she knocked on the cracked office door.

"Yes?" I forced a smile.

"Travis wanted me to bring this by for you to look over," she said as she walked the papers over to me. "He wants you to call him when you're done looking it over."

"Ight, thanks," I smiled. "Tell him I'll give him a buzz."

"Thanks, Mr. Simms."

"Please, just call me Kris."

She smiled as she exited the office.

I graduated from FAMU in 2006 with a degree in economics. Upon graduation, I immediately moved to Atlanta. While in Atlanta, I attended graduate school at Georgia State University and received my masters in economics.

I currently work for the United States Federal Government as an economist with the Center of Disease Control and Prevention in Atlanta. I'm also an adjunct instructor at Georgia State, where I teach an Intro to Economics class once a week on Wednesday night.

I could hear Micah's voice.

I don't know how I got myself into this shit. I don't know how we got to this point in our life.

I love my wife. I swear, I love my wife. I've gotten myself in too deep and I don't know how to get out. I love my wife, but I love Micah, too.

I never thought I would be the one doing the cheating, that was Dwight's job.

He was the notorious cheater in the group.

What the fuck am I doing?

What the fuck have I done?

Part Seven:

Back to Tallahassee

92

Dorian

The end of the day couldn't come fast enough. It was Friday, Labor Day weekend and pay day all rolled into one. I couldn't wait to enjoy these three days off from work.

Brandon knocked on the door, walked in the office and asked, "What are you doing in here?"

"Ready to get the hell up out of here!"

"I can't wait to get on the road," Brandon replied.

I walked over to a filing cabinet to retrieve a folder and said, "I can't believe you convinced Kory and me to go on this trip—especially me. I don't wanna see y'all band like that."

He smiled and said, "Nigga, stop fronting. You know you a Rattler at heart. I know you really wanted to go to FAMU, but settled for Bethune-Cookman. It's ok. We all make mistakes in life."

"You got jokes," I laughed.

"Tell me I'm lying," he said.

I closed the file cabinet, headed back to my desk and said, "I'm only going because I want to hear Gov. Reed speak tomorrow."

"It's gonna be a fucking media circus out there," Brandon said. "I ain't looking forward to that part of the trip."

"Hopefully we'll run into my brother while we're down there. I spoke to him yesterday and he said that he was riding down to Tally with some of his friends tonight. Maybe we can set something up."

"That's what's up. Kory is excited about the trip. I think it'll be good for all of us."

I looked at my best friend and said, "You and Kory are becoming really good friends, huh?"

"Yeah. He's a good guy. We mesh well together."

"What is Micah gonna do this weekend? Is he still getting up with his friends like he does every Friday?" I asked.

"He said that all his friends and co-workers were going out of the town for the weekend. I invited him on the trip, but he declined. He said he'll probably go spend some time at his brother's place." Brandon shrugged his shoulders.

"Is everything alright between y'all?" I asked.

"Yeah, that I'm aware of. What makes you ask that?"

"Just a question."

Brandon said, "Oh. Anyway, let me get back so I can hurry up and get this work done."

*****

Keston

I yelled in pleasure, "Damn, bae, you 'bout to make me cum!"

"Bust that shit for me," Phoenix said as the steamy shower water hit my backside.

"OH, MY GOD," I screamed in pleasure.

He gripped me tighter at the waist and started to pound my ass even harder than before.

"Oh, shit," I yelled as I was about to explode.

"Get that nut," he said. "Get that nut!"

He stroked it harder... and harder... and HARDER!

In a pure euphoric state, I yelled, "Oh, my God!" I felt my nut shooting up my body. With one last stroke, he hit all the right spots and that creamy white stuff erupted from my dick like a volcano. I screamed in pleasure. Moments later, Phoenix pulled out and screamed as he reached that desired state of pleasure.

When we both were done, I turned around and we kissed as the water beat down our faces. He smiled and said, "Damn, I love you."

"I love you, too."

After we both got dressed, Phoenix headed into the kitchen to make a quick lunch. I stayed in the room and finished packing for the trip. When I joined him in the dining area, he had just finished making us a turkey and cheese sandwich. I looked at him and smiled while I ate my food.

"Why are you looking like that?" he asked.

"Just thinking," I smiled. "Everything in my life feels so right at this moment."

He smiled and said, "I don't know what I'm gonna do with you being gone."

While he took a bite of his sandwich, I said, "Phoenix, it's only for the weekend. I'll be back before you know it."

"I know, but still," he pouted. "I have to keep myself entertained someway."

"What do you have planned?" I asked.

"I have a few ideas," he grinned.

"Like what?"

"Well, for one, I need you to come over here."

"Over where?" I asked.

"Over here," he motioned me to come to him.

"Why?" I wondered what he wanted.

"Kes, just come here. I wanna show you something."

I curiously walked over to him. He turned me around really fast and started to pull down my jeans.

"Phoenix," I pleaded as I tried to put up a fight. "I gotta get on the road."

"I know," he bent me over and spread my ass apart. "But a few minutes won't hurt."

The next thing I knew I felt the invasion of his tongue in my ass.

"Shit," I moaned.

I sighed.

Yeah... another few minutes won't hurt.

It won't hurt at all...

93

Zach

I was pressed for time. I ended up staying on campus later than normal and then got stuck in traffic because of an accident on the way home.

When I walked in the house, Dray was in his office, on the phone, working on something for his Rolling Stone job. I kissed him on the cheek then hurried off to the shower. Once out of the shower, I began to pack my clothes for the trip this weekend.

Just as I finished putting the last of the items into the suitcase, Dray walked in the room and said, "Sorry it took so long for me to come help you, but I had to take care of that stuff with Rolling Stone."

"It's cool, Dray," I smiled as I looked around the room to make sure I didn't forget anything.

"Do you need any more help?"

"Naw, I think I pretty much got it. Kes should have been here about twenty minutes ago, so hopefully he's on his way." I closed the suitcase and drug it over to the door.

Dray sat down on the bed and said, "Well, I hope you enjoy yourself, but don't do anything I wouldn't do."

I looked at him, forced a smile, shook my head and then said, "I'll try my best not to."

When I got the text from Kes stating that he was a few minutes away, I motioned for Dray to follow me downstairs. As soon as we reached the living room, he said, "Where are y'all staying?"

I looked at him and sarcastically replied, "At a hotel."

"Separate rooms?" Dray asked.

"Umm, yeah," I shook my head.

I know what he was hinting at. He wanted to know if Dwight and I were gonna be in the same damn room at the same damn time.

I said, "Dray, we are four grown ass men with careers. I want you to think about the question you just asked. What sense does that make? I think we all have enough money to get our own fucking hotel rooms!"

The doorbell rang before he could reply.

"Coming!" I said as I headed over to let Kes inside.

He stepped inside, smiled and said, "You ready to get this thing on the road?"

"I was ready half an hour ago."

"Sorry," Kes replied as Dray appeared around the corner. "I was a lil busy."

"Umm, hmm, I bet," I smiled.

He smiled and then greeted Dray. After they exchanged hugs, Dray said, "Kes, can you do me a favor?"

I looked at Dray with concern. Kes eyed him with suspicion and said, "Sure, what's up?"

Dray pointed to me and told Kes, "Don't let him do nothing crazy. You know how he can get when he's away from home."

"And how do I get?" I asked, staring at Dray.

Sensing the tension, Kes laughed and said, "Dray, we're just going to Tallahassee for a few days. There isn't much you can do there."

"I know. I was just joking," Dray smiled. "Calm down, boy."

I shook my head and rolled my eyes.

"Y'all have a good trip and get my baby back home safely," Dray said.

"Bye, Dray," Kes smiled as he grabbed my luggage and headed out.

I turned to face Dray. We embraced with a kiss and then he said, "I love you. Be safe."

"I love you, too," I said as I headed out of the house, ready to get this Labor Day weekend started off right!

*****

Kris

I tried my best to comfort my wife. I said, "It'll be ok."

With worry on her face, she said, "But what if it is my child? Kris, my past is rearing its ugly head. She's so beautiful. I have to keep my composure around her. A mother knows her child and I'm convinced that girl is my daughter. I know she is."

"Rozi, calm down," I pleaded with my wife. "Just calm down."

Ever since she came home, she has been stressing about this kid in her class, who she thinks is her daughter.

"People are gonna start asking questions," Rozi said. "What if she starts to ask questions?"

"Baby, don't worry about that this weekend. You and the kids are spending some time with your mother and your brothers. Eric is the only person in your family, besides me, who knows about this kid. I know it was a long time ago, Rozi. Everyone makes mistakes, baby. But unless you want your family to start digging into your past, you have to control yourself this weekend. You can't let your family see you like this while they're up here in Atlanta. Just have fun with your family, baby."

There was a knock on the door.

I looked at her and said, "When I get back from the trip, we'll sort through everything, ok?"

She took a deep breath and said, "Ok. I've gotta put my game face on for my family this weekend."

When I opened the door, Kris and Zach were standing at the door.

"OH, MY GOD!" Rozi screamed as she rushed Zach. "I haven't seen you in so long!"

Kes smiled at the embrace.

After she hugged Kes, she turned back to Zach and said, "How has everything been?"

"Everything is good, Rozi," Zach smiled.

"Kris told me you moved to Atlanta. How do you like it so far?"

"Baby," Kris interrupted. "You know how you and Zach can get and we don't have time for that. We gotta get on the road. We're already behind schedule."

She looked at Kes and Zach and said, "Who's driving?"

"I am," Kes stated.

In a playful tone, she said, "You better get my husband back home safe and sound, you hear me?"

"Yes, ma'am, Mrs. Simms," Kes smiled.

After I hugged and kissed my kids, Rozi said, "Y'all boyz be safe on that road. Drive the speed limit. Kris, call me and let me know that y'all made it, ok?"

"Ok," I kissed my wife. "Remember what I said. Keep it under control and we'll talk about it when I get back."

"I got it," she smiled as we walked out of the door.

"I love you," I said.

"I love you, too," she said as she watched us put my luggage in the car.

As we pulled out of the driveway, Kes blew his horn as Rozi and the kids stood at the door and waved bye-bye.

94

Dray

As soon as Zach was gone, I sat down on the couch and looked around the huge, empty house. It wasn't empty with material shit, it was empty with warmth.

Something was missing. I couldn't put my finger on it, but something was missing.

I turned on the television and flipped through a couple of channels before quickly turning it back off. TV has never really been my thing. That was Zach's shit.

Sitting alone in this house wasn't gonna cut it. As an idea popped in my head, I smiled and reached for the phone. Within a few rings, he said, "Hey, Dad! What's up?"

"At the house and wanted to see if you wanted to come over for the weekend."

"You're in New York or Atlanta?" Nolan asked.

"Atlanta."

"Dang, Dad. I would love to come but one of my friends from school is coming over to spend the weekend. I know we could probably go to your house, but his dad already talked to mom, so I can't."

"I understand," I replied.

"We can do next weekend, though," he said excited. "Will that be ok?"

"We can make that work," I said as I realized I had to find a way to get Zach out of the house while Nolan was here. Maybe I can take Nolan out of town for the weekend. I don't know. I'll have to figure it out.

"So next week it is, Dad," Nolan said excited. "Dad, I love you but I gotta go. Mom is making me clean up my room before TJ comes over."

I sighed, "Well, enjoy yourself. Have some fun for me, too."

"Ight, Dad. Love you. Talk to you soon."

"I love you too, Nolan."

I placed the phone down on my lap, looked up to the ceiling and exhaled. Something has to give.

I don't have friends down here in Atlanta. Yes, Phoenix is here for the moment, but he resides in Chicago. All of my damn friends are back in New York. Zach doesn't seem to be stressing like me. All of his damn friends are here.

I've gotta get out more. I've got to meet some new people. I've gotta do something.

There is Phoenix's best friend, CJ Wright. He plays basketball for the Hawks and he lives here in Atlanta. Maybe we can start chilling. We hit it off really well when we were at Phoenix's crib in Chicago. I definitely can't deny the fact he was kinda sexy. Naw, let me stop that shit right now!

Just as I got off the couch to grab something to drink, the phone started to vibrate. It was Phoenix. I answered, "I was just thinking about you."

"I hope it was good thoughts," Phoenix stated, as I opened the fridge and grabbed a bottle of Green Tea.

"Of course," I smiled.

"I know Zach is gone with Kes for the weekend, so what you got planned?"

"Nothing, really. I was just trying to figure that shit out. My son just said he was too busy to chill with me," I laughed. "So I'm just winging it right now."

"Perfect!" Phoenix said.

"What's perfect?"

"You can come to Vegas with us."

"Vegas? Who else is going? CJ?" I asked with a smile on my face.

"Why did your voice change when you mentioned CJ's name?" Phoenix asked.

"What?"

"It's like you wanna see him or something, like you were excited to have him on the trip. You feeling CJ?"

"Naw, man, it ain't even nothing like that. I was just thinking about our time at your place back in Chicago. He seemed like a cool ass dude. I just wanted to get to know him a lil more. That's it."

"Umm, hmm," Phoenix said. "CJ is a no-go. He's down in Florida."

"What's he doing down there?" I asked.

"He went to go visit his dude."

"Oh," I replied. "So who else is going?"

"My other best friend, Keon Douglass."

"Keon that plays for the Brooklyn Nets?"

"Yep. Keon is cool. We're all in this game together, so you can be yourself, feel me?"

"Yeah, I feel you," I replied in response to our sexual orientation.

"I'll break the ice, if that's cool with you," he said.

"That's cool," I stated as it was gonna be interesting to meet another successful, rich, DL dude, who just happened to be a celebrity.

"The plane is leaving in a couple of hours, so head on over to my place."

"That's what's up, but I don't have any clothes ready. I ain't ready to go to Vegas."

"Who gives a fuck," Phoenix said. "Dray, if you're gonna hang around me, you gotta live life on the edge. Be spontaneous. Just jump up and say let's do this, let's go there and deal with the consequences later. God blessed you with this one life. Make the best of it. Seize the moment. We can get some clothes when we get there."

"I hear ya, Phoenix."

"I'm serious, Dray. You ain't got shit to do here, unless you're about to get into some trouble while Zach is gone. I don't think you're that kinda dude, so go head and meet me at my house in about an hour. K-Doug is on his way over here now. I'm ready to get to Vegas! My hand is burning, nigga. I just need to throw away some money. I gotta get rid of it ASAP!"

"Phoenix, you're a mess," I laughed. "Let me at least pack some underclothes and I'll head on over there."

"Ight. Time is of the essence, so hurry."

"I will," I hung up the phone.

I smiled.

I was heading to Vegas!

*****

Zach

When we arrived at Dwight's place, Kes turned to me and said, "You gonna get Dwight?"

"That's a negative," I replied. "I don't do his wife like that."

"Damn. You and Lexi still beefing?" Kris asked. "I thought y'all squashed that shit at the wedding."

"I never came at her the wrong way. She came at me wrong. She was the one who didn't want me at the wedding. She was the one who tried to get Dwight to stop being my friend. She is the one who tried to force him to choose between his best friend and his family. Who does that? The day of the wedding, she supposedly squashed the shit, but she still acts funny. Kris, I don't have time for that. I'm too old for those kid games."

"I hear ya, Zach," Kris replied as we sat in the car.

"I'll just call him," Kes said.

"You know what, I'll go in," I opened the front passenger door.

As I approached the house door, she immediately opened it. Lexi looked at me for a second and then planted a smile on her face.

"Long time-no see, Zachariah," Lexi reached over and gave me a hug.

"Yeah," I forced a smile. "It has been a minute."

"Please come inside," she said. "How is everything? I hear you live in Atlanta now."

"Yeah, I moved back earlier this month."

"I know," she said as Dwight came around the corner.

I turned and looked at her. She forced a smile.

After I hugged the kids, I turned to Lexi and said, "Well, it was nice seeing you again. Take care."

"You too," she smiled as Dwight kissed all his kids.

Once he was done, the kids left the room and went back to what they were doing. Before we walked out of the door, Dwight looked at Lexi, shook his head and said, "Don't call me unless one of my kids are sick or if it's a life or death matter. If it isn't, I will hang up the phone. Don't believe me? Try it."

She threw the middle finger.

"You too," he said as he walked out and slammed the front door.

When we got to the car, Dwight put his luggage in the trunk and then said, "I know y'all ain't gonna make me sit in the back. My legs are to long for that."

"Well, I'm driving," Kes said.

"So I guess you're telling me to move to the back with Kris," I said looking back at Dwight.

"Pretty much," Kris laughed.

"Only because it's you, nigga," I moved and sat behind Kes.

Kris was behind Dwight.

Right before we pulled off, I said, "Let me use the restroom right quick before we get started."

"Me, too," Kris said as he got out of the car with me.

Kris rang the doorbell. Lexi came to the door and looked at us like we were crazy.

"Can we use the restroom before we get on the road?" Kris asked.

"Oh, yeah, sure," she smiled as she let us inside.

Kris waited and held a small conversation while I headed to the guest bathroom. As I walked through the house, I could see why Dwight was pissed all the time. There were dishes in the sink. Some of the kids' toys were on the floor. She needed to dust. She needed to vacuum. What the hell does she do all day? It ain't like her ass gotta work.

I shook my head and kept my comments to myself. This was neither the time nor the place. Wanting to quickly get out of there, I pissed, washed my hands and headed out.

When Kris saw me, he headed in the direction of the bathroom.

"Thanks," I said to Lexi as I approached the front door.

Right before I left, she said with an attitude, "I know what you're doing."

I turned around and said, "What was that?

"You heard me. I said I know what your faggot ass is doing. Just let me make one thing perfectly clear. I don't like you, ok. I never liked you. I only deal with your ass because I have to. I know why you brought your nasty, sneaky ass down to Atlanta. The moment you arrived, my husband changed. I know what you're doing. I know what y'all are doing. Y'all think I'm stupid, don't cha? I ain't stupid. You and that motherfucker in that car out there keep on fucking with me and I got something for that ass. Keeping trying me like I'm stupid. I know what the hell is going on!"

"Listen," I stared at her, keeping my voice down, mindful that their kids were in the house. "I don't know what your problem is, but it isn't me. Let's get that straight first off. Secondly, if I wanted your man, there is nothing you could do to stop it. Know that, ok. If I wanted your man, everything you have now… will be…POOF," I said as I blew some of my breath in her face to exaggerate my point, "Gone like the motherfucking wind. Thirdly, I don't want your man. I need you to understand that. Let that shit marinate in your thick ass skull. Fourthly, I'm in a relationship and have been for nearly the past eight years. So, I repeat, I don't want your man. Fifthly, your husband isn't gay. It'll probably be in your best interest to stop saying or suggesting such matters. Lastly, I'm too much of a man to call you a bitch, but you need to grow the fuck up. Seriously."

Kris cleared his throat as he came around the corner. He stared at us with a look of concern.

Lexi stared at him and then to me. She said, "GET OUT OF MY FUCKING HOUSE! BOTH OF YOU! GET OUT RIGHT NOW!"

Dwight and Lexi's oldest son, nine-year-old Brennan, ran into the foyer and looked at the scene. He approached his mother and stood next to her side.

"GET OUT!" she said again. "GET OUT OF MY HOUSE!"

"Gladly," I said as we stepped out.

She slammed the door shut.

As we walked back to the car, Kris said, "What the hell was that about?"

I shook my head but I never answered.

I was already over it.

95

TJ

Nolan's house was just as he described it. As Ray turned into the driveway, I smiled. Ray parked the car, reached into his pocket and gave me five-twenty dollar bills. He said, "You still got your debit card on you, right?"

"Yes, sir."

"How much money you got on it?"

"Uncle Killa called and I told him that I was going to chill at my homeboy house. He said that he was gonna deposit some money in my account so I could go shopping or whatever. When I checked it the other day, he had deposited like five hundred dollars. So I really don't need your money, Ray."

"Naw, keep it anyway. It's always good to have a little cash on you just in case you can't get to an ATM."

I smiled. I wish Jodi knew I was swimming in money. Maybe she might really start taking me seriously.

Ray looked at me and said, "You better behave yourself in this lady's house and act like we raised you with some manners."

"Ray," I smiled as I opened the car door. "Calm down, I got this!"

He shook his head and smiled.

As I grabbed my bag, I phoned Nolan to let him know we were outside. He excitedly replied that he was coming to the door.

Ray being Ray, he followed me to the door. Nolan opened a few seconds later and said to Ray, "Nice to meet you, Mr. Shaw."

Raidon looked down at me. I could suddenly feel my heart about to beat out of my chest. Raidon was not Mr. Shaw. Daddy was Mr. Shaw.

Even though Ray was my daddy, too, daddy and Ray weren't legally married and if Ray said that his name wasn't Mr. Shaw, Nolan would start to put two and two together. I looked at Ray with pleading eyes for him to keep quiet. He looked back at Nolan smiled and said, "Nice to meet you too, Nolan."

Just as I breathed a sigh of relief, Nolan's mom appeared around the corner. Damn, she was beautiful. She smiled as she got closer to the door.

"It is so nice to finally meet you, TJ," she said as she reached down and hugged me. She smelled good, too. "Nolan has been talking so much about you."

After she exchanged greetings with Ray, she told us to go put our stuff down. Right before Ray and Miss Tasha started to talk, I hugged Ray bye and then ran off with Nolan.

The weekend had officially begun.

*****

Kris

Every time Zach and I looked at each other, he continued to give me the look of *don't say shit about what happened earlier with Lexi.* I kept my best friend wishes and left it alone.

We were well into the trip when the conversation turned into relationships. Keston said, "Kris, Rozi is so damn beautiful."

"Yes, she is," Zach interjected.

"And y'all have beautiful children," Dwight added.

"Thanks y'all," I smiled as an image of my family appeared before me.

"So how did you and Rozi meet?" Kes asked. "When I came apart of this group of friends, y'all were already together."

"It's a long story," I said.

Kes looked in the rearview mirror and said, "We ain't got nothing but time."

"Well, Rozi and I go back a long time. I knew Rozi back in high school back in Miami."

Keston said, "Kris, Rozi went to high school with us? I don't remember her. What was her last name then because her face or name doesn't ring a bell?"

"You and Keston did go to the same school," Zach said to me. "I forgot about that."

"I thought Rozi was from West Palm Beach," Dwight added. "Isn't she Eric's sister?"

"Who is Eric?" Kes asked.

"Rozi McDaniel is her maiden name," I said.

"Eric is an ex-boyfriend of mine," Zach replied. "And yes, Eric and Rozi are siblings."

I said, "Keston, Rozi didn't go to school with us. She's from West Palm Beach. Palm Beach and Miami is only an hour drive, if that. Rozi was best friends with the girl I dated in high school. After the girl and I split, I lost contact with Rozi and we all went our separate ways for college. I came to FAMU. My ex-girlfriend went to Florida and Rozi attended Spelman. When I was in college, I ran across Rozi in the mall in Atlanta and that's how we reconnected. When Micah's mom got sick in 2004, he used to fly me back and forth to Norfolk, Virginia, during the summer so we could still chill. During one of those flights, the plane had an eight-hour layover in Atlanta, so I called Rozi and chilled at her place. Chilling with Rozi is what made me originally realize that Micah had cheated on me."

"Wow," Dwight said. "That shit was so long ago."

"Yeah, man," Zach said. "I think it was summer 2003. That's when Micah was acting strange. Something was most definitely going on with him. Y'all remember that?"

"I know I do," I sighed.

Dwight said, "That's when he got ole girl pregnant."

"That's right," Zach said. "Micah got Rozi pregnant and he was working extra hard to pay for the abortion so no one would find out. After he gave Rozi the money for the abortion, Micah returned back to being himself."

"Wait," Kes said as he kept his attention on the road. "You married the chick your ex-boyfriend cheated on you with?"

"Man, she helped me get over Micah," I said.

"That's weird," Kes said. "But whatever floats your boat."

I thought about Rozi's current situation.

"So riddle me this," Kes said. "Does Rozi know about your past with Micah?"

"Yes," I replied.

"Rozi knows that you and Micah used to be an item? Rozi knows that you used to fuck dudes?" Kes asked shocked.

"Yes," I said.

"Was this before or after the marriage?" Kes asked.

I said, "Rozi knew everything about Micah. I couldn't hide it. One time while Micah and I was still an item, I was at her house relaxing for the weekend. It was nothing sexual, just as friends. Anyway, I went to use the restroom and like a dummy, I left my phone on the coffee table. The phone rang and the pic I had of Micah and I kissing flashed across the screen. When I came back to the living room, she called me out on it. It was no need in me lying. In fact, it only bought us closer together. She has never judged me."

"I wonder if she thinks about your past and if you still have feelings for dudes?" Kes asked.

"I've often wondered that myself," Zach added.

"Y'all listen," I said. "I need your help, well opinion."

"What's up?" Dwight asked as he turned and looked at me.

"Y'all can't tell anybody," Kris said. "I'm serious, only three people in the world know about this—Rozi, her brother, Eric, and me. That's it. Y'all my boyz and I need it to remain between us."

"You know we ain't gonna say shit," Zach said.

"Kris, what's going on?" Dwight asked.

I said, "Earlier in the conversation, we talked about Micah and the fact that he gave Rozi the money for the abortion."

"Yeah," Zach eyed me with suspicion.

"Two things," I said.

"Ok, the first?" Dwight said.

"Rozi confessed to me that the baby was never Micah's baby."

"So Micah paid for an abortion and it wasn't his kid?" Dwight asked. "That's fucked up!"

"What do you mean the baby wasn't Micah's?" Zach asked.

"Rozi met two dudes around the same time."

Kes said, "Oh, Lawd! This gonna be some shit made for Maury."

"Micah was one of the dudes, and some other dude who went to FAMU at the same time was the other. Anyway, over a matter of time, she met both dudes at a club or whatnot. Micah was the second dude she met. She and the first dude kicked it off and started fucking. She said that the dude was from Atlanta and was going to school at FAMU. He wanted to make Rozi his girl. Rozi wasn't too keen on it but she kept fucking with the dude when he would come to Atlanta because the dick was good. Then one weekend they got into an argument over something and Rozi ended up going to a party with her friends that the Omega's from Morehouse were throwing. She met Micah at that party. They chilled for the weekend and before he came back to Tally, they started fucking. So, keep in mind, this is when Micah and I were happy in our relationship. Micah would often ride with his brother, Morgan, to Atlanta. While he was there, he'd fuck Rozi. The problem arose when Rozi came up pregnant. She told me that those were the only two dudes that she had fucked that year. She swore on our children lives she was telling the truth. So, I believed her. That's beside the point though. She told Micah that the baby was his because she honestly thought the baby was his. At the time, she had been fucking him more than she was fucking the other dude. When Rozi went to the doctor, he told her she was ten weeks pregnant and she thought she was eight weeks pregnant. The times didn't add up. There was no way in hell the baby could be Micah's because she wasn't having sex with him when the doctor told her how many weeks she was."

"So I guess she never told Micah," Zach said.

"Correct. She never told Micah that he wasn't the father," I said.

"So," Dwight added. "Like I said earlier, Rozi took Micah's money and paid for an abortion and it wasn't even his kid."

"Rozi never had the abortion," I admitted.

"WHAT!" both Zach and Dwight yelled.

"The day she was scheduled to have it, she went to the clinic and she couldn't do it. The nurse talked her out of it. With Eric's help, Rozi went into hiding from her family. She made excuses as to why she couldn't come home. She said she was working or school was really kicking her ass, shit like that. Rozi agreed to give the child up for adoption. So, she carried the baby to term and once she delivered the baby girl, she signed the papers and never saw the girl again."

"Wow," Zach said.

"What prompted Rozi to tell me this story was when Rozi was almost done with college, she saw a baby girl at a store. One look at the girl and she knew the child was hers."

"A mother knows her child," Kes said.

"But, we have a bigger problem now," I implied.

"What's that?" Dwight asked.

"That same girl has grown up now and that girl is a student in one of Rozi's classes."

"GET THE FUCK OUT OF HERE!" Zach said.

"How does Rozi know that's her child?" Dwight asked.

"She doesn't have concrete evidence, but again like Kes said, a mother knows her child."

"Wow," Kes said. "Just wow."

"Ok. This is the real issue at hand," I said.

"What's that?" Zach asked.

"What would you do if you knew who the real father was?"

"Does the real father know about the baby?" Dwight asked.

"No," I shook my head. "She never told him."

"And you know who the father is?" Zach asked.

"Yes, you and Dwight know him, too. We all went to FAMU."

"Was he in the band?" Dwight asked.

"No."

"A million niggas went to school with us so I ain't 'bout to kill myself figuring out who it is," Dwight said.

"This is why I asked y'all not to say anything. I'm torn. I feel like that man has a right to know, but Rozi is my wife. I'm supposed to be on her side. Also, let me clarify. I don't know the dude personally, I know him through the two of you," I said as I looked at Zach and Dwight. "I've also wondered what if that dude has a family now or whatnot. What would this news do to him and his current family?"

"As a man, I'd want to know if I had a kid out there," Zach said.

"Kris, who is the real father of the kid Rozi gave up for adoption?" Dwight asked.

"Your other best friend, Amir Knight," I admitted.

"Stop playing, Kris," Zach said.

"I'm not playing," I pleaded. "Rozi told me what the dude name was. I never told anyone until today. I've kept it to myself for all these years."

"So you're trying to tell me that my best friend since high school has a kid out there that he doesn't know about?" Dwight asked.

"Yeah," I sighed.

"Kris," Dwight said upset. "Why would you tell me this knowing that Amir is my homeboy? I can't keep this from him!"

"Dwight, you said you wouldn't say anything," I said.

"He needs to know that he has a daughter out there. That shit ain't fair and it ain't right," Dwight said.

Kes looked at me in the rearview mirror.

Dwight said, "You need to get your wife to tell Amir the truth, because if you don't, I will. And it's as simple as that!"

96

Dorian

Brandon was driving and we had been on the road for at least an hour. I was in the passenger seat and Kory was sitting directly behind me. They were talking about work, but I tuned them out and listened to the radio.

I often wondered what kind of music my brother was into. I know I was more of a neo soul dude and I loved my gospel. I vibed to the likes of India.Arie and Jill Scott, but my favorite artist was none other than Musiq Soulchild. His soulfulness just puts me in another world.

I turned down the volume when my phone started to vibrate. I exhaled. It was my dad. I motioned for the two of them to lower their voices and I answered, "Sup, Dad?"

"Hey, Dorian, how is everything?" he asked.

"Everything is good," I replied happy that he seemed upbeat. "You seem happy today."

"I haven't been in as much pain the last few days," he said. "Whatever the doctor is doing is working. I've had a good couple of night's rest."

"That's good to hear," I smiled.

"Yeah, you haven't checked on your old man in a little while so I was calling to make sure you were ok."

"Sorry. I've been really busy with work."

"I understand. Have you made contact with Paula?" he asked.

I exhaled.

I haven't told my dad that I've met Zach and I haven't told Zach about our father's medical condition. In fact, except for one time,

I've yet to mention our father to Zach. I don't know how Zach really feels about Duane and I would like to get to know Zach and build something with him first, before all that outside stuff affects our bond.

"Are you there?" he asked.

"Umm, yeah," I said. "Just know I'm working on everything. I'm working on it."

"Dorian, I don't have much time left. Yes, I feel better today, but my days are still numbered. Please make this meeting with Zach a reality for me before I leave this Earth."

"I'm working on it, dad," I said frustrated.

"Ok. Well, I don't want to interrupt you. Enjoy your weekend and don't forget about me down here."

"I won't forget about you. We'll talk soon," I hung up the phone.

Right before I turned up the music, Brandon looked to me and said, "Everything ok?"

"Yeah," I sighed. "Everything is fine."

*****

TJ

After I got settled into Nolan's room, his mom came upstairs and asked us what we wanted for dinner. Being modest, I said, "It doesn't matter to me."

"Well, I want some pizza," Nolan said.

"Is that ok with you, TJ?" his mom asked.

"Yes, ma'am," I smiled as I remembered to use my manners.

"Well, I'm ready when y'all are," she smiled.

"I'm hungry now," Nolan said.

"Ight then, let's head on out," Miss Tasha said as we both jumped up ready to get something to eat.

When we got into Miss Tasha's silver, BMW x3, Nolan took his seat in the front and I sat directly behind him.

This shit was nice. All leather. It smelt good and the bitch was clean. I could see myself driving something like this when I get older.

As Miss Tasha backed out of the driveway, she said, "So where do y'all want to go?"

"Anything is ok with me," I said. "Papa John, Pizza Hut. It doesn't matter."

Excited, Nolan chimed in, "TJ, you gotta try out Fellini's."

"What's that?"

"It's a pizza place. They've got the best pizza and the slices are like so big!"

"Umm ok," I shrugged my shoulders.

"Mom, can we go there?" Nolan asked.

"If it is ok with TJ," she smiled as she looked in the rearview mirror.

"It's fine, Miss Tasha."

"Then Fellini's it is!" she said.

While she drove, she and Nolan engaged in a small conversation about school. In the midst of their conversation, an image of my mother appeared. That ever lagging question of *what would life be like if my mother was alive* lingered in my mind.

Would I be a different person if my mom, April, was here? If she was alive, would I still be living with daddy? Would I be living in Atlanta? Would we be back in Orlando? Would mom and daddy be together? Would Ray still be in my life? Would I have other brothers and sisters now?

I don't like being an only child.

I want someone to play with. Sometimes, I want a kid brother or sister I can fuck with, someone I could have a relationship with. I love my life, but it would be so much better if there was someone I could talk to and see eye-to-eye.

It'll never happen though. Both Ray and Daddy are too busy sticking each other in the ass.

That shit gotta hurt. My stomach turned at the thought. *Whatever floats their boat, I guess.*

"TJ, are you okay?" Miss Tasha asked as she looked in the rearview mirror.

"Yes, ma'am," I smiled.

"So Nolan tells me that you're new to Atlanta," she said. "How do you like it?"

"Atlanta is cool. Elijah and Nolan have helped to make the transition better. I still miss Charlotte and I miss my friends there, but moving here wasn't my decision to make. That's one of the negative things about being a kid, you don't have much say in important matters."

"You're very articulate for a thirteen-year-old kid," she said.

"Thanks," I smiled. "I've learned a lot. When one of your parents has a doctoral degree in education, you don't really have much of a choice but to be in the books."

She smiled and said, "I wish more of our young black men had the same attitude as you. A lot of the young men I see only want to play sports or pursue a rap career. There is more to life than being in the entertainment field."

I just stared at her.

Bitch, my daddy was about to become a pro athlete until he got injured and realized he couldn't play anymore because of his heart condition. Daddy's best friend, my Uncle Killa, plays in the NFL. She's too old to be judging people like that.

"So, your mom is here, too?" she asked.

"My mom passed away when I was three."

"Oh…wow… sorry to hear that," Miss Tasha said.

"It's ok," I sighed.

"So you have a stepmom?" she asked.

I stared at her in the mirror. Damn, she was nosey as fuck! I see where Nolan get that shit from now.

"Did you hear me?" she asked. "I asked did you have a stepmom."

I forced a smile and said, "Umm… something like that."

"Something like that?" she asked.

"Yeah," I nodded my head, getting aggravated. "Something like that."

"We're here," Nolan said as she turned into the parking lot.

She looked up at me in the mirror again. I forced another smile, relieved that we had arrived at the pizza joint.

Realizing that she was intruding into unwanted territory, she forced a smile and dropped the subject.

When she parked the car, she cleared her throat and said, "Let's eat!"

97

Kory

As Brandon continued on the drive, I said, "So, I've been thinking."

"About what?" Brandon asked.

"Our conversation from the other day at lunch."

Brandon quickly looked at Dorian and then put his attention back on the road. Dorian looked back at me.

"What about it?" Brandon asked as he looked in the rearview mirror before putting his attention back to the road.

"So you just cheated on your boyfriend without even taking into consideration how he'd feel?"

"That was years ago," Brandon said.

"What's your boyfriend name again?" I asked.

"Micah," Dorian answered for Brandon.

I said, "So, were you just cheating because you were cheating with the NBA baller, or are you just a cheater? Is this who you really are?"

"Excuse me?" Brandon said offended. "You don't even know me like to say something like that!"

I said, "I wasn't trying to be rude. I'm just saying does Micah make you happy? Why are you with the dude? Why would you cheat on someone you love?"

Dorian turned around and looked at me. Brandon stared at me in the rearview mirror.

I continued, "People can say what they want about me. I've made some mistakes. I've did some shit I'll regret for the rest of my life. I've never been proud of that one thing I did, but I can't take it back so I'm forced to live with it. Even then, the person who did that wasn't me. That was not Kory. I know y'all don't care about that. Nonetheless, anyone who knows me knows that I've never been one to hold my tongue. I've always been the person to tell the truth. I've always been the dude to keep it real. When I see something is wrong, I'll always address it. My old best friend back in college used to get mad at me for pointing out the truth. He didn't wanna hear it, but I told his ass anyway. So, I consider y'all my new friends down in Atlanta. And because you're a friend to me, I'll keep it real with you."

"So what do you see, Mr. Matthews?" Dorian asked me. "What made Brandon cheat on Micah?"

I said, "Just from the way you've talked about Micah in the past, something tells me that something is missing in the relationship. I don't know why y'all hooked up and I could be way off base, but something in my gut tells me that y'all hooked up out of obligation. Maybe it was out of a rebound relationship or something on those terms. Yes, the two of you love each other, but like many relationships, you're just there out of obligation, because that's just the way it is. You say your dude is a bottom, but you let the NBA baller dick you up all over the fucking country. It's clear that you like both dick and ass. Why wouldn't Micah want to spend the weekend in Tally with you? Isn't that where y'all met? Didn't y'all both go to school down there? Something tells me he has his own plans. He can do what he wants to do knowing for certain that you ain't nowhere to be found. There is a completely different side to you, Brandon. What you present to the public isn't the real you. Dorian knows the real Brandon. I don't think that's the only time you've cheated on that dude and I don't think it will be the last."

I stared at Brandon. He stared at me and said, "You don't know shit about me to be making such accusations."

"I'm just stating what I see," I said. "That's all."

*****

Zach

After Dwight stated his demands to Kris, as it related to the Rozi and Amir situation, a great wave of tension bombarded the car.

Kris spent the next part of the trip looking out of the window and sending text messages. Dwight stared out of the window. Kes just bobbed his head to the beat of the music. For once, I must say it was relaxing to just sit in silence. I needed this moment to be in my thoughts.

As I turned my head towards the window, I exhaled. I could see and hear moments from my counseling session with Dray yesterday:

After the silence was broke, Dr. Bynum got straight to the point by saying, "Are the two of you still sexually active?"

I stared at the piece of artwork that hung on the plain white wall. The artwork was an abstract piece of work and was painted in earth tones. I loved earth colors. They were so warm and inviting.

I zoomed in on Dr. Bynum. He stared at the two of us, waiting for an answer. I heard his question I just didn't feel comfortable talking about my sex life to this stranger.

After a moment of silence, Dray looked to me and then over to Dr. Bynum and said, "We just recently started having sex again."

"Again?" Dr. Bynum asked as he made a notation on his yellow legal pad. "Prior to recently, when was the last time you had sex?"

Dr. Bynum looked at me; I stared at him. Dray said, "It had been about five months."

"Dr. Finley, why the stoppage?" Dr. Bynum asked me directly.

"There was a lot going on in our lives," I replied.

"Can you be more specific?" Dr. Bynum asked as he looked me directly in the eyes.

I said, "I don't understand what our sex life has to do with this meeting. And if I'm honest, I don't feel comfortable discussing my sexual life with my partner to some complete stranger."

Dr. Bynum said, "In my experience, I've learned that sexual issues, along with finances, are usually the root causes of a lot relationships going south. What I'm trying to do here is continue to put the pieces of this puzzle together. Like I said in the last meeting, I want to build a rapport with you so that you trust and feel comfortable with me. I'm here to help you and Drayton have stable ground again."

"Zach, just answer the man's question," Dray said upset.

"Don't demand me to do anything," I said cutting my eyes to Dray. "I do what I want, when I want and how the fuck I feel like it. Don't get in front of this man and act brand new, ok."

Dray shook his head. His body language told me that he wasn't happy with my lack of interest in this session. I cut my eyes to Dr. Bynum and he was writing down another set of notes. When he looked up, he said, "So what exactly do you want from these meetings? What do the two of you plan to achieve from the counseling sessions?"

Dray instantly replied, "I want it to go back to where it was."

"And where was it?" Dr. Bynum asked.

Dray answered, "When we first met, it was like we lived to see each other. We were on one accord. We did for the other without thinking. I would give anything for this man. I loved him with everything inside of me. Now, something is missing."

Dr. Bynum looked at me; I looked at him.

Dray continued, "I want my relationship to be strong, honest and open. We're not on a stable foundation. I'm not ready to give up everything that we've worked so hard to build."

"Are you ready to give up?" Dr. Bynum looked at me.

"I'm here aren't I?" I asked.

I could see Dray shaking his head. Dr. Bynum continued to stare at me with an emotionless face.

"Listen," I cut. "Dray and I are both very strong willed people. We are both very guarded. I'm very private. I've always been that way since I was a kid. That's just in my DNA."

"So, again I ask you," Dr. Bynum said. "What do you want from these meetings? What do you plan to achieve from these counseling sessions?"

"I want to get my relationship back on solid ground. I want things to go back to the way they were," I said.

"I'm just gonna be frank with you, Dr. Finley," Dr. Bynum said. "I can't help you if you will not openly talk to me. I can't help you if you continue to keep the walls up around me. I'm trying to open you up, and for the second week, you've meet me with walls of rejection. I'm never this forceful with my clients, but Dr. Finley you're not my average client. You're usually the one who sits in my seat. You know the next set of questions I will ask. This presents a challenge to me as I have to find a new way to approach this unique situation. I'm trying to find ways to talk to you, but you have to open up and allow me to do my job."

Tired of his lashing, I stood up and said, "Are we done?"

"Zach, sit down and stop acting so fucking bitchy all the damn time!" Dray

demanded.

"Maybe you didn't hear what the fuck I just told you a few minutes ago," I said looking to Dray. He was starting to piss me off. "Don't demand anything of me, ok. I'm not your child. That's what Nolan is for!"

Anger quickly appeared on his face.

When I turned to Dr. Bynum, he was writing more notes down. When he looked at me, I said, "Sir, this is nothing against you, but I'm just not feeling this shit today. I have other pressing, important issues on my mind, and this meeting with you is not on the top of my fucking list. Dray, I'm sorry that I wasted your time today and Dr. Bynum I'm sorry I wasted yours. Maybe next week will be better but right now you won't get anything out of me. I'm not in the mood and I refuse to sit here and waste all of our times."

My attention was placed back in the car when I felt a tapping on my thigh. I looked over at Kris and he said, "Kes asked you a question."

"Sorry," I cleared my throat. "What's up Kes?"

"I was just thinking," he said. "How did the counseling session go yesterday?"

Dwight instantly turned around and said, "What counseling sessions?"

"Dray and I are working on repairing our relationship," I said.

"So you're seeing a counselor?" Dwight asked visibly upset. "When the fuck did this shit start?"

"Why can't he see a counselor to work on his relationship? What does it have to do with you, Dwight?" Kris asked with a smirk on his face. "Y'all fucking? You and Zach fucking or something?"

Kes looked at me in the rearview mirror.

Ignoring Kris, I said to Dwight, "Yes, Dray and I have been seeing a counselor. Yesterday was our second meeting."

"So when were you gonna tell me about this?" Dwight asked.

I snapped, "I didn't know I had an obligation to tell you everything that happens in my relationship with Dray. I could have sworn I was in a relationship with Dray, not Dwight."

"So, it's like that, Zach?" Dwight asked.

"Dude, what is it with you?" Kris asked. "Are y'all fucking? Dwight, you came over to the other side? You fucking with niggas now?"

"KRIS, SHUT UP!" Dwight said pissed off. "DAMN!"

Kes looked at me in the rearview mirror.

"Don't get mad at me," Kris said to Dwight. "Get mad at yo'self, nigga. You had all those years to get up with Zach. I ain't stupid. I can put two and two together. I've known the two of you for fourteen years. We've all been best friends for fourteen years. I know the history. I see the reaction in the car." Kris turned to me and said, "I heard the altercation with Lexi today."

"What happened with Lexi?" Dwight asked.

"It doesn't take a rocket scientist to figure out that something ain't right in the water," Kris said continuing to look at me. "So what's really going on here? Is Dwight the reason why you really moved to Atlanta?"

"What happened with Lexi?" Dwight asked again.

Determined to get the heat off Dwight and me, I turned to Kris and said, "Are you and Micah still fucking?"

"What?" Kris asked shocked.

Taking a page out of his playbook, I said, "I've known you for fourteen years. We've all been best friends for fourteen years. I know the history. And you still haven't answered my question from last week. Are you happy with Rozi? Do you still wish you could have one last shot at a life with Micah? Based on your answers, or lack thereof last week, it doesn't take a rocket scientist to figure out that something ain't right in the water. So what's really going on here? Are you and Micah still getting it in? Is that the real reason why you're always the first one to dip on our Friday night's out? Make me understand, Kristopher K. Simms. Make me understand."

Kes interjected, "Can we change the topic please? This shit is getting out of hand. Ain't nobody fucking nobody but Phoenix and me. Period!"

98

TJ

We headed back to Nolan's place after dinner and his mom didn't do any more prying into my family life.

When we got back to the house, Nolan and I headed upstairs and immediately begin to play videogames. While we played some fighting game, I took the chance to look around his room.

He had every fucking electronic machine known to man, just like me. He had a big ass room, too. We were some lucky kids and I couldn't deny it.

His mom was a divorce attorney so that's how she made all of her dough. His dad was some big wig at some company that spoiled the fuck out of him. While we were very different, we were also just alike.

Playing fighting games wasn't my thing, but I played along since Nolan was so happy to have someone challenge him.

After about an hour of playing that boring shit, I said, "Man, you don't got Madden or 2K in this bitch. I like sports, nigga."

"I got an old one," he said disappointed. "I'm not really into sports like that."

"What year is it?" I asked.

"Madden 13."

"Damn, man, that like three years old," I said in amazement that in all these video games, he didn't have the latest sports shit.

"I told you I ain't into sports like that," he looked at me. "But we can play it if you want."

"Yeah, let's do that," I said.

As soon as he got up to retrieve the new game, my phone started to ring. When I saw the name, I smiled and quickly answered, "HEY, UNCLE KILLA!"

I could hear him smiling through the phone when he said, "My favorite nephew. How's it going?"

"It's good," I smiled. "I'm at my homeboy house playing video games. We 'bout to play Madden."

"I hope you're playing with my team," Killa said.

"You already know, Uncle Killa," I said as Nolan walked over to the game console. I'm 'bout to make daddy and then put him on your team just like how y'all was in college."

"That's what's up. Make sure you tear dat azz up like how your father and I used to do back in the day."

"That's the only way, Uncle Killa," I smiled.

"Did you check your account?" he asked.

"Yes sir," I replied. "Thanks but you ain't have to put that much money in there. I was only going for the weekend."

"Yeah I know, but you should go and buy yourself something nice. You know you gotta stay fly being my nephew."

"I know," I smiled.

"Well, I was just calling to check on you. My plane is about to depart."

"Where are you going?" I asked.

"Las Vegas," he replied.

"It ain't no NFL teams in Vegas," I said confused.

"With the season starting next week, most coaches give their players the weekend off to relax their bodies one last time before the rigors of the season starts to affect us both mentally and physically. There is a convention that some of the players attend every year, this weekend in Vegas."

"Oh," I said. "Well, have fun for me and thanks for everything Uncle Killa."

"Let me know how many tickets you gonna need for your friends when we play the Falcons in Atlanta this year, ok?"

"Ok, I'll let you know."

"Love you TJ. Be safe."

"Love you, too, Uncle Killa. You be safe, too."

Nolan was staring at me when I hung up the phone. He said, "Uncle Killa? What kind of name is that?"

"You don't know who Killa Davis is?" I asked bewildered.

"No, am I supposed to?" he asked.

"Ok…how about Kameron 'Killa' Davis?" I asked.

"Naw… not ringing a bell," he nodded his head.

"Wow. You're really not into sports. What do you do all day?" I asked.

"I play video games, duh," he looked at me like I was stupid. "So who is Killa, or Kameron 'Killa' Davis?"

"While I make my daddy on this old ass Madden, you should Google him," I said.

Nolan looked at me.

"I'm serious," I said. "Google him. You're sitting amongst royalty, lil boy."

"Whatever," he laughed as he grabbed his iPad.

*****

Zach

After four testy hours in the car, we finally arrived in Tallahassee. I never imagined the trip would have turned out like this. Tempers were hot, emotions were high. Everyone except Kes was on edge.

"So what y'all wanna do?" Kes asked.

"I wanna see the band," Kris said.

Dwight said, "I'm hungry. We can check out the band tomorrow at the damn football game."

Kris turned to me and said, "Zach, what you wanna do?"

"I need some liquor in my system. Fucking 'round with y'all got my damn pressure up."

Kris smirked and said, "Well, it is what it is. I'm down for whatever."

"I say let's go to the hotel, get checked in, shower up and head out for dinner," I suggested.

"Sounds like a plan to me," Kes said.

"Let's do it," Dwight said as we headed deep into the heart of the city.

"Damn, I miss this place," I said as we drove through the city. "There are so many memories in good ole Tallahassee."

"Ain't that the truth," Kris said as he placed a phone call to Rozi.

When he got off the phone, I said, "So yesterday was just a bad day for me and I think I took it out on Dray and the counselor."

"What happened?" Kris asked.

"Do y'all remember my old roommate, Kyran Barr?"

"That nigga that you got into the fight with?" Dwight asked.

"Yeah, him," I said.

"What about that crazy muh'fucker?" Dwight asked.

"I had a dream about him," I said.

Kes looked up at me in the rearview mirror.

"What was it about?" Dwight asked.

"Well, he got out of prison and he came looking for me. In my dream, he found me and he tried to kill me. As he was aiming the knife at my throat, I woke up and couldn't go back to sleep. The scary part about this shit is that he gets out of prison on September 23rd."

"He gets out of prison on your birthday?" Kes asked.

"Yes."

"He gets out this year?" Dwight asked.

"Yes," I said.

"Wow," Kris added.

"I know he's in Arkansas but something inside of me is scared," I sighed.

"That man ain't looking for you," Dwight said. "Besides, it ain't no way in hell he gonna find you in Atlanta."

I said, "I just got an eerie feeling in the pit of my stomach. But that was only the beginning."

"What else happened?" Kris asked.

I continued, "I couldn't go back to sleep so I was tired all damn day. On the way to work, I got a $300 speeding ticket. That was strike number two. When I was leaving campus to go to the counseling session with Dray, I saw that someone had hit my brand new car. It wasn't a big dent, but the fact that someone hit my shit and left pissed me the fuck off. Now, I have to pay to get that shit repaired. I haven't had the car a month and some non-driving motherfucker done put a dent into it. That was strike three. At that point, I had reached my bullshit quota for the day. I just wanted to go home, get something to eat and go to sleep. But no, that wasn't an option as I had to go that damn session with Dray. Sitting in the counseling session listening to that man try and pick apart my sex life was the icing on the cake."

"Wow," Kes said.

"Yeah, yesterday wasn't a good day. Dray was pissed off. I left him to talk to the counselor his self. I wasn't about to spend another minute in that place. When he finally got home, he was ready to come for me, but I knew I was in the wrong and I tried to explain the type of day I had. Realizing where I was coming from, he backed off the impending attack and then made me dinner. He just left me alone in my thoughts last night. So I say that to say that if I offended any of you in the car this evening, excuse me and forgive me. It's just a lot of shit on my mind."

Soon after we arrived at the hotel and we all checked into our separate rooms.

"Thirty minutes," Kes said. "Let's all meet down in the lobby for dinner in thirty minutes."

99

Dorian

We arrived in Tallahassee and headed over to the band practice field. Brandon was so excited. We parked and navigated through the thick crowd standing on the sideline watching the FAMU band go through their first routine of the year for tomorrow's game. As Brandon mingled with old drum majors and old friends, Kory and I just stood there and watched.

Neither Kory nor I wanted to be at this practice. After about thirty minutes of standing there, we both decided to go back to the car and just wait for Brandon to return. This wasn't our venue.

"He needs to hurry up," Kory said. "I'm starving."

"Shit, me, too."

After the practice session, Brandon finally rejoined us and we headed directly over to a restaurant to eat. We spent a good portion of the night at Applebee's. It wasn't anything fantastic, but it got the job done. The drinks always made me feel damn good.

When we finally left, we headed back to the hotel. I was tired as a dog, but Brandon and Kory seemed to be energized while downing the drinks.

I couldn't hang.

After a long night with Eric last night and a long day at work, and after this drive, I was ready to call it a night.

After I showered, I picked up the phone and started to text Zach. I wanted see if we could still get up tomorrow sometime. Before I got in the bed, I walked over to the hotel balcony, stepped out and looked at the view of the city.

The night air made everything even more relaxing. When I cut my eyes down, I paused. I stared a little longer, but it was clear that they *were* together.

What was Brandon and Kory doing sitting on a bench outside the hotel talking? What was up with that?

Something about the two of them ain't right. I've gotta keep my eyes on that shit.

I passed it off on the liquor, but even at dinner, I could have sworn that they were flirting with each other.

"Whatever," I replied as I headed back into the room and went directly for the bed. I'm too tired for that mess.

If Kory is feeling Brandon, I just hope he knows what he's getting himself into.

I hope he knows…

*****

TJ

Jodi had me cheesing like a giddy school girl. I smiled and said, "Yeah, girl. You already know I do."

Nolan was stretched out on his big ass bed, surfing the internet on his tablet.

"Whatever, TJ," Jodi said through the phone. "It's getting late, so I better get some sleep."

"Dang, you gonna leave me already?"

"Ain't you with Nolan?" she asked.

"Yeah," I replied. "He ain't worried about me though."

"Yeah, but it's rude," she said. "You're his company and you're talking on the phone to me."

I sighed and said, "Yeah, I guess."

"Boy, I need to get my beauty rest. I'll call you."

"Ight, Jodi."

"BYE JODI!" Nolan yelled.

She laughed and said, "Tell him bye."

"She said bye," I repeated to Nolan.

He smiled.

"I'll call you, TJ. Bye."

When she hung up the phone, I jumped up and down like a lil kid.

"I don't know how you pulled that shit," Nolan said. "Jodi is the finest girl in school and she ain't ever give no other dude the time of day."

"That's because she don't like y'all lame ass Atlanta niggas," I said as I took my seat on the small couch in his room.

There was knock on Nolan's door. Miss Tasha opened the door and asked, "How is everything going?"

"It's good," Nolan said.

"Is Nolan treating you ok, TJ?" Miss Tasha asked.

"Yes ma'am," I smiled.

"Good," she said. "I'm really tired and about to get in the bed. I made some chocolate chip cookies if you guys wanted some. There is some milk in the refrigerator. I've had a long day so please don't make too much noise. Y'all boys enjoy your night. I promise I won't wake you in the morning."

"Thanks, mom," Nolan smiled. "And we'll keep it down."

"Thanks, Miss Tasha. Goodnight."

She smiled and closed the door.

"My mom's cookies are the best," Nolan said. "We gotta get some later."

"That's what's up."

Nolan walked over to me and said, "I still can't believe you know a football player."

"Man, I've met a lot of them," I replied. "When I lived in Charlotte, Uncle Killa would pick me up in the summers and he would take me on trips and shit. I've met all kinds of professional athletes and entertainers."

"My dad is big," Nolan flaunted.

"Really? What does he do?"

"He's an executive at some magazine. He knows a lot of important people, too," Nolan added.

"That's what's up."

Here this nigga was trying to compare my life to his. Yes, his father may know some important people, but I've met the important people. I've played ball with the important people. I've had lunch with the important people. I've played video games with the important people. There is a clear difference. But I wasn't gonna spoil his pride. If he wanted to believe his daddy was important then so be it.

We headed out of his room and down the stairs to retrieve the warm cookies. After I poured a glass of milk, I joined Nolan at the kitchen island.

He leaned over the counter and said, "So tell me this."

"What?"

"What's up with yo' boy?"

"Who?" I asked as I dipped the cookie into the sea of milk.

"Elijah. Seems like he just changed all of a sudden."

"You know him better than me," I said eating the cookie. He didn't lie, that cookie was good as fuck. "I thought y'all were friends."

"We are friends," he said. "He's just been different lately."

"Differently how?" I asked, remembering that Eli said Nolan had been acting differently.

"Man, fuck it," Nolan said. "I'm just gonna put it out there."

"What?" I asked. "What happened?"

"Between you and me," he whispered. "I think that nigga gay."

"So," I shrugged my shoulders.

"So?" Nolan replied dumbfounded. "You wanna hang around a gay nigga?"

"If Eli is gay, and I put a big emphasis on IF, why does it matter?"

"Cause that shit ain't right," Nolan said.

"Has Eli come at you in a gay way?"

"No," he said.

"He's never made an advance at you?"

"Naw," Nolan shook his head.

"So what the fuck it gotta do with you?" I asked. "Let that man live his life."

"My mom taught me that being gay ain't right. Bishop Reed teaches us the same thing, too. It's a sin and he's gonna go to hell for it."

"Are you perfect?" I asked.

"What?"

"Are you perfect?" I repeated.

"No."

"So why are you judging that man?" I asked. "Since you wanna get biblical, you probably commit sins every day, but like most people, you look over your shit and only see what's wrong in the other person. I don't even know why you talking about that man like that. That shit ain't cool. Eli is supposed to be your friend. He ain't even here to defend his self and you trynna call him gay. And like I said, if he is gay, that's his business. That don't got shit to do with you."

"Why you protecting him?" Nolan asked.

"I ain't protecting nobody," I replied. "What I'm doing is being fair. Eli's sexual orientation, or hell, anyone else for that matter, has absolutely no impact on your life, so why should you care if someone is gay or not. If you are a true friend, you'll be a friend to the person regardless of who they like to have sex with."

Nolan stared at me for a second then said, "Let's go play some more games."

After we played another round of games, my eyes were starting to get faint. It was almost one in the morning and I never really stayed up this late.

There was, however, something familiar about Nolan. I just couldn't put my finger on it. It was like he looked like someone I knew. I just couldn't place the face.

That shit was starting to bother me. I hated when I couldn't figure shit out.

A couple of times during the night, Nolan asked me why I kept looking at him. My only response was, "You remind me of someone, but I can't figure out who it is right now."

People can say what they want about my personality or my attitude, but I am very observant and I try to be fair. Daddy and Ray taught me that. Sometimes it's better to let the other person talk as you can learn a lot from just listening.

Some people say I'm like Daddy with my temper and I agree that I need to work on that. But in my opinion, that's where the comparisons stop. Unlike Daddy, I am fair. I like to stand up for the right thing, at least I try too. Like tonight for Elijah, I stood up for my friend.

I know Eli is gay but that shit ain't Nolan business. I meant what I said though. Even if someone is gay shouldn't stop you from being their friend, if you were truly friends to begin with.

I'm seeing a side of Nolan that needs to grow the fuck up. I know we're all teenagers and shit, and maybe living with two black gay male parents has forced me to see life from a different angle, but some of Nolan's rants are just dumb. Maybe he needs someone like me in his life to teach him some shit that his mom and his retarded ass church ain't teaching him.

I live in the real world, with real life issues. Ain't nothing wrong with the bible, but those bible holding muh'fuckers are the ones with the most God damn problems. They are the fakest muh'fuckers out here, telling me what I need to do with my life when you ain't even practicing the shit ya damn self. What kinda fuck shit is that?

When this game ended, we both agreed it was time to call it a night. After I changed into my pajamas, I turned to Nolan and asked where was I supposed to sleep.

"You can sleep in the bed with me or you can sleep in the guest room or you can sleep on the couch in my room. It's up to you."

As I made my way towards his bed, I jokingly said, "If I get in here, don't be trying none of that homo stuff. I ain't gay, nigga."

I guess he didn't realize it was a joke, so he stared at me for a second then replied with an attitude, "I ain't gay, either."

"Yeah," I shook my head as I got down towards the foot of the bed. "That's what they all say."

100

Zach

I needed that release at dinner. It felt good to be around three friends without the drama that rode with us in the car. I could tell that Kris was still worried about his situation with Dwight, but he didn't let that interfere with our night at dinner.

I downed a couple of drinks—quite a few drinks—to help ease some of my issues away, even if it was only for the moment.

When we got back to the hotel, we all went our separate ways and agreed to let each other sleep in tomorrow. The game didn't start until six in the evening so we would have more than enough time to drive around town and reminisce about our times in Tallahassee. Luckily, Florida State's football game was on Monday night, so that would most definitely help with the traffic.

I showered and got in the bed. It felt so good to be alone, in a comfortable king sized bed made for a king like me.

I had been texting Dorian throughout the night. He wanted to meet up tomorrow while we were both in Tallahassee. I was most definitely down for that!

I know it was late, but Dray was on my mind so I phoned him. There was a lot of noise in the background when he answered.

"Where are you?" I asked.

"VEGAS!" he yelled into the phone. "GETTING FUCKED UP BABE AND IT FEELS SO DAMN GOOD!"

"What the hell are you doing in Las Vegas?" I asked confused.

"PHOENIX INVITED ME," he said. "I WENT WITH ANOTHER ONE OF HIS FRIENDS. IT WAS SO SPUR OF THE MOMENT. I'M SO HAPPY I CAME!"

I smiled. I was happy that he was having fun. "Well, don't gamble away our bank account," I joked.

"I WON'T!" he said. "HOW'S THE TRIP?"

"It's ok, just in the room about to get some rest."

"COOL!"

"Well, I'll let you go," I sighed. "Have fun and take a drink for me."

"OK. I LOVE YOU! DON'T WORRY ABOUT THE CAR REPAIRS! I'll TAKE CARE OF IT FOR YOU!"

"Dray, why are you yelling?"

"I'M NOT YELLING," he yelled. "PHOENIX WANTS ME! I'M GONNA GO NOW, OK!"

I laughed and said, "Ok. Good night and I love you, too."

Right as I hung up the phone, I flipped off the lamp and turned on my side. It was so quiet. So peaceful. So relaxing. This has been one long ass day.

I often complain about everything that is wrong in my life, but I know that I'm beyond blessed. There are so many people that wish they could be where I am in my life.

If my grandma were living, she'd tell me to shut up and be thankful for everything God has bestowed upon my life. It may not seem like it but I am thankful. I am thankful and I'm blessed.

While Dray and I don't always see eye-to-eye, I love that man and I know he'd move mountains to make sure I was happy. I have three close friends in Dwight, Keston and Kris, that will take a bullet for me. I have my mother who won't let a fly hurt me. She has really stepped up to the plate over the past few years. And now I'm getting to know my blood brother. What more could I ask for?

Again, I am beyond blessed.

After I said a quick prayer, I sighed and closed my eyes. This sleep was going to be good as fuck!

And then there was a knocked on my door taking me out of my subtle bliss. In only my boxer briefs, I got up and walked over to the door, wondering who the hell was there.

When I saw the face, I looked to the sky and exhaled. I turned on the hall light and unlocked the door.

There stood Dwight.

Damn, he was fine.

He had on a black wife beater, black basketball shorts, black socks and some black Nike slides. He had something behind his back.

With most of my body behind the door, I said, "Dwight, what do you want?"

He removed his hand from behind his back and there was a bottle of liquor. He smiled and said, "For old times' sake?"

I just looked at him. There was an awkward moment of silence.

He said, "So, you're not gonna let me in?"

I just stared at him.

"Can I come in?"

I exhaled and continued to stare at him…at his body…not really sure what to do…

~To Be Continued~

Life of a College Bandsman

Upcoming Titles:

Life of an EX College Bandsman 8: Growing Pains

Life of an EX College Bandsman 9: Nothing Lasts Forever

Life of an EX College Bandsman 10: Is He the Reason

Life of an EX College Bandsman 11: The Finale

About the Author

Known mostly as BnTasty by his online reader-base, Jaxon Grant started his writing conquest in June 2008, on Da Site, which was a popular stories website for gay and bisexual men. With his initial publications, Jaxon captivated his audience and created a healthy following that urged him to move outside of the confines of those who flocked to Da Site to read his material. Now, after many years of growing and understanding his skills as a writer, he's brought his work to a national audience.

Jaxon has written with compelling thoughts that tackle the issues we face as Americans, not just in the LGBT community. In his unique style, he uses the elements of drama, mystery, suspense, romance and tragedy to further the depth and scope of his work.

Jaxon was born and raised in Orlando, Florida. He attended Florida A&M University (FAMU) and majored in Social Science Education with a concentration in Political Science. While at FAMU, Jaxon was a member of the marching band, the world renown FAMU Marching 100.

Please be sure to visit his website, www.jaxongrant.com, and sign up for his newsletter to receive important updates from Jaxon. You can follow Jaxon on Twitter and Instagram @jaxon_grant. Finally, you can text Jaxon to 88202 to receive new release alerts directly to your phone.

Made in the USA
Las Vegas, NV
22 August 2021